DOMESTICATING DRAGONS

DAN KOBOLDT

BAEN

A Baen Books Original

Baen Publishing Enterprises
P.O. Box 1403
Riverdale, NY 10471
www.baen.com

ISBN: 978-1-9821-2511-0

Cover art by Dave Seeley

First printing, January 2021

Distributed by Simon & Schuster
1230 Avenue of the Americas
New York, NY 10020

Library of Congress Cataloging-in-Publication Data

Names: Koboldt, Dan (Daniel C.), author.
Title: Domesticating dragons / by Dan Koboldt.
Description: Riverdale, NY : Baen Books, 2021.
Identifiers: LCCN 2020044397 | ISBN 9781982125110 (trade paperback)
Subjects: GSAFD: Science fiction. | Fantasy fiction.
Classification: LCC PS3611.O333 D66 2021 | DDC 813/.6--dc23
LC record available at https://lccn.loc.gov/2020044397

Printed in the United States of America

10 9 8 7 6 5 4 3 2 1

To Sadie, our favorite miracle.

CHAPTER ONE
Reptilian

Three years, five months, and thirteen days after my dog died in the canine epidemic, I walked up to the door of Reptilian Corporation wearing a suit I couldn't afford. The company leased a shining 20,000-square-foot facility in downtown Phoenix. I'd seen plenty of fancy buildings before, but this one took the cake. Ten stories of glass and steel nestled in a verdant landscape of trees, shrubs, and actual *grass*. It looked like a strange mashup of biotech and an Ivy League campus. The irrigation bill alone had to cost a fortune. I put my hand on the warm metal door handle and paused to take a deep breath. Six years of work had brought me to this moment. *Don't blow it.*

I tugged the door open. A rush of cool air greeted me, carrying with it the faint metallic smell of recent construction. The lobby alone was the size of an aircraft hangar. I approached the security desk just inside, where a redhead in a sharp business suit greeted me.

"Can I help you?"

"I'm here for an interview."

"I didn't know we were interviewing."

Damn, she was gorgeous. Probably twenty years old and so far out of my league it wasn't even funny. *Focus, man.* "Well, it's more of a meeting."

"Your name?"

I'd made the mistake of glancing upward and found myself staring at the dragon frescoes painted on the ceiling three stories up. It looked like a reptilian invasion of the Sistine Chapel. They were *obsessed* with dragons here. "Noah Parker."

She tapped out a few keys. "There you are." The desk between us looked about a hundred years old. It was probably one of those reclaimed wood jobs, an old ship or something. She slid a black portable flatscreen onto it, in a weird juxtaposition of traditional and modern. I looked around but didn't see a stylus.

"Where's the pen?"

"It's a palm scanner."

"Right, of course." I reached out to put my right palm on it, like it was no big deal. Like I spent every day passing through state-of-the-art security at one of the nation's hottest biotech companies. Light bloomed beneath my thumb, and her computer chimed softly.

She printed a security badge with VISITOR in bright red letters across the top, just above my picture. Which looked to be my DMV photo, not the most flattering image ever. I grimaced. "Thanks."

"Take the elevator to the seventh floor. Someone will meet you in the lobby."

I clipped on the badge so that the fold of my suit jacket hid most of the horrific photo. "So, what's *your* name?"

She shook her head. "That's need-to-know information."

"Well, maybe I need—"

"No, you don't."

Ouch. I stood there with my mouth open for a good half second. "Did you say seventh floor?"

"Seventh floor." She'd already turned back to her flatscreen.

I wasn't off to a good start. The awkward interaction shook me up. I caught the next elevator and sighed in relief that I had it to myself. The doors hissed open on the seventh floor to reveal an empty lobby. I stepped out and glanced around. Glass doors lined both sides of the atrium, their glowing red access panels making it clear that I wouldn't be allowed through. "Hello?"

The muted click-click of heels echoed from behind the door at my left. It slid open to reveal a dark-haired woman with a slim tablet and a face I recognized. My breath caught. It was *her*.

Evelyn Chang was one of the top genetic engineers in the country. I'd met her once at a conference when I was in grad school. She was at Cal Tech back then, but already making a name for herself. I doubted she remembered me. She smiled. "Noah Parker. I was just reading your dissertation."

"Oh." I didn't really know what to say. "What do you think?"

"Your biological simulator sounds promising. Does it work?"

My simulator was a computer program that read in a genome sequence and predicted the organism it encoded. A company like Reptilian would naturally be interested in its commercial applications, even if I hadn't written it specifically to get their attention. "It's not perfect. But the results so far have been really encouraging."

"That's good to hear. How about a little tour?"

"I'd like that." More than I dared tell her.

She led the way through the secure door from which she'd come. I followed, my head still spinning from the fact that Evelyn Chang had been reading my paper. The hallway opened into a wide two-story chamber. The air felt uncomfortably warm, maybe ten degrees above ambient temperature. Sunlight streaked in through circular skylights that, oddly enough, reminded me of the hydroponics closet back home.

"This is the hatchery," Evelyn said.

"I didn't realize you hatched the dragons in-house."

"Only our prototypes. Most of our orders get shipped out as eggs."

I counted eight steel-and-Plexiglas doors on either side, but only two that seemed to be in use. Which was odd. I mean, the place had a license to design *dragons*. With Evelyn here running the show, you'd think the hatchery would be booming. Maybe I wasn't getting the whole picture, but I filed this away for later.

The far door opened to admit two people in white jumpsuits pushing a wide cart between them. I scrambled aside. A foam cushion topped the cart. In the center of that rested an oblong stone about the size of a watermelon. It had the color of desert sand: pale yellow beneath a whorl of reddish earth tones.

"Hey, Jim," Evelyn said. "Mind if we have a look?"

The white-clad orderlies paused but kept their hands on the cart. Dark-tinted masks obscured their faces. How did Evelyn know who they were? My eyes slid down to the stone. My breath caught.

"Is that—"

"A dragon egg. Go ahead, you can touch it."

I felt nervous doing so. The thing looked so *fragile*. If I damaged it, there was no way this meeting would have a happy outcome. Still, this could be my only chance to ever touch a dragon egg, so I figured I might as well. I laid my palm on it. The shell felt rough, almost porous. "Oh my God," I whispered. "It's *warm*."

Evelyn smiled. "Fresh off the printer."

One of the white-clad staffers, presumably the one called Jim, cleared his throat.

"We should let them get it into the pod," Evelyn said.

I nodded and forced myself to lift my hand. The memory of that warmth lingered, though. I watched them wheel it away and into one of the active incubator rooms. Well, even if nothing came of this meeting, I had a pretty good story to tell.

Evelyn led me through another set of doors and back into the world of ambient temperature. We encountered no one else in the long, sterile hallway. A muted hum came through the wall on the right-hand side. It was faint, but unmistakable: the whir of server cooling fans. Maybe it was just my anticipation, but I could sense the power of those machines. The nearly limitless potential.

Her office, a rectangular room almost as large as my studio apartment, waited at the end of the hallway. Glass windows on two walls offered a stunning view of downtown, only partly obscured by the exotic plants growing in pots along the windowsills. I'd taken enough botany to recognize the Venus fly traps, sundews, pitcher plants... all carnivorous species.

I tried not to ponder the significance of that.

Evelyn gestured me to the thick leather guest chair, on the near side of the most notable piece of furniture: a wide steel desk in the shape of a half-donut. She took the much-plainer swivel chair in the donut-hole, perching on the edge as if she might pop back up at any second.

I settled into the guest chair with a squelch. I winced. It must be one of those chairs that made awkward noises whenever you moved. *Just what I need*.

"How much have you tested your simulator code on other organisms?" Evelyn asked.

"Quite a bit, actually. I worked my way up to frog before I hit the limits of our computing resources at ASU."

She smiled the knowing smile of someone who didn't face that problem. "Are there any other limitations, beyond the computing requirements?"

"It needs a high-quality genome sequence. The more annotation content, the better."

"What species do you think would be the toughest to run on it?"

"If you mean biological and legal complexity, then it's obviously human." *But that's the easy answer.* A Genetics 101 student could get it right. I ran through my mental list of test simulations. "But if you mean genomic difficulty, I'd say one of the gymnosperms." Plant genomes were nasty things: large, repetitive, lots of copied genes and pseudo-genes. "Norwood spruce, maybe."

She gave a sharp nod, as if my answer pleased her. "Do you know what I'm going to ask next, Noah Parker?"

"Whether I've run it on the dragon reference?" That was the genome sequence Reptilian had assembled to produce their synthetic reptile.

"Well, have you?" she asked.

"I haven't, for three reasons. First, it would take more computer than I've got. Second, the public version of the dragon genome is still a little rough." Right then I remembered that she'd probably played a big role in that project. I cleared my throat. "No offense."

Evelyn shrugged. "We never claimed it was more than a first draft."

"Well, the third reason is, I'd want to compare the results to live subjects."

"You could have just bought some of our dragons," Evelyn said.

I can't even afford this suit I'm wearing. "Why didn't I think of that?"

"In its current form, the simulator only models physical characteristics. Is that true?"

"Yes. That's what most end users are interested in." Biotech and seed companies cared mainly about physical traits, things that affected the bottom line. Still, they had deep pockets, so my university was happy to issue the licenses. Reptilian hadn't licensed it yet, but I hoped that was where this was going.

"What about behavioral traits?"

The question caught me by surprise. As much as I'd enjoy modifying a few of my younger brother's behaviors, that had never been my focus. *So why is it hers?* "They're a lot more complex. Harder to predict from genetics alone."

"Tell me about it." She shook her head. Then she seemed to get an idea and stood. "I want to show you something."

I followed her out of her office and down another hallway to door labeled *Holding Facility*.

She pressed her palm to a biometric scanner, which glowed green in response. The door hissed open. "This is where we keep dragons after hatching."

"You keep live dragons here?" I couldn't imagine why. The unhatched eggs would be low maintenance. Living dragons, not so much.

"Just some of the experimental models." Evelyn stopped before a large window that let out into darkness. She activated a control panel and hit a button. Light bloomed on the other side of the glass. It was a holding cell, about ten feet square, and a large scaled *creature* the size of a Labrador lay curled up in the corner. Dark, leathery wings rested against the serpentine body.

"This was one of our early prototypes," Evelyn said.

The dragon's eyes flicked open. It uncurled and stretched, almost like a cat, and rolled to its clawed feet. It was much bigger than that, though. About the size of an adult mountain lion, by my guess.

I took a step forward and put my fingertips on the glass. "I've never been this close—"

The dragon hurtled forward and slammed into the Plexiglas. Right in front of my face. It hissed and snarled and bared its teeth and threw itself at the Plexiglas again. *Wham.* I scrambled backward and, and nearly fell. "Jesus!"

"They're a little wild," Evelyn said.

"Yeah, no kidding."

She switched off the lights again. Darkness hid the dragon's body from view, but not its eyes. They glowed with a fey light, watching me without blinking. I shivered as I followed Evelyn back to her office, doing my best to ignore the repeated thuds of the dragon hitting the Plexiglas. *A little wild, my ass.* Were it not for the barrier, that thing would have ripped my head off.

No wonder they needed a biological simulator.

CHAPTER TWO
The Waiting Game

I left Reptilian with a good impression and a handful of vague promises. Evelyn said that they'd proceed with a license for my simulator. If it did as I promised for their genetic engineering team, she might even be able to bring me on.

My car stuck out like a fresh pimple among the glittering sedans in Reptilian's parking lot. It was technically a sedan, too, but the previous owner had welded the back doors shut for reasons that remained unclear. I'd bought it in a police auction with the little cash I scrounged together in my last year of graduate school. I never even bothered locking it. Replacing a broken window would probably cost more than the jalopy was worth. I climbed in, whispered a prayer, and hit the start button. It sputtered into life, thank goodness. If I left it here much longer, I'm sure the company would have had it towed.

I drove away, watching Reptilian's shining building shrink in the rearview mirror. Picturing my foot in the door — because it was. If they licensed my simulator through ASU, I'd have to send them the source code. All of it could have been done through electronic channels, but they'd asked me to come in. That meant something. Even if Reptilian claimed they weren't hiring now, even if we didn't talk any specifics about a job, this was an audition. All I had to do now was nail the call-back.

But here's the ugly truth about academic software. There are few of the strict programming rules like those you'd find at a commercial shop. In other words, we don't have to write perfectly clean code, even to get published in journals like JCB. I stood behind my simulator's functionality, but the code that ran it might have gotten a little sloppy in some places. I spent the next week polishing it up.

In that time, Reptilian signed their license through ASU and paid the fee, which told me that they wanted it pretty badly. That was good. There was something I wanted badly, too, and they were the only place to get it.

I could have sent Evelyn the code when I'd finished, but 3 a.m. e-mails didn't seem like the best approach for a hopeful job applicant. So I set a timer-delay, and the message kicked off at the far more respectable time of 9:30 in the morning. Let her think I was a responsible early riser, when in truth I was dead to the world, sleeping off the effects of the necessary caffeine binge. I finally roused myself at around 10:45, got dressed, and put my phone on maximum volume. Evelyn might need to peruse the code and run some tests, but it shouldn't take too long.

At any moment, I'd get the call. The official word that Evelyn wanted to bring me on. I kept my phone beside me at every moment. I couldn't even shower, for fear it would ring right after I put the shampoo in.

But the day came and went, and no phone call. No e-mail reply. I started to panic a little. Maybe Reptilian Corporation's servers flagged my e-mail, so she never got it. That happened sometimes when you sent programming code around. And like a moron, I'd forgotten to switch on message tracking, which would have told me when she opened it.

I started another e-mail to her, asking if she'd gotten the code, but forced myself to delete it. *Be patient*. I didn't dare let her glimpse how much I wanted the job. How I needed to get in there and see what those servers could do.

That night, I couldn't sleep. My brain concocted all kinds of scenarios in which Evelyn didn't get my simulator code, or couldn't open it, or read through it and changed her mind about me. When I finally did fall asleep, I had nothing but self-doubt nightmares in which I showed my incompetence to the entire scientific community.

The next morning, I awoke groggily to the soft chime of an incoming message. She'd replied to my e-mail with a single sentence:

Thanks for sending this; I'll be in touch soon.

This response reassured me—she'd gotten my message, and now could review the code—but my confidence fled in about ten seconds. First, why did she take an entire day to get back to me? Her message implied that she hadn't even *looked* at my code yet. How long was that going to take? I knew, intellectually, that she had a regular job to do on top of recruiting people like me, but the vagueness of "soon" rankled. Maybe that meant four hours from now, or maybe it meant a month.

There was nothing to do but wait.

The day slipped away without further word from Evelyn. I started to doubt myself. I replayed the meeting in my head, wondering how I might have blown it. Maybe the code didn't impress her enough. I pored over it line by line for another day. Sure, some parts were a little rough around the edges, but this was Evelyn Chang. She could connect the dots.

So what the hell was taking her so long?

When I didn't hear from her the next day, panic set in. I felt a strong and foolish temptation to go down to Reptilian and beg for a job. I'd probably never have made it in the door, and I'd certainly be flagged as a total nutcase. But I couldn't think of anything else to do.

Thankfully, some of my friends from grad school invited me out for margaritas. Their treat. I drowned my angst in tacos and cheap tequila. *Way* too much cheap tequila.

The next morning brought too-bright daylight and a lot of regret. My head felt like someone had put a vise on it and kept tightening the damn thing over and over. I wanted to sleep it off, but a persistent buzzing jarred me awake. It was my phone, vibrating against the glass-top nightstand.

I fumbled for it and looked at the screen, wincing at the brightness of it. The blurred figures resolved into a phone number I recognized. "Oh, God." I scrambled out of bed to my desk. *Where the hell are my notes?*

On the third ring, I coughed up half a lung and it tasted like tequila-soaked tacos. On the fourth, I hit the answer button. "Hello?"

"Noah Parker."

"Yes?"

"It's Evelyn Chang."

"Hello." It took a lot of effort to keep the strain out of my voice. Christ, why couldn't I have slowed down last night?

"My team and I reviewed your biological simulator. It's impressive."

"Uh, thank you." I held my breath and crossed both fingers.

"This morning, I convinced the board to make an exception to our hiring freeze."

I pumped my fist in the air. "Really?"

"We can bring you on as a trainee."

Ugh. That didn't exactly have the ring of *staff scientist* like I wanted it to. In the academic world, post-doctoral trainees were glorified graduate students. Cheap labor with no prestige, no authority. I didn't know what it meant at Reptilian, but I doubt it entailed unfettered access to their lab and equipment. "I see."

"You're disappointed."

"No, just surprised." I recentered myself and tried to remember that job within those walls was probably all I needed. I could work my way up. *All I need is access.* "But hey, I'm ready to learn."

"Good." She sounded pleased.

"When would you like me to start?"

"How about today? I'd like to get that simulator code talking to our design software as soon as possible."

I stifled a groan. I hadn't shaved in three days, and I needed a shower that I probably couldn't afford the water for. But the sooner I started, the sooner I might climb my way out of poverty.

I checked my watch. "See you in an hour."

CHAPTER THREE
INVENTOR PROFILE

Name: Simon Redwood
Companies Founded: 13
Claim to Fame: The Dragon Genome Project
Current Venture: Reptilian Corporation,
    a genetic engineering firm

Many successful businesses arise to address a real-world problem. In the case of Reptilian Corporation, that problem was hogs.

Feral hogs are the descendants of domestic hogs that escaped (or were released intentionally) from captivity. Most forms of livestock depend on humans for food and protection, and don't last long in the wild. Not so with feral hogs. They don't simply survive in the wild. They *thrive*.

A feral sow breeds once or twice a year, producing a litter of four to six young. They can eat about anything—grasses, roots, mushrooms, acorns—but given the choice, they prefer domesticated crops. Corn, rice, and soybeans are particular favorites. A pack of feral hogs (called a *sounder*) can wipe out a two-acre farm field overnight.

An Invasive Species
With each generation, feral hogs develop longer hair, larger tusks, and other traits that help them survive in the wild. A fully grown adult animal weighs a hundred pounds and has no natural predators. As recently as a decade ago, feral hog populations were growing

virtually unchecked in the southwestern United States. They drove out natural species, destroyed grazing grounds vital to ranchers, and devoured entire farm fields. Ironically, the species that we bred as livestock made food more expensive.

Five years ago, a thousand scientists, ranchers, and wildlife experts convened in Phoenix, Arizona to discuss the hog crisis. Everyone agreed on one thing right off the bat: the methods tried so far weren't working.

Feral hogs are nocturnal, and their incredible sensory perception—especially smell and hearing—helps them avoid humans during daylight hours. They hole up in the most unforgiving of environments, like swamps and briar patches, that most humans can't get to. These behaviors have frustrated would-be hunters and trappers, who make only a small dent in feral hog populations.

The Redwood Solution

Simon Redwood is no stranger to tough problems. The eccentric, wild-haired inventor has often proposed unconventional—if not entirely successful—solutions to some of our world's most daunting scientific challenges. Solutions like SolarMesh, the roll-up solar panel system that brought power to much of the Caribbean after last year's devastating hurricane season. And no one will forget MedicFT, the medical triage robot that Redwood claimed would replace the modern emergency room.

It isn't clear who invited him to the convention in Phoenix, but he got five minutes on the podium, and made them count.

"The only way to effectively control hog populations is the introduction of a new predator," he said. "A synthetic organism designed to hunt feral pigs in the wild."

Many in the audience uttered a groan. Synthetic biology was an often-maligned branch of the life sciences. Synthetic biologists had thus far developed single-cell organisms, like bacteria and brewer's yeast. Efforts to make larger, more complex animals always failed.

The creature that Redwood proposed was a new level of ambitious. A carnivorous reptile with a lizard's claws, an alligator's teeth, and a taste for "the other white meat." Few in that convention hall in Phoenix believed that it would succeed, but all of them were desperate. And no one had any better ideas.

The Dragon Genome

The first step to reach Redwood's vision was to create a genome sequence for this so-called reptilian predator. Even with advances in DNA sequencing, the cost of this endeavor went considerably beyond what the farmers and ranchers could provide. Given the agricultural industry's lobbying power and their keen interest in addressing the feral hog outbreak, Redwood felt certain that the funds could be had to undertake this venture. He didn't name his campaign the "Synthetic Reptilian Predator Design" fundraiser. Nobody would back such a thing. Instead, he proclaimed it the Dragon Genome Project.

Dragons have captivated human imagination for millennia. They've also inspired a certain primal fear. Wouldn't it be incredible to bring that myth to life? A two-minute video posing that question appeared online at the start of the fundraiser. It had to be faked—clips of dragons living in the wild, feeding their young, and casting long terrible shadows across the path of fleeing gazelle—but it was, in a word, majestic. Simon Redwood never formally admitted to creating it. But he never denied it, either. In an era when crowdfunding campaigns seem to be everywhere—and often fail to attract any donors whatsoever—the DGP met its goals within three weeks. Part of that was simply Redwood's name. It's no secret that he enjoys support from legions of fellow dreamers. And funders as well: Angel investors have been betting on his ideas for years.

Of course, the idea of creating a synthetic animal raised ethical concerns. Environmental groups threw a fit about it, and made fairly cogent arguments about the possible dangers, and the ecosystem impacts. The public seemed to pay little attention. The magic of dragons was simply too strong. By the time the project funded, Redwood's scientific endeavor already had tacit approval from the EPA. They wanted the hog problem addressed as much as anyone.

With the financing secured, Redwood's team began assembling the genome for his synthetic predator. As source organisms, they used sequences from various members of the animal kingdom. Reptiles, mostly, but some rodents as well. The dragon genome would be an amalgam of nature's cleverest and most resourceful hunters.

To Build A Dragon

Fast forward a couple of years, and Simon Redwood's dream seems well within reach. The so-called Dragon Genome specified a lizardlike creature about four feet long, with razor-sharp teeth and claws, whose circadian rhythms and night vision made it a nocturnal hunter. Its olfactory and taste receptors are fine-tuned to feral hogs, and the slender build lets it prowl the unforgiving habitats that they prefer.

At least, that's what the instructions said.

Unfortunately, Mother Nature did not bend so easily to the whims of a synthetic genome. Try as they might, Redwood and his team could not get an egg to hatch. Feral hogs continued to plague the Southwest, and many of the farmers and ranchers who'd backed Redwood's project from the get-go wondered if they'd made a mistake. The donors for the crowd-funded research project began grumbling about having their donations returned.

Those were grim days for Simon Redwood. He disappeared into his private laboratory, working round the clock to crack the secret of bringing his creation to life. Six months later, he emerged once more, gaunt, emaciated, but triumphant. A clutch of "dragon" eggs appeared viable and was about to hatch.

Hog Hunting

Redwood's reptilian predator was the answer to every rancher's prayer. They proved adept nocturnal hunters and targeted only feral hogs, just as the inventor had promised. They were short-lived, too: thanks to a built-in amino acid deficiency, Redwood's dragons only lasted for around ten days. Yet it was hard to argue with the results. At three designated test sites in the American Southwest, feral hog populations fell precipitously following the dragons' release. Just as Redwood had predicted, a synthetic predator succeeded where so many others had failed.

Following the success of early trials, Redwood built a company around the synthetic dragon design. The Dragon Genome might be public domain—that was a federal requirement for publicly-funded genome sequencing—but the aptly named Reptilian Corporation holds exclusive rights to the mysterious process that uses it to produce living reptiles. Admittedly, Redwood had little experience in the corporate sector himself. For help, he turned to an old friend who had been his roommate at Stanford.

Robert Greaves, who had studied chemical engineering and then law, was then a VP at Bingham Pharmaceuticals. He left considerable stock options and a high-profile clinical trial behind to lead Redwood's new venture. This looks to have been a fortuitous move. Ranchers, farmers, and even conservation agencies lined up to purchase the hog-hunting predator. Analysts estimate that Reptilian Corporation earned tens of millions of dollars in its first two years.

Not everyone was happy with Reptilian's success. Animal rights groups continued to protest the use of a predator as unnecessarily cruel. Environmental organizations raised concerns about possible ecological consequences. These complaints only intensified with reports of the reptiles living independently in the wild, claims which Greaves was quick to dismiss. He maintains that the reptilian predators can't survive on their own for more than a couple of weeks, and that tests conducted by his team confirm that they are only targeting feral hogs.

Though demand for the hog-hunting predator seems to have slowed, Reptilian Corporation has recruited some of the best genetic engineering talent in the country to build upon their early success. Greaves handles the day-to-day operations at the company, leaving Simon Redwood free to do what he does best.

Dream.

CHAPTER FOUR
Intercepted

My jalopy was the first thing to let me down. I threw myself into the driver's seat with twenty-two minutes left in my promised hour and jammed the ignition button with my finger.

The engine made a high-pitched whine but refused to turn over.

"Aw, come on." I waited three seconds and tried it again. This time, the car didn't so much as whimper. "Shit!"

I bailed out and ran to the bus stop. Nineteen minutes. In a sheer miracle, a bus from the red line pulled up a minute later. I jumped on and grabbed a ceiling loop, swaying in the crowded aisle and sweating as the minutes ticked down. I had fourteen left. Then ten minutes. Reptilian's shiny building swung into view at last. I hit the bell and jumped off at the next intersection.

Damn, it was stifling outside. Heat rolled off the sidewalk like it was a furnace. I half-walked, half-jogged the two blocks to Reptilian Corporation's mirrored building.

I checked my phone as I walked into the blessedly cool lobby. One hour and two minutes had passed since I'd hung up with Evelyn. I figured that was within the margin of error.

The same redhead waited at the reception desk. *Well, then. Batter up.*

"Well, we meet again," I said.

No flicker of recognition crossed her features. Maybe she was a robot. "Can I help you?"

"I'm Noah Parker."

She looked back to her screen. "And?"

Her dismissiveness put me off. It was one thing to do that to an interviewee, but I worked here now, damn it! I cleared my throat. "Well, it's my first day today."

Her brow furrowed prettily, which almost made up for the total lack of eye contact. "I don't have anything on the schedule."

Oh, God. Please tell me it wasn't a dream. "I just found out an hour ago."

"Who's your supervisor?"

"Evelyn Chang."

"Really?" She actually looked at me, in all my sweat-soaked glory, for more than half a second. "You're a *designer*?"

"A trainee, technically," I could feel the grin on my face.

"How did you pull that off?"

I put my hand on the desk in front of her, palm down. "Bribery." I lifted my hand away, revealing a tiny pewter figurine.

"*Ooh.*" She picked it up. "It's a little dragon! Is it for me?"

"Yep."

"Thank you." Her voice was an octave higher, too. She gave me a mock-serious side look. "I suppose I should print you an ID card."

"If it's not too much trouble," I said.

The ID printer spit out a plastic badge a second later. She clipped on a magnetic fastener and slid it across. My horrible DMV photo stared up at me, but I loved reading the words right below it.

Noah Parker
DESIGN

"You can go straight to the elevators from now on," she said.

"I don't know. What if you decide to tackle me?"

A faint smile played across her lips. "I'll call up and let her know you're here."

"Thanks."

"I'm Virginia, by the way."

So, suddenly I *did* need to know. "Nice to meet you." I fled to the elevators before I messed things up.

Maybe this won't be so bad after all.

Here's what was odd about the elevator. I could have sworn I hit the button for the seventh floor, but it stopped at five. The doors opened, revealing a huge guy in a buzz cut and dark suit. And I mean *huge*. He had to be six and a half feet tall, three hundred pounds. Built like a linebacker.

"Noah Parker?" he asked.

I almost said no. It must have been my survival instincts kicking in. "Uh, yeah. That's me."

"I'm Ben Fulton, chief of security."

"Nice to meet you," I said. "Do you work for Evelyn?"

"I work for Robert Greaves." He gestured to the hallway to his left. "Right this way, please."

I hesitated. "I think I'm supposed to go to seven."

"Not yet. This is your security interview."

"Oh. I didn't know there was one."

His smile had no warmth to it. "We like it to be a surprise."

I followed him down a rather plain hallway to an unmarked white door. He wrapped his big hand around the steel handle and held it there a half-second. Soft blue light glowed between his fingers. Then the door emitted a soft click, and he pushed it open.

A hidden biometric scanner. It piqued my curiosity a little. We passed through a room lined with flatscreen monitors showing security feeds from around the complex. There had to be fifteen or twenty screens, and they shifted views every five seconds or so. That made for at least a hundred separate cameras. Two in every hallway, at a minimum.

I followed Fulton took into a tiny, austere room that waited beyond. There was a square wooden table in the middle with chairs on either side. He settled into the larger of these, which left a notably smaller chair for me. It was about the size of a student's chair in an elementary school. I felt like someone's pet bird on a perch.

"So, you're a local boy, huh?" Fulton set down a manila folder with a government seal on the front, and my name on the tab.

A federal background check. *Are they for real?* "More or less. I grew up in Mesa."

"And you went to ASU."

I grinned. "Go Sun Devils."

"Evelyn Chang went there, didn't she?"

"For graduate school," I said. "We had the same thesis advisor. Dr. Sato." I shouldn't have I added that. He probably already knew, and if he didn't, it would sound weird. The last thing I needed was this guy digging into that particular fact. It was true, but also not a coincidence.

"So, what drew you to Reptilian Corporation?" he asked.

"You guys are doing some cutting-edge stuff with genetic engineering."

He looked up from his folder. "Really?"

I shrugged. "Customizing an organism from the genome up is pretty ambitious. A lot of people didn't think you could build a successful business out of it."

"Yeah, well, the jury's still out on that."

That was news to me. From everything I'd read, Reptilian Corporation was killing it in a time when most nascent biotechs had failed. "Still, I like the systems approach to genetics. And I think my simulator could help with things."

He frowned. "You're really here for all the genetic engineering stuff?"

"Of course." I paused. "Does that surprise you?"

"A little bit. Whenever I ask what brought people here, they always talk about the dragons."

Oh, crap. I'd forgotten how much people went nuts for them. "Yeah, sure. Dragons are awesome. I assumed I didn't even have to say it."

"But everyone *does* say that, Parker. They go on and on about dragons until I'm ready to throw up."

I tried a smile on him that I didn't feel. "Then I guess I'm a pleasant surprise."

"I don't like being surprised."

No, you like to do the surprising. My palms started sweating. It took a conscious effort not to wipe them on my new dress slacks. I couldn't do that, because if I lost this job I'd have to return them. "Good to know."

"There are plenty of biotechs employing genetic engineers," Fulton said.

"Not as many as there used to be."

"Still, someone like you probably got interest from both coasts."

I said nothing, even though he was spot-on. When my thesis came out, my phone *did* start to ring. A few of the big pharmas were sniffing around, and some of the rising biotech startups. Several universities sent out feelers, too, though they tended to start with Dr. Sato. That was often how people took the next step in academia, via personal connections. I suppose the same could be said of me, but the step I wanted to take was right in Reptilian's door.

Fulton raised his eyebrows at me.

"I'm sorry, was that a question?" I asked.

"Did you have interest from other companies?"

"A little," I said. "I never called them back."

"Then let's return to my original question. Why do you want to work at Reptilian?"

"I already said why. Your genetic engineers—" I stammered in my own defense, but he cut me off.

"Bullshit. Geeks like you can work anywhere, so when you go someplace, it's personal."

More personal than you know. Damn, this guy was good. I had to give him something, because it was kind of obvious that I needed a second reason to come to this company for this job. Clearly, I couldn't tell him the truth—that I intended to use the company's resources for my own designs, and probably sabotage a dragon. A flash of inspiration came. "You're right. There was something else that brought me here."

He smirked knowingly. "Spill it."

"Simon Redwood."

Fulton rolled his eyes. "Oh, hell. You're one of *those.*"

A Redwood fanatic, he meant. "Come on, man," I said. "You have to admit he's a genius."

"He's off his rocker."

"Well, I think he's brilliant," I said. "Been following his moves since I was a kid. And I dreamed about working for one of his companies, so here we are."

"Fine." Fulton set down his tablet with an air of resignation. He almost seemed a little disappointed, too. "Now you get to hear about the house security policy."

I covered my heart-thumping relief with sarcasm. "Oh, I can't wait."

"You will wear your security badge at all times. You won't attempt to access any restricted areas."

"Where am I allowed to go?"

"The seventh floor and the parking garage. That's about it, unless you're invited by a superior. Everything else is a restricted area. You'll have no expectation of privacy while in this building, but everything about your work here is considered a protected trade secret. Do you understand what that means?"

"No talking about work outside of work," I said.

"Exactly."

Somehow, even though I'd made it past the tough questions with this guy, I started feeling *more* intimidated by him. Maybe his sheer size had something to do with it. He occupied at least seventy percent of the room. It occurred to me that with the risks I'd probably be taking, I might want this guy on my good side. *So what's he into?* Well, I didn't know much about him, but I had a guess. "Can I ask a question?"

"Knock yourself out."

"What's he like?"

"Who? Redwood?"

"No." I waved that off like we'd covered it already. Then I leaned over the table and lowered my voice a little, as if afraid to say it out loud. Truth be told, I almost was. "Robert Greaves."

"Oh." He offered a half-smile, and I could tell I'd won a point. "He's the smartest man I know. And he operates on a level that most people don't appreciate."

"Is it true that he only wears black?"

He barked a laugh. "Don't believe everything you read, kid. He doesn't waste brainpower on unimportant things, that's all."

"Will I get to meet him?"

Fulton snorted. "Keyboard monkey like you? Probably not." He smiled to soften it, though.

"Ah well, worth a shot." I sensed the security interview coming to an end, and I wanted to leave on a high note. "Anything else we need to cover?"

"Officially, no."

"All right, what about *unofficially*?"

"Just a friendly word of advice. Don't hit on the help."

I started to stammer a response, because I didn't know what the hell he was talking about.

"The redhead in reception," Fulton said.

"Oh." Damn, he really *was* watching everything. I held up my hands. "Message received."

"Good. You can head on up, now."

"Thanks," I said.

So much for leaving on a high note.

CHAPTER FIVE
The New Guy

I took the elevator up to seven, where no one was waiting. I suppose I could have lingered in the lobby, but I imagined I could feel Fulton watching me over the security cameras. If he saw me waiting, he might decide to fill my time with more invasive security questions.

I tiptoed through the hatchery, where the same pair of white-garbed staffers ignored me. I watched as they entered one of the hatching pods and team-lifted an egg, rotating it forty-five degrees. They lowered it back into the foam holder with exaggerated slowness. *Like a mother with a newborn infant.* Sunlight bathed the entire pod like a spotlight. Warm air spilled out the open door; it had to be almost a hundred degrees in there.

I might have remembered it wrong, but this seemed to be the same egg from my last visit. The skylights for the other pods remained closed, which cloaked their empty egg-beds in twilight. Maybe I'd caught a lull in the design-print-hatch process, but the stillness to the place worried me. No eggs meant no dragons, and as far as I knew, dragons were the company's main source of revenue.

I hurried into the open door of Evelyn's office. She sat behind no less than six holo-projector screens but had her eyes on one and was speaking into a headset. "Yes, Robert."

The back of the screen was opaque, but I had a feeling she was on a video call with the big boss. I started to retreat, but she spotted me and beckoned me inside. When I tried to back out, she beckoned harder.

"We'll get it done," she said. "Okay. Bye." She eased the headset out of her hair and smiled at me, showing white teeth. "Noah Parker."

"Sorry I'm late. I didn't know there would be a security interview."

She waved off my apology. "It's been a crazy morning all around."

Tell me about it. I gestured at where the screen had been. "Was that Robert Greaves?"

She nodded. "He's breathing down my neck about the wild dragons. Which is why I'm glad you could get started. Come on, I'll introduce you to our team."

We passed through a set of Plexiglas doors to an odd-shaped room. The walls formed a hexagon. No, a pentagon. Five walls and five cozy workstations encircled a lab instrument the size of a minivan. I caught glimpses of it as we walked around to the right. Robotic arms zoomed back and forth on titanium guide poles, like an oversized 3D printer.

"What's with the robotic arms?" I asked.

"That's our biological printer."

I sucked in a sharp breath. "The God Machine." I'd heard whispers of the instrument that turned genetic code into viable dragon eggs. I couldn't wait to see it in action.

"Ha! You heard about the nickname."

"It's sort of public knowledge." Then I saw the tall stacks of high-end grid servers behind them. *Switchblades.* A new class of high-end computers, and there were *dozens* of them. Completely secure, nearly limitless on-premise computing resources. After working so long and so hard to get here, being this close to them sent a chill down my spine.

We approached the first workstation, where a thirty-something engineer hunched over his keyboard. The engineer part was just a guess; he had the intense stare and terrible posture that usually came with a highly organized mind.

"This is Brian O'Connell," Evelyn said.

The man went on typing, oblivious to fact that we stood right behind him and Evelyn had just said his name.

"Brian?" Evelyn touched his shoulder.

He flinched and tore his eyes from the screen with obvious reluctance. "Oh, hey."

"This is Noah, the new design trainee."

We shook hands. His wrapped mine like a warm blanket. He smiled in a friendly way beneath his dirty-blonde goatee, a spot-on match for the uncut hair. Between that and the comb-over, he looked almost like a monk. But his eyes burned with blue fire, even as they slid away from mine back to his screens.

"Brian wrote the code for our biological printer," Evelyn said.

"The thing that built the dragon eggs? I'm impressed," I said.

He mumbled something that might have been thanks. Evelyn ushered us out into the next workstation, where a dark-haired girl sat with excellent posture, typing no less than 120 words per minute. She turned to greet us with a big smile, perfect teeth and everything. Right then, Evelyn's phone buzzed and she had to step away. Leaving me alone, to fumble out my own introduction.

"Hello. I'm Noah. The, uh, new guy."

She shook my hand with delicate fingers. "Welcome! I'm pretty."

"Oh." Her self-awareness threw me for a loop. "I agree."

She giggled. "No, I'm *Priti*. Priti Korrapati."

Oh my God. I felt my face heating and wished I could melt into the floor. "Right. Sorry about that."

"Happens all the time."

"So, what do you do for Evelyn?"

"I'm a designer. Started out in plants, made the jump to reptiles."

I gave her a side-look. "What kind of plants? *Arabidopsis*?" That was the one of the best-studied plants in the scientific community. The rest of the world knew it as mustard weed.

She smiled and shook her head. "*Oryza sativa.*"

"Rice? No way!" Rice was second only to corn in research dollars. The big agribiotechs put a lot of money into genetic engineering. "In the private sector, I'm guessing."

"You guess correctly."

God, I loved her accent. I wanted to keep her talking. "How does that compare to biotech startup world?"

"It's quite similar, actually. Perhaps a bit more intense."

"Perform or die."

"Maybe not that drastic. But you have the idea."

Evelyn reappeared; a stray hair hung across her face. "Sorry about that." She gripped her tablet so hard I thought she might break it.

"Everything all right?" I asked.

"Yes, but we'll have to cut this short. They want me upstairs."

"No problem." I turned back to Priti. "Nice to meet you."

"Likewise."

I rejoined Evelyn and moved on to the next workstation, which I thought might be mine. But a heavyset guy in a ball cap slumped in the chair, either deep in thought or totally asleep.

"Frogman?" Evelyn whispered.

Did she just say Frogman?

He woke like a hibernating bear. His eyes came into focus. "Evelyn. S'going on?"

"This is our new designer, Noah Parker."

"Paul Myers." He gave me a friendly nod. "Good to meet you."

"Did she call you Frogman?"

"Everyone does. Did my graduate thesis on *Xenopus.*"

"I'll bet that's useful." Frogs were a great model for developmental traits. Amphibians were about as close as you could get to dragons and still be in a valid genetics branch. I had to admit that my weak point in genetics might lie in the developmental realm. *I'm going to need to talk to this guy.*

He didn't seem like much of a talker, though. He offered a noncommittal grunt and put on noise-canceling headphones. Evelyn quietly beckoned me out, into the second-to-last workstation. No one sat in the chair, but a half-circle of empty energy drink cans said the place was occupied. If I had to guess, I'd expect whoever sat there was probably in the nearest restroom.

"That's Wong's spot," Evelyn said. "He had to fly home to get his visa renewed, but he should be back in a couple of weeks."

"Where's he from?"

"China."

That caught my attention because I'd been dabbling in Mandarin as a second language. "What part?"

She pursed her lips, as if reluctant to answer. "Shenzhen."

"Oh." Shenzhen was home to China's government-sponsored research laboratories. These were basically the genetic engineering version of sweatshops. The government recruited the best and brightest right out of high school, and worked them eighty hours per week, fifty-two weeks a year. Most of them slept in the lab. At the end of each month, the least-productive ten percent of the workforce got their walking papers. "How long did he last?"

"Two years."

"Jesus."

"He kept his sense of humor. You'll like him." She ushered me into the fifth workstation, a kind of wedge-shaped cubicle about six feet wide and ten feet long. "Here's your spot."

A leather chair and glass-top desk took up one half of it. A conveyor belt from the God Machine took up the other half. I sidled up to it for a better look inside. Warm air flowed through the gap like a furnace. *There they are.* The grid servers gave off a gentle hum. Their LED screens cast a soft blue light on the titanium inner frame. The robotic arms had gone still, obscuring my view of the central printing chamber. Conduits and cable guides kept all the wiring neatly organized, and I couldn't see a speck of dust. Clean as a spaceship.

I liked a good clean lab. It spoke to the people in charge. I started to say as much, when I noticed the strange device on the floor beneath the printing chamber. It looked like something out of the Atari museum, a jumble of black plastic and looped wires about the size of a shoebox. Old-school status lights blinked erratic green and amber at the base. "What's that?"

"That's the Redwood Codex."

Redwood Codex. The words carried an aura of intrigue. "What does it do?"

"It's the secret behind Simon Redwood's successful prototype. But that's a story for another time," she said. "You want to try logging in?"

I really wanted to ask more about Redwood, but she looked like she was in a hurry. "Sure thing."

She gestured me to the chair. I slipped into it and rolled up to the flat glass table. But there was no keyboard or mouse or anything. "Where's the—"

She took my wrist and guided my palm to the cool glass surface. A narrow line of blue-white light traced my fingers, followed by the muted glow of a palm scan. A soft chime sounded, and then touch-controls illuminated in the glass: keyboard, finger-pad, and some kind of an intercom. Two feet in front of my face, an opaque square appeared in midair. I fought the urge to wave my hand through it.

Projection monitors. Oh, my sweet lord. I didn't think I'd get them, too. I exhaled slowly, and my fingers found the keys. There was even faint tactile feedback as they slid into place. Incredible technology. "I'm in."

Evelyn's tablet beeped. She glanced at it, frowned, and let out a little sigh.

"What's wrong?" I asked.

"Nothing you need to worry about." She shook her head, as if to clear it. "The systems group already ported your simulator code to our servers. Now you'll just need to customize the interface to our design program."

"What are you using for that? GeneDesign?"

"No. It's something we cooked up in house." She reached across to touch a button on the keyboard. A new application bloomed on the screen in front of me.

"DragonDraft 3D," I read. "Never heard of it."

"It's our interface to the Dragon Reference. Every gene, every variant, every regulatory sequence."

I sensed a hint of pride in her voice. "You wrote this, didn't you?"

"It's my claim to fame around here."

"Well geez, if you've got that then I imagine the dragons pretty much design themselves."

"In the hands of the right person, absolutely. Let me show you." Her narrow fingertips danced across the keyboard. "We'll start a basic flying model."

A grayscale dragon appeared in mid-screen, rotating slowly in two dimensions. It was a clunky low-res image. The triangular head reminded me of a viper, but the neck and body resembled a lizard on steroids. Evelyn hit a key, and the dragon spread its wide, leathery wings.

Evelyn tapped another key to bring up a window of slide controls: *Body Size, Wingspan, Musculature,* and at least a dozen others. "We've mapped the genetic basis of key physical traits." She slid down *Body Size,* and the dragon shrank. She nudged up *Claw Length,* and the talons on the feet grew from meek to downright frightening.

She tinkered with more of the feature sliders, and I noticed something about the draft interface. Whenever she slid a feature downward, the number in the top right of the screen jumped up from zero. When she slid it the other way, the numbers descended. If it got to zero, the slider wouldn't move up another hair.

"What's this number up here?" I asked.

"Feature points. They govern how many advantages we can give to any one dragon."

"What if you need to increase something, and you're at zero?"

She shrugged. "You have to take them from something else. Speed for stamina, body size for cranial capacity, that sort of thing."

"Seems a little restrictive," I said.

"Remember that dragon you saw on your interview?"

"The wild one? Yeah."

"What if it were twice as big and three times as smart?"

"Oh." I chuckled. "Good point."

"Besides, we're trying to develop a prototype that's calmer and less predatory."

That surprised me a little. According to everything I'd read, Reptilian's hog-hunting dragons were a commercial success because of their aggressiveness. "Why would you want to do that?"

"A predatory dragon has only limited market potential," she said.

"What would you do with a . . . non-predatory dragon?"

"Do you know how many dog owners there are in the US?"

"That's easy. Zero." A few years had passed since the outbreak of the canine epidemic, but dog populations still hadn't recovered. Every descendant of the gray wolf proved susceptible to the contagion. That meant all dogs, no matter the breed. The epidemic had originated in Asia but quickly spread to other continents. There was no cure. No stay of execution. Once your dog developed the telltale lesions on his muzzle, it was too late. We kept waiting for them to announce a cure or some kind of treatment. Lots of smart people tried. Companies, too—after all, dogs were a billion-dollar business. None of it mattered. Nothing could stop the epidemic. After the fourth or fifth failure of a promising therapy, we stopped getting our hopes up.

"*Before* the epidemic," Evelyn said.

I shrugged. "Probably twenty million."

"Try forty-five million."

"Wow, that's a lot. But dogs aren't coming back anytime soon."

"That's the point."

Realization dawned on me then. "You want to sell dragons . . . as pets?"

"If we can produce a domesticated model, yes."

I wanted to tell her she was crazy, but it probably wasn't the worst idea. "All right, I'll give it a whirl. How do I design one?"

"Design privileges are something you'll earn over time."

"Oh." I didn't have to fake my disappointment.

"It's your first day, Noah," she said.

And I'm an unknown quantity. "I guess have to prove myself, huh?"

"Everyone does."

"Any suggestion for how I do that?"

Evelyn smiled. "Get your simulator code up and running. Then we'll talk."

CHAPTER SIX
INTERLUDE

I was twelve when I first got interested in genetics. My brother Connor was ten, and we spent every waking minute together. That's probably why I noticed the little changes. He started to tire more easily, whereas I had boundless energy. He couldn't jump as high as he used to.

No one believed me, though. I tried telling my mom how there were some days when he couldn't keep up with me. And that he had trouble getting to his feet sometimes. He'd get on all fours, then push his butt up in the air, and finally come back on his thighs. It looked weird. But she worked all the time to support us. Every night when she got home, I think she was just grateful to see we were still in one piece. She didn't see Connor the way I did.

Right up until the day he fell while we were out playing and couldn't get up. She believed me that time. She called an ambulance.

Somehow, we bypassed the emergency room and landed in something called the PICU. Pediatric Intensive Care Unit. That was probably a good thing, because it brought Connor in front of a rarity: a doctor who actually gave a damn.

She was an older lady, short and sharp-eyed. She wore a bright floral blouse beneath a well-worn lab coat. If it weren't for the coat and the stethoscope, I'd have mistaken her for someone's grandmother. She bustled in while a nurse was checking Connor's vitals. "I'm Dr. Miller. Want to tell me what happened?"

"They were playing outside," Mom said. "He fell and couldn't get back up."

"How hard did he fall?"

Mom looked at me, and so did Dr. Miller. I squirmed under their gazes. "Not that hard. It was more of a trip." I didn't volunteer the fact that I was the one who tripped him.

Connor didn't either, but made a face at me behind their backs. The nurse left, and Dr. Miller began her own examination.

"He's behind in his growth curves," she said.

My mom waved this off. "He's always been small for his age."

I smirked at Connor, who stuck out his tongue at me.

"Any staring spells or seizures?" the doctor asked. Her East Coast accent stretched out the vowels, which made her a little hard to understand.

"None that I saw," Mom said. She looked at me for confirmation.

I shook my head.

Dr. Miller took out a reflex hammer and tapped Connor's knees. His legs jerked out, but only slightly. She frowned and lifted his legs one at a time to examine his ankles. "Any problems with walking or running?"

"He runs slow," I volunteered.

Connor punched my arm.

"His heel cords are a little tight," Dr. Miller said.

"Is that significant?" my mom asked.

"By itself, no," Dr. Miller said. "But with sudden ataxia and the diminished reflexes, it could be the early signs of a muscle disease."

"Oh my God," Mom whispered.

"Are you the biological mother?" the doctor asked.

"Of course, I'm his god—" she began, but caught herself. "Yes. Why would you ask that?"

"They can run in families. Have you had any health issues? Especially muscle weakness or problems walking?"

"No."

"What about fatigue?"

"Who doesn't have some fatigue?"

Dr. Miller barked a laugh. "Fair point, Mrs. Parker. Does his father have any health concerns?"

Connor and I waited for the answer, both of us holding our

breath. Mom *never* talked about our dad. He took off when I was four. Connor had no memory of him. I thought I did sometimes—vague flashes of a deep voice and dark beard—but I couldn't be sure.

Mom frowned. "We're not in touch. But I don't think so."

"I'd like to do further testing to rule out genetic disease."

"What does that involve?" Mom asked, in a tone that meant, *what does that cost?*

"We'd look at a panel of a couple hundred genes. Have you unlocked their sequence data?"

Every newborn in Arizona had their genome sequenced, though the results were "locked" in a data vault, only to be consulted if there was a problem.

"No. I don't like the idea of that information being out there," Mom said.

"It will stay confidential, as part of your medical records."

"Can you guarantee there won't be some kind of a data breach?"

Dr. Miller paused. "No. But your genome is like the money in your bank account. You have to take it out to use it. Otherwise, what's the point?"

"Are there any alternatives?" Mom asked.

"A muscle biopsy. It could confirm the diagnosis, though it's a more primitive test." She lowered her voice. "Not to mention uncomfortable."

In the end, my mom gave over. She signed the papers to unlock our genome data for genetic testing.

The following week, the pediatrician called with news: Connor had a genetic variant in a gene called BICD2. That was short for *bicaudal D homolog 2*, and mutations in it caused a dominant form of spinal muscular atrophy. Mom and I didn't have the variant. Dr. Miller explained that it was probably a newly arisen change, a so-called *de novo* mutation. Every person has fifty or sixty *de novo* mutations that they didn't get from their parents. It's a quirk of nature: The low-but-measurable error rate from copying our genetic code. Most mutations happen outside of genes, so they have no serious consequences. Connor was just unlucky.

There was a problem, though. Connor's mutation had never been seen in a muscular atrophy patient. Or in the DNA of healthy people, for that matter. The genetic testing laboratory classified it as a Variant of Uncertain Significance, or VUS. It might cause disease, or it might not. The lab couldn't say for sure. Insufficient evidence, they claimed. They wanted to know if it would be possible to get a sample from Connor's biological father.

"Never gonna happen," Mom said.

Dr. Miller understood, but her hands were tied where the diagnosis was concerned. Connor's variant remained a VUS.

In some ways, that almost made things worse. Without an official diagnosis, we didn't know what to expect for Connor's future. Some mutations in his gene caused only mild muscle weakness. Others caused a severe and progressive disease. The uncertainty hung over our family like a specter. Maybe he had the disease and would start getting worse. Maybe he had something else entirely. BICD2 disease had no cure. Because of the uncertainty, Mom couldn't get him into any clinical trials. All she could do was sit back and watch.

Twelve-year-old me called bullshit on that. If there was no way to prove that Connor's mutation caused disease, well, I'd just have to invent one.

CHAPTER SEVEN
Design 48

The utility of a biological simulator in a place like this was obvious, at least to me, but I'd still have to get the design team on board. I believed in my program's logic—so did Evelyn, or she wouldn't otherwise have brought me in—but integrating it with the existing design program was a major challenge. It had to be seamless, built right into DragonDraft3D so that the designers could run simulations at every step of their process. That's a lot harder than it sounds. The design interface was unknown territory. I had to understand it inside and out before I could do anything.

I probably put in seventy or eighty hours that first week. Day blurred into night. One particular advantage of installing a new software package into Reptilian's systems is that I was temporarily granted high-level administrative access. And so, while my main focus was installing the simulator code for everyone, I also created a private virtual workspace for myself. A place where I could tinker with genetic code and dragon designs without anyone knowing about it. As long as I kept file sizes reasonable and didn't use too much computing power, this little testing ground would give me a private sandbox.

I was going to need that privacy. Indirect as it might seem, the path was pretty clear to me. Get my simulator up and running. Establish myself as a key part of the design team. Then I'd have access to the company's computing resources and their all-important God

Machine. That's when the real work, the work I'd *actually* come here to do, could finally begin.

At the moment, however, dragons were the bread-and-butter. The visual models produced by DragonDraft3D were clunky, monochrome things. The general shape and number of limbs were correct, but that was about it. My simulator already offered a dramatic improvement, but I knew I could do better. The company's private servers—the Switchblades—offered more computing power than I'd ever imagined. So I expanded my code as I went, adding new subroutines and deeper features. The designs evolved into ever more precise biological models. Evelyn was going to love them. I'd have shown her right then, but it was Sunday. How did it get to be Sunday?

It was probably for the best—I still hadn't tested the latest updates. But first, I needed coffee. My legs carried me out of the pentagonal design lab. Only when I passed through the sealed door did I notice that the entire room had a soft, deep hum to it when the God Machine wasn't running. It had a smell, too: a faint hint of metal and oil beneath the hot silicone.

The door whispered shut behind me, dampening the noise. A new aroma wafted to my nose, and I followed it like a moth to a flame. Down the white LED-lit hallway, around the corner, and into the break room. Evelyn had pointed it out once on my tour, and I'd mentally bookmarked it for a closer look. A rectangular glass table sat in the center of the room, flanked by half a dozen ergonomic chairs.

Swedish-made furniture, by the look of it. High-end stuff. But my tired eyes skimmed right across it to the counter on the far wall. There was a *second* machine in the building that made dreams come true. This one dispensed not dragon eggs but liquid delight from a dark master. The screen brightened as I got near it. A wonderful array of drink options beckoned. I pressed the rectangle that read *Cappuccino*.

The panel flashed a confirmation, then opened a new window: a live camera feed of the machine's interior. My cup took shape in red plastic on the metal platform, the 3D-printing arms spinning around it as they shaped it. The instaplastic material hardened in seconds, while puffs of steam announced that the milk was ready. Part of me thought this was too cool, too *easy* to be real. So when the panel slid open to reveal my serving of freshly-made coffee, it was quite a moment.

I cradled the still-warm cup in my hands, brought it close. There was even a little Reptilian Corporation logo etched on the outside. Steam drifted up from it. I closed my eyes and inhaled. "Ah, sweet elixir."

Frogman shuffled in, headphones on. "Hey." He hit the button for black coffee.

I watched the vidfeed over his shoulder. "This is a hell of a coffee machine."

He grunted. "They like us well-caffeinated."

"They?"

"The board of directors."

"Oh." I nodded sagely. "I suppose I thought Robert Greaves called the shots here." That's what most of the industry-analysis articles claimed. Redwood, despite his founding the company, let his old friend run the day-to-day.

"Who do you think runs the board?"

Good point. "Is Simon Redwood around much?"

"If he is, I haven't seen him."

I felt a small stab of disappointment, because I wasn't lying when I told Fulton that I had a slight Redwood obsession. Granted, Frogman didn't strike me as the most observant person in the world. Redwood could probably dance a jig in the corner of his module and he might not notice.

I swirled my cappuccino, admiring the perfect froth level. On my way back to my workstation, I noticed that all the designers were working on Sunday, too, other than the mysterious Wong. Everyone at Reptilian went the extra mile. I hoped I'd live up to the reputation.

Thanks to the caffeine infusion, I banged out a couple more hours of work before heading home.

Monday couldn't get here soon enough.

I crashed hard that night. When my alarm went off at six a.m., it was painful. But the promise of showing off my simulator got me up and moving. I beat most of the designers to work, but not Evelyn.

She sat behind her desk, sipping espresso behind a phalanx of holoscreens.

I knocked softly. "How would you like to test drive the new biological simulator?"

She craned her head around a screen to look at me. Her brow furrowed. "You look exhausted."

I shrugged, uncomfortable under the sudden scrutiny. "I was up late."

"Again? You've been putting in a lot of hours, Noah."

"Have I? Hardly seems that way."

"Seventy-six hours last week, based on the server logs."

"I like to keep busy." And I hadn't realized she'd be keeping tabs on me, either.

"You should pace yourself. But since you brought it up, let's see what you've done," Evelyn said.

I came around her desk. "Already sent it to you."

She brought up DragonDraft3D in a new holoscreen and loaded a design. "This is the original dragon, the hog-hunter." She launched the simulator with a flurry of keys. A three-dimensional dragon shimmered into view, rotating slowly in full color. It was lithe but muscular, with impressive sets of teeth and claws. The scales had a dull brown and green color to them that reminded me of Texas dustbowls. I mentally celebrated the fact that I'd thought to go full color.

Evelyn gasped.

"Do you like it?" I asked.

"It's very impressive." She put two fingers on her touchpad and spun the model around. "The physical traits look spectacular."

"I thought so, too." *And I didn't even cheat.* I could have, too. I could have taken photos of the real-world dragons that hatched from Reptilian's eggs, and made sure my simulator predicted them perfectly. But that would only work once, and someone at Reptilian would probably be able to figure it out pretty quick. I didn't dare risk coming off as dishonest.

"There's another model I want to try it on." She tapped a few commands. "Will your simulator run in real-time?"

"It should." The simulator would work on any organism, theoretically, though I'd done most of my testing on higher-order animals.

She loaded a design labeled *48* and launched the simulator. The visualization took longer to load this time, even on the fancy servers.

"It's a little slow," Evelyn said.

Ouch. I couldn't resist a parry. "You must have made a lot of modifications."

Her cheeks flushed a little, and I wished I'd hadn't said that. *Typical Noah, open mouth, insert foot.*

"Then again, I haven't had access to your level of computational firepower," I said. "I'm sure there are things I could do to speed it up."

The simulator finished loading, and the image of the resulting dragon appeared in midair in front of us. Right away, I could spot the differences from the hog-hunting model. An almost friendly stoutness had replaced the sleek lines of the hunting model. All the sharp edges had been smoothed out, from the ridges on the back to the size of the claws and teeth. They'd practically made it *playful*. From the size of the cranium, it would be smarter, too.

"This is a very different dragon," I said.

"It's meant to be."

"Not for hunting hogs, I hope?"

"More like playing with kids."

I gave her a sidelong look. "You're serious about that domestication thing, aren't you?"

"There's a huge market if we can produce the right reptiles for it."

Again with the market talk. A hint of worry began nagging at the back of my head. "So how close are we?"

"Not very. Our dragons want to be predators."

"That's not too surprising, given the genetic sources," I said. The Dragon Genome was a composite based on the genomes of lizards, snakes, and rodents. Predator instincts would be strong. "What have you done to tweak it?"

"Already more than I thought necessary. Physical traits, intelligence, metabolism, the works."

"I assume you brought down some of the hormones."

"If we lower them any further, the thing won't want to get out of bed."

"Do you mind if I . . ." I gestured at the design.

She slid over. "By all means."

I slid up next to her and scrolled through the design in DragonDraft3D. *Jeez, she's not kidding.* I counted no less than thirty genetic modifications to the endocrine system. "Wow. Not bad."

She smiled. "You're not the only one who can put in seventy hours a week."

"Touché." I scrolled down the list of enhancements. "I don't see any neurotransmitter mods."

She grimaced. "I don't trust those. Too unpredictable."

"They're a billion-dollar industry, you know." Second only to lipid-lowering medication, the last time I checked.

"Without a way to predict the outcome, I've been reluctant to tamper with those networks."

I shrugged. "A little mood-centering might go a long way. Otherwise it's running on survival instincts." Most wild animals lived by instinct: fight, eat, mate, survive. You almost had to target those pathways to domesticate something.

Evelyn sighed. "It can't hurt to try. Any recommendations?"

"I'm partial to serotonin receptors."

She rolled back in her chair and gestured at her desktop panel. "Go ahead."

I felt the grin spread across my face. "Really?"

"Sure. I'm in edit mode anyway."

I pressed three fingers down on the glass to resize the keyboard— she must have teeny tiny hands—and found the right menus in DragonDraft3D. To Evelyn's credit, there were modification commands for every neurotransmitter pathway I'd ever heard of.

I kept mine subtle: first, structural change on the serotonin reuptake channel, to slow it down. Serotonin stimulated positive reinforcement: the longer it stuck around, the more a dragon would be content with its current stimuli.

Of course, satisfaction might not be enough to counteract the wild aggression of the juvenile Evelyn had shown me. A secondary adjustment couldn't hurt. Dopamine seemed like the best option. I didn't dare tamper with dopamine release; that would be akin to putting the animal on heroin. Instead, I goosed up the sensitivity of the receptor to help the dragon *get happy*, as they say.

I double-checked the modifications and nodded to myself. "Let's try that."

Evelyn copied my three-finger shortcut to resize the keyboard. "Looks like you're getting comfortable with our systems."

Whoops. I'd spent so much time on them the week before, I didn't realize how familiar it felt. "I'm a quick learner," I said, chiding myself for such carelessness. The less she knew about how comfortable I was with their systems, the better. They still hadn't taken away my sysadmin access.

"So it seems. But we've made enough tweaks to this model. I think it merits a live test." She hit a bright red rectangular button in the top right corner of the keyboard.

"What was that?" I asked.

She smiled, and her eyes glowed with joy. "The print button."

It took a lot of self-restraint not to run back to the design lab. By the time we got there, the God Machine had already whirred into motion, its robotic arms bobbing and weaving like the needles of a possessed sewing machine.

"How long does it take?" I asked.

"Seventeen minutes, give or take," Evelyn said.

I pulled up the design simulation on my workstation while we waited. The specs looked good, but I didn't really have a way to guess at the dragon's aggression. If they really wanted to tap into the consumer market, the dragon would have to be gentle as a lamb.

Finally, the arms of the God Machine went still. My conveyor belt purred into motion. I peered down into the darkness of the print chute. A round shadow appeared and zoomed toward me. Color bloomed when it hit the light: chestnut brown, with flecks of black and ivory. Kind of like a sparrow's egg, except this one was the size of a small watermelon.

"God, it's gorgeous," I breathed.

"I never get tired of seeing them come out of the printer," Evelyn said.

"This one looks different from the one I saw on my tour."

"They're all unique. Like snowflakes."

"Even eggs printed from the same design?"

She shrugged. "The patterns are always similar, but there are subtle variations."

"Hmm. Biological noise?"

"I suspect it's from the Redwood Codex."

"I can't wait to hear what that is. Other than a fire hazard, I mean."

She laughed. "That fire hazard is the reason we produce living dragons, and our competitors do not."

"What does it do?"

"You'd have to ask Simon Redwood."

Oh, please be serious. I'd have killed for five minutes him. "Sure. Where's his office again?"

"He doesn't have one."

Damn. "Have you met him?"

"Once, very briefly." Her eyes glowed.

I leaned close to her. "What did you think of him?"

"I thought, this man is crazy as a loon." But she smiled, and I knew she was kidding. In fact, I got the distinct feeling that maybe she was a Redwood believer, too.

The arrival of the hatchery staffers prevented me from asking a hundred more questions about Redwood. The handlers hefted our freshly printed egg into their foam-topped cart and whisked it away to the hatchery.

"They don't waste any time, do they?" I asked.

"We don't like the temperature to drop more than a couple degrees. And the hatchery staff are . . . attentive."

Now there's an understatement. "When will the egg be ready to hatch?"

"Almost two weeks."

"Aw, why so long?"

"We've pushed it down as much as we could," Evelyn said. "Any faster and the lungs won't develop by hatching."

"It's going to kill me to wait that long."

Evelyn gave me an indulgent smile. "That's what I said about Design 36."

CHAPTER EIGHT
Distance to Target

Reptilian took over my life, expanding like a gas to fill the entire vacuum of free time. I had an air tablet hot-linked to my workstation, so I could work whenever I wanted. Of course, that way lay madness. There was nothing to do but wait until Design 48 was ready to hatch, at which point things would get incredibly busy. I had to find something to fill the gaps.

In college and early grad school, I had all kind of hobbies. Ultimate frisbee, trail running, pickup soccer. I spent almost as much time outside as I did inside. Grad school eventually put the kibosh on that: the round-the-clock work schedule and tiny living stipend didn't leave much room for recreational activities. What little time I had left, I used to spend with my ex-girlfriend, Jane.

Now, for the first time, I had a regular work schedule. And more importantly, a regular *paycheck*. Sure, it was a trainee's salary and there were student loans to pay off, but it was still more money than I'd ever seen. The health insurance was better, too, though it came with strings attached. To avoid stiff surcharges on my premium, I had to log regular physical activity. They called it a *wellness incentive* but it was essentially forced exercise. I refused to run or ride a bicycle in Arizona's oppressive heat.

Thousands of acres of rugged desert and sparse timber still surrounded the Phoenix's outer limits. Tonto National Forest, Gila Reserve, all the big-name parks were within reach. I bought myself pair of decent hiking boots and went exploring.

It got me outside and gave me something to do, but I grew bored of it. Even after I almost fell off a boulder trying to take a selfie with a saguaro cactus.

I couldn't stop thinking about Design 48. Between my tweaks to the serotonin system and all the adjustments Evelyn's other designers had already made from the hog-killing dragon, it was hard to imagine our prototype wouldn't be compatible with domestic life. Even so, a sharp little sliver of doubt began to poke at the back of my head. This was the *forty-eighth* attempt to domesticate Redwood's reptilian predator. Evelyn knew her stuff, too. I'd seen that not just in her design, but in the underlying code of DragonDraft3D. It was encouraging that she'd wanted to print a prototype based on changes we'd done together, but I still felt like I was missing something.

On the walk back to the parking lot after said boulder incident, I passed a young couple headed out into the park. Both of them stared so hard at their watches that they nearly walked right into me.

"Thirty-five degrees, fifty-six point two zero nine minutes north," the man said.

"Same here," the woman replied. "Fifty-six point two zero nine."

The numbers sang to me. *What strange voodoo is this*?

"Excuse me," I said. "Do you mind if I ask what you're doing?"

"We're on a geocache," the woman said.

"Oh. Right." I nodded as if this made perfect sense.

"You have no idea what that is, do you?" she asked.

I laughed. "Not a clue."

"It's like a treasure hunt with GPS. You navigate from one waypoint to the next, until you reach the end."

"So you just, what, use your phone?"

The man shook his head. "Not reliable. You want a dedicated GPS unit, or a watch." He held up his wrist so I could see it.

A hobby with tech gear? *Sign me up*. "Thanks. I'll let you get back to it." I hustled past them toward the trailhead. Hiking was a bust, but this geocache thing might hold some promise.

Come on, this was basically following a satellite-guided treasure hunt. How hard could it be?

I found out a week later when I set out on my first-ever geocache. I'd opted for a higher-end GPS watch, figuring that even a slight technological edge might save hours of frustration. Hundreds of geocaches existed right under the noses of Phoenix metro residents, and twice as many could be found in the surrounding desert. I opted for one of the latter, a geocache called Lone Luna.

The cache was *supposed* to be a straight shot from the parking lot southwest about a mile and a half. The moment I turned off the highway, a loud steady crunch from underneath the jalopy's worn tires announced a gravel parking lot. *Perfect.* The description for this cache said something about it being straight down a trail, so I'd opted to wear sneakers instead of my hiking boots.

Trouble was, once I'd parked and while I waited for my watch to sync with satellites, I didn't *see* any trails. My watch double-beeped its readiness; sure enough, the distance to target came up as 1.55 miles.

"Time to find this thing."

Five steps later, a sharp pain jabbed the top of my foot. "Ow! Shit!" Barrel cactus. I'd been looking at my watch and walked right into it.

The worst thing about barrel cacti isn't running into one. It's what comes afterward. The spines are curved like fishhooks. I spent two torturous minutes extracting myself from that mess while the sun beat down mercilessly on me.

Distance to target: 1.54 miles. Not an auspicious start.

I skirted the barrel cactus, stumbled on a pile of loose rocks, and caught a thistle-branch right across the midriff. "*Damn* it!" I plucked the branch free with my pocketknife so that it wouldn't prick me again. This didn't qualify as a trail in my book. I had to backtrack to get around the brambles.

Distance to target: 1.56 miles. *Son of a bitch.*

So far, I didn't understand the point of this hobby. The treasure-hunt aspect appealed to me, but raw desert terrain offered little comfort for crossing terrain. If I wasn't careful, I'd walk into a ravine or step on a rattlesnake.

I plucked the last errant thorn from my midriff, stifled a sigh, and pressed on. The land sloped down into a shallow vale, where the brambles mercifully gave way to hard dirt. The only obstacles were occasional patches of creosote and bur sage, which I skirted while trying to keep my bearings. The distance to target ticked steadily downward, until I had less than a tenth of a mile.

Strangely, after fighting my way from one torturous hazard to the next, I kind of looked forward to finding this thing. I picked up my pace to a jog, stumbling over loose rocks and clumps of dead weeds. I dodged a last patch of creosote and saw the target: a moon-white boulder about four feet tall. How it had come to rest here, I couldn't even begin to guess, but I knew the logical place to hide a cache when I saw it. Hell, it even fit the name of the cache.

Well, where is it?

I skirted the boulder, expecting to find a box or container or *something* at the base. But I came up empty. Worse, I noticed someone had scrawled curse-words on the side of the boulder. Someone else used a marker to just write the word "Boo." Clearly, I wasn't the first geocacher to get this far and not find the prize.

There was no cache any longer.

"Well, shit." In retrospect, maybe I should have checked the comments or something. It sucked not having a tangible object to mark my first geocache, but I figured the boulder was good enough.

You'd think that after coming this far and failing to find a cache at the end of it, I'd be sick of geocaching. But that's the thing about me: coming this close only made me want it more.

CHAPTER NINE
Aggression

During the incubation period, everyone at work tried to concentrate on something but Design 48. I finished fine-tuning the behavioral module and showcased it to the other members of the design team. Evelyn schooled me on some of the finer points of DragonDraft3D. She challenged me with test cases—adapting dragons for various physical environments and lifestyles.

I didn't know if it was unusual for the Director of Dragon Design to train a new employee, but I didn't ask. Maybe Evelyn needed something to fill time during the endless wait as much as I did.

The points system in DragonDraft3D made the design process more challenging. I suppose the purpose was to prevent us from creating a super-predator. I could create a big, strong dragon that was too dumb to fly, or a clever dragon that couldn't claw its way out of a cardboard box. I understood the safety angle, but it seemed to me that the whole system prevented one from designing something that matched people's expectations for dragons. But that was a problem that only mattered once we cracked domestication. The original Reptilian product, the hog-hunter, fulfilled its purpose well. Only the amino acid deficiency—the ecological failsafe—kept it within the point restriction.

At last, the incubation period ended. I may or may not have been staring at the holo-clock on my desk when Evelyn showed up. "Are you ready?"

"Sure." I stood and followed her through the airtight doors to the hatchery. Warm air smothered me like a blanket, and I had to shade my eyes against the bright skylights. The sparrow-egg lay on the other side of the Plexiglas, resting on an honest-to-god nest of straw and synthetic grass.

Evelyn and I settled into two of the six conference room chairs that lined the window. I glanced over in time to see her lace her fingers, close her eyes, and whisper something.

"Did you just say a prayer?"

She smiled and looked down at her hands. "Every little bit helps."

"You really care about your designs, huh?"

Her smile fell away. "It's not just this design. This company needs a domesticated dragon, or we won't stand a chance at hitting our sales target."

"How can that be? No one else makes dragons."

"There's only so much demand."

"What about zoos, and wildlife parks?"

"They don't generally go for animals with a two-week shelf life. Most of our sales are to ranchers and farmers."

"There are plenty of those, aren't there?"

"Sure. The only problem is that our dragons are too good at their purpose. Hogs aren't as big of a problem now."

I laughed and knew how nervous it sounded. "You're making me worried, Evelyn."

"We should be worried. If nothing changes, we'll be operating a very expensive factory for something no one can buy."

Oh, shit. "How long do we have?"

"Without domestication? Probably a month."

"Christ." I felt like I'd been kicked in the gut. If the company went under, all my recent efforts would have been for nothing.

"Don't worry, I'm sure we have it this time." Evelyn checked her watch. "Should be any minute now."

I forced a chuckle. "Oh, come on. Is it really that precise?"

"Usually."

I'd never witnessed a dragon hatching, let alone one that I'd helped design. Now that the wait was over, it was hard to imagine that just two weeks ago, I'd watched the egg roll out of the God Machine.

A small part of me fear that nothing would happen. That it had all been some heartless ruse.

Then the egg trembled. I grabbed Evelyn's arm, probably a little ungently. "Did you see that?"

"You know, I'd forgotten what it's like to see your first egg hatch."

I hardly heard her, because a fracture appeared down the middle of the egg. "Look!"

The crack widened, spawning other fractures left and right across the eggshell. Something sharp and triangular poked its way through. My chest hurt, and I realized I'd been holding my breath. I forced myself to breathe.

One of the white-garbed egg handlers entered the hatching pod. Judging by the height and the husky build, it was the one named Jim. Nice guy, but as quiet as they came. He carried a stainless-steel bucket.

"What's in the bucket?" I asked.

"Raw beef. He'll try to get the hatchling to eat from his hand." Her brow furrowed, and she leaned forward.

The dragon's claws followed its snout, and it ripped the egg in half. Little pieces of it stuck to the dark green scales, which glistened wetly in the sunlight. The dragonet lifted it head, blinking its catlike eyes. A pink tongue flicked out of its dark snout. It turned toward the handler.

"It smells the meat," I whispered.

The handler drew a long piece of bright-red meat from the steel bucket. He tossed it in a gentle arc. The dragon skittered out of the way.

I chuckled. "He's quick, isn't he?"

"That's the fast-twitch muscle response."

"The Olympic sprinter gene?" It was called alpha-actinin 3. Years ago, researchers had found that having mutated copies of the gene makes your fast-twitch muscles behave like slow-twitch ones, which makes you a better long-distance athlete. In contrast, almost all Olympic sprinters had two functioning copies, and thus plenty of fast-twitch muscle fibers. "Nice touch."

"I thought so."

"We might want to put the endurance mutations in, though, if you're trying to make a pet. A game of fetch doesn't exactly require quick reflexes."

She gave me a side glance. "Maybe you are right, Noah Parker."

The dragonet put its snout down, tested the meat, then, snapped it up. It tossed its head back to finish it in a single gulp, like a dolphin flipping a fish. The handler took out a second piece but didn't throw it. Instead, he held it out so that it swung back and forth, a tempting high-protein pendulum.

"Now's the real test," Evelyn said.

I nodded, too anxious to talk.

The dragon's head moved back and forth in time with the meat. It spread its wings, then folded them along its back. And crept forward, tasting the air. The handler stood motionless, the proffered meat held out at arm's length.

"Come on, buddy," I muttered.

The dragonet crouched. Oh my God, he was going to eat it! I made a fist in pre-emptive celebration. Then it leaped past the meat and clamped its jaws around the handler's arm.

Evelyn gasped. "Oh, no."

The handler stumbled back into the wall, shaking his arm. The dragonet held on, thrashing against him. Bright red points of color bloomed in the white sleeve. The door flew open, and two men in khakis ran in. One had a wooden pole with a wire loop at the end. He slid this around the dragonet's body and pulled it taut. Held the thing still while the other one approached and jabbed a syringe into the dragonet's neck. It slumped to the floor while the bleeding handler made a hasty exit. I suppose he went right to medical. The two guys in khakis lifted the dragon's unconscious form—at least, I *think* it was unconscious—and carried it out.

Evelyn and I sat there in silence, almost shell-shocked.

Finally, I said. "So, I guess we haven't cracked domestication."

"That was nearly as bad as Design 32." She shook her head, and sighed. "Know what this means?"

"Back to the drawing board, I'm guessing?"

She didn't answer but bit her lip and looked away. Which surprised me a little, given that she'd been in this position forty-seven times before. Hell, I'd have thought that my present might even be a boon: maybe I could help make the design even better. But she didn't look excited at the prospect. If anything, she looked worried.

What isn't she telling me? "Come on, it's not like this is the first design that didn't work."

"Exactly. The board's patience with us won't last forever."

Her tone gave me a chill inside. I had another card in my back pocket, but I wasn't sure I wanted to play it yet. Then again, if things were really so precarious, then Evelyn needed a win. "What if my simulator could predict behavioral traits?"

"You told me it didn't."

"That's true. But a while back, I did some tinkering with a module for basic temperament."

"Define 'tinkering.'"

"It's still experimental, but it attempts to simulate basic behaviors."

"How quickly could you get it up and running?"

She hadn't asked if the module actually worked, which was a hell of a compliment. "Assuming I can find the code, just a few days," I said, hoping both parts were true.

"We could design a few models and choose the one with the best temperament," she said, almost to herself.

"Is that a yes?"

"It's a yes, Noah Parker. But work fast."

CHAPTER TEN
INTERLUDE

ASU's accelerated graduate school program was unique. In a period of six years, you got your undergraduate degree and a PhD, compared to the typical eight or nine years. I plunged headlong into the genetics curriculum. Three years in, I was starting to make the shift towards a dissertation project. However, I'd also picked up a beautiful but temperamental distraction.

Her name was Jane. We met in a pottery class, of all places. I only took it to meet the fine arts credit, but Jane was an art history major. She took classes in just about every medium. She preferred two-dimensional stuff like sketching and painting, which is why it had taken her so long to get around to clay.

We started dating in early fall, and by winter we were spending almost every day together. Because I was still living at home with Mom and Connor, Jane and I spent most of our time at her place. She had a dingy two-bedroom apartment close to campus, so it was convenient. Of course, she also had a crunchy, tree-hugging roommate named Summer who I couldn't stand, but nobody's perfect.

Jane and I would sit on her lumpy couch and binge old Aaron Sorkin TV shows. She needed me there to keep her steady, but I didn't mind. It was easy. After two years of working my ass off with no social life, I liked easy.

My course work suffered, though. I admit that. I missed some classes, and I didn't put nearly enough time into my laboratory work.

The unexpected turning point came in springtime. March 15th. I remembered because it was the ides of March, and I expected a vaguely threatening prank phone call from Connor at any moment. *Beware the Ides of March.* My phone did ring, but it wasn't him. It was mom.

"I should take this," I said.

Jane rolled her eyes and refused to hit the pause button.

"Hi, Mom," I whispered, stepping outside to Jane's tiny porch.

"Connor," she said. Her voice sounded thick, and I thought maybe she'd gotten into the box wine a little early.

"No, it's Noah. You called me."

"Connor," she said again. "He fell. We're at St. Luke's."

I don't have a distinct memory of hanging up or running to my car. The next thing I knew, I was shoving my way into a cramped hospital room to find Connor in a paper gown. He looked pale, but at least he was conscious.

"What happened?" I blurted out.

"He fell down the stairs," Mom said. Her eyes were red-rimmed, but she was holding it together.

"*Halfway* down the stairs," Connor said. "I tripped, that's all."

"You said your legs gave out," she said.

"It was an accident. Could have happened to anyone."

He didn't believe that; though. I could see the uncertainty on his features. Damn, it was hot in the little room, and my sudden arrival had put everyone on edge.

"What happened to your face?" I asked.

He brought his hand up to his cheeks, feeling around. "What do you mean?"

"You must have hit it, what, five or six times?"

"I didn't—" he started, and then smirked when he caught on. "Oh, really?"

Mom swatted at me, but a smile flickered across her face. Our banter always either calmed her or annoyed the tar out of her. Often it depended on the status of the box wine. I wondered if she'd tapped it already that afternoon.

Dr. Miller barged in and said without preamble. "Hello, Parker family."

"Hi, Dr. Miller," we chorused.

"What happened?"

"He collapsed on the stairs," Mom said.

"Halfway," Connor said.

Dr. Miller did her routine exam of Connor's extremities and reflexes. She ordered an MRI of his legs to be sure it wasn't a circulation issue, but her frown told us what she really thought.

"How bad is it?" Mom asked quietly.

"He should avoid stairs as much as possible," Dr. Miller said. "Physical activity is only going to get harder for him, and we don't want to risk a more serious injury."

After that, her bedside speech was more of the same. The disease continued its relentless course, and all we could do was take steps to help Connor avoid further injuries. He didn't seem to be hurt this time, but we were lucky. Things like broken bones would be very hard for him to recover from.

I left the hospital in a kind of stupor. We'd gotten lucky this time, but the accident offered a grim reminder of the future Connor faced if I didn't do something about it. Which meant I had to buckle down and get back on track, if I wanted to go through with my plans.

"Where did you go?" Jane demanded, the moment I got back to her place.

"The hospital."

"Why?"

"Connor fell," I said.

"I didn't know what happened. You just *left*."

She didn't ask about him or his condition. She never asked. I'd told her everything when we first started dating, but she didn't like the idea of me "playing God" so she tuned it out. Now, I remembered the pale look of fear on my brother's face, and her attitude made me furious. "I have to go," I said, not looking at her.

"Again? Why?"

I took a breath and forced myself to meet her eyes. "Because it's over. We're done."

I stormed out of her apartment and didn't look back.

The rest of the breakup involved things I'd rather not put into words. It was hard, but I escaped relatively unscathed. Or so I thought. Only later did I realize that I'd left something important at her place: my backup data drive. Of course, I realized this after spilling a soda on my laptop, causing it to go dark. With my *entire* thesis work on it. Six months of coding and debugging that, as it turned out, had never made it to the cloud because of Jane's crappy wi-fi service. I needed my drive, and getting it was going to suck.

As my car rumbled down the narrow street beside her run-down building, the familiar stomach-tightness settled in. I didn't want to face Jane, especially so soon. But I backed out now, I'd never work up the courage again.

I blamed my Systems and Data Recovery instructor for this impending awkwardness. He'd instilled me with my obsession over backing up stuff on portable hard drives. I thought I was so damn clever to keep it at Jane's place, both so it would be in a different physical location from my home laptop, and so I could work on my project whenever I was there. In retrospect, it would have made more sense to keep it at Mom's house.

I coasted into an open spot and put it in park. Shut it off and prayed that the trembling whine didn't represent my jalopy's final death rattle. I climbed out and didn't bother locking the doors. Two of the door locks didn't work anyway.

My feet found the solid spots in the sea of broken pavement that passed for a sidewalk up here. Loose gravel crunched under my shoes. As I climbed the rickety stairs, I tried to focus on what I was going to say. A month had passed since I'd last been here, but the stomachache felt like it had never stopped.

The sun had bleached the door's paint to a sickly sea green. Pale, colorless voids marked the spots where the numbers (2-0-8) had fallen off years ago. I knocked four times, half hoping that no one would answer. Muffled sounds from the other side dashed those hopes. The cheap deadbolt clicked.

The door swung open wide enough to reveal the face of Jane's roommate, Summer. Thin braids of her blonde hair hung in disarray around her thin face. She saw me and wrinkled her nose. "What do *you* want?"

I managed not to snarl, but only just. Summer and I had never gotten along. "I just came for one of my drives."

"Jane's not here."

Faint sleep lines marked the right side of her face, even though it was almost ten in the morning. I pretended not to see them. "It's a shoebox in her closet."

"Doesn't ring a bell."

The first tendrils of cold dread settled about my shoulders. "I think I stashed it on shelf in the corner. Where you wouldn't see it."

"I'm pretty sure she burned everything of yours."

"Not this." I whispered it like a prayer. Even Jane at her worst would know what the drive meant to me. Would she have destroyed it? God, I hoped not. "At least let me look." My mouth twisted and fought me, but I managed to add, "Please."

Summer let out a long sigh, like I was asking her to give up a kidney or something. "Fine." She turned and walked away, leaving me to push the door open so I could come in. I made a beeline for Jane's bedroom.

"She didn't come home last night," Summer called over her shoulder.

I shook my head. "Not my business anymore." And not my problem, either.

"She didn't come home the night before, either."

The way she said it rankled me. Like she saw the wound and wanted to rub salt in it. I glanced back. "Don't you have a rave to get to?"

She snickered and stalked off to the kitchen.

Jane's room smelled like her, felt like her. Charcoal sketches plastered her "art wall" opposite the door. She sketched constantly, mostly vague cameos of total strangers she saw during the day. She'd gotten even better since I'd been here last, but I knew her style in the way that you know your parents' handwriting. The ghost-faces that stared back at me might be mistaken for black-and-white photographs.

As many times as I'd been here, I never felt comfortable in this place. I tried not to look at Jane's bed. Did my best not to check where the pillows were, and whether or not the sagging mattress bore two indentations instead of just one. I didn't want to know.

The closet door hung ajar, and Jane's mishmash of clothes—almost all of them black or blood-red—made a bruised tangle inside. I reached over them, back to the corner where I'd stashed my box.

Nothing. "Shit!" I whispered. Stupid of me to think she'd leave it, after the way things ended between us. *Stupid, stupid, stupid.*

"Hi."

I flinched at the quiet, familiar voice. Jane stood in her doorway with her art-bag and easel draped over her shoulders. She'd dyed her hair again, a yellowish green. Such a waste of her natural color. She was alone. Probably just coming back from drawing class. *Damn Summer for making me think otherwise.*

"Hi," I said.

"What are you doing here?"

"I came to get my hard drive, the one with the backup code." *Please let it be here.* How long would it take me to rewrite that simulation engine? A couple of months, at least.

"What for?" Jane asked.

"I need something on it."

Her lips trembled. "I think that's the last of your stuff."

"Yeah." I fought to keep my face still. Sadness, bitterness, and longing all fought to show themselves on it. *I have to be strong.*

She looked down and away from me. "Bottom right corner."

I crouched and fumbled beneath her clothes. My fingers closed on the familiar smooth cardboard. I dragged the box out. *Still feels heavy.* I fumbled the lid open, not daring to breathe. The hard drive nestled inside in a pile of packing peanuts. Relief flooded me. I sagged against the closet door. "Thank the lord."

"Is that all you came for?" Her voice carried a dangerous undertone.

Uh-oh. "Well, yeah, I—"

She scoffed. Turned away from me. "It's fine. Just go."

We stood there in awkward silence. A part of me wanted to stay. The foolish, impulsive part. The wiser part knew that I should leave. And I might as well do that before I lost my nerve. "Well, see you." I walked to the door, trying not to look at the pillows or the bed, or her face.

As I slid past her, she shook her head and muttered, "Asshole."

I halted in my tracks. A spike of anger flared up in me. "What, for taking what's mine?"

She sniffed and covered her eyes. Couldn't even look at me. "Whatever. You should go."

She didn't mean either thing. I knew that, and I wavered. It would be so easy to go back three steps and put my arms around her. *She'd let me do it, too.* Maybe the relief of holding her again would help me get past the pain.

That's the thing about Jane: she was the worst thing and the best thing that had ever happened to me. The allure of that emotional roller coaster ride beckoned. But I couldn't let myself slide into that dangerous comfort zone again.

"That's what I'm trying to do," I said.

Summer poked her head out of the kitchen. "What's taking you so long, jackass?"

Such a delightful roommate. I glared at her and stalked out. I didn't even close the door. That old Jane-induced darkness threatened to bubble up inside me. I clenched my jaw and shook it off. *It's over now. It's done.*

And I had work to do.

CHAPTER ELEVEN
Domestication

My behavioral module code was in better shape than I remembered. Maybe I'd suppressed all memories from my last few weeks with Jane. I don't know. But I was grateful now, because it took me less than a week to get the functionality integrated into my biological simulator.

Meanwhile, the rest of Evelyn's design team started working on Design 49. First, they tried modulating the protocadherin genes that governed reward response. The idea was that customers could reward-train tame behavior, a practice that often worked with birds. It might have succeeded for us, were it not for the fact that newly born dragonets are ravenous. Customers wouldn't withhold food when they needed to. Not only that, but the herpetologists raised the valid point that hatchlings had to eat, or they wouldn't thrive.

Next, the designers tried jacking up the dopamine, figuring that a happy dragon would be less likely to maul its owner. They were wrong; we didn't need a focus group to predict the lawsuits that would follow.

I thought my module might be able to help. It scored aggression with some rather complex modeling of stimulus-response and synaptic pathways. Basically, it estimated the balance of neurotransmitters in the animal's brain and matched those against the known chemicals underlying aggression.

"What's the output?" Evelyn asked me when I told her it was done.

"There are a few readouts, but the one you'll want is probably the aggression score. It goes from zero to one hundred."

"Higher being more aggressive?"

"Exactly. Tame animals should be below fifty. Ferocious, bloodthirsty predators should score in the high nineties."

"What would score one hundred?"

"I'm not sure any living creature would." I paused. "Maybe the T-rex from *Jurassic Park*. *Too bad I don't have access to that genome.*

She smiled. "I love that book."

"Me, too." The scientist in me knew that DNA molecules are too fragile to endure for millions of years, even encased in amber. But damn, what a great story. Crichton died too young.

"Run any domestic animals yet?" she asked.

"I ran *Canis familiaris*." Better known as the domestic dog. "It scored a twenty-nine."

We both sighed and shared a moment of sadness.

"Did you have a dog?" she asked.

"Yep. Bailey. He was a golden. What about you?"

"Fan-fan. She was a—"

"Shih Tzu?" I guessed.

She smiled. "Am I that predictable?"

I shrugged. She was proud of her Chinese heritage, and it made sense that she'd own the classic Chinese breed.

"What about Design 48?" she asked.

"I didn't run it yet. I was waiting for you."

She tapped a few commands to bring the design up in DragonDraft3D. I showed her how to activate the behavioral module. Then she ran the simulator, and the now-familiar image of our most recent failure shimmered into existence over her desk. The scores came up, too. Aggression was at 87.

"Well, I think I see the problem," I said.

She chewed her bottom lip. "I'll spend some time testing it. Thanks, Noah."

"Hope it helps," I said.

A few days later, Evelyn called a meeting with the whole design team. We crammed into her office. There weren't enough chairs, so I ended up on the floor between Brian O'Connell and the Frogman. Korrapati took the extra seat. That's when a Chinese guy rolled in on a foot-scooter, one of those motorized jobs that you balance on to zoom around. But he was riding it *indoors*.

"Am I late?" he asked.

"Wong!" said everyone at once. In my head, it sounded like *Norm!*

"Welcome back." Evelyn gestured at me. "Andrew Wong, this is Noah Parker. Our newest hire."

The newcomer's forehead crinkled as he flicked off his scooter. "We are hiring now?"

"He's a trainee," Evelyn said.

Wong kicked up his foot-scooter and shook my hand. "You must be very good, very good, Noah Parker. Glad to have you here." He talked a mile a minute. His smile was the picture of open friendliness, so I think he really meant it, too.

I felt everyone's eyes on me, and it made my face hot. "I don't know about that."

"Noah's behavioral module is working, and not a moment too soon," Evelyn said. "Design 48 failed in hatching."

By mauling the handler, I couldn't help but think.

Everyone groaned. I took this to mean they'd experienced this before.

"Too bad," Wong said.

"I've convinced the higher-ups to let us design another prototype, but it may be our last."

"Whose turn is it to have design privileges?" Korrapati asked.

"Pretty sure it's mine," said the Frogman.

Evelyn put both of her hands flat on her desk, as if holding herself up. "I'm thinking we will have a competition among all designers. Noah included. The best domestication prototype gets to be printed."

"How will you decide which design is best?" O'Connell asked. "We should have some criteria."

"We'll use the aggression score in Noah's behavioral module as a baseline metric."

This brought a wave of protests.

"Aw, come on!"

"That's insane!"

"Using the score gives Noah an unfair advantage. He *wrote* the simulator," O'Connell said.

I fought the evil grin that wanted to spread across my face, because he was absolutely right. It wasn't as significant an advantage as it appeared—the simulator scored the genetic code, after all—but it would give me an edge.

"Perhaps, but he has the least experience at dragon design," Evelyn said. "That makes it a fair contest, in my opinion."

The protests quieted to a grumble. Even though I couldn't ignore the tension in the room, my mind already raced ahead to the design challenge. This was my chance to prove myself to the rest of the team. But it went beyond showing that I belonged here. Whoever cracked domestication would establish the baseline prototype for all future designs. *And maybe get free rein with the God Machine besides.* My heart rate quickened at the thought.

I snuck a look around the room. O'Connell was openly pissed, probably about my simulator playing such a critical role. Korrapati looked thoughtful. The Frogman's face held no emotion; he was impossible to read.

Wong grinned. "I like a competition."

Hell, that's the scariest reaction of them all. Not that I was too surprised. Anyone who survived two years at Shenzhen would have to be taken seriously.

"What's the deadline?" Korrapati asked. She sat with perfect posture, taking notes in a little Moleskine notebook. Because of course she was. She'd probably be a hell of a competitor, too.

"One week from today," Evelyn said.

"Not much time," said the Frogman.

"You can score your designs as much as you want in the interim. That okay with everyone?"

A few mutters answered her, but at least no one spoke up.

"Good luck," Evelyn said.

O'Connell stomped out without a word. The Frogman followed on his heels.

"Noah, hang back a minute," Evelyn said.

Uh oh. Maybe this was the part where she told me that the simulator *was* an unfair advantage. That I couldn't compete. I still didn't have a good rebuttal for that argument. I'd overcome my lack of experience with DragonDraft3D pretty fast, and she probably knew it.

Evelyn smiled. "So, Noah Parker. What do you think?"

"The competition's an interesting idea. I just don't want to step on any toes." *If I win, they'll say it was because of the simulator code.*

Evelyn shrugged. "You should consider it an opportunity to show you can be part of the team."

"Fair enough." It occurred to me, then, that a gesture of transparency might be the right opening move. "I'd like to make one more modification to the simulator code."

"Is it critical?"

"No, but it might help the spirit of the contest."

"I don't know."

"Aw, come on. Let me at least show you what I want to do."

She sighed. "All right."

"Would you mind pulling up the latest code?" I skirted around her desk so I could see the holoscreens straight on. She brought it up in a new window, which brought the current total to eight. Biotech news feeds, e-mail, and some kind of security monitor. My eyes wanted to wander, to see what the DDD got to see, but I forced them front-and-center on my code. At Evelyn's gesture, I took over the keyboard and scrolled down to the spot I wanted. "Know what this is?"

She glanced over it, wrinkling her brow in concentration. Then her eyes widened in realization. "A phone home?"

"Bingo." I was impressed, not just that she recognized it but that she knew the old-school term. It was a special subroutine deep within the simulator that sent me a message every time the code was executed.

"You like keeping an eye on things," Evelyn said.

"When I write them, absolutely. But here's what I had in mind." I changed the recipient of the "phone home" from my address to the alias for Evelyn's design team. Now it would send every single simulation run to the entire group.

Evelyn laughed. "Real-time scoring? This will be a good competition."

"I think it will," I agreed.

And I'm going to win it.

The design team didn't waste any time. By the time I reached my desk, my updated simulator code had already sent out two results.

O'Connell: 82.69.

Korrapati: 76.18.

Not bad for an opening salvo. And even though my shoulders

tensed at how quickly the rest of the team was moving, it told me two useful things. First, O'Connell and Korrapati already *had* models they were working from. At least two existing prototypes had entered the competition field. Second, it confirmed what I suspected: everyone wanted to win this contest just as badly as I did.

I pulled up Design 48 on my computer. Given that it had failed— and failed spectacularly—I figured no one would mind if I claimed it as my starting model. Otherwise, I'd have to create one from scratch, and I still had to get comfortable with DragonDraft3D. That being said, all the customizations didn't really belong to me. So I made a copy of Design 48 and removed all the team's modifications. That left me with a barebones dragon that would score embarrassingly high on the aggression scale.

Maybe that's not such a bad idea.

"Eh, what the hell." I ran the design through my simulator. The 3D holographic model sprang into existence in front of me, beside the projection monitor. It looked much as I remembered, but slightly more predatory, with a lean body, rippled musculature, and a streamlined head.

Parker: 93.78

Out in the design lab, someone snorted. Sounded like the Frogman, but I couldn't be sure. *Good.* I'd just as soon surprise them.

These grand plans survived about two minutes. Without Evelyn there to guide me, I had no idea what I was doing in DragonDraft3D. Scientifically, I knew what avenues to explore first—temperament pathways, neurotransmitter controls, that sort of thing—but finding these and adjusting them while keeping within that damn "points" system proved tedious work. Design 48 represented weeks of work by multiple engineers. God knows how many little tweaks they'd made. The disadvantages kept piling up.

Evelyn snuck up on me. "How's it going, Noah?"

"Rough," I said. "Not because of DragonDraft3D," I added quickly. "I just need to get used to it."

"I could give you some more instruction," she said.

I waved her off. "I don't think that would be fair to the others."

"But you've never designed a full prototype before."

I grinned. "All the more reason for you to be impressed when I do."

"I admire your confidence, Noah Parker. Good luck."

She click-clacked out and went in to confer quietly with Wong. Then she dropped in on Korrapati. Rallying the troops, as it were. I tried not to begrudge her a few words of encouragement. The rest of the team probably needed it more than I did, given how many designs they'd seen fail.

Wong: 79.23

"Damn," I muttered. That put me squarely in fourth place, and I was fairly certain the Frogman wasn't playing. So it was effectively last place, and a long hill to climb in front of me. There was so much to do, I hardly knew where to start.

Back to basics, Noah.

In their unmanipulated form, our dragons were wild animals. That had been clear as day when Evelyn showed me that one during my interview. Clearer still when Design 48 had attacked the handler. It didn't surprise me, given the diverse collection of predators that gave rise to the dragon genome. Thousands of years of evolution had written those survival instincts. It wasn't something I could undo in five minutes. I had to chip away a little bit at a time, like an ice sculptor.

First things first, I figured it wouldn't hurt to make the dragon slightly less dangerous. Besides, physical traits were the easiest to change. I reduced the claw length and tooth size. Cut back the size a little bit, too, because all things being equal, a smaller dragon would pose less of a threat to the staff. These changes freed up some feature points, which I figured I'd need soon enough.

While I was at it, I reduced the running speed and slowed the reflexes a hair. The less dangerous, the better.

Now I was swimming in feature points, and it was time to cash in. I flipped over to neurological enhancements and began the more delicate dance of mood alteration. I tempered the stimulus-response pathways to more moderate sensitivities but cranked down serotonin re-uptake to keep the neurons firing. Then a splash of baseline dopamine expression, to make the dragon a bit happier all the time. On paper, it seemed like my prototype would make an ideal domesticated dragon. Time to see what my simulation code had to say.

Parker: 85.42

Damn. I'd made some headway, but I hadn't even caught up with

O'Connell. It was 5:30 by then, quitting time, and the end-of-day test rounds started to roll in.

Korrapati: 76.18.

Wong: 77.89

O'Connell: 79.30.

I should probably stay late and try to close the gap, but I couldn't gather my scattered thoughts. My shoulders and neck ached from hunching over my workstation. I decided to clock out.

One day down, seven to go. And I'd already fallen behind.

CHAPTER TWELVE
The Leaderboard

I stayed up until 2 a.m. reading papers about animal behavior and domestication. A poor decision, but I was desperate. Then I had a horrible dream about wolves attacking the humans that tried to domesticate them. I woke up in a tangle of sheets to the persistent bleat and blinding glow of my multialarm. The volume and brightness told me I'd overslept. *Shit.*

It was 7:45, not as bad as I thought. The jalopy fired up on my second try. I slurped hot coffee on my way in. Scalded my tongue something fierce, but it got my neurons firing. By the time I hit my workstation, I had four new ideas I wanted to try to get that aggression score down. If the field hadn't changed much since yesterday, I might even catch up.

My naive optimism lasted right up until I logged in. E-mail alerts flooded the screen.

Korrapati: 69.20.
Wong: 76.89
Wong: 75.01
Wong: 73.93
Wong: 72.55
Wong: 70.48
Wong: 69.12
O'Connell: 73.11

Well, crap. So Korrapati stayed late, O'Connell came early, and Wong never even left. *Jesus.* I rolled back my chair and leaned over the divider. Wong slouched behind his wall of empty drink containers, with no less than four projection monitors hovering in front of him.

"Hey Wong, busy night?"

He swiveled enough to grin at me. "Very busy!"

"You ever sleep?"

He shook his head. "Sleep when we domesticate the dragon."

I chuckled and returned to my desk. *That's the Shenzhen work ethic, all right.* I couldn't argue with the results, though; according to the latest simulation run, Wong had the lead. I pulled up my own prototype and started modifying the mitochondrial pathways. Mitochondria produce energy for cells, and thus affect numerous processes, from stress response to memory to overall longevity. The little power plants even have their own genetic code, a tiny circular chromosome with a couple hundred genes. Most engineers don't even touch the mitochondrial genome, because it already works quite well. Mutations tend to cause subtle degenerative diseases.

But it occurred to me, in my sleep-deprived morning state, that the speed and ferocity of Design 48's attack had required a lot of mitochondrial energy. Maybe tamping down the energy production wasn't a bad idea. Nature had done some of the hard work for me already—we already knew dozens of mutations that altered energy production and overall function of the mitochondria. I selected a couple of these, put one back, chose another. Like a shopper at a genetic engineering supermarket.

Parker: 82.18

Well, I still hadn't broken 80 but that marked a big improvement. Even better, I doubted any of the other designers thought to try this route. The mitochondrial genome is so tiny, it's easy to forget.

I turned my attention to brain development. So many of the critical neuronal connections form well before an animal is born, so it stood to reason that with some rewiring early on, we might get a better handle on temperament. But unlike the mitochondrial changes, I couldn't go browsing the natural catalogue of brain development mutations. They tend to be lethal. That simple, unavoidable fact hinted that perhaps I shouldn't be tampering with such a crucial element of dragon biology, but . . .

Korrapati: 58.63.

Hell, I had nothing to lose.

I plunged into the dark recesses of developmental neurobiology. The genetic program that controlled this process was like an elegant orchestra—genes turning on and off in rhythmic fashion, new patterns rising and falling as the vital connections formed. I harnessed those elements and rewrote their playbook. Well, maybe that's an overstatement. I nudged their genetic fate a bit here and there. I forged new links between sensory perception, memory, emotional response.

My free points plummeted as DragonDraft3D recomputed the intelligence quotient. The dragon *seemed* smarter, though in fact what I'd hoped to grant it was awareness. Awareness of itself, its surroundings, and its human owners. A reptile that relied on intellect more than instinct might see the long-term benefits of human partnership. *Time for the real test.* I sent my new prototype to the simulator.

Parker: 62.61

"Holy crap," I breathed.

No one snorted with derision this time. The air hung heavy with tense concentration. I knew they had to be thinking, *How did he do that?*

I smiled and got right back to it. Maybe it was my imagination, but DragonDraft3D felt easier to navigate. I'd been so focused on the tough developmental changes that I hadn't noticed it happening. The further I climbed up the learning curve, the more naturally my next moves came to me. At first, Evelyn's interface design felt almost random. Now I saw this higher-order structure to it: physical to intellectual to behavioral capabilities. I could probably design my current prototype from scratch in under an hour.

Those days blurred together into an endless block of caffeine-fueled design. The competition consumed every part of my mind, to the point where I forgot to consider that winning this contest was just a means to an end. The deadline crept ever closer, and I began to close the gap on the rest of the team.

Then we hit the fifty-point plateau.

Korrapati got there first. Her prototype hit 51.33, then 50.08. On her next run, it bounced back up to 50.73. I didn't notice this until later—I'd forced myself to stop checking the scores the moment they came in. I was still in the low sixties. My competitors' successes only harmed my productivity, and I couldn't afford to fall into a slump.

"Noah?"

I recognized Korrapati's voice, but it took a moment to register the fact that she'd spoken to me. Everyone in the design lab had pretty much stopped talking to each other as we hit the home stretch of the competition. I leaned back. "Priti. Hey."

"Have any plans for lunch? The food trucks are here today."

I nudged my insulated lunchbox farther under my desk. "That sounds great."

Should I invite Wong? He hadn't eaten, or even moved from his chair. But he'd insist on riding his scooter, which would take forever. Besides, I kind of wanted to hear what she had to say. So I left him and followed her to the elevator. A couple of dungaree-clad wranglers occupied the one that stopped for us. We rode it down in silence. That silence pressed on us as we made our way past the desk.

"Hey, Virginia," I said.

She brightened. "Hi, Noah!"

Korrapati did a double-take. Inwardly, I smiled.

A parade of hybrid-fuel trailers lined the curb on the street outside Reptilian's front door. The bright, garish paint jobs assaulted my eyes like an attack of mismatched tropical birds. The lines in front of most of them were three deep.

"What do you feel like?" Korrapati asked.

"Ooh, how about Asian fusion?"

"Are you suggesting that because *I'm* Asian?"

Oh, hell. "No, I, uh—" I stuttered.

She flashed me a perfectly wicked smile. "Just messing with you."

I scowled at her, mock-serious. "You are vicious."

"Only when I want to be."

"Shouldn't the person at the top of the leaderboard be the nicest right now?"

She schooled her face back to neutral quicker than I'd have thought possible. "That's only temporary."

"Seems to me you're the one to beat."

She stopped short at a lime green food truck. "Well, here's your Asian fusion."

Asian-Mexican fusion, I didn't dare say. I ordered something that held a prominent place at the top of the truck's digital menu. My order arrived in a cardboard box in about two minutes. The cardboard didn't quite burn my hands, but it weighed over a pound.

We sat on the thick concrete curb that doubled as a security barrier for Reptilian's glass entrance.

"What did you order?" she asked.

"Something called carnitas fries." I flipped open the box lid. The aroma set my mouth to watering. "Sure smells delicious."

"You chose well. That's their specialty."

"What did you get?"

"Grilled cauliflower."

I tried and failed to conceal my reaction.

"What?" she laughed. "It's good."

"Oh, I'm sure." *If you're a rabbit.*

We ate in silence for a moment. The carnitas fries were still piping hot, but damn good. I couldn't identify half of the toppings that weren't meat, but I ate it all anyway. We made small talk, while I waited for her to tell me what this lunch was really about.

"How do you like working at Reptilian?" she asked.

"It's good. Challenging." I paused. "And a little different than I expected."

"How so?"

I shrugged. "I thought we'd be churning out a lot more dragons, for one thing."

"We used to," she said, with an almost wistful air. "That's all I did, when I first started here."

"And now?"

"I suppose the demand tapered off. For wild ones, at least."

I feigned seriousness. "So basically, what I'm hearing is that you hogged all the dragons."

She gave a little gasp but smiled. "I make no apologies."

"Well, if we can crack domestication, there should be plenty of work to go around."

Her grin faded, and the sharp lines found their way back to her face. "Yes. Domestication."

There's the opening she wanted. I braced myself, because I half-expected she was about to tell me that I had no chance at winning this competition.

"I'd like to learn more about how your simulator scores aggressiveness," she said.

"I posted the code. You should be able to read it."

"Yes, I could read ten thousand lines of code. Or I could simply ask you."

I chuckled. "Good point. Well, it's a mixture model with two primary dimensions: the chemicals in the brain—"

"Neurotransmitters?"

"And hormonal regulators, yes. The other dimension tries to capture psychological intent. You know, what drives the animal."

She nodded along as I spoke, as if unsurprised.

She probably did *read the code but wanted me to confirm it.*

"Is there any sort of a manual threshold? A minimum value they won't go below?"

I smiled. "At around fifty, you mean?"

"Yes."

She's stuck. The realization gave me a glimmer of hope, because if Korrapati couldn't improve, maybe I could catch her. Then again, it didn't seem fair to hold up the best designer in the group out of pure selfishness. "It sounds like you've found the best answer, but for only one of the two dimensions. I'm guessing the first one?"

Her eyes widened enough to confirm it.

"Yeah. Intent is a much harder nut to crack," I said. "There's so much latent instinct buried in the dragon genome. Stuff we probably don't understand at a deeper level."

"Thousands of years of evolutionary pressure, much of it subtle."

"Exactly."

"Thank you for the insight. You didn't have to help."

"No problem. This contest is just for fun, right? We should be helping each other."

Furrows appeared in her brow. She stopped eating. "Have you ever heard the joke about the campers and the grizzly bear?"

"I don't think so."

"These campers encounter a grizzly bear with her cubs, so they take off running. One of them asks, *do you think we can outrun her?* And the other one calls back, *It doesn't matter if I can outrun her. I just have to outrun* you."

I chuckled. "Okay, I have heard that one."

"It's kind of similar to the leaderboard, don't you think?" she asked.

"How so?"

"We all want to win the contest. But given the company's financial crunch, the most important thing is not to come in last."

"Why?" I felt like coming in last was almost a guarantee for me at this point.

"The worst performer might not have a job when this is over."

I felt like she'd punched me in the gut. "Do you think Evelyn would do that?"

"She might not have a choice."

"Well, that kind of sucks." It made sense, though. Evelyn needed designers who could meet tough challenges. And hell, I'd given her a way to score us, to make our performances quantifiable. *I'm such a moron.*

Korrapati sighed and squared her shoulders. "Well, I guess I'd better get digging. Thank you for the help."

"Sure. But I think it's only fair that I share my ideas with the rest of the team."

She pressed her lips together but nodded. "That's your choice."

When I got back to the lab—feeling nervous, guilty, but oddly satisfied from the carnitas fries—I did just that. Sent an e-mail to the whole design team about the nature of the aggression score and my best guess on the cause of the fifty-point plateau. Of course, none of them believed me. They pushed ahead with their designs, figuring they could get around it.

Wong: 50.34

O'Connell: 50.28

O'Connell: 50.42

Wong: 50.83

Wong: 50.65

Wong: 50.18

Wong: 50.30

"Give it up, Wong," I called over the divider.

He rolled out far enough to look at me. "No giving up."

"You're not in Shenzhen anymore."

A cloud passed over his face. "Without this job, I go back."

"Why wouldn't you want to stay?"

He shrugged. "H-1 visa rules. If I lose job, or company closes, I must return."

"Reptilian's not going to close."

"I would like to have your confidence."

"Come on, Wong. This company makes dragons for the world. It's invincible."

He turned back around to his monitors, shaking his head. "No company is invincible."

I'm not sure why Wong's offhand comment rattled me, but it did. If Reptilian folded, its assets would be sold off piecemeal. The God Machine first of all. Now that I thought about it, achieving dragon domestication seemed simple by comparison. *There has to be a way to crack it.*

And by God, I'd find it or die trying.

CHAPTER THIRTEEN
Trifecta

The next days flew past in a blur. I hardly slept. My quest to crack domestication consumed every waking minute. I studied the neurological pathways that Evelyn had coded into DragonDraft3D. Hell, I even started reading cat blogs, in case that might turn up something useful. For this brief period, I was practically a model employee. Putting the company's needs first.

Ironically, my poor old jalopy provided a flash of inspiration. I'd blown half of my first paycheck on a repair bill that involved the mechanic literally jamming a screwdriver down the front grille to help hold the radiator in place. I didn't dare use the A/C for fear of overheating the engine. A car without A/C in Phoenix is pretty much a self-made torture device, but at least I was able to get around.

About a week after the outrageously-priced repairs, the jalopy started making a new sound. It registered somewhere between squealing tires and the screech of a rodent just caught by a bird of prey. The car still drove, but it unnerved me. What if it broke down on me? I'd be stranded halfway between home and work. Worse, I'd be relegated to the wilderness of public transportation again.

I'd grown too accustomed to the jalopy's convenience, balls-hot as it might be. I couldn't go back.

It reminded me of a story I'd read about cat domestication. Unlike dogs, which were simply captured as puppies and raised to be tame by human handlers, cats sort of domesticated themselves. It happened in ancient Egypt, at around the time that modern humans developed agriculture. Once they were able to grow enough grain to last for more than a few days, ancient Egyptians started storing it in granaries. Which inevitably drew rodents. Whose abundance drew the wild cats. Which got to stay because they killed the rodents.

Genetic comparisons of domesticated cat breeds to their wild cousins revealed a surprising phenomenon: some of the most significant differences were in pathways involved in fear. In other words, the cats stuck around because they were *afraid* of having to go back and live in the wild. Their fear overcame the instinct for independence.

Fear might be the answer we needed.

I hardly noticed when the jalopy carried me to work without incident. I don't remember passing Virginia at the front desk or taking the elevator up to the seventh floor. All I remember is planting myself at my workstation and starting a new modification to Design 48. I didn't use my carefully-tweaked prototype with all the adjustments—that model was approaching the fifty-point plateau like the rest of the competing models. If I was right about this, I'd break through. But I didn't want the others to know I had.

Evelyn stopped by to see how I was doing. "Fear response, Noah?"

"Yep." I didn't look up. I couldn't look up. I had to keep going, or I'd lose track of things in these complex genetic pathways.

Evelyn stood there long enough that I could sense her concern. I took a breath and looked back at her. "What's wrong?"

"I think you made a mistake."

"Where?"

"You've put in an imprinting locus, haven't you?"

"Yes." That was a keen insight. *Man, she really knows her stuff.*

"But you haven't linked the fear response to sensory neurons. They won't be afraid of their human handlers."

"They're not supposed to fear us."

Her brow furrowed. "You lost me."

"They're supposed to fear life *without* us. Without food and warmth and shelter."

"Hmm . . ." Her eyes lost focus for a minute. "Combine that with the behavior and reward response, and the survival instinct . . ."

"There's your trifecta," I said.

"Domestication by evolutionary instinct."

"Seems weird, doesn't it?" I asked. Weird and just plain *wrong*, to make dragons so dependent on us. But if it took a self-domesticated dragon to keep this company viable, I'd give them one.

"No one else has tried this. I'll be interested to see how it does."

I waited until she'd left before running it through the simulator. Design 48 had scored 93.78 originally, and now the only thing I'd changed was the domestication trifecta. Which, by the way, didn't involve any of the other genes I'd tweaked over the past week, so any gains here should add to what I'd already done there. Of course, I was still in last place, probably twelve points behind the crowd just above 50.

Parker: 81.62.

Jesus. I'd shaved off more than twelve points. That, added to my other prototype, would probably be enough to get below the fifty-point plateau.

But not by much. If I'd had more time to tinker with the behavioral traits, I might have gotten close to the others. Then this would give me a clean victory. But I was behind, and nearly out of time. Still, I could technically win Evelyn's contest.

Of course, if I did, everyone else in the design team would hate my guts.

Not that I'd blame them, but it's just too damn convenient when your own simulator code seems to block out competitors and let you win at the eleventh hour. They'd probably throw a fit to Evelyn. Hell, I would in their shoes. I wanted to win so badly. To prove myself. Oddly enough, that reminded me of something Evelyn had asked me to do when the competition started. It wasn't to prove my genetic engineering abilities. It was to prove that I could be part of the team.

A reminder flashed on my screen. Fifteen minutes until Evelyn's deadline. That wasn't much time. I exported my trifecta into a "patch"—a set of changes that anyone else could bring into their DragonDraft3D models. The only question was where to send it. My first thought was Korrapati. She'd put a ton of work into this, and I liked her. But then again, if what she'd said was true, whoever lost this might get fired. The company would never let Korrapati go, and even if they did, she'd find another job in about two seconds. I was more worried about Wong because of his visa situation. He was good, but if some higher-up decided it was simpler to lay off a non-citizen, he'd be screwed. And I hated the thought that he might go back to Shenzhen.

Wong: 50.11

Wong: 50.12

I chuckled. If I wanted a sign, there it was. So I sent my patch to Wong with a brief note: *Try this.*

In essence, that meant I was throwing in the towel myself. I forced myself away from my desk and tried to eavesdrop on my neighbor over the white noise. I heard the incoming message beep, then Wong's fingers playing across the keys. He drew a sharp breath. Silence ruled for five seconds. Then he rolled out in his chair and met my eyes with as stony an expression as I'd ever seen on him. All the chipper facade had disappeared.

He doesn't know if he can trust me. We had only a few minutes to go, after all. But I gave him a nod, hoping he'd at least try it. He stared at me another moment, then rolled back in.

His fingers danced on the keyboard. I glanced at the clock. A minute to go.

Ding. Incoming message. I held my breath and pulled it up.

Wong: 37.93.

"Yes!" I pumped a fist, while the lab erupted into cheers and curses and laughter.

"My God, Wong!" Korrapati said.

"What did you do?" O'Connell shouted.

Wong rolled out of his workstation with a big smile on his face and shrugged, like it was no big deal.

I grinned so wide my cheeks hurt. Part of me still couldn't believe it had worked. "Congratulations, man." I reached across the divider and shook his hand.

Evelyn click-clacked into the lab. "Well, it looks like we have a winner! What was your secret, Wong?"

Wong looked at me. I could tell he was about to share the credit, but I put a finger across my lips. *This is your moment, buddy.*

"No secret. Only hard work," he said.

"And a lot of runs in the simulator," I said. "Twice as many as anyone else. You earned it, Wong."

Evelyn looked happy enough to dance. Her face *glowed*. "I appreciate your hard work, everyone. Save your designs. We'll try Wong's next, but we may need a backup."

Inwardly, I groaned. The best parts of my design were already part of Wong's. *Let's hope I'm not the backup.*

"Noah, do you have a minute?" Evelyn asked.

"Sure." I followed her to her office, my heart already sinking. Even my best-scoring models put me in a distant last place in the competition. Maybe she expected better. But hell, they couldn't have scored the competition without my simulator code. I clung to that sliver of reassurance while Evelyn brought me in and shut her door. Then I kept my mouth shut and let her steer the conversation.

"Did you enjoy the competition?" she asked.

I laughed and shook my head. "You know what? I did. It really helped me learn DragonDraft3D."

She nodded. "I think everyone on the team doubled their experience using my poor little application."

"It's really nice. I like the interface."

She waved off my compliment, though her eyes twinkled. "So, what do you think of Wong?"

"He's good. The score was a crusher."

"Funny how he made such a significant gain, in such a short time."

"Maybe he was snowballing us." I said.

"Maybe. But there was only one other designer who made such an improvement in one shot." She tapped her fingertip on the desk. "Something tells me that if I looked at his prototype, I might find your trifecta."

Uh-oh. I looked down at my shoes.

"Ha! I knew it," she said.

"Is collaboration against the rules?"

"Not at all. Frogman and O'Connell worked together on a few of their models. But I'm surprised you gave it to him."

I shrugged. "He had a good design already. I just helped with the final push. Besides, you were right."

"About what?"

"You said I'd like him, and I do. I don't want him to go back to China."

"You deserve some of the credit."

I shook my head. "All that matters is the prototype works."

"We'll know soon enough. I'm authorizing six eggs."

"*Six?*"

She put her hands on her hips. "Do you believe in the design, or not?"

"Well, yeah, but—"

"Management's not going to let us hit the print button forever, Noah. We should use it while we can."

My stomach danced with butterflies, half nerves and half excitement. "Whatever you say, boss."

She put in the authorization—it took director-level clearance to print that many eggs from the same prototype—and we went to Wong's workstation to watch them roll out of the God Machine. They were about the same size as Design 48's egg, but slightly rounder. I'll never forget the color: chestnut brown, with faint swirls of mahogany. I wanted to touch one, to put my hand on the still-warm shell and try to sense the promise within. But Evelyn's override automatically summoned the entire hatchery staff. They invaded the design lab with a convoy of egg carts and formed a white-jumpsuited human chain to move the eggs out. I couldn't have gotten near one if I tried.

I wandered over to Wong, who sat in his chair with a dazed expression on his face. "Six eggs, huh? That seems like a lot."

"Crazy."

"So what did you name your model? Design 49?"

"Not design anything. I go with PetWong."

I laughed. "That's perfect."

"If it works." He shrugged. "I figure Wong means hard worker, at least."

"It'll work," I reassured him. "It *has* to." Otherwise, all my carefully laid plans might have been for nothing.

CHAPTER FOURTEEN
HIATUS CONTINUES

PHILADELPHIA, PA—The American Kennel Club confirmed this morning that its beloved National Dog Show remains on hiatus this year. AKC officials first suspended the competition—televised each year on Thanksgiving Day—four years ago, as the canine epidemic took hold in North America.

"The few folks lucky enough to have a show-quality dog still alive are keeping them under quarantine," said AKC President Patricia Hernandez. "They don't want to risk exposure, and we can't blame them."

Canine facial tumor disease (CFTD) was first reported in South Asia and bore a striking similarity to another disease that affects the Tasmanian devil, a marsupial once native to Australia, but today found only in Tasmania. Researchers identified both diseases as transmissible soft-tissue tumors that are spread by physical contact with an affected animal. Dogs' natural social tendencies makes them particularly vulnerable to the spread.

CFTD typically manifests as visible and painful tumors affecting the nose, mouth, and snout of infected animals. These tumors soon metastasize into the lymph nodes and lungs, requiring euthanasia within four to six weeks. Radiation and chemotherapy fail to halt the progression of the tumor, and efforts to develop a cure have been unsuccessful despite considerable funding from both government organizations and private industry. As a result, canine populations plummeted more than ninety-five percent in most parts of the world.

The precise origin of CFTD is controversial. Some organizations believe it "jumped" from Tasmanian devils to dogs. Others, including the international task force assembled to address the epidemic, have suggested that CFTD came out of a research laboratory, possibly one devoted to genetic modifications of canine species.

According to the AKC, some dog owners have kept their pets alive using strict quarantine procedures. So-called "canine clean rooms" prevent exposure to other dogs, which is the most common route of infection. Yet even these extreme measures sometimes prove unsuccessful. Canine populations continue to decline. Dog parks remain empty.

With this bleak outlook, many families who lost dogs to CFTD are turning to other species for pets. The number of households with cats, hedgehogs, domesticated pigs, or more exotic pet species have more than tripled in the last three years. Even so, man's best friend leaves behind a void that's difficult to fill with other animals. Canine instincts made them imminently trainable, and hundreds of years of specialized breeding allowed dogs to take on many roles in our society, from sniffing out explosives and contraband to assisting the visually impaired and providing emotional support. Perhaps other animals will be able to perform some of these tasks, but for the vast majority, the loss of dogs is sorely felt.

CHAPTER FIFTEEN
The Herpetologist

For the next two weeks, I ran Wong's design through the simulator code over and over. The amount of effort he'd put into engineering it astonished me. They were sensible changes, too. Wong knew his stuff, and he'd given his design a great foundation. Between that and my so-called trifecta, the reward-survival-fear feedback loop, it might be enough to tame the wildest of reptiles.

I saw little of Evelyn during the gestation period. She met with the board almost daily, and never came out of those meetings looking pleased. The executive team had lined up a second series of funding that could keep the company going, but the investors made it contingent on the successful hatching of a domesticated prototype.

By "successful," they pretty much meant *no maulings*.

Our director's trepidation was not lost on the design team. The fact that we had little to do until the prototypes hatched didn't help either. Engineers like to be busy, and I was no exception. We were all jumpy as desert hares. Even the permanently chipper Korrapati grew quiet and spent most of her time in her cubicle with headphones on.

Finally, the day of the hatching came. I'd come in early to run the design through my simulator one last time. Every benchmark looked solid, as far as I could tell. Maybe that's why I felt the pressure more than most: this hatching would probably seal the fate of my design simulator, at least at Reptilian. And if it couldn't work here, I wouldn't have a good excuse to run a certain other simulation I'd been dying to try.

It was around 9:30, and I began pondering a coffee break to kill some time. Just as I got up, Evelyn click-clacked into the design lab. "Everyone? It's time."

We all stood and followed her out. Korrapati, Wong, and O'Connell led the way. I trailed after them, with The Frogman lumbering along beside me. He kept his headphones on and made no attempts at conversation, which was probably for the best. I was too nervous to talk.

Please, God, let this work.

We had the observation room to ourselves. Someone had moved our six eggs into the larger hatching room on the other side, where each of them nestled in a thick bed of foam and synthetic nesting material atop a steel table. Heat waves radiated up from the steel surface, which kept the eggs right at 95.2 degrees. A great temperature for hatching dragons, but it had to feel like an oven for the white-clad staffers.

Two pairs of them were hard at work rotating the eggs one final time. Then they lined them up against the Plexiglas, like newborns at a hospital nursery. The door opened to admit a middle-aged man was dressed like Indiana Jones, right down to the broad-brimmed hat. He'd grown out the beard, but I still recognized him from his show on *Animal Planet*.

"Is that—?" I began.

"Tom Johnson," Evelyn said.

No one in the United States knew more about herpetology than Tom Johnson. He'd advised the Dragon Genome Project, and personally captured most of the reptiles that were sequenced for it. Sure, they could have gone to zoos and collectors to get samples, but the minds behind the DGP wanted as much wild variation as possible. That meant getting some dangerous snakes and lizards from not-so-nice parts of the world. The video of Johnson wrestling a Komodo monitor in Indonesia had gone viral and drawn considerable public interest in the project.

"Sweet Jesus," I breathed. "Not taking any chances, are you?"

Evelyn laughed. "No, we're not."

"Why didn't we bring him in before?"

"He's been on an expedition in South America."

Seeing him right there through the glass had me starstruck. "What's he like?" I found myself asking.

"Oh, Tom?" Evelyn seemed surprised by my interest. "He's fascinating. Not hard to spot across a room, either."

"What do you mean?"

She shrugged and looked away.

I nudged her with my elbow. "Got a little crush on him, don't you?"

"Maybe."

I couldn't take my eyes off him. *Hell, maybe I've got a man-crush myself.*

Johnson made a quick pass and then went back to stand beside egg number four. He waited almost expectantly, like a professor expecting an answer from one of his students. It wasn't even a minute later that the egg trembled and a vertical fracture split the top in half. A gray, toothy snout appeared. Then a clawed foot. My chest hurt— I had to remind myself to breathe.

The hatchers started to edge forward, like they were going to help. Johnson wasn't having it. He ushered them to the door and followed them out.

"Wait, is he leaving?" I asked. "Are we sure we want it hatching unsupervised?"

"Be patient, Noah," Evelyn said.

I clamped my mouth shut. *Easy for you to say.*

We watched in fascination as the dragonet fought its way out of the shell. The egg-pieces clung to one another, thanks to the sticky goo underneath, so it was a bit like watching an ant stuck in honey. The goo itself coated the dragon and dripped in slow motion to the hatching room floor.

Johnson reappeared with a huge tray of meat. The hatchers tried to follow him, but he shut the door with them on the outside.

The first dragonet had wriggled free of its shell by then. It was gray-brown in color. Slender and lizardlike. Its tongue flicked in and out. It looked over as Johnson approached.

Here we go. If the dragonet shied away, even from the offer of food, that would be a really bad sign. Wild animals put survival even before nourishment.

The dragonet held still, watching him. Johnson tossed it a piece of meat. The dragonet hesitated, then leaned close and snapped it up.

Evelyn gasped. "Look at that."

"It's good. Very good," Wong said.

Johnson had another piece of meat ready, but he held it out a few feet away. This was the real test, to see if the dragonet would come to him. The meat swung idly back and forth like a pendulum. The dragonet's little head followed the motion.

"Come on, come on," I whispered.

Evelyn said nothing, but clenched her hands together so hard, they turned pale at the knuckles.

The dragonet shrank back for a moment, and I felt sure we'd failed. *Too much fear.* What was I thinking? Had we really gambled the future of Reptilian Corporation on the cats of ancient Egypt?

The Frogman muttered something that sounded a lot like *some trifecta.* O'Connell snorted. I could already sense who was going to take the fall for this latest failure. Not Wong—his design was undoubtedly similar to all the others before I'd helped him. No, they'd pin this on the guy whose simulator scored all the designs. Whose last-minute patch had effectively chosen the winning prototype.

I'm such a moron, I thought.

Then the dragonet stalked forward to snatch the meat from Johnson's hand. Gulped it right down. Paused, then actually nuzzled the man's leg. Evelyn and I laughed out loud. Even the stalwart Johnson looked surprised. He glanced up, saw Evelyn, and gave her the thumbs-up.

Evelyn blushed, and I couldn't blame her. *This is ten times better than Animal Planet.*

One by one, the dragon eggs hatched in the pod. One by one, Johnson enticed them with strips of raw meat. He took his time, offering the dragonet tiny morsels and retreating while it ate. He retreated less each time, until he stood over the dragonet while it chewed. He held the last piece out between two fingertips, just close enough that the reptile had to come to him to get it.

Every time, the dragonet took the bait.

And every time, Johnson would rest his hand on the little scaly head for a couple of seconds. Just long enough to establish physical contact, to imprint that vital physical link between survival and the human master. I might know my way around the genome, but Johnson could charm a snake out of its skin.

It took an hour and a half to get through all six hatchings, but I hardly noticed. My mind spun with the implications of a domesticated dragon. The market potential and the customization opportunities. There should be no way for the company to fail now. The others encircled Wong and offered congratulations. Korrapati sounded earnest, O'Connell grudging. But a win was a win, and we needed one.

The next morning when I got to work, the design lab was empty. The God Machine sat still and silent, except for the ever-present hum of the servers. Their LED lights blinked in enticing patterns, awaiting the next design. Or the next run of my simulator code. Here I was, probably close to winning full-time designer status at a company that might not exist in a month. I tore my eyes from the servers and went to look for Evelyn.

Her office was empty, but I found her in the conference room with Korrapati, Wong, and O'Connell, watching something on the screen.

"What's going on?" I asked.

"Robert's holding a press conference."

This ought to be interesting. I slid into a chair just as Greaves took the stage. As always, he wore khakis and a black turtleneck, a desert version of Steve Jobs. I'd have been nervous as hell in front of all those microphones, but Greaves leaned in and made eye contact with the front row of reporters. He smiled with perfect teeth and dropped the bombshell. "We've developed a domesticated reptile that's safe to keep in the home."

There was a moment of stunned silence, and then a flurry of reporter inquiries hit him all at once.

"How much will they cost, Mr. Greaves?"

"Aren't they dangerous to humans?"

"Robert! When can we see one?"

"Soon," Greaves promised. "As you know, our company has struggled to develop a foothold in the marketplace, despite having a creature unlike any in the world."

"Does a tame dragon change that?" asked a reporter.

"It's hard to say. We successfully hatched six dragons this morning. They'll be auctioned off at this time tomorrow." Greaves looked right at me, or at the camera, I mean. "I don't want to frighten anyone, but . . . there's a chance these will be the only tame dragons ever produced."

I don't think I heard anything after that. The sound of the blood in my ears drowned everything out. I looked at Evelyn. "What did he mean by that?"

She shrugged and looked down at the table.

O'Connell stood. "What the hell do you think he meant?" He stalked out.

Korrapati looked frightened, and even Wong seemed a little shell-shocked. I thought about him going back to Shenzhen and felt a wave of sympathy.

"Maybe it's just marketing talk," I said. "You know, to drive up the prices." I pointed at Evelyn. "You said he knows what he's doing, right?"

"I did say that."

"Well, I hope you're right."

She sighed. "Me, too."

I don't remember the rest of the afternoon, only the next day. The day of the auction. There was no point in trying to get any work done before it started. Evelyn recognized that and hosted a little bagels-and-juice party in the conference room. It was a nice gesture, but hardly enough to break the tension over the design team.

She perched on the chair at the head of the table, not touching her bagel. Korrapati sat on her right, with the posture of a queen. She looked stiff as a board, though. Wong lounged on across from her, but I detected a hunch in his shoulders, too. O'Connell and the Frogman had the day off. Hell, they were probably out interviewing for other jobs. If I'd been smarter, I would have been too.

The logical part of my brain tried to argue that Greaves knew what he was doing; that the ominous statements about the company's future were meant to drive up the prices. But no matter how they spun it, this was the first market test for domesticated dragons. If it went poorly, we'd all be out of a job.

"What do you think will happen?" I asked Evelyn.

"I can't say, but the first auction will be a bellwether for the others."

"They're going up one at a time?"

"It was Robert's idea."

Evelyn had used her director's clearance to get us a live feed of the auction on a massive projection monitor at the front of the room. The screen showed digital map of the world and a numeric countdown. Five minutes to showtime, the bidder registrations began to flash on screen. We couldn't see the names, only the geographic region and a buyer's ID number. Which was kind of a shame. I'd have loved to know who was bidding, and whether or not they had deep pockets. Still, they were all major urban centers. All over the world, too. That seemed promising.

The timer crept down to zero, and then the screen showed a minimum bid of five thousand dollars. Zero bids. Hell, I could have swung that much, and maybe I should have. I didn't much care for dragons, but it would be a consolation prize if my whole plan fell apart.

I held that morose thought for the few seconds. Then madness erupted on the live feed. Bids rolled in right on top of one another, from all over the world. London, Jerusalem, Oslo, Buenos Aires. Three bidders in Tokyo, four in Los Angeles. The price quickly hit double, triple my salary. Even if I'd squeezed every asset and favor and loan possible, I'd never have been a player.

The minimum price rocketed past five million, at which point most of the bidders dropped out. Three remained: Beijing, Abu Dhabi, and Silicon Valley. I began quietly rooting for the Valley, in hopes that we might get to make a personal delivery. Hell, it might even boost morale, to think that one of our first dragons lived close by.

The three finalists kept bidding the minimum increment until about 5.5 million. I guess at that point, Beijing had finally had enough.

"Oh my goodness!" Evelyn said.

I glanced up at the screen, and thought I was hallucinating.

Beijing: 7.7 million.

Silicon Valley and the UAE got the message. They made no more bids. Thirty seconds later, Beijing officially won the world's first domesticated dragon. I had to admit, it seemed fitting somehow.

I shook my head. "Someone in China sure wanted one of these."

Evelyn kept her eyes on her table, and suddenly appeared quite interested in her fingernails.

"You know who it is, don't you?"

"Do you assume I know everyone in China?"

"Not everyone, no," I said. "But I'll bet you know who was bidding."

She shrugged, still not meeting my eyes. "I have some suspicions."

That's as good a confession as I'm going to get.

The Chinese government, then. I couldn't say I was very surprised.

None of the other auctions reached 7.7 million, but they all got pretty close. Hell, there were goddamn *sultans* jumping in toward the end. Wong, Korrapati and I cheered with each one. All told, the six dragons brought in close to forty million dollars. Cash.

"Jesus, that's a lot of money," I said. And it wasn't even counting the next round of investor financing. "So, what happens now?"

Evelyn had fallen silent over the last ten minutes or so. Now, her eyes looked off at something unseen in the distance, and glittered. "Now, Noah Parker, we get to build *dragons*."

CHAPTER SIXTEEN
Evolution

So much changed over the next few months. The marketing department dove into a hiring blitz—now that we had something to sell to the consumer market, we needed an actual sales force—and they wasted little time. Our so-called "Design 49" wouldn't entice any customers; if anything, it served to remind people that our first forty-eight designs failed.

The company underwent an evolution of its own. The marketing department, which had doubled in size after the influx of cash, decided that *Reptilian Corporation* sounded too dry, too technical for the broad consumer market that we hoped to tap into. After many discussions with the executive team—to which I was not invited—they decided that the Build-A-Dragon company fit the mission better.

PetWong also died in committee, no surprise there. Instead, the marketing folks named our domestication breakthrough "The Rover" and branded it as a dragon for the family home. The press coverage from the auction had brought in a flood of orders, enough to keep our egg printer running for months straight.

With the push of a button, we could have swung into mass production mode right then and there. But Greaves set a firm maximum quota of dragons so that the production line only occupied half of our output. The rest were reserved, as he put it, for "design and innovation."

"I don't understand it," I said to Korrapati, when we were out for lunch. We'd started going to the food trucks together once every couple of weeks. It wasn't a romantic thing at all—even though she was gorgeous, I think we both realized that a relationship between designers in our little lab was a recipe for disaster. Or at least, that was the vibe I seemed to be getting, so I saw the wisdom of it.

But we both loved food, so we made the food trucks a little good-luck tradition.

"What don't you understand?" she asked.

"Why aren't we churning out Rovers to fill those orders, so that we can make a pile of money?" I shook my head. "Maybe I'm bad at math."

"I've seen your code, and I don't think that's it."

"Oh. Thanks," I said, and I could feel the heat in my cheeks.

"You're bad at *economics*."

"Ouch."

"It's basic supply and demand, Noah. The harder they are to get, the more people want them. And the higher price we can charge for each one."

"Maybe we could still charge the price and sell a crapload."

"This is better. It gives the company a solid cash flow, while not taxing our infrastructure too heavily."

It made sense, though I grumbled to myself that a taxed infrastructure would make my life easier. If everyone was super busy, my unsanctioned side project could hardly attract notice. With the God Machine churning out eggs constantly, I might even print one or two off the books.

I couldn't argue with that. In the wake of Wong's victory, the sense of competition among designers grew even stronger. The hog-hunting dragon (renamed "The Guardian") and the Rover marked important milestones for Build-A-Dragon's design team, but there were other market opportunities. Other niches to fill. All of us wanted to design breakout model number three. As the newest member of the design team and with no official credits yet, I still had to prove myself before I'd have full access to company resources. I had big plans for them.

The others, as far as I could tell, were swinging for the fences. O'Connell and the Frogman were working on a large flying model.

Korrapati had tackled a stouter version of the Rover for police and military use, which would be in high demand since all the police dogs died off. Wong wouldn't tell me exactly what he was doing, but said it was "big, very big."

I figured as long as everyone was going big, I might as well go small.

I got to work early and well-caffeinated. With the entire design team actively working on new prototypes and running my simulator, we constantly fought over computer resources. Of course, no matter how early I got in, some people never seemed to leave.

"*Nihao, Wong Xiansheng,*" I called over the cubicle wall, knowing he'd be there.

Wong rolled out of his workstation with his crooked little grin. "Good morning, Noah Parker."

"How are the blades?"

"Not busy."

"Good. So, you ready to tell me what you're designing?"

He shook his head. "Still top secret."

I laughed. "All right, then I'm not telling you mine."

He rolled back into his workstation. I logged in and started a new prototype based on the Rover model. Evelyn wanted that to be the starting point since we had proven domestication. I reduced the body size to the smallest setting DragonDraft3D allowed. This dragon would be tiny. Less than a few pounds. The small size freed up a lot of feature points, which I fed into intelligence quotient. A tiny, *clever* dragon. To my knowledge, we'd never printed something like this before.

Then I reduced some of the other traits—tooth size, claw length, muscle mass—so I could spend some points on wingspan. A tiny, clever, *flying* dragon. I might as well enjoy this. For coloring, I chose light brown and sage green. Desert colors. It seemed appropriate, somehow.

I hit the Print button. The God Machine whirred, and my conveyor belt squealed into motion. The egg arrived a few seconds later. It had a reddish-brown tint and couldn't have been bigger than a softball. It rolled off the conveyor belt onto the integrated scale, which took a measure on every printed egg and compared it to the expected weight. At least, that's what was supposed to happen. Instead, a red error message flashed on my monitor:

PRINTING FAILURE

Strange. The egg looked fine to me. A bit on the small side, sure, but technically sound. Another message flashed beneath it:

Weight: 0.0 kg

That wasn't right; even this egg should be about half a kilogram. Maybe the scale was off. I moved the egg over against my workstation so that I could give it a closer look. The weight tray looked a tad off-kilter, so I jiggled it a few times. It settled flat. A new bright-red warning message from my monitor demanded my attention:

REPRINTING

"Shit." I searched for the abort command, but the God Machine had already swung into motion. Before I could stop it, my conveyor belt whirred. An identical egg slid out. This time, the scale registered the correct weight at 0.50 kilograms. Damn thing must have been jammed before. Now that the weight matched the expected value, DragonDraft3D made a record of the successful printing and sent a pickup request right to the hatchery.

Jim arrived within minutes, when I was still tinkering with the scale to figure out what went wrong.

I glanced up. "Hey, Jim. It's right here." I handed them the egg, which I'd set on my lap while I fiddled with the scale.

"Is this a joke?" Jim asked.

I blinked. *He actually spoke to me.* And here I thought him an egg-obsessed robot. "What?"

"This can't be within spec," he said.

"Hey man, good things come in small packages."

He shook his head but set the egg carefully in the middle of the transport foam with both hands. "Nobody sneeze."

They rolled it out. My workstation beeped with an incoming message. Evelyn was passing along a custom order. "About time," I said.

I sat down and got to work on it, which is why I forgot all about the softball-sized egg that had rolled behind my workstation.

CHAPTER SEVENTEEN
INTERLUDE

The fact that my biological simulator worked so well for Reptilian is less circumstantial than it might seem.

After things ended with Jane, I'd poured myself into my thesis project. Initially, I'd started simple, with the genome of a tiny bacterium that only needed a handful of essential genes to survive. Once it worked on that, I expanded the simulator to more complex bacteria, then multicellular organisms. Many of the essential functions worked the same way in mice, fish, and chickens as they did in humans. Over the next two years, I continued expanding and testing its capabilities.

With each new advance came a cost, though: the computational power required to run it. Modeling the vast complexity of living creatures didn't scale in linear fashion, but exponentially, as the genes and their products interacted in ever more sophisticated manners. I got about as far as frogs before I hit the limits of ASU's computing resources.

That brought me to the office of my thesis advisor on a Wednesday morning in late spring, when the oleander bushes along Thunderbird Road were in full bloom. Dr. Sato sat in his swivel chair, nodding off over an actual book spread open on the desk in front of him. His ancient coffee maker spat and hissed, drizzling dark brown liquid into the waiting carafe. The place always smelled of those two things: old books and fresh coffee.

"Morning," I said.

"Oh!" Dr. Sato reared back, his eyes wide. "Hello, Noah."

"Sorry to startle you." I kept forgetting to make a noisier entrance, so he'd rouse before I came in. It was early enough yet that he hadn't had his two cups.

"No apology necessary." He gestured to the threadbare chair just inside the door. "I suppose you're here to ask for more compute."

I sank into the chair, which had to be older than I was. "How did you know?"

"Call it a lucky guess."

"I thought you didn't believe in luck."

"It's not that I don't believe in it. I just prefer hard data. Case in point." He shuffled the papers on his desk and came up with a grey-and-white striped sheet with a university letterhead. "Would you care to guess which software package consumed the lion's share of our department's computing resources in the past month?"

I grinned. "The porn filter?"

"That was number three. Ahead of it by a significant margin were two processes, 'NPsim' and 'NPdesign.'"

Damn. I really should have come up some more creative names for my programs. "Well, those could be anyone's."

"The initials give it away. You do love making your mark on things," Dr. Sato said.

"You've got me there."

"I just got off the phone with the department chair. There's good news and bad news."

"Okay." I tried to ignore the lump in my throat. Maybe I'd finally crossed a line with the computing power. But my simulator was a hungry beast, and each more complex genome brought me tantalizingly closer to human. *Just a few more months.*

"The bad news is that you'll have to find a new place to run your simulator. We can't allow you unfettered access to the university computing resources any longer."

Oh, no. A cold uncertainty welled up in my stomach. "Well, where am I supposed to run it?"

"That brings us to the good news," Dr. Sato said. "I met with the rest of your thesis committee met yesterday to review your dissertation. You've made incredible progress."

"Oh." I hadn't given any thought to defending my thesis and finishing my PhD. "Thanks, I guess."

"We think you're ready to defend."

The words hit me like a physical blow. "So you're not just cutting me off, but you're kicking me out, too?"

Dr. Sato set his coffee down and brought the full weight of his gaze on me. "It's time for you to move on, Noah. Ideally, to somewhere with significantly more resources."

"I-I . . ." Words failed me for a moment. I sighed. "I wouldn't even know where to start."

He harrumphed and plucked another sheet from a pile on his desk, seemingly at random. "I've taken the liberty of compiling a list of research institutions with top genetic engineering programs."

For a career scientist, this was the traditional path—you moved to a new institution at nearly every stage, to maximize your network of collaborators and find the right academic home—but I didn't think of this as a career. This was a means to a very specific end. I took the sheet and scanned it. Stanford, Michigan, UC Davis, Emory. Great programs and solid reputations. But they were so far away from Connor and Mom. A tightness formed in my chest, squeezing away the comfort I normally felt in Dr. Sato's cozy office. "Is there nothing closer?"

"Not with the resources that you're likely to need."

"Oh."

"You look like you swallowed a lemon," Dr. Sato said.

"Sorry. It's a lot to take in." I forced a calmer expression onto my face. "I just don't want to have to move away."

"A change of scenery might be good for you."

I gave him a side-look. "What makes you say that?"

"You've worked hard for this. Especially in the last two years."

"You make it sound like that's a bad thing."

"That's not what I meant. But you should take some time to enjoy life, Noah. Before you look up and realize most of it has gone by."

"There will be time for that when the simulator is done."

"When will you call it done?"

"When it can scale up to human."

"And presumably, there's one particular human at the top of your list."

His directness caught me off guard. He knew about Connor's situation, of course, but we hadn't had the open conversation about the connection to my work. "Is it that obvious?"

"To me, yes. But it raises an important question about your eventual goal. What is it that you hope to do?"

I *did* know that part. "Prove that my brother's mutation is the cause of his disease. Then he can qualify for gene therapy trials." Spinal muscular atrophy had been an early success for gene therapy, and I knew for a fact that the BICD2 study was still enrolling. We'd tried to get Connor in, of course, but they wouldn't accept anyone with a Variant of Uncertain Significance. The stakes of the trial were too high.

"You're convinced that it is," Dr. Sato said.

"Absolutely."

"Let's say your simulator supports the idea. Do you plan to call his doctor and tell them to change medical records?"

"Well, not exactly." This was the fuzzy front end of my plan, the part I felt less certain of. "I guess I'll present them with the evidence and try to get them on board."

Dr. Sato chuckled. "You haven't been around a lot of medical doctors, have you?"

I bristled. "Actually, I've met quite a few." Mostly when I'd tagged along to Connor's appointments.

"Yes, but you saw the patient-facing doctor. Now we're talking about engaging them as a professional."

"I *am* a professional." Or I would be, at least, by the time this happened.

"Your project is research, which gives you a lot more freedom. When it comes to patient care, however, the clinical guidelines are much stricter."

A touch of anger bubbled up inside of me. "So they'll just ignore what I say, because it's *research*?"

"If all you have is a computer program, yes. Clinicians want experimental evidence, not just computational predictions."

"I'd love to experiment on him, but he continues to refuse that idea."

Dr. Sato smiled. "As he probably should. But I was thinking more about *animal* testing."

"Aren't animal models pretty much locked down?"

"The classic ones are tightly regulated, yes, ever since the canine epidemic."

Not for the first time, I cursed the name of CFTD. No one had proved that it was artificially created, but there were strong suspicions. It not only robbed the world of dogs but ushered in a boatload of legal restrictions on genetic modifications of animals. Institutional Animal Care and Use Committees had existed before the outbreak, but now they held as much power as the review boards for human research. "Getting all the approvals would take a long time." *Which Connor doesn't necessarily have.*

"What about a synthetic model?"

I wrinkled my nose. Synthetic biology was a relatively new branch of biomedical research, the kind that created new animal and plant species by engineering their genomes from scratch. Because they didn't exist naturally on Earth, researchers had a lot more leeway on genetic research. A number of commercial firms had come in and tried to make a profit from synthetic organisms. "Oh, is Unicorns-R-Us still in business?"

"No, they closed up shop last year," he said.

"What about Custom Chimeras?"

"Just filed for bankruptcy."

"Damn. What's happening to all of them?"

"The same thing that happens to many startups. They each have a wonderful idea, but no way to make money from it." He tilted his head, as if a new thought had just intruded. "Have you heard of Reptilian Corporation?"

I had, of course. It was impossible to live in Arizona and not hear about the hog-hunting dragons. "Oh yeah," I deadpanned. "Those are the guys who do identity testing on dog poop, so you can sue your neighbors when they don't clean it up."

"That's Doo-doo Digital, as you very well know."

I couldn't fight the grin. "I just wanted to hear you say it."

Dr. Sato frowned. "Maybe I was mistaken about your readiness to defend."

I held up my hands in mock surrender. "All right, all right! Tell me about this Reptilian Company."

"Reptilian Corporation." He found a glossy magazine beneath one of the stacks of paper on his desk—*Southwest Business Journal,* one of the few magazines still doing print—and flipped it open to a two-page spread about the company. The white-haired man in the feature photo looked familiar.

"Is that Simon Redwood?" I asked.

"It's his company. Number thirteen, if I'm not mistaken."

"Well, that's one selling point."

"Are you a Redwood believer?" Dr. Sato asked.

"Oh, absolutely. I couldn't even tell you why." I shook my head. "There's just something about him."

"I really thought his space elevator was going to work."

"Yeah, that was a shame. He's got some killer ideas."

"That's not all." Dr. Sato tapped his finger on the photo and drew my attention to the backdrop. It was a server room, with tidy grids of dark gray servers. The LED patterns on them were arranged in a distinctive double-X pattern.

I gasped. "Are those Switchblades?" The next-gen computers weren't due to hit the market for another month. Rumor had it, the waiting list was already a year long. Redwood must have gotten early access. And God, he had *dozens* of them.

"Reptilian raised a lot of capital."

"Why don't they just do it all in the cloud?"

"That's a good question." Coming from Dr. Sato, this was a real compliment. He *loved* good questions.

"Maybe they have something proprietary that they don't want anyone to know about."

"Lots of VCs are still under Redwood's spell. And they're in Phoenix."

"Shut *up,*" I said.

"Right in the downtown. They're not hiring, but a former student of mine, Evelyn Chang, heads their design department."

"*The* Evelyn Chang?"

"Yes." He smiled fondly. "She's done well for herself."

I stared at the photo, wondering what in the hell this Reptilian Corporation did with all that computing firepower. If I worked there, I could not only run my simulator, but maybe put Connor's mutation into a living organism. Two birds with one stone. "I would love access to a place like that."

"I would strongly recommend you call it a career opportunity, rather than *access*. A next step for you and your career."

I tapped the magazine. "Get me an interview there, and I'll call it whatever you want."

Dr. Sato sighed. "I suppose I could put in a good word, but I want you to do something for me in return."

"Anything."

"I want you to remember that you're entering the private sector."

I rolled my shoulders, feeling defensive. "I know that."

"Corporate America is a different world, Noah. A less forgiving world. You'll have to learn to play their game if you want to last long enough to achieve your goals. You need to make yourself indispensable."

"Okay. How do I do that?"

"Oh, that's easy." He smiled. "Figure out what they need, and make sure you're the person who can give it to them."

CHAPTER EIGHTEEN
Cancellation

Ten days later, I'd just started a new design of a nonflying prototype for urban use when a calendar notification materialized on projection monitor four.

Hatching event.

"What the—" I began. Then I remembered the softball-sized egg for the little smart dragon. Even though my snarkiness had faded a bit since designing that model, I kind of wanted to see it hatch. At the very least, a tiny genius dragon against the stiff hatchery staffers was a matchup I didn't want to miss.

Sunlight streamed from seven of the hatching pods' windows; we were running at full capacity. But all the pods held run-of-the-mill Rover models. My pint-sized creation was nowhere to be found. I went back and checked my calendar, which showed that the egg should indeed be hatching today. I couldn't find it, and the rest of the design team had gone to lunch, so I walked down to Evelyn's office. "Evelyn?"

She peeked out from behind a virtual wall of projection monitors. Eight, to be precise. Anything more than six meant she was super busy. "Good morning, Noah."

"It's one-thirty."

"Already?" She shook her head. "Where does the time go?"

"I hate to bother you, but I think one of my designs is missing," I said.

Her brow furrowed. "Which one?"

"Model 86. I designed it ten days ago."

Her mouth fell open. Then she pursed her lips and looked away from me. "That design was canceled."

"By who?"

"Me."

I bit back an unkind word but couldn't keep all the anger from oozing into my tone. "You want to tell me why?"

She looked at me flat-eyed. "You sank all of the feature points into intelligence."

"What's wrong with that?"

"I assumed it was a joke."

More like proving a point, I didn't say. Truth be told, it probably wasn't the most marketable idea. But I still wanted to see how it would turn out. "So what happened to the egg?"

"Quarantine."

That meant Build-A-Dragon's desert facility, which was somewhere outside the city and off limits to regular employees. "That's too bad. It's still a viable design."

She sighed. "Look, Noah. We don't have the luxury of building any dragons we want. Robert expects us to produce viable prototypes for new product lines."

"Which would be easier if he lifted the point limits. That's the point."

She pursed her lips. "I don't think that is going to happen."

"Why not?"

"I brought it up with Robert today. He's made up his mind."

"I don't see how we'll do much more than a basic pet, if that doesn't change."

She smiled. "We'll just have to get creative."

"I guess." I turned to leave.

"Sorry about your little design."

"Yeah," I said, thinking, *not as much as I am*. A smart little dragon would have been a lot of fun. Not that I cared too much. I still didn't give a crap about dragons.

I tromped back to my desk and collapsed in the chair. I felt no motivation at all to open up DragonDraft3D to start a new prototype. The point limitations were going to be a problem. My master plan hinged on creating a dragon that was strong and smart, with enough endurance to stress-test genetic therapy. If I couldn't figure out how to print a dragon egg that went beyond the point limitations, I might never be able to do the experiment.

My workstation made a sudden crackling noise, like a glass window about to shatter. I thought it might be a bad cooling fan. I shoved aside a pile of papers that had accumulated on both sides of the tower to get a better look, which is when I saw it. The duplicate egg.

"Oh, *shit.*"

I picked up the egg to take it down to the biowaste disposal drop-off. I felt bad for wasting the egg, even though Evelyn had canceled the design. Incredibly, the thing still felt *warm*. Almost hot. It must have rolled to the perfect spot to catch the outflow of heat from the God Machine.

I wondered if it might still be viable. The God Machine was always on, so the egg might not have had a chance to cool.

According to company protocols, I should have called the hatchery staffers to come get the egg. But I was pissed off. Not just about my design getting canceled without a heads-up, but with the leadership's dogged insistence on keeping the point limits in place. The simmering anger made me want to do something reckless. I dug my insulated lunch box out of my satchel and shoved the egg into it. It made that crackling noise again.

"Uh-oh."

How long did an egg take to hatch? Maybe half an hour, maybe less. I grabbed my keys and hustled out.

I've never felt as open and exposed as I did crossing the design floor. Why the hell did we need this open floor plan, anyway? I avoided eye contact with the other designers, and prayed Evelyn wouldn't choose that moment to come talk to me. I made it to the hatchery door. *So far, so good.*

I opened the door to find Jim and Allie bearing down on me, a loaded egg-cart between them. I'd have turned around and gone the other way, but I couldn't cross that floor again. Instead, I slipped in and pressed myself against the right-hand pod so they'd have room to pass.

"Hey guys!" My voice cracked a little. Sweat dripped into my eyes.

God, it's hot in here. How they could stand to work all day in those white jumpsuits, I'd never understand. Hopefully they wouldn't notice how much I was sweating.

Allie ignored me. Jim grunted something that might have been a greeting. They never took their eyes from the egg on the cart between them. Right then, I could have taken my little egg out of the lunchbox and handed it over. *That* would get their attention. But my eyes fell to the one already on their cart, yet another cookie-cutter Rover design. That's all we'd ever produce, if the top brass didn't come around on those point restrictions.

Screw it.

I forced myself to walk to the far door. I pushed it open, bracing for the blinding red lights and the wail of the biological alarm. Nothing happened. Silence never sounded so wonderful. I hit the button for the elevator and didn't breathe until it came. The doors hissed open. I sagged in relief when I saw it was empty. I scurried on and hit the button for the lobby.

Ding. Seventh floor. The doors hissed open to reveal the towering frame of Ben Fulton, Build-A-Dragon's security chief.

Oh shit oh shit oh shit.

"Mr. Parker," he said, stepping on.

I edged over as close to the wall as I could. "Mr. Fulton."

"Keeping out of trouble?"

I forced a smile. "As best I can."

He hit the *Close Door* button. The elevator shot downward. At around the third floor, the egg decided to crackle again, loud enough that it could be heard through the bag and over the hum of the elevator gears.

Fulton looked over at me, his eyebrow raised.

I'm sure my face was red as a tomato. I fumbled with my bag. "Forgot I had some hard candy in there."

He grunted and turned to face the front again. I wasn't sure if he'd bought it. What if he demanded to look in my bag? He wouldn't without cause, though. He seemed like a standup guy. Still, I'd just as soon not get caught for something this stupid.

The doors opened at ground level. Fulton sauntered off without so much as a backward glance. I took what felt like my first breath in a while.

I prowled across the lobby to the parking garage. I paused just before the door. The moment I crossed that threshold, I'd break the law. The FDA considered dragons and other synthetic creatures to be "genetic engineering products." Registration was mandatory, and Build-A-Dragon kept a close eye on registrations. I could be fired for this, sending years of hard work and preparation down the drain. Even if that didn't happen, getting caught with an unregistered dragon would put me under a lot of scrutiny, which I certainly didn't want. It seemed like a silly gamble for an egg that had no guarantee of hatching.

Then again, there might never be another tiny, smart dragon egg printed again.

Did I really want to see it hatch so badly?

Hell yes.

CHAPTER NINETEEN
The Little Emperor

We took great care to orchestrate the hatching of new prototype dragons at Build-A-Dragon. They heated the hatching room in advance to make sure it maintained the optimal temperature. A synthetic nest and a team of well-trained handlers ensured that nothing disturbed the dragon before it was ready to hatch.

Having smuggled an egg out of the building illegally, I didn't have such luxuries. By the time I got the egg home, the dragonet had punched through the shell with his snout. I swept aside the dirty dishes on my kitchen table and set the egg in the middle. Then I ran to the closet and dug out my old-school incandescent desk lamp. The thing hogged energy like nobody's business—I kept it mainly to run up the energy bill for my jerk of a former landlord—but its sixty-watt bulb produced a little heat. I switched it on and tilted it toward the egg.

The snout, which had been poking out of the hole it made in the shell, quickly disappeared inside of it. I must have scared him.

"It's all right, little buddy," I whispered.

The egg trembled. A single claw poked through the hole the snout had made.

"Yeah, that's it." I wondered if I should help him break the shell. What had Johnson done? I couldn't remember him assisting the hatching process itself. He'd been kind of hands-off until the dragons got free.

The claw shot downward, slicing through the eggshell like a Boy Scout unzipping a tent. The reddish-brown egg split apart at the seam. The two halves clattered to the table in a puddle of amniotic goo, revealing a curled-up little reptile the color of desert sand.

He was so tiny, so comically small, that I laughed out loud. "Well, look at you!"

He uncurled his neck and looked at me with bright little emerald eyes. My breath caught. I could see the intelligence there, the cleverness. It was like he knew me and what I'd done and how he'd come to be. Ten seconds out of the egg. I mean, he *knew*.

"Ho-ly crap," I whispered.

He blinked and flicked out his tongue, as if sampling the sound of my voice.

Shit, the imprinting exercise. I'd almost forgotten.

I ran to the microfridge and yanked it open. "Come on, let there be some raw meat."

I shoved aside the takeout containers and spotted a plastic-wrapped package behind them. Sliced pork shoulder, which I'd planned to grill out on the balcony. "Yes!"

Meanwhile, the dragonet had stood on shaky legs, teetered back and forth, and then tottered closer to the desk lamp.

I ripped the plastic off the package and dumped the meat on the cutting board. Found my steak knife in the sink, and started slicing the steaks into long, jagged pieces. The dragon's little head pivoted in my direction.

"Cutting as fast as I can," I said.

He flicked his pink tongue in and out.

I grabbed a fistful of the meat and walked back to the table. "Here you go, little dude." I took one piece and dangled it before him.

He unfolded wings from his back. Lamplight shone through their paper-thin webbing. I leaned closer so he wouldn't have as much ground to cover. Imprinting was fine and good, but if he hurt himself, it's not like I could run to the vet with my unlicensed prototype dragon.

He lowered his wings and spread them out to either side, like a gymnast on a balance beam. He crept toward me, his nails clicking faintly on the wood. Catlike eyes fixed on the meat, as it swung back and forth between my fingers. Six inches away, he paused.

Crap.

"It's all right," I whispered.

He held still, his eyes flickering back and forth between me and the meat.

Well, if he didn't want to make this easy, neither would I. "All right, forget it." I shrugged and turned around.

I made it two steps when I felt the draft of cold air against my neck. Leathery wings wrapped around my face. Tiny claws dug furrows into my bare arms.

"Son of a bitch!" Survival instincts kicked in; I dropped the meat and fled into the living room.

The dragonet released me and fluttered down to the floor to claim his prize.

I shook my head. "You little punk."

He cocked his head at me, then started eating. Or tried to, at least. I'd cut the pieces the way Johnson had, for a decent-sized Rover hatchling. This little guy didn't have the jaws or the teeth for it. I let him tug away for a couple of minutes—mostly out of pettiness, for the scratches he gave me—and then cut one of the pork chops into half-inch cubes.

"Here." I tossed one to him in a gentle, rainbow arc.

He scrabbled aside and let it plop to the floor, leaving little oily splotches where it bounced. He looked at it, then back at me.

"Go on. It's all right."

He approached the cube warily, like a panther stalking its prey. He tested the meat with his tongue, then snapped it up in a single gulp.

"See? It's good."

He lifted his snout and made a high trill, like a gargling songbird.

I laughed. "Is that your way of asking for more?"

I tossed him another cube. This time, he snatched it out of midair and swallowed it in a single gulp. I fed him another five or six pieces in similar fashion. "That's probably enough for now, eh?"

He trilled again.

"All right, one more."

I washed up while he wandered around the kitchen. Now that he'd stuffed himself with pork, he seemed to move less like an agile reptile, and more like a bowling ball with legs. His stomach bulged out. I hoped he wasn't going to start throwing up. I sat on my couch, suddenly exhausted. The whole cloak-and-dagger thing took a bigger toll than I'd have guessed. The dragonet sidled up and stared up at the couch-cushion, as if sizing it up.

"I don't think you should—" I started.

He leaped up, flapping his wings like a crazed turkey, and scrabbling for purchase on the front of the cushion. He cleared the edge and tumbled over, ending up in a little heap against the back of it. I resisted the urge to help him. Touching him this soon, when he felt vulnerable, might scare him. Not to mention the dignity factor. Intelligence and pride were linked in most animals, and I'd given this one more intelligence than any dragon we'd ever printed.

So I looked away and pretended not to notice while he found his footing.

He propped himself up in the center of the cushion. Not necessarily close to me, but not as far as way as he could have been, either. He folded his wings to his back and perched like a statue. Regal as a king on the throne.

No, an *emperor* on the throne.

"I think we should give you a name," I said. "Would you like that?"

He trilled an affirmative.

I pulled up a list of famous emperors on my phone and try them out. "How about Julius?"

He flicked his tongue out and shook his head, like a dog coming in from the rain.

Guess that's a no-go. "All right. Augustus?"

Another headshake.

"How about Nero?" A small part of me hoped he'd agree. It not only sounded cool but reminded me of one of my favorite old school sci-fi movies.

He shook his head again, but less vigorously.

We're getting warmer. I tried a few more Romans, with no luck. Maybe I should try some East Asian emperors. Just before I pulled those up, I saw another name from Ancient Rome. Something about it felt fitting. "What about Octavius?"

He didn't react at first. I swear, I could see the wheels spinning in his tiny, clever head. Then he put his snout up in the air and crooned a high, happy note.

I laughed. "All right, all right. Octavius it is."

He flopped around on the couch a bit more, but eventually settled in and dozed off. It was kind of cute to watch. I watched his little chest rise and fall and wondered, *what am I going to do with you tomorrow?*

CHAPTER TWENTY
Facing the Music

It dawned on me, as I got ready for work the next day, that I hadn't really thought this whole hatch-the-dragon-at-home thing through. I had no way to contain a nascent reptile in my condo. Or to keep him fed, for that matter. The frozen pork might hold him for now but based on what I'd seen of the training manual, I'd need to get him some real food, soon. But they still expected me at work, and it was too late to call in sick.

So I locked down my condo as best I could while Octavius ate breakfast.

"Hey," I said to him.

Octavius looked up from his pile of hastily chopped pork.

"I have to leave for a while." A little part of me found it ridiculous that I was trying to talk to a day-old reptile. "Will you be okay here on your own?"

He chirped once and went back to eating, which I took as a yes. I think he understood, though he also tried to follow me out the door as I left. This created another ten-minute delay as I coaxed him back inside and did the explanation all over again.

Bottom line, I got to work half an hour later than usual. The whole way there, I worried about leaving Octavius for so long. I had no idea how the little dragon would handle being alone for nine hours. Maybe I should have locked him up, but I wanted to build his trust and didn't think that was the best way to start. I kept mulling this over on my way in, and it distracted me enough that I didn't notice Evelyn waiting for me in the design lab until I nearly ran her over.

I stopped short. "Evelyn?"

She straightened, as if she'd been lingering but didn't want it to seem that way. Strange. She usually had a senior staff meeting first thing in the morning. Why would she skip it? A cold knot of discomfort started to form in my belly.

"Noah Parker." She didn't smile. If anything, her face showed as little emotion as I'd ever seen on it. "Would you come to my office?"

"Now?"

"It's important."

It wasn't really a request, either. I nodded wordlessly and followed her. *Crap, they already know.* I wasn't sure how, but my money was on Fulton. Maybe he suspected me in the elevator or saw something on his omnipresent security cameras. It didn't matter. The guy was good at his job. I screwed up somehow, and now it was time to pay the piper.

In Evelyn's office, she took her chair, gestured me to the one facing it, and pressed the switch to activate the hermetic seal on her door. I didn't look at her as I sat down. The palms of my hands grew damp with sweat.

"I had a meeting with Robert this morning," she said, without preamble. "About what you've done."

Shock and fear paralyzed me, like a rabbit that hears a hawk scream. I forced a swallow down my dry throat. "Okay . . ."

"We want to keep this quiet."

She slid a legal-sized, sky-blue envelope across her table. It had my name typewritten on the front.

I didn't need to read it to know what it said. I'd been around long enough to see a few people get the dreaded blue envelope from HR. I tried to pick it up but couldn't get my fingers to cooperate. I guess my hands were shaking. I palmed it across the cool glass to myself, clutched it against my chest, and stood to leave. I didn't say anything. There was nothing *to* say, really. *This is the end.*

"Well, are you going to read it?"

"Don't need to," I mumbled.

She wrinkled her brow and frowned at me. "Open it, Noah."

I sighed. "Fine." I flipped open the envelope and yanked out the folded letter. A second, rectangular sheet fluttered to the floor. White-blue-white-blue-white-blue. It looked like a check. I snatched it up and looked. Yeah, it was a check all right. For half a year's salary and made out to me. "W—what is this?"

"Cracking domestication has made this company solvent, at least for the moment. I told Robert it's only right to reward the designer who helped make it happen."

"It was Wong's design—"

"He told me about your help. I also checked his code and recognized your trifecta in it. So I told Robert we had two designers who should share in the credit."

"You . . . talked about me to Robert Greaves?" The thought of him hearing my name gave me a little spike of pleasure. But I hardly noticed that against the wellspring of relief that flooded me. *I'm not in trouble.* My plan was still in motion.

"He really believes that design is the key to our company's future. It's a new era for us, Noah."

I half-fell into the chair. The relief and shock turned my muscles to jelly. "I don't know what to say."

Evelyn smiled. "Say that you'll help me bring more dragons to the world."

"Try and stop me," I said.

CHAPTER TWENTY-ONE

THE ROVER MANUAL
THE BUILD-A-DRAGON COMPANY
ROVER INSTRUCTION MANUAL, DRAFT 37 REV 1

Dear Owner,

Congratulations on your purchase of a Rover (TM) from the Build-A-Dragon Company! This manual contains important information on keeping your dragon healthy and happy (and your family safe) for your time together. Please read it carefully. If you have any questions or concerns about your new pet, DO NOT ATTEMPT TO RETURN IT.

Instead, please call our 24-hour, multilingual customer support line. One of our Dragon Specialists will be happy to assist you.

Delivery and Hatching

By the time your Rover egg arrives at your door, the gestation period will be about halfway complete. Detailed instructions for incubating the egg will be included. Please read and follow them with care. Dragon eggs require vigilant temperature control. When the egg begins trembling and crackling, it is nearly ready to hatch. Keep it in a secure area, and make sure you have raw meat on hand to complete the vital imprinting exercise.

Your Dragon's Crate

The crate that accompanies your Rover was custom-designed to serve as his house within your family home. In other words, don't throw it away. Put the crate in a corner of your household away from any fans, electrical outlets, and sources of cold air. This will be your dragon's fortress of solitude while he lives with you.

Do not, under any circumstances, allow children or small pets to enter the crate.

Feeding and Hydration

Like any pet, your Rover should be offered food and water on a regular basis. We strongly recommend the Build-A-Dragon RepChow food, which contains a careful balance of protein, grains, and vitamins to keep your dragon healthy. If you insist on feeding him other food, aim for a combination of 60% protein, 20% vegetables, and 20% starches. For protein, pork is best, as our dragons seem to prefer it to other meats. However, he will also eat beef, poultry, or fish.

Be sure to keep your dragon well-hydrated by offering 8 to 12 ounces of good clean water with every feeding. Sports drinks, soda, juice, and other beverages are not recommended. The Build-A-Dragon Company cannot assume any liability should you give your dragon alcohol.

Scale, Tooth, and Claw Care

You should have noticed that your dragon has scales, teeth, and claws. If it didn't, we probably wouldn't be able to call it a dragon, would we? In this section, you will learn about how to properly care for these parts of your pet.

Scales are your dragon's protective outer skin. As such, you should make sure that they remain intact and well cared-for. If you notice any dry patches, rub them gently with baby oil twice a day until the scales are back to normal.

Your dragon may molt once every 6-8 months. This is normal. There is no need to mail the molted skin back to the Build-A-Dragon company.

Dental care is vital to keep your Rover model healthy. You should brush his teeth every time that you brush your own. Just don't use the same toothbrush.

The nails on your dragon's feet will grow throughout his lifetime.

He will use them to dig, scratch, scrape, maim, and climb. If the nails grow too long from disuse, they may become uncomfortable. Provide a scratching post and encourage your Rover to use it instead of walls or furniture. If the nails get too long, you can trim them with the Build-A-Dragon ClawClipper. You can also ask your veterinarian to clip or grind the nails. Good luck with that.

Exercise and Play Time

Regular activity and play time will give your dragon a healthy lifestyle. Rovers love to play games like hide-and-seek, chase, fetch, and ambush. You can also take him for walks or hikes. Given the choice, however, a well-fed Rover will usually sneak off to take a nap. Instead, encourage your dragon to do some light activity following meals. You might think about doing the same, tubs!

Dragon Safety

Remember that your dragon, while friendly, is still a capable predator. He may attack birds, small animals, or other dragons if given the opportunity. Over time, he will grow loyal to the members of your family. He may protect them against real or perceived threats. Please keep this in mind if you or your children engage in any contact sports.

Keep your dragon in a fenced area or on a leash at all times. Unlike the hog-hunting reptile, the Rover is not meant to live in the wild and cannot survive more than a few days on its own.

Like many animals, dragons are territorial. Keep visitors and small pets away from your Rover's crate and feeding areas at all times. If your dragon brings a shoe, child's toy, or other object into his crate, he considers it his property. Reclaim it at your own risk.

Do's and Don'ts

DO give your dragon a name and begin calling him by it right away.

DON'T choose Rover. That's ours.

DO let your dragon explore your home, backyard, and neighborhood.

DON'T let your dragon out of sight as he explores. Especially if there are other pets or small children in the vicinity.

CHAPTER TWENTY-TWO
Clipping Wings

I drove home on a cloud, exhilarated at both the bonus and having kept Octavius a secret. For the moment, at least. Other hurdles loomed ahead—like keeping an unlicensed dragon in my condo within city limits—but I'd dodged the main bullet.

Of course, all this assumed that he'd remained in my condo in the nine-odd hours since I'd left this morning. I hurried upstairs to my door, fumbled it open, and shut it quickly behind me. My condo waited in injured silence.

"Octavius?" I crept toward the kitchen. The bowls of food lay empty on the wooden table, both of them licked clean. "Anybody home?"

A smattering of spilled cereal pieces on the floor provided the first clue that something was amiss. They formed a messy trail to the pantry, where the cereal box and three others had been ripped apart. It looked like a trashcan after a raccoon's gotten into it.

Okay, so he was a little hungrier than I thought.

I'd reasoned that with all the reductions to physical traits, he might not have the same appetite as our prototypes typically did. Swing and a miss on that logic. He was an omnivore like most of our dragons, but he must have been starving to resort to processed grains. It wasn't the mess that really bothered me, but the silence. If he'd given up on the cereal and gone looking for better food, where was he? Half-chewed cereal pieces formed a trail that led around the counter, out of the kitchen, and straight at the balcony.

Did I lock the balcony door? My heart plummeted even as I stalked across the living room and fumbled it open.

I stepped out into warm Phoenix sunset, scanning the horizon for a little flying form. At the same moment, it occurred to me that I'd had to lift the latch to open the door, which meant it couldn't have been closed from the outside. So there really wasn't a way he could have been out here. Which meant the cereal-breadcrumbs were a red herring.

Or a trap.

I spun around at the door, which I'd left half-open. Dark green wings spread wide as Octavius shot through the gap toward me.

"No!" I jumped and caught his legs. He came down thrashing, battering me with his wings. I cursed and clung to him long enough to charge back inside. I tossed him at the couch. He caught wing and tried a U-turn on me. I kicked the door shut in time for him to slam into it. He screeched in indignation, flung himself at it again, and collapsed in a heap on the floor.

"No, Octavius," I said. "You'd die out there!"

I collapsed on the couch to catch my breath.

That had been a close one. If he'd gotten out and flown off, I doubt I'd have found him again. Nor did I think he'd be able to pick out my balcony from the hundreds of others like it in my condominium complex. I could hardly go posting "MISSING: Illegal Dragon" notices around the neighborhood. Not unless I wanted Fulton to show up at my door.

Once the panic subsided, I dug the last of the frozen pork out of my microfridge and sliced it into dragonet-bite-size pieces. Octavius played dead on the floor, but his tongue betrayed him, flicking in and out at the smell of the raw meat.

"Come on, I know you're hungry." I set the bowl on the floor and backed off three paces, so he wouldn't feel threatened.

After another minute, he revived miraculously, and scampered into the kitchen to devour the still-frozen meat. I wanted him to stay so badly, but not because I forcibly kept him prisoner. Here he was a day out of the shell and had already manipulated me into nearly letting him escape. Something that clever wouldn't be foiled for long, especially since I had to leave every day to go to work. I needed him to *want* to stay.

I cleaned up the cereal mess while he ate. We kept looking at one another without being obvious about it. The weird sudden tension between us made my shoulders ache. I retreated to the couch and started drawing up the plan to better secure my condo. Octavius wolfed down the rest of the meat and waddled in from the kitchen. He didn't try to climb up on the couch this time, but circled and stretched out on the floor, just out of arm's reach.

"Feeling a little gun-shy, huh?" I asked.

Not that I could blame him. Being manhandled and thrown bodily back into my condo undoubtedly represented the most traumatic thing he'd gone through in his short life. That's assuming the destruction of half my pantry hadn't traumatized him. I'm guessing it hadn't.

He seemed so morose that I felt like I should offer something, anything, to give him a glimpse of freedom. "Tell you what. If you promise not to try and escape, we can watch the sunset out on the balcony."

He perked up and trilled an affirmative with the carefree enthusiasm of youth. I slid the glass door open and went first. Then I had to use all the self-restraint I could muster as he crept out after me and looked up at the open sky. He hopped up onto the other plastic deck chair so suddenly that I almost grabbed him.

I forced myself to breathe as he settled down to watch the big orange heat-lamp drop below the horizon. The deep longing on his face was a powerful thing to behold. Freedom and blue skies pulled at him in some primal way.

I watched him out of the corner of my eye, weighing his too-short claws and too-small teeth against the harsh environment of the Arizona desert. He wouldn't last a week out there. No matter how clever he might be.

"Listen, buddy." I made my voice as soft as I could, like I was trying to talk Jane down from one of her episodes. "I know that you'd love to go out there and fly free. But you never find your way back to my condo."

He lifted his head and chirped three syllables at me; they sounded eerily like *yes, I would.*

"It's not safe out there. Especially for a little guy like you."

He cocked his head while I said that. Either he didn't understand the words, or he thought I was a total moron.

"This is Arizona. Everything out there is dangerous, and you barely have teeth or claws." I couldn't bring myself to tell him that I was the one who'd reduced all his normal dragon features, basically to prove a point.

He crooned a soft, plaintive note and laid down again. Which only made me feel worse. He'd probably never be able to do much outside, certainly not without me watching over him.

I sighed. "Sorry, buddy. Looks like you're stuck with me."

His gaze wandered away from me and to the glass door, which glowed with the ruddy haze of approaching sunset.

CHAPTER TWENTY-THREE
Disturbing Signs

When I shared the good news about cracking domestication, Mom forcibly invited me to a celebration dinner in Tempe. Connor was still living at home while he finished engineering school, so I didn't mind going. I got there early but didn't see his car. Maybe he was out somewhere, gallivanting around. Getting home late for dinner. *Such a slacker.*

My mom opened the door on my second knock. "Hi, honey!" She squeezed me into her usual too-long hug, an embarrassment mitigated only by the unparalleled aroma of roast beef.

"Smells good in here," I said. "Where's Connor?"

"Where do you think? In his room."

"I didn't see his car out front. Did it break down again?"

She looked away from me. "We sold the car."

"The Conmobile! You're kidding me." I shook my head. His junker was the only vehicle that made mine look decent. "Why?"

"He doesn't drive so great anymore. It's hard with his legs."

"He's never driven so great, if you ask me." I brushed her off and went to give him some crap about it while the insults were fresh.

His door was closed. From beyond came the muted sound of machine-gun fire, interspersed with Connor yelling out orders. I banged on the door. "Con Air!"

The video game went silent. "Yes'm?" he called. His own version of *yes ma'am.*

"I'm coming in, so turn off the porno."

I shoved his door open. The room was cleaner than usual, which meant Mom was cleaning it for him. The only mar on the cleanliness was a series of pockmarks all over the carpet, almost like footprints, but round. A grin found its way to my face. "What, are you doing a pogo stick in—"

Then I spotted the cane leaning up against his chair, and the barb died in my mouth. "Shit. What happened?"

He shrugged. "It's just temporary. Been having some balance problems."

I didn't buy that. When someone with a muscular disease needed support, it was only temporary until they needed something more. "What about the physical therapy?"

"I'm taking a break from it."

"It's supposed to help you keep your strength up."

"Then you do it." He tugged off his headphones and flung them on his desk, where a monitor flashed the words YOU ARE DEAD in bright red letters.

I didn't want to pick a fight when I'd just arrived, so I nodded at his monitor. "Is that Halo 16?"

"It's Halo 17."

"You dog! How did you get early access?"

"It's been out two months."

"Damn." I'd essentially given up video games to focus on my thesis work, but I still missed them. "I didn't even realize."

"It's probably for the best, since you're not that good at it."

Oh, I know he didn't. "I think I have a few minutes to remind you who's the alpha brother."

"Bring it on!"

We played for probably half an hour, during which time Mom opened a bottle of wine and shouted increasingly slurred threats down the hallway. At last, I set down my controller with an air of finality. "Must be your lucky day."

"Keep telling yourself that, dude."

I couldn't resist a parting shot. "Can you gimp it down to the kitchen or do you need me to carry you?"

"Psh." He grabbed the cane and let it clunk me on the head on his way out to show what he thought of that. Then he raised his voice. "No, Noah, I'm not playing another game. Mom's waiting for us!"

Judas. I cursed and scrambled after him, but he beat me to the table and left me with most of Mom's ire.

"It's half cold already," she said.

"Looks *amazing*, Mom," I said.

"It really does," Connor said.

"You're the best cook in a hundred miles, I've always said it."

"In the entire state, if you ask me."

She tried to keep frowning at us, but the corners of her mouth twitched upward. "I expect clean plates."

"You bet," I said.

"Noah'll even do the dishes," Connor added.

Double Judas.

The second dinner ended, he compounded the betrayal by claiming he had a study group session. He disappeared into his room, and I swear I heard the sound of distant video game gunfire. I didn't want to abandon Mom, though, so I cleared the table while she loaded the dishwasher. I double-checked to make sure he wasn't within earshot, then lowered my voice. "How long has he had the cane?"

"About two weeks. I insisted, after he kept falling." She was careful not to make eye contact.

"Why didn't you tell me?"

"He doesn't want anyone to know."

"Why not?"

"You know how he is." She shrugged. "Besides, it's only temporary."

I gave her a dubious look. We both knew that was a lie. "Any luck with the clinical trials?"

"Dr. Miller has a resident monitoring the registries for us."

That meant *no*, he hadn't qualified for any. And he'd continue not to qualify, as long as his mutation has its "uncertain significance" status. I didn't have the heart to voice the thought, though. The whole situation sucked. It really did.

No one was going to fix it for us, either. It was all on me.

CHAPTER TWENTY-FOUR
Customization

To be fair, work was keeping me busier than ever. I'd hardly settled in my chair in the lab the next morning when I heard the click-clack of heels approaching.

"Good morning, Noah," Evelyn said.

"Morning," I said. I wished I'd stopped for coffee. If she was on me this early, it meant a long day.

"We had some new orders come in."

"How many?"

"Six."

"Jesus." A single custom dragon usually took me a few hours. I was looking at a two-day workload, at least. "Did we have a sale or something?"

"The new ad campaign rolled out."

"Of course it did," I muttered.

Build-A-Dragon's customization program was currently the company darling. It allowed us to squeeze the maximum revenue out of one-percenters, the kind of people who could afford not only to buy our dragons but have them customized to their whims. The enormous profit margins for those underwrote our whole department. Every new marketing campaign brought a deluge of custom orders. These went into a queue of sorts, and Evelyn's team took them pretty much at random.

"Which order's the priority?"

"They're all the priority," she said.

"All right, then pick two." I knew it would make her crazy. In Evelyn's perfect world, I'd get them all done at once, in record time, and she'd bask in the praise of the company board. But a good dragon design, a worthy design, didn't happen instantly.

She consulted her tablet, which was hotlinked into my workstation. She pulled up the order queue on my monitor, scanned the entries, and highlighted a couple. "These two," she said. "They're new customers and paid for express delivery."

Express delivery was something of an inside joke at Build-A-Dragon, but I didn't say as much. We might get to the orders a little sooner, but designs took a certain minimum amount of time no matter how quickly a customer wanted them. Then again, if someone was willing to pay extra for the appearance of a faster turnaround, Build-A-Dragon was more than happy to let them.

"I'm on it," I said.

"I was also wondering if you'd like to develop another prototype."

"I like the custom jobs," I said, by way of avoidance. In truth, I was a little gun-shy after she killed the design that produced Octavius. Despite the early morning wakeups, I'd already taken a shine to the little guy. But I couldn't exactly tell her how I'd gotten the market research, so I had to let it go. "They're keeping me plenty busy."

"The customs are important, but they're short-term jobs. We need to think about the larger plan, and that means new prototypes."

I sighed. I'd have to pay the piper sooner or later. "What do you have in mind?"

"I was thinking a long-range flier."

"Ooh," I said, betraying my eagerness. There was something inherently fascinating about a dragon that could fly. Korrapati's short-range suburban flier—called the Harrier—were pretty good at it. The high metabolism gave them a lot of energy, and we made sure their bodies were light enough that they could maneuver as well as any bird. We were already shipping a lot of those, especially to urban areas where a smaller dragon made sense.

The long-range flier prototype was another story. O'Brien and the Frogman did their best, but because of the infamous point restrictions, the largest flying dragon got the smallest brain. The so-called Pterodactyl flew decently enough during our field trials to get the thumbs-up for manufacturing, but no one thought to point out that these took place in a large open space out behind the building. Soon after it hit the market, we learned that the Pterodactyl had a frightening tendency to crash into stationary objects.

Some genius had started an internet petition to rename it the "Terribledactyl" and collected a thousand signatures. Sales plummeted, and they pulled the model from our catalog.

"It's an obvious gap in our product lines right now. Customers want a dragon that can fly faster and farther."

"Without crashing into things?"

She cracked a hint of a smile but forced it away. "It won't be easy, Noah."

"Not with the point limitations, no."

"You're good at solving problems. You showed that with the trifecta."

She knows me too well. But my mind had taken a different tack already. A long-distance flier would necessarily have strength, agility, stamina . . . traits that might be useful for other purposes. "I suppose I could give it a shot."

"After the customs."

"Right."

"Thanks." She click-clacked away.

I sighed and got to work. The first custom order was a household dragon. Small frame, slow-growing, and a coloring that came right out of a five-year-old girl's imagination. It took a certain kind of overindulgent parent to throw down the cash for one of our dragons and let it be pink with white polka dots.

I opened DragonDraft3D on the computer and started a basic flightless Rover model. We had walkthroughs and preloaded configurations for dragons like these, but I liked to do them by hand. That way every dragon had the mark of Noah Parker on it. Maybe one day that would be worth something.

This customer wanted a mild temperament, which meant tuning the oxytocin receptor to high efficiency. No claws, obviously, so I knocked out a few keratin genes. I trimmed back the growth time on the scales so they'd end up small and pliable. Pigmentation came next. I have to admit, my fingers fought me on the colors they'd requested. Pink and white just felt *wrong*.

Every step I took, I ran through the biological simulator to ensure viability. Dragon biology, malleable as it might seem, required a delicate balancing act. Since I'd curtailed the physical traits, I could have given the birthday job a larger cranium, but I didn't think that was a good idea. Intelligence contradicted loyalty in dragons, and this one would need a lot of love. Especially once it got a look in the mirror.

I hit the Print button, and the God Machine got to work. Ten minutes later, a hot pink egg slid out on the conveyor belt.

I shook my head. "You've got to be kidding me."

Wong chose that moment to pop his head over the divider. "Very nice, Noah Parker!"

I groaned. "It's a custom."

"You should get a matching shirt."

"Get back to work, will you?"

I opened another window on my system to make sure hatchery staffers had gotten the transfer request. I had to get that thing out of my line of vision as soon as possible but Build-A-Dragon didn't want designers so much as touching the eggs. It was hard to argue with them about not trusting me with fragile objects, though. I spilled something on my desk or my person about once a week.

Two white-garbed hatchery staffers appeared a few minutes later.

"Hey guys," I said.

"Hey," they answered, in a distracted sort of way.

The hatchery staffers had grown even more obsessive in their care of dragon eggs since business picked up. Then again, they *did* spend a lot of hours in the relentless heat of the Arizona sun. Dressed in stifling white jumpsuits, no less. Anyone who did that every day was bound to end up a little sun-touched, as they say.

I ate lunch at my desk—peanut butter and jelly sandwich, as always—and flipped over to the secret, not-officially-ordered design. A design that carried a genetic change of uncertain significance. I'm not sure why I didn't just go to Evelyn and tell her about this part of my plan. My instincts told me that giving a dragon a progressive muscle disease wouldn't hold much appeal with company leadership. Dragons were our products; sending out intentionally defective ones might reflect poorly on us. Even if it were for good reasons, like helping my brother and others like him. Besides, the old adage probably applied: it was easier to ask forgiveness than permission. His variant went in, and the dragons would either replicate his disease or they wouldn't. My simulator backed my prediction: its modeling of the dragon with Connor's variant foresaw gradual muscle weakness and progressive loss of strength. That's because my simulator thought like I did. I went back to the code itself and made the tweaks so it essentially ignored the spiked-in variant. The genetic sabotage was ready, and the failsafe effectively disabled. Now all I needed was the right dragon to put it into.

In the meantime, I started in on the next order. Basics first: body type, maximum size, growth rate, coloring. The current customer wanted an attack dragon. Lean, muscular, and jet-black. I glanced over the rest of the form. The heavy claws were an obvious choice. Same with the spiked tail and extra rows of canine teeth. The buyer certainly knew his business.

The sales department had redacted the name of said buyer, but I could make an educated guess. Dragons like these usually ended up in the hands of rich criminals. They'd paid for on-site hatching, too, which meant our staff would oversee the hatching and deliver the live dragon to the customer in person.

I altered the hemoglobin gene to give it higher efficiency. Then I wiped out one of the dopamine receptors, so the dragon wouldn't be easily sated. These traits meant the cranium had to be small. This dragon would operate mostly on instinct, which worked well for attack models. Dragons were already natural predators. Take away their senses of empathy and self-preservation, and you had yourself a killing machine.

The simulator kept me in check; sometimes I went too far with the musculature or claw size. Two steps forward, one step back. I didn't bother with wings; it would be too heavy to fly. It was late afternoon by the time I found the right balance. One perfect killer dragon. I made a note on the dietary guidelines (lots of meat, preferably raw) that customer service could pass along to the buyer. I gave it an aggressive-model flag in our system, too, which meant the customer would receive all the usual disclaimers about dangerous animals. Much of the legal framework for Rottweilers, pit bulls, and other dangerous dogs had been adapted so that it applied to synthetic organisms as well. If your dragon maimed someone, you were responsible. Rumor had it that Greaves had retained a powerful lobbying group to make sure that attack dragons weren't banned altogether.

I hit "Print" and put in a transfer ticket while the God Machine got to work. Funny how the egg often hinted at the dragon inside it. This one slid out of the printer like a shadow. The marbled black-and-gray shell seemed to absorb the light all around it.

Jim and Allie arrived, and wheeled their cart into position beside the God machine.

"Hey guys," I said, earning two silent nods in response.

They did a team lift on the egg—it was heavier than it looked, and company protocols required this anyway—and eased it into a shallow foam receptacle on the cart.

"This is a—" I started to say. I'm not sure what happened next. Maybe one of the wheels gave out or something. But the cart buckled, and the handlers shouted in alarm. Jim tried to catch it, but he was on the wrong side. Allie couldn't hold the weight on her own. Instead, she threw herself under it. Didn't even hesitate or anything. She grunted when it hit her but held on with both hands.

"Shit!" I half-fell out of my chair to help her.

I had trouble getting a grip on the egg's slippery-smooth surface. *Damn, it's heavy*. I couldn't lift it on my own, but I kept it from crushing her.

Jim kicked the cart to one side, straddled Allie, and gripped the egg in a bear hug. I squirmed out of his way. He grunted and heaved the egg in a dead lift. Allie scrambled out from under it.

"Are you all right?" I asked.

"Yeah." She unzipped her headgear and pushed it down. Her jet-black hair tumbled loose about her face. She grimaced. "I'll grab another cart."

"Maybe I should get it," I said.

"I'm fine." She limped out.

Jim stood there holding the egg, his arms taut with the effort.

"You want to put that down?" I asked.

He shook his head. "I got it."

Then Allie was back, and they tried the whole thing again. The cart held this time. Thank God the egg hadn't broken; I doubted they'd have taken it well. Allie pressed her hands to her right side and gasped.

"Maybe you should see the doctor," I said.

"Right after we get the egg situated."

Jim pushed the cart out and she limped after it, pulling the damaged one behind her. I might as well have been a painting on a wall now that they had the egg in their possession.

In all the commotion, I forgot to tell them to put it in a solitary incubator.

CHAPTER TWENTY-FIVE
TECH SUPPORT

Build-A-Dragon Support Chat Transcript
Operator: Li-Huei Chang
Date: August 23rd

System: We appreciate your patience. A support operator will be with you in two minutes.

System: We appreciate your patience. A support operator will be with you in one minute.

Charles Smith (trainee): Hello, and thank you for contacting the Build-A-Dragon Company. May I have your name, please?

Guest 5: Maria Domingo Sanchez.

Charles Smith (trainee): Good afternoon, Mrs. Sanchez.

Guest 5: It's MISS Sanchez!

Charles Smith (trainee): Of course. Miss Sanchez. How can I help you today?

Guest 5: Something's wrong with my dragon.

Charles Smith (trainee): What seems to be the problem?

Guest 5: It got fat.

Charles Smith (trainee): I'd be happy to help you with that. I see you have a Rover model. Is that correct?

Guest 5: Yep. His name's Drago Malfoy.

Charles Smith (trainee): Bravo on the literary reference. Adult Rovers should be sixty to eighty pounds. How much does yours weigh?

Guest 5: I don't know, 140?

Charles Smith (trainee): Just to confirm, miss, you have standard Rover model that weighs 140 pounds?

Guest 5: That's right.

Charles Smith (trainee): Good God! What have you been feeding him?

Guest 5: He likes to hang out under the table, so I guess it's mostly what we're eating. Hamburgers, pizza, chicken wings. Chili cheese burritos.

Charles Smith (trainee): Is that all? No dessert?

Guest 5: Oh, he's got quite the sweet tooth. Cakes with extra frosting. Cookies. Deep-fried Oreos are his favorite.

Charles Smith (trainee): I'm afraid that the reptilian digestive system is not designed to handle high levels of sugar and saturated fat.

Guest 5: In English, please.

Charles Smith (trainee): Stop feeding your dragon so much junk food, Miss Sanchez.

Guest 5: Well, what should we feed him?

Charles Smith (trainee): Most of our customers feed their dragons genuine Reptilian dragon food, and they stay quite lean.

Charles Smith (trainee): The dragons, that is.

Guest 5: Did you just call me fat?

Charles Smith (trainee): I absolutely did not, Miss Sanchez.

Guest 5: You think I'm fat, don't you?

Charles Smith (trainee): I certainly wouldn't know.

Guest 5: Let's see you pop out three children and maintain an ideal weight!

Charles Smith (trainee): That certainly would be a stretch for me, Miss Sanchez. But back to the dragon . . .

Guest 5: What about it?

Charles Smith (trainee): Changing his diet should help considerably, but I might also recommend regular exercise.

Guest 5: Well, he likes sports.

Charles Smith (trainee): Outstanding. Any sports in particular?

Guest 5: Baseball, golf, tennis . . . And football, of course.

Charles Smith (trainee): Your dragon plays football?

Guest 5: He doesn't play, he watches it on TV like everyone else.

Charles Smith (trainee): Ah.

Guest 5: He devotes a lot of hours to it already. I'm not sure we can add more.

Charles Smith (trainee): You understand that watching sports on television doesn't really count as exercise, right?

Guest 5: Says who?

Charles Smith (trainee): I suppose that's a toss-up between physics and reality.

Guest 5: Psh. I'm in decent shape and that's all I do.

Charles Smith (trainee): I'm not going to touch that one, Miss Sanchez. May I ask, do you generally keep your Rover indoors or outdoors?

Guest 5: About half in, half out.

Charles Smith (trainee): So, I assume you let him out during the day, and bring it in at nightfall?

Guest 5: No, I meant LITERALLY half and half. He's stuck in the doggie door.

Guest 5: That's why I'm talking to you.

Charles Smith (trainee): I'm afraid that the Build-A-Dragon company cannot be held liable for property damage due to negligence.

Guest 5: I don't give a damn about the door. I just want to get my dragon unstuck from it.

Charles Smith (trainee): Do you have any vegetable oil in the house? Perhaps in bottom of the deep fryer?

Guest 5: How do you know I have a deep fryer?

Charles Smith (trainee): Call it a lucky guess. Does that mean you have some?

Guest 5: We got plenty.

Charles Smith (trainee): If you rub oil generously about the dragon's middle, I think you'll be able to ease him out of the door.

Guest 5: I'll give it a try. For now, I have to sign off for dinner.

Charles Smith (trainee): Well, I'd hate to come between you and a meal. Good evening, Miss Sanchez. Thank you for contacting The Build-A-Dragon Company.

CHAPTER TWENTY-SIX
Desert Encounters

I tried to go back to work, but the incident with the egg and hatchers kind of shook me. After my third false start on the next custom order, I decided I should just call it a day and go home. Not so long ago, heading home meant I'd play Russian roulette with the jalopy and head to my empty, crappy apartment. Now, I had Octavius to come home to. And more importantly, I'd spent most of my bonus on a much nicer form of transportation. It was my one concession to the flash and glam of the Phoenix lifestyle, a car I'd dreamed of owning since childhood.

A Tesla Model S, bright red.

I paused to unplug it—charging your battery on the company's grid was part of the benefits package—and put my thumb on the biometric scanner. The car beeped, the security system disarmed, and the driver's side door hissed open.

I never, ever got tired of that sound.

I slipped into the driver's seat, put my hands on the wheel. I inhaled the scent of Nappa leather while the retinal scanner verified that it was me.

"Good afternoon, Noah" said the car. Her voice, which sounded like the computer from "Star Trek," was another thing I never got tired of hearing.

"Hello, gorgeous," I said. "Let's go home."

The seatbelt slid across. The car backed out and began the

seemingly endless ascent up the exit ramp. The windows dimmed automatically when we got outside the garage. I fiddled with the console to find some 80s music.

The Tesla got me home in twenty minutes—leaving in mid-afternoon had its perks—and parked itself in the garage beneath my condominium building. This was one of the prefab "green" complexes that they'd built all over Scottsdale. I could have afforded a swankier place downtown, but I liked the fact that they generated their own power. Totally off the grid. My corner unit had a balcony and fifteen hundred square feet of bachelor pad.

Another thirty or forty years of gainful employment, and it would be all mine. Of course, that depended on remaining employed, which was by no means a guarantee.

The condo door slid open at my touch. Fluorescent lights flickered on.

"Octavius?" I called.

No answer. He was probably asleep, as usual.

I dug a diet soda from the high-efficiency mini fridge and took it out on the balcony. Nestled between two stone gargoyles I'd picked up at a yard sale lay a football-sized dragon the color of sandstone. He kept till as a statue, but the detail was far better than any carving I'd seen.

"There you are," I said.

The dragon stirred. One bright eye flicked open to look me up and down. He stretched and hopped over to nudge me with his snout. He'd grown since hatching, and he was getting stronger. Between that, his ever-sharper teeth, and the rapidly growing claws, I figured he could hold his own against the average house cat. I rubbed the dry patch of scales behind his ears. "Missed you, buddy."

He had the run of the condo while I was at work, whether I wanted it or not. There's just no way to corral a dragon that can work doorknobs and pick locks.

I took a slug of the soda, savored the rough cool slide of it down my throat, and sighed.

Octavius looked up at me and made an inquisitive sound.

"Just a rough day at work," I said. "Trust me, you don't want to know."

He looked back at the sunset, and a flash of wistfulness crossed his features. Just a momentary flash, but I caught it. He wanted to be out there, I could tell. But if I let him roam free, someone might find him. If word got back to Build-A-Dragon, they'd eventually figure out who had printed his egg. Then I'd be on probation if I was lucky or fired if I wasn't. Either way, I'd win some scrutiny that I didn't want. Not with the progress I was making on my flying dragon.

Still, I felt bad about keeping Octavius shackled here with his metabolic deficiency. I flicked him on his shoulder to get his attention. "Let's do something fun this weekend. You and me."

He spun around in a circle and uttered two high syllables. *Frisbee?*

"No, you destroyed the last one, remember?" I asked.

He shook his head, denying it.

"We lost the other one in that lake Wednesday after *someone* got distracted by a butterfly. I won't say who."

He ducked his head and looked down at the ground.

"What about a geocache?" It would take us out into the desert beyond prying eyes. I hadn't been in a while, and it helped me clear my head. Maybe I'd figure out what sort of dragon made the most sense to host my unsanctioned genetic testing. Besides, I was still tied with SumNumberOne on the leaderboards, and if I didn't log another cache soon I'd drop into the #2 slot. "We have to follow clues to track down a prize."

He perked his head up, intrigued but not sold on it.

"I'm pretty sure there's a good cache up in Tonto," I said. "We'd go past a restaurant that makes the *crispiest* bacon . . ."

He jumped up and crooned happily, nearly knocking me off my chair in the process.

"All right, buddy, if you insist."

Because of the crappy night's sleep, we got a later start than I wanted the next morning. We were going after an ambitious geocache in Tonto National Forest, three million acres of cactus-studded desert and with the occasional evergreen ridge thrown in. The drive alone was about an hour; I got breakfast on the way. I parked the Tesla in a remote parking lot and set out on foot. As soon as I couldn't see the parking lot, I let Octavius take wing. He flitted left and right overhead as I hiked up the trail.

Tonto might be rugged, but it was still close enough to Phoenix that I expected to run into some other people. Hikers, for the most part. Other people were taking out their non-canine pets for some desert time. I counted three ferrets, two guinea pigs, and an honest-to-god cat on a leash. Every time, I had to call Octavius back and hold him so he wouldn't tangle with some ridiculous pet. After the third instance of this in the first half mile, I was kind of used to it. The foot traffic thinned out as we got farther from the parking lot. We had a quarter mile to cover until the first clue, so I let Octavius scout ahead.

There was a chance I'd run into another person or two. I figured I'd handle it. I expected it. What I didn't expect was to navigate a sharp turn and come face to face with Ben Fulton. He was wearing dungarees and a faded ball cap, so I almost didn't recognize him.

"Parker?" For a moment he seemed just a startled as I was.

"Hey." I made a dedicated effort not to glance up to see where Octavius was. "What's up?"

"What brings you out here?"

I tapped my watch. "Geocaching. You?"

"Just stretching my legs." He glanced over my head and frowned.

My heart sank. He must have spotted Octavius. I had no idea what I would say to explain his presence.

"Well, I'll leave you to it. Be safe."

He brushed past me on the way to the parking lot. I stood frozen for a moment. *What just happened?* I snapped out of it and searched the skies frantically for Octavius. I spotted movement at least, near the tops of some saguaros that lined the parking lot. Yes, there he was. Darting low and fast among the tops of the cacti. He seemed to be getting stronger and took to wing more easily than usual. It was curious, really. I'd given most of the design points to intelligence, so his physical traits got only a pittance. Still, he was growing into a powerful little flier. It occurred to me that a flying dragon, one that had to pull its body through the air, was the true test of muscle performance. Maybe that would be the best reptilian model for Connor's mutation. A model that would demonstrate that his variant caused disease after all.

A realization jarred me back from that line of thought. Octavius was not alone. Another flying shape about his size zoomed around the cacti. Similar coloring, too. *How in the world?* It was another little dragon. They chased one another around, but it looked more playful than aggressive. Then someone whistled, and the strange dragon broke off. It swooped down to the window of a large black pickup. Fulton's pickup. I'd seen it in the parking garage at work enough times to know.

Fulton has a dragon, too. Maybe his was authorized, but I doubted it. The thing looked too much like Octavius for it to be a coincidence. Why would he, of all people, take the same risk? What did it mean? I pondered this as Octavius glided back to me, looking especially pleased with himself. Maybe he understood, or maybe he'd just enjoyed seeing another creature just like himself. He landed on the split boulder and stared back at the parking lot, where Fulton's pickup disappeared behind a cloud of dust. Maybe he didn't know what to make of it. I sure as hell didn't.

"Ready to find the prize?" I asked. "It's supposed to be at the base of a boulder."

He tilted his head and chirped two questioning syllables that sounded uncannily like *boulder*.

"A big rock, taller than this." I stood and lifted my arms straight up. "It'll be along the trail, about half a mile up. Think you can find it?"

He took off and zoomed ahead, following the trail as it wound down into the desert scrub. He circled back two minutes later, trilling his excitement. That was promising. He landed on my shoulder and prodded me with a clawed foot.

"Ow! All right, buddy," I said. "Easy with the claws."

I picked up the pace, kicking the occasional rock with my boots to send it skittering across the hard-packed dirt. Two minutes later, we crested a ridge that looked out over a wide basin of saguaro and rocky-strewn sand. A ten-foot boulder rested a few feet off the path. That had to be the one. But I couldn't see the cache itself, because there was a girl standing right in front of it.

There are too many people in this goddamn park.

"Hello," I called.

She jumped and turned around, startled. I started to stammer out an apology. Then a bundle of black hair and teeth jumped up right in front of me, grunting and snapping at my knees.

"Whoa!" I took a step back out of instinct.

At first, I thought it was a boar, or a wild hog. Its mottled brown and black hair blended well with the desert terrain. The only thing that stood out was the hemp collar around its neck. *It's a goddamn pig.*

Octavius hissed and lifted his wings as if he was going to swoop down to attack. No surprise there. The first of his kind had been bred to hunt animals like this.

I put a hand on his clawed feet to restrain him. "No, Octavius."

He rewarded me with another hiss, but I held him fast and backed away.

"Riker! Come!" the girl commanded.

The pig obeyed with obvious reluctance. It retreated, never taking its eyes from us. Giving us a snarl, too. Which Octavius was happy to return.

"Sorry to startle you," I said. "Are you here for the geocache, too?"

"Yes, we—" she began. "Noah?"

I got a better look at her face, and it clicked. Her name was Summer Bryn, and she was the tree-hugging roommate of my crazy-ass ex-girlfriend.

CHAPTER TWENTY-SEVEN
Suspicions

"Well. Summer Bryn," I said.

"Noah Parker."

Seeing Jane would have been worse, but not by much. She had sunglasses on, so the glare I felt was probably my imagination. "Didn't expect to see you," I said. *Or Ben Fulton, for that matter. Why did I have to pick Tonto today?* "We're, um, on a geocache."

"So are we."

"Right."

More awkward silence. These memories started flashing through my mind of the terrible shouting matches with Jane. Summer really had seen the worst of me.

"What's that thing on your shoulder?" she asked.

"Haven't you seen a dragon before?"

"Not in person. I might have seen one on a geocache once, out in Red Mesa. It ran off before I could get a good look."

"That wasn't a dragon. They don't live in the wild."

"Then I guess I haven't. I just figured a dragon would be more, um..." she paused. "Impressive."

"Tsh." Granted, it's not like I'd impressed a bronze or anything, but Octavius was still special, in a way. "Size isn't everything."

"I should hope not."

Octavius seemed to know we were talking about him. He flicked his tongue out at her, one of his rudest gestures.

"Hey, now, be nice," I told him, fighting the grin that wanted to spread on my face.

Summer clipped her mangy pig on a leash. She'd grown her hair out. She looked lithe and healthy, which only served to twist the knife that the reunion planted in my gut.

Octavius never took his eyes from the pig. I had to pry him loose from my shoulder one claw at a time.

"Did you find the marker?" I asked.

"Maybe."

How did she get so tan, anyway? All I ever did was burn. The SPF50 saved me from the worst of it but kept me pale as a ghost. "Not going to tell me, huh?"

She shrugged. "It's against the rules."

"Fine, be that way," I said.

"I think I will," she said. "See you in another few years."

She stalked off with the pig in tow, which meant she'd found the marker and was headed to the next one. I watched her go, wishing I'd thought to say that. She'd always liked to get the last word.

We could have just followed her, but that would be cheating. Besides, it would be far more enjoyable to beat her fair and square.

I pointed Octavius to the boulder. "Right there, buddy," I said. "Find the marker."

He glided to the boulder, circled it once, then settled down at the base. He chirped at me; he had it already. It was a brick, half-buried in the dirt, with a number stamped on the top. At least she hadn't buried it. I put the coordinates in my watch. About a third of a mile.

"Come on buddy," I said. "We can't let a girl beat us."

Karma came promptly back to bite me, because there was no catching Summer and Riker. We caught glimpses of them from time to time as we approached a marker, but they built a lead and kept it. I'd figured we'd be quick to catch them; Octavius and I were *good* at this stuff. But she didn't miss a beat.

It was ridiculous.

Finally, we reached the endpoint. Octavius found the case in a hollowed-out log. It turned out to be an old can of WD-40, sawed off and capped with a plastic lid. I took this off and dumped the contents into my hand. There were some McDonald's toys, a couple of matchbox cars, a G.I. Joe, a pack of gum. I plucked out the micro-USB drive and plugged it into my watch to log the find. Octavius got to pick out the prize. He nudged a glass marble with sky-blue whorls with his snout.

"That what you want?" I asked.

He crooned the affirmative. I took the marble and left our own little token, a tiny pewter dragon figurine. I made sure the lid was on tight before I put the cache back. Then I obscured a couple of footprints I'd made in the loose dirt—no need to make it too easy for the next guy—and headed back to the parking lot.

Jeeps and SUVs now occupied most of it. A light coat of sand-dust covered all of them, too, from the constant comings and goings. I finally had cell service again, so I couldn't resist the urge to check my league stats. I'd hoped today's cache would put us ahead. *Still tied for first. Damn.*

There was a little picnic area beside the line of cars. I caught a flash of movement there, and Octavius hissed. Riker shot past, in hot pursuit of a neon green frisbee. He reared up to snag it out of the air. Not a bad show of talent, for a pig. He raced back to Summer and ruined the performance only a little by refusing to give her the frisbee.

She saw us and made a big show of checking her watch. "I was about to call the rangers. Thought maybe you got lost."

"Your concern is touching."

"Did you find it, or do you need some help?"

"Funny," I said. She thought she was *so* smart. "You know what the WD stands for, in WD-40?"

"No, what?" She threw the frisbee again and brushed an errant strand of hair out of her face.

"Water displacement."

"For real?"

"That's why it's used to prevent rust."

"You're such a nerd."

Riker had the frisbee and came trundling back for another round of tug-of-war.

"Yeah, I know. I even named my pet after a 'Star Trek' character," I said. "Oh, wait. That was you."

"Hey! Riker's a good name."

They were a good team, too, though I didn't say that. Right then it hit me. Riker was the name of the first officer on "Star Trek," and the captain called him Number One.

"Oh my God," I muttered. *I really hope that's a coincidence.*

Summer glanced at me. "What?"

"Nothing." I thought about leaving, but my curiosity got the better of me. "So the geocaching thing. You don't happen to go by the name SumNumberOne, do you?"

That caught her off guard. She gave me a sort of side-look. "How do you know that?"

I shook my head. "Unbelievable."

She gasped, and even let go of the frisbee. "You're NPdesign."

"Yeah."

She chewed her lip. "This is weird."

"What are the odds, right?"

"Took you long enough to tie me on the leaderboard," she said.

"Just wait until next weekend, when we pull ahead."

"I'm not too worried about it." She yanked the frisbee away from Riker and threw it again. A perfect, level throw, just far enough to make the pig work for it.

"We're doing Big Mesa Star," I said.

It was a lie, at that point. Big Mesa Star was a legendary five-marker geocache in Big Mesa National Reserve. It had the highest difficulty rating, so finding it probably would put us on top. She had to know that.

She snorted. "Good luck with that one."

"Thanks," I said. "See you in another few years."

CHAPTER TWENTY-EIGHT
The Prototype

I should have been more reluctant to design another dragon prototype after Octavius's design was canceled, but the challenge of designing a better flying model intrigued me. I brought up the Pterodactyl design that O'Connell and the Frogman had put together and perused it at length. Honestly, it was pretty good. They'd invested most of the feature points on wingspan, musculature, and endurance—the holy three traits of flight-capable animals—and devoted what paltry ones remained to intelligence. It was probably what I'd have tried first, too.

Having seen the results of the "Terrible-dactyl," however, I figured I should take a different route.

First, I curtailed each of the holy three traits—which would undoubtedly limit the flight capability—and moved those over to intelligence. My simulator showed that the resulting dragon would have better flight control, with a reduced range. But I was still worried about whether the dragon was smart enough to navigate in three dimensions. The instinct of flight wasn't bred in the same way its hunter and predatory instincts were. There were, as far as I knew, no flying organisms that contributed DNA sequences to the Dragon Genome.

So I robbed Peter to pay Paul once again and goosed up the intelligence even more. This time, the simulator showed that the dragon would hardly fly at all. Not that it *couldn't* fly, but it chose to spend most of its time on the ground. Maybe it simply knew the limits of flight and preferred to save them for emergencies. Wild turkeys did that, so there was biological precedent.

But I could already hear the nicknames customers would produce for a flying dragon that never flew. "No-fly" or "Flying lemon" or "'Fraid-of-flier." I scratched that model and started over.

Project Condor, as I started calling it, was doomed from the beginning. It wasn't that I didn't know how to make a big, badass dragon. I sure as hell did. But balancing size with agility and intelligence while staying within Build-A-Dragon's guidelines was virtually impossible.

I was at my desk, muttering curses to myself, when Evelyn stopped by for a status update.

"Noah, you are talking to yourself," she said.

"Was I? Jeez. Sorry."

"Are you making any progress?"

"Not really." I was happy with the body size and cranial capacity, but the simulator said the dragon wouldn't fly. The wings were too short. "You're asking a lot."

"I know it's a hard design," Evelyn said. "That's why I gave it to you."

"If you really want all of those features, I need some wiggle room with the point restrictions," I said.

Evelyn chewed on her lip. "How much wiggle room?" she asked.

"Maybe twenty points," I said.

"That many?"

I shrugged. "Otherwise it's hard to make it smart enough *and* strong enough."

Caution warred with ambition on her face while she considered this. "Do what you have to do," she said at last.

I felt a thrill that I tried not to show. A chance to go outside Build-A-Dragon's restrictive guidelines? Talk about a game-changer.

I had a few orders in the queue, but nothing pressing. I opened DragonDraft3D and entered an override sequence to put the program in "experimental" mode, allowing designs beyond Build-A-Dragon's strict parameters.

The God Machine wouldn't print an experimental egg without director approval, but I felt confident that Evelyn would grant it. An improved flying model, if it sold well, would be a major coup for her with the company's top brass.

It was tempting to amp up everything: body size, wingspan, intelligence. To make something like the dragons out of legend that Connor was always prattling on about. I had to admit, it would be kind of sweet to create something like that and simultaneously use it to get him his long-awaited diagnosis.

But I'd never get Evelyn's approval to print *that* egg, much less permission from Robert Greaves. Even so, a scaled-down version of it, a *promise* of such perfection, might convince them to lift the point restrictions permanently. And the fact that it would provide a perfect model for Connor's mutation? Just a side benefit.

I cracked my knuckles. "Let's do this."

The first thing I did was push the wingspan out to three meters. I couldn't entirely resist the liberty of sanctioned boundary-breaking, so I tweaked the metabolism and bumped up the cranium capacity. Then the fast-twitch muscle response. This dragon wouldn't just be able to fly. It would swoop, glide, pivot. It would dance in the air. But it would also hold a secret: my brother's so-called variant of uncertain significance. This was the model for it. I knew it in my bones. A strong, smart flying dragon would test its muscles in countless ways, just like a boy would. I couldn't ask for a better model system.

If I was right about it, the muscle weakness would arise over time, and even then, it would mostly affect the lower limbs. With a muscle biopsy, I could compare their leg tissue to that of a dragon without the VUS under a microscope. Muscle cells from BICD2 patients had a striking visual feature called Golgi fragmentation. Basically, the compartments that move things around the cell are scattered and disorganized, rather than centrally located. If I could prove that cells containing Connor's variant had the fragmentation, it should convince the doctors that it caused his disease.

Then again, these were a lot of *ifs* and *shoulds*. The thing is, few aspects of genetics can be predicted with absolute certainty. But I figured that an in-demand prototype to satisfy a key niche market was as good an excuse as I'd ever have to test out a model system.

Besides, if I managed to create a flying dragon that started out strong and deteriorated months or years later, they might give me a goddamn promotion. Even so, there was a risk here. If it became a mainline prototype, the design would get all kinds of scrutiny. Evelyn would check the design herself before she gave the print approval. She wrote DragonDraft3D, so it was very possible that she'd put in features that I didn't know about. Features that might detect subtle acts of sabotage. I'd made all kinds of tweaks to muscular genes to get the flier's performance where it needed to be. Hopefully she wouldn't notice one more.

I sent the print orders to Evelyn at around two o'clock, which happened to be the busiest part of her day. She was usually double-booked for meetings and prepping for her board briefing. Sure, I was gaming the system a little bit, but the less attention she could give my design at this stage, the better.

The God Machine began purring a minute later. *Jackpot*.

The egg came out almost perfectly round, and the shell pattern was my favorite to date: whorls of green and blue with just a hint of orange. I paused a moment before calling the hatchers. I put my palms against the smooth surface. It was warm, almost hot to the touch.

I'd gone outside the guidelines. Maybe more than I should have. But I knew one thing: the results would be spectacular.

CHAPTER TWENTY-NINE
Big Mesa Star

Everyone who tackled the Big Mesa geocache started at the same place: a rock-strewn parking lot that served as the trailhead for half a dozen hiking paths. Unlike most caches whose instructions and routes were fixed, this one had an interactive start. You "rolled the dice" from your phone in the parking lot and took whichever numbered trail you were told to. That way you couldn't easily solve it by trial-and-error alone. This, and a dozen other little tricks like it, explained why only a handful of cachers had beat Big Mesa in the past five years.

Terrain was another factor: the steep ridges and deep canyons were not only hard to cover, but also wreaked havoc on the GPS tracking. There were five interim caches, and you had to find them all to have a shot at the final one. The few people who'd actually logged the cache were quiet about it. They didn't drop hints or anything, which is unusual among geocachers. Most of us are braggers. Then again, we're also pretty competitive, and the more people who solved Big Mesa, the less prestigious it would be.

We let the Tesla take us there on autopilot so that I could review the cache clues, the comments of those who'd tried, and the notes from my own failed attempts. Octavius flitted around the car; he could sense my nervous excitement. On one hand, this was the hardest geocache we'd ever attempted. On the other, if we logged the find, we'd really stick it to Summer and her mangy first officer pig. Talk about a win-win.

"Thirty seconds to destination," the car told me.

I'd already decided that if I saw Ben Fulton's big truck in the lot, I'd abort this mission. He hadn't spoken to me since our run-in at the desert. It seemed wise to follow his lead. He was pretty high up in the company. Part of Robert Greaves' inner circle. He could probably do whatever he wanted. In contrast, I was a junior designer who fully intended to use the company's resources for personal gains. The less he knew about me, the better.

"Arriving at your destination," announced the car.

There was no big black truck in the parking lot. *Good*. I really wanted to tackle Big Mesa. The only other vehicle was a dusty Jeep Wrangler 4x4 with the doors removed. I caught a flash of blonde hair, and there she was. SumNumberOne.

"Aw, come on!" I said.

She wore a white tank top and sage green shorts, bright and clean colors that left me feeling drab by comparison.

I parked and walked around to the hatch to change into my hiking boots. "You just had to ruin this, didn't you?"

"I'm pretty sure we were here first," she said. She did some kind of yoga stretch on the bumper of her Jeep. Her hiking boots bore multiple layers of red dust and wind-blown sand. She was *really* flexible, too.

Somehow my boots ended up tied together. I muttered a curse and started over. "Only because I told you what I was doing."

"It's a free country." She gave the Tesla a little double-take. "Nice car."

"Thanks." I didn't know if she was being sarcastic or not, but it *was* a nice car.

Octavius climbed out onto the raised hatch-lid and stretched out. Riker ran over and started grunting at him. Octavius preened and pretended not to notice.

"What kind of pig is that, anyway?" I asked.

"No idea," she said. "He's a rescue."

"You didn't get a genetic test?" They were all the rage among livestock-as-pet owners, for establishing breed purity in the show circuits.

She shrugged. "What would be the point?"

"To see what he is." That's the first thing I'd have done. But let's be honest, I wouldn't have adopted a stray animal of unknown genetic provenance in the first place.

"He's a pig who needed an owner. That's all that mattered."

There was no sense in arguing with her. I'd learned that years ago, and I didn't need another lesson.

She had her phone out, then. It was like I wasn't even there anymore. "Trail four," she said. "Come on, Riker!"

They took off at a good pace, without so much as a goodbye. I watched her go longer than I should have.

Now they had a lead on us. We could make up time once we got started, though. I sure as hell wasn't going to lose to her again today.

I got my phone out and rolled the dice to set my own geocache attempt in motion. I had to be careful not to screw with it: you could only roll once per day, and then you were committed.

Which is why, of course, it had to be four pips staring back at me on the screen.

"Well, crap," I said.

Competitive geocaching has a sort of honor code. You don't tamper with the waypoints, remove the caches, or make them impossible to find. There's nothing worse than spending half a day on a geocache that some jerk decided to mess up.

Summer had to know we were following her. Well, not following, but on the same trail. We saw her and Riker a few times, so I'm sure they saw us.

The first waypoint marker was a metal plate inside a hollowed-out log. I knew that much from the comments I'd seen online. I got right to the coordinates and found the log, but there wasn't anything metal in view. Which was odd, because Summer had clearly found it and moved on.

I got down on all fours so I could see deeper into the cavity. There it was, right at the very back. I had to reach all the way up to my shoulder to get it. The desert-eaten wood of the log scratched me up pretty good. Maybe that's just how she'd found it, and she was only putting it back where it was.

Maybe.

The second waypoint was a single number chiseled into a chunk of limestone. According to the instructions, it should have been "visible from the trail." We lost ten minutes checking rocks farther and farther from the waypoint, finding no such marker. Ten minutes under the unforgiving sun, which grew hotter by the minute. The desert was quiet. A rustle from the ridge to my left made me turn, thinking it was Summer coming back to gloat. I didn't see her but caught a glimpse of…something. Some kind of animal. For a second, I nearly thought it a dragon. That told me I was spending too much time in the sun. At last, I went back to the waypoint and looked at the nearest rock. The side facing up was dirty and grit-covered. I shoved it over and sure enough, there were the numbers.

By the time we found the third waypoint marker—which someone had "accidentally" dropped right into the middle of a spiny cactus—I knew these weren't coincidences. Someone was screwing with us. It didn't take a genetic engineer to figure out who that would be.

Until then, I'd been keeping a respectful distance. Telling myself it wouldn't be fair to watch her find each waypoint and put it back. Well, forget that. If she was trying to sabotage us, I'd be happy to pass her up and return the favor.

"Come on, buddy, let's hustle!" I told Octavius. I picked it up to a fast jog. Not the safest thing to do on a desert trail, but I didn't care.

We finally caught up to them in the basin, a wide sort of valley with towers of red rocks all around. She and the pig were searching the ground beside the trail. They were so focused, they didn't even notice us coming up.

They hadn't found it yet.

"Having trouble?" I called.

She glanced up, saw us, and mumbled, "Damn it."

My watch beeped to tell me that we'd reached the right coordinates. Summer and Riker were about twenty yards farther down the trail. The terrain of the basin was flatter and more barren than what we'd seen so far. Not a single log or boulder in view. Time to break out the secret weapon.

Octavius was perched on my shoulder, taking a break. I tapped his claw and whispered, "All right, buddy. Find the marker!"

He took off and started an aerial grid search. He swept over the rocks up and down the trail, did a little loop-the-loop over Riker's head just for kicks, and eventually settled on the arm of a big saguaro. It was fifteen feet tall and two-armed, so an old one. Seventy-five years, minimum. Something had drilled a hole in it at shoulder level. I leaned close but couldn't see anything, and I hadn't thought to bring a flashlight. Damn.

Summer was watching me, too. She must have spotted the hole, and her frown said she'd not noticed it before. Good.

Now, I'm not the kind of person to go reaching into strange holes in cacti in the middle of the desert. But there's another unwritten rule when you're in a competition like ours.

Be brave to the point of stupid.

"One way to find out," I said. I took a breath shoved my hand in there blind.

Summer gasped.

Of course, that's when the woodpecker decided to come back.

The Gila woodpecker is small but scrappy, with a red spot on the top of its head, zebra-pattern wings and a brown body. This one must have had a nest in the saguaro, because it started dive-bombing my head and cawing at me.

"Son of a bitch!" I shouted. My arm was at a funny angle in the cactus. I couldn't get loose.

But I could hear Summer laughing just fine. My face grew hot; I'm sure it was bright red. *Goddamn woodpecker.* I tried batting the thing away with my other arm. "Octavius!"

Octavius swooped down from where he'd been circling and tried to catch it, but the woodpecker was too quick. It ducked into one hole in the cactus and popped out another.

Hell, I might as well just go for it. I reached down into the cavity inside the cactus. Way down, until my shoulder was right against the spines. My fingers closed around something hard and rectangular. It felt like a pack of gum, which would be an odd choice for a cache. I eased it out of the hole and retreated about ten yards from the cactus. Octavius returned to my shoulder without being told. The woodpecker gave us a final chewing-out and disappeared.

"Check it out." It was a polished piece of antler, with coordinates carved scrimshaw-style into one side. I plugged them into my watch.

Summer made a disgusted sound and started walking toward us.

I guess I could have been a gentleman and handed it to her. But there *was* the honor code to think about.

So I let Octavius take the carving and plunk it back in the woodpecker hole, before she could say anything.

"Thanks a lot," she said.

I smirked at her. "Say hey to the woodpecker for me."

We finished two points on Big Mesa Star before it got too hot. I really wanted to keep our lead on Summer, but I also didn't want to collapse of heat exhaustion. Big Mesa was going to take me a while. But if it put us above SumNumberOne, all the trouble would totally be worth it.

CHAPTER THIRTY
Disputed Dreams

Even though I had to keep Octavius on the down-low, there were limits to that secrecy. They ended squarely with Connor, who'd never forgive me if I had access to a dragon and didn't show it to him. Pronto.

Granted, there was a danger this might give him the wrong idea: that I was in this for the dragons. That's why *he* would want to do it. Hell, that's probably why most of my fellow designers did it. But I had an ulterior motive and the dragons were just means to an end.

Most of Connor's mechanical engineering classes were online. It took him about twice as long as it should have, but at least he didn't have to get to a physical classroom to earn a passing grade. That was yet another crappy part of dealing with a chronic degenerative condition: so much of the modern world expects a young man in his twenties to be healthy.

Sunday seemed like a good occasion to pop in on Connor and mom. I called ahead to give him the heads-up, and he answered on the second ring.

"N-zymatic."

"Hey, C-section."

He laughed. "I hate that one."

"I know. What are you up to?"

"Killing Nazis. What about you?"

"I'm on my way over. Got something to show you."

"Is it subpar video gaming skills? Because I've seen those."

I snorted. "You wish."

"Die, you Hitler-loving scum."

"I hope you're talking to the game," I said.

"Uh, sure. Let's say that."

"Are you going to tell mom I'm coming over?" I quietly hoped it would win me some kind of a hot cooked lunch. Octavius had cleaned out all my deli meat, so I was down to PB&J at my place.

"She's not here, bro."

"Where is she?"

"Some kind of a wine bus tour. It runs all day."

Well, that explained the full-volume Nazi slaughter. I told myself it was a good thing, because Mom probably needed a break. "It might be for the best. I don't want to freak her out."

The background noise of machine-gun fire halted suddenly. "Why, what are you bringing?" Connor asked.

"It's a surprise." And furthermore, I didn't want to say it over the phone.

"Come on, give me a hint."

When were kids, I used to catch all kinds of creatures outside and bring them in to keep as unauthorized pets. More than once, I'd lost track (or control) of a reptile in the house, only to have it reappear weeks later. Usually when Mom was just waking up. It occurred to me that, by bringing Octavius over, I might be daring history to repeat itself. "Let's just say it's a riff on one of my classic misbehaviors."

He snickered. "Like that narrows it down."

I got there about ten minutes later and had to ring the doorbell two times before the door's deadbolt snicked open. Connor was nowhere to be seen within; he must have unlocked it with his phone. Over my protests, Mom had let him have access to the home controls after I moved out.

I noticed the tracks right away, a veritable spiderweb of narrow wheelmarks in the carpet that ran parallel to one another. It served as a kind of advance warning, so that I could steel myself not to look surprised when I found him sitting in his wheelchair in his room. It was the same one, of course, but now it seemed almost like an extension of him. He'd even wrapped the right-side handle with camouflage duct tape, an old gamer's trick we developed as kids to steady the wrists of our desk chairs. He was making good use of it, too, judging by the score in the top right of his massive projection screen.

"I thought this game didn't come out until next month."

"It doesn't. I got into the beta program."

"How?"

"By being awesome."

"Seriously."

"A buddy from the engineering program hooked me up," he said.

I watched as he equipped some kind of machine gun and used it to mow down a line of charging Nazis. "It looks awesome."

"Yeah, it is. I'd let you play, but you'd just be a liability."

"Right. You have all the cool stuff, and I don't." I was going to enjoy this. I cleared my throat. "Octavius?"

My little dragon winged in through the doorway, circled once, and landed on the handle to his chair. Connor shouted and almost fell out of it. "Jesus! What is that?"

"That, little bro, is my dragon."

"No fricking way!"

"He goes by Octavius."

On hearing his name, Octavius leaped into the air again, flapping his little wings like a crazed bat. Connor followed his every move, as if hypnotized.

"All right, you little show-off." I grinned and patted my shoulder.

Octavius folded his wings and crash-landed onto the approximate area I'd indicated. His claws dug into my skin as he fought to keep his balance. I gritted my teeth against the pain, because I didn't want to ruin this moment.

"Octavius, this is my brother Connor."

Connor gaped and struggled to find words. "W-where did you get him?"

"Where do you think?"

"I thought people couldn't buy them yet." He jabbed an accusing finger at me. "You said we couldn't get them."

"Well, some of us get access to video games, and some of us get access to dragons."

"He looks too small to be a Rover."

That caught me off-guard. "You know about the Rover?"

"Of course. Did you not think I'd keep tabs on the coolest company in Phoenix?"

"He's not one of our production models. He's kind of an accident, actually." I told him the story of the too-small dragon egg, how Evelyn canceled the design, and the haphazard dragon hatching I conducted in my condo.

"Dude, you should have called me."

"I was terrified to say anything to anyone. If they found out at work, I'd be in deep shit."

"Why? He seems like the best accident ever."

"They're kind of strict about stuff that comes out of the hatchery."

"Greaves is worried about the public image, huh?"

Jeez, he *was* keeping tabs. "Don't even get me started. He also has this feature points system that keeps getting in the way of my designs. That's why I came up with Octavius's design in the first place. To send a message."

"That tiny dragons are awesome? Message received."

He was so wowed, I almost wanted to hand Octavius over right then. But I'd done the imprinting and keeping him close to me was the only way I could be certain the company would never find out.

Whether or not I was getting attached to the little guy was completely beside the point.

"That reminds me, you can't tell anyone about this. My record's squeaky clean at the company and I need it to stay that way, for phase two."

"What's phase two?"

"That's where I introduce your mutation and prove that it causes disease."

"I don't know what that's going to accomplish. Other than putting a dragon in a wheelchair."

"It's a proof of principle. If it gets you a formal diagnosis, then maybe you qualify for a drug trial. Or even gene therapy." And I could even lay the groundwork for that, with Build-A-Dragon's resources.

"It's never going to work," he said.

"Let me worry about the science. At this point, you're only qualified to play video games."

"This isn't about science." Connor pointed at Octavius. "Look at what you've made. It's something tangible. Something *real*. How are you not just astonished by it?"

"I'll admit that the dragon thing is cool, but I have bigger plans for that place."

"As usual, you're focused on the wrong thing. I'm fine, dude."

I looked at his wheelchair and remembered how slow he'd been to climb back into it when Octavius scared him. He wasn't fine. He was stubborn, and shortsighted, and unwilling to take my help. "Yeah, you're something. I should go."

"Come on, don't be like that."

"It's fine." I turned away from him. "I want to slip out before Mom gets home."

He tried a different tactic. "She'll be just as ticked if you don't wait for her."

But she'd be just as ticked if she came home to find I'd brought a reptile into her house. *Again.*

"We were never here."

His jaw tightened. "See you."

I walked out, with Octavius on my shoulder. He looked back at Connor and made a soft chirp, as if confused. *That makes two of us.* The renewed sound of machine-gun fire followed us down the hallway and out the front door.

CHAPTER THIRTY-ONE
The Short Happy Life

Between Summer's interference in our geocaching and Connor's sudden lack of enthusiasm, weekends were really starting to suck. Hell, maybe I should have gone on Mom's wine tour. It was almost a relief to get back to work. Besides, Evelyn had told me that one of my customs would be hatched in-house, so I kind of wanted to watch.

When a customer ordered one of Build-A-Dragon's mainline production models, like the classic Rover, they got an egg in the mail with specific instructions on how to make it hatch. It was just easier to ship an egg than a live dragon and allowing the customers to hatch the dragon themselves was vital for the imprinting. For custom dragons, however, the clever folks in marketing realized that hatching them in Build-A-Dragon's facility was yet another thing for which we could charge a premium. The owners of the pink-and-white birthday dragon had opted for this.

When the appointment reminder flashed up on my screen, I grabbed my lunch and hurried to the viewing gallery on the employee side.

They had the garish egg nestled in a soft nest in one of the large incubation rooms along the south wall. A nice-looking Latino family sat on one of the benches in the viewing gallery with the nervous excitement of first-time dragon owners. It was hard to miss the little girl. She looked about eight or ten, and literally bounced with excitement. Her dress was a bright shade of pink that, unless I missed my guess, would be a perfect match for the birthday dragon I'd created.

The parents were really spoiling her. Their smiles said they knew it, too. Hell, after watching the girl press her face against the glass for the third time, I kind of wanted to see her reaction myself. There was a man sitting in the back row, off by himself, in a dark suit and sunglasses. I didn't recognize him and wondered if maybe he was the family's security guard.

A scaled pink-and-white nose poked out of the eggshell. The family at the observation window clapped and cheered. Watching them hug one another with rapt excitement on their faces made me forgive myself for creating such a ridiculous dragon with my arts.

The pink dragon tumbled out of the shell, blinked uncertainly at the sunlight streaming in, and stood on wobbly legs. I had to admit that it was kind of cute. The delighted girl squealed loud enough that I heard her through two Plexiglas walls. The noise didn't put the dragon off, though; my tweaks of the neurotransmitter system had seen to that. It only knew how to love and be loved. This showed in the way it capered for them along the glass, turning its body back and forth to be admired.

We were all so focused on the birthday dragon that we didn't notice the second hatching in the incubator room. I hadn't even realized there was another egg in there. If I'd seen it, if I'd recognized the mottled grey shell, you can bet I'd have hit the panic button.

Because that was the attack dragon, and it had a different sort of programming entirely.

The hatchers didn't realize anything was wrong until a blur of black scales shot across the room. Until the attack dragon clamped its jaws around a certain pink-and-white neck. Until it was far, far too late.

The birthday dragon made a pitiful sound, its tiny mind incapable of processing the idea that something could harm it. I swear that the attack dragon paused just to be sure it had our attention. Then it wrenched its head in a sharp movement. The birthday dragon's neck snapped with a sickening crunch. It went limp and tumbled to the floor.

A quick-thinking hatchery staffer dropped the curtain on the observation window, but the damage was done. The little girl was an inconsolable pink ball of screams and tears. Her mother was crying, too, and her father's face was furious. They'd probably be suing us. But the man in the dark suit and sunglasses showed no reaction. It was like he expected it to go down this way. Right then, I realized who he was: the buyer for the attack dragon, who had come to take delivery.

I sat there with my PB&J in my hand for a long time, too stunned to move. I'd never really seen one of our attack dragons in action before. The thing was just so *fast*. Merciless, too. Part of me felt terrible for what had happened to the birthday dragon. The other part felt a harder, colder truth. *I design one hell of a dragon.*

CHAPTER THIRTY-TWO
LATEST TRIAL FAILS

BOSTON, MA—Hopes for a cure to canine facial tumor disease (CFTD) were dashed last week by the announcement that a promising immunotherapeutic agent failed in animal trials.

Canizumab, developed by the animal health division of Bingham Pharmaceuticals, had shown the most potential of any therapy tried so far.

CFTD's sudden appearance and unusual properties have baffled scientists. While population-scale epidemics have been documented in other species—including a similar transmissible tumor disease in the Tasmanian Devil population of New Zealand—natural or acquired resistance typically allows a subset of the population to survive. No such resistance has yet emerged among canines.

One reason CFTD has proven so difficult to treat is that the tumor cells hide themselves from the immune system of an infected dog. Normal healthy cells produce a protein, called MHC, that helps the body distinguish its own cells from invasive pathogens or unhealthy cells, such as tumors. Early investigations of the tumors of infected dogs, however, revealed that the cancer cells do not produce MHC.

"MHC proteins help the immune system distinguish between a dog's own healthy cells and invading or infected ones," said Dr. Ellen Marley, a cancer immunologist at Johns Hopkins University who was not involved with the trial. "By not producing them, CFTD renders itself invisible to one of the body's best avenues of defense."

Early on in the epidemic, scientists sequenced the genome of

CFTD tumor cells and found that they harbored thousands of DNA mutations—far more than most human tumors. Strikingly, many of the mutations were shared across all tumors. They disrupted genes that normally helped dogs fight infections, recognize unhealthy cells, and remove them. The pattern of shared mutations is unusual and led scientists to believe that the tumors might somehow be transmissible from one dog to another. Subsequent investigations uncovered evidence that this was, at least in some part, true. Most cases of CFTD emerge after contact with an infected dog. Because the tumors are initially small, many owners did not realize their dogs were infected until they had spread it to other animals. Worse, there appears to be a latent means of environmental infection for some dogs. A sidewalk or dog park visited by a single infected animal can give rise to new cases days or weeks later.

Many researchers believe that immunosuppression by the tumor cells is key to their survival (and the host animal's demise). Canizumab, by targeting this mechanism, was expected to help a dog's immune system clear the tumor cells before they took hold. The drug passed initial safety trials late last year.

"Canizumab targets two therapeutic mechanisms simultaneously," said Dr. Jonathan Fisker, senior scientist at Bingham Pharmaceuticals, after the conclusion of the initial safety trials. "First, it inhibits the immune cell checkpoint that tumors leverage to evade T cells. Second, it boosts the immunogenicity of tumor cells to make them better targets for immune elimination."

A phase II trial began almost immediately to prove efficacy. This is where it seems that the drug's performance saw some challenges. Though it was well-tolerated by infected and healthy dogs alike, the drug failed to stop the relentless onslaught of CFTD. There was no significant difference in survival or tumor burden between dogs that got Canizumab and ones that received the placebo. The announcement of the trial's failure sent biotechnology stocks tumbling on Thursday.

The outcome is not only disappointing for investors, but also for the millions of dog lovers around the world who hoped Canizumab would bring our furry companions back. Worse, the high-profile failure makes it even less likely that other biotechnology firms will invest in new CFTD research in the near future.

CHAPTER THIRTY-THREE
Strange Allies

For the rest of the week, I waited for the fallout from the birthday dragon incident. I jumped every time someone passed my office, thinking it was Greaves coming to yell at me. Or worse, Fulton arriving to escort me out of the building. I figured it was only a matter of time until one of the customers spoke to a reporter, and the online news channels started bashing us again. Then the ranks of the protestors outside our building would swell again, and I'd have to leave even earlier to get to work on time.

The guilt ate at me. I should have told the hatchers about the attack dragon so that they kept it in solitary. No one *knew* that—once the eggs left the God Machine, they fell under the hatchery staff's purview—but I could easily take the blame for this. Hell, if the fallout was really bad, they might even fire me. I confessed these fears to Evelyn, and she told me not to worry about it. It was a hatchery issue, not our department. I wasn't sure I believed that.

The week dragged on forever. I only got through it by looking forward to Saturday, when I thought we had a good shot at finishing Big Mesa Star. I'd rested, I'd planned, I'd checked the rankings of geocachers far too often. I'd also scoured the boards for hints of how to find the waypoints on trail number four. Only a handful of people had completed the Big Mesa star, but the most recent had only been a month or two ago. That told me it was beatable.

I hadn't slept well all week. Every time I closed my eyes, I saw the attack model snapping the pink dragon's neck. Heard the nauseating crunch of bone and cartilage. It was like a song I couldn't get out of my head. Saturday morning was no exception, so I just got up, roused Octavius, and drove out into the desert.

Fog still shrouded the rocks of the parking lot at Big Mesa Star; that's how early we were. Octavius still dozed in the passenger seat while I laced up my boots. We had the lot to ourselves; even the highway traffic was quiet.

Then I heard the steady rumble of a big truck coming down the road. Luckily, I hadn't woken Octavius yet. Dragons were becoming more common in Arizona, so it was reasonably safe for us to take these little excursions into the desert. I wasn't brave enough to stroll around with him in downtown Scottsdale or anything, but out in the desert people knew better than to ask too many questions. Still, this close to the road, it would be just my luck to encounter a park ranger or something. I edged closer to the Tesla as the truck rolled into the lot with fog lights ablaze, crunching gravel beneath its oversized tires. When the lights swept over me, I finally got a look at the profile. *It's not a truck. It's a Jeep.*

"You've got to be kidding me," I muttered.

I tried to ignore it and lace up my boots as quickly as possible. Which would have worked, except the Jeep parked haphazardly right next to me.

"Still trying to beat me?" Summer called.

"Don't flatter yourself. I'm trying to beat Big Mesa Star."

Riker popped up in the back seat and grunted at us. "Hush!" she told him.

Octavius stirred once but went back to snoring in my passenger seat. *Some watch dragon.*

"So. How many times have you tried Big Mesa Star?" she asked.

Once last month, and another time about a year ago. But I didn't want to admit it, so I shrugged.

"This is our third try," Summer said.

"Wow. Really?"

"I keep losing signal in the basin." She had the doors off her Jeep, so I had a good view as she put on her boots.

God, she's got long legs.

I figured I might as well pony up some honesty. "It's our third try, too."

"Ha! I knew it."

"Yeah, well, we're serious this time." After the week I'd just had, I really needed to win something. "Didn't get as far as I thought I would last weekend. Some of the markers were *a little hard to find*." I made the last bit slow and accusing.

She looked at me flat-eyed, not giving anything away. "Maybe if you're nice, they won't be."

It wasn't that I'd been *trying* to be mean to her. It had just come naturally. It reminded me, strangely, of the attack dragon that had killed the birthday dragon. Which I still felt terrible about but had come down to pure instinct. Just like my instinct of sniping at Summer back when she'd started becoming a problem for me and Jane. But that was the past. We'd sparred so often, Summer and I, that Jane got a little jealous. Which was ridiculous, if you actually listened to the barbs we exchanged, but whatever. All that stuff was well in the past and I intended to keep it there. "I can try that."

"This geocache is hard enough as it is."

"That's for damn sure." I chuckled. "Maybe we should help each other." The words came out before I really gave them thought. Then again, if we sabotaged one another like we did last time, neither of us would get the cache. Watching her might be informative. *It might even help me figure out how to beat her.*

She gave me a side-eyed look, as if she'd heard that thought. "What are you proposing?"

"An alliance."

"Until the cache is found?" She mulled this for a few seconds. "Deal."

"How far did you get last time?"

"Two points. But I marked the coordinates of the next one, so I can go straight to it."

"So did I."

She held her wrist beside mine for a double-check. That's when I realized we had the exact same watch.

"Hey, we match," I said.

"Yours looks like it was in a plane crash."

I noted that her watch didn't have a scratch on it, though the wristband showed some age. "Psh. It just means we're more willing to get dirty." I walked back to the car and roused Octavius from the Tesla. "We've got some company."

He craned his neck past me to get a look at them. When he recognized them, he raised his wings and started hissing.

"None of that, now," I said. "They're friends today. Got it? Friends."

He cut off the hissing, but never took his eyes off Riker.

Summer clipped the pig onto a retractable leash. "You ready?"

"After you, Number One."

She snorted. Riker took the lead down trail #4, pulling at his leash like a rotund sled dog. It started off at a gentle incline, heading right down into the basin. I told Octavius to scout ahead; it never hurt to have eyes up above. Summer and I kept comparing the distance to target on our watches. If those numbers started to jump around, it meant we were losing GPS signal, and couldn't trust any directions. We'd have to backtrack and start again.

Riker kept his snout to the ground, sniffing everything. Now that I thought about it, a pig's peerless olfactory abilities could be useful on a geocache. He seemed fairly well trained, too. More than Octavius, at least, which wasn't saying much.

"I've never seen a dragon like yours," Summer said.

"He's one of a kind," I told her.

"A customized one?" Her eyebrows went up a little. "You must be doing well."

"Well, I sort of get the employee discount," I said, by way of avoidance.

"I thought you were all about playing God with *human* DNA. Back when, you know . . ."

"Yeah," I said. "I'm still working on that." *But maybe not hard enough,* a little voice inside me said. Causing dragon-on-dragon violence didn't offer much in the way of accomplishment, though. That poor little birthday dragon. It shouldn't bother me as much as it did.

"With dragons?"

"It's complicated."

We walked in silence for a moment.

"Have you heard from her?" she asked, meaning Jane.

"Not for a long time." I knew better than to stay in touch. I didn't want to hear about whatever guy she was dating, or what color she'd dyed her hair. Just thinking about it tore at me. "You?"

"The same."

We fell into silence. I sure as hell didn't want to say more about her, and from Summer's tone, it sounded like she felt the same. Well, not exactly the same. I doubt her heart hurt the way mine still did when I thought of her. At least they weren't in touch anymore. That would have made it even more awkward than it already was.

Octavius came to the rescue. He glided back a minute later, trilling a little victory call.

"I don't speak dragon, but that sounds promising," Summer said.

"Yep, I think he found it," I said.

We crested a ridge, and Octavius led us right to a metal trail marker sign, the kind that told you how far it was back to the parking lot.

"Oh. It's just a mile marker," Summer said.

Our watches beeped, though, which meant we were in the right location. And Octavius kept dipping his head down at the sign. I searched the ground around it but saw nothing. "I don't see anything."

Octavius gave a sharp trill.

I crouched to inspect the sign itself but saw nothing on the front. I craned my neck to look at the back of it and saw the little metal tube. It looked like stainless steel, and shinier than the sign's cheap metal.

"No way," I breathed. Hidden in plain sight. Geocache designers loved to get cute like that. I gave it a little tug, and the tube came free from the back of the sign. Two circular magnets had held it in place.

"Bingo," I held it up for Summer to see.

"Are you serious?"

I found the tube's cap and flipped it open. A slender, flat piece of metal slid out, with coordinates stamped plainly on the front.

"Damn, so he found it after all." She gave Octavius a considering look. "Smart little dragon, isn't he?"

I scratched him behind his ears. "That he is," *The smartest one in the world.*

CHAPTER THIRTY-FOUR
Instincts

We hiked almost a mile to reach the next marker. The day was heating up by then, and the waves off the desert rocks promised a scorcher.

"So, you're working for the enemy," Summer said.

"Since when is Build-A-Dragon the enemy?"

"They're messing with nature."

"Please don't tell me you're still into that organic, tree-hugging stuff."

She glanced back long enough to narrow her eyes at me. "If by 'organic' you mean plants not genetically modified or doused with pesticides, then yes."

"I don't think our dragons are harmful to nature. They can't even survive in the wild."

"Then why do you make them?" she asked.

I shrugged. "People want them," I said. I should do more to defend my employer, but my heart wasn't in it.

"People wanting to buy something doesn't make it right," she said.

Her watch beeped before I could reply.

"Is that the waypoint?" I asked.

"Yeah."

My watch beeped a second later. That wasn't good, because I stood slightly in front of her. The terrain was already interfering with the GPS.

185

I grunted. "I'm worried we're already off. But it should be close."

We began an informal grid search, looking for anything out of the ordinary. Usually it was something man-made: a coffee can, a birdhouse, a little statuette, something like that. I'm not the giving up type, but after fifteen minutes I was losing hope fast. Summer's shoulders had slumped a little. She started checking her watch again.

Then Octavius let out a trill of victory. He flitted back to circle my head, then flew over to a place in the canyon wall.

"We've got something!" I called. Summer and Riker hurried over.

The waypoint was a metal spike, the kind they used in old railroad tracks. Totally driven into the rock wall, with a face about an inch across. It took a tiny dragon to spot something like this. I leaned close to it, saw the faint outline of typescript, and knew we had it.

"This is it," I called over my shoulder. "Ready for the coordinates?"

"Hit me," Summer said.

The numbers were etched in tiny, block-like print. Summer punched them into her watch while I read them off. We did a double-check, just to be sure.

"Three quarters of a mile," Summer said.

"We'd better get moving," I said. I rubbed Octavius behind his ears. "Good eye, little buddy!"

He took off and zoomed around us as we hiked up. Maybe I praised him too much, but honestly, we probably wouldn't have found it without him. And now he was really lording it over Riker. Gliding back and forth, humming a little song to himself that sounded uncannily like "We are the Champions" by Queen. I'd have said something, but after Summer's comments about Build-A-Dragon, I wanted him to rub it in.

I'm sure that's why Riker was so eager to sniff out the next marker. I let Octavius fly ahead, but the pig wasn't about to let the dragon be the hero again. He bounded ahead, too, ignoring Summer's calls for him to slow down. We picked up our pace, but the animals were both faster across the rocky terrain. The cliffs rose on each side of us, too, not quite a box canyon but close. Riker disappeared through a switchback ahead. Then we heard him give a sharp bark. A surprised, fearful sound.

"Shit!" Summer said. She ran into the switchback. I hustled in right behind her, not knowing what to expect.

She stopped so fast that I almost crashed into her. Her body had gone stock-still. Riker's snort became a low whine. He was about six feet in front of her, in a little cut-out in the canyon wall. I didn't know what the problem was until I heard it. The dry, quivering buzz that terrified anyone who spent time in the desert.

Rattlesnake.

"Easy, easy now," I whispered. I put my hands on Summer's shoulders and pulled her back. Slowly. We didn't stop until there were ten feet between us and the rattler. Unfortunately, Riker cowered on the far side of it, penned up against the canyon wall. He had nowhere to go. The rattler lay coiled up between him and the trail.

Summer made a soft little sound, almost like a sob. "We have to help him!"

I scanned the ground, desperate to find a stick or something. No dice. I could try smashing it with a rock. That was risky, though. It would lash out at something. Probably the pig. The last thing I wanted to do was make it look like my fault. If that thing bit him . . . well, I doubted we could get him to a vet in time.

"Damn!" I hated feeling helpless. Especially in front of her.

Riker feinted left and then right, looking for a way out. The rattler's head moved with him. It uncoiled slowly, closing in for the attack. Its black tongue flicked in and out. I wondered if I should turn Summer away, so she wouldn't see it happen. But I couldn't move. It was like watching a car wreck in slow motion.

The rattler rose up and reared back.

"No!" Summer cried.

I sucked in a sharp breath and braced myself. Then I felt a brush of air on my cheek. A scaly missile shot past me in a blur.

Octavius.

He slammed into the rattler like a meteor. The momentum carried both dragon and snake to the ground against the hot red stone. It happened so fast, I couldn't move. Octavius came up with the snake's neck in his jaws. He set his feet and wrenched it in a figure eight. *Crack.* The snake went limp, and the rattling faded. Summer and I stood there in stunned silence. Octavius rammed the rattler's head against the rock wall a couple of times for good measure, then spat it out. I scrabbled forward, grabbed its tail, and slung it away.

Riker bounded to Summer. She crouched to hug him. I wanted to do the same thing. It's not like I loved the mangy animal, but she clearly did. It was a tender thing to watch. It softened me on her.

I held out my arm, and Octavius flew to it. "Where did that come from?" I asked.

He trilled softly at me, as if not certain himself. God, but I was proud of the little guy.

Summer came over, still cradling a trembling Riker. For the first time, she looked Octavius right in the eyes. "Thank you."

Octavius basked in her gaze, practically preening.

"Is he all right?" I asked, meaning Riker. He'd tucked his snout under her arm.

"Traumatized, but he'll survive."

"Let's get the hell out of here."

"Yeah."

We didn't even discuss the idea of continuing. We agreed to meet the following Saturday to try and finish. I let her mark the spot in her watch, but sort of *forgot* to save it in my own. Unless she was a horrible person—a prospect that seemed less and less likely—she'd realize I couldn't continue without her. It meant we'd get together again, maybe on purpose this time.

Octavius had his instincts. I had mine.

CHAPTER THIRTY-FIVE
Icarus

I waited and waited for some fallout with the attack dragon incident, but the hammer never came down. Which I found very strange. It's almost like the executives wanted to pretend the incident had never happened. The PR department must have gone into overdrive, to put out that fire before it started.

Between that and the imminent test run of my flier model, I couldn't focus on anything else. Custom orders in my queue started piling up. Korrapati and Wong, to their credit, helped pick up the slack. When I got four or five designs deep, they'd sneak up and grab one, and get the order done without so much as a word.

Every time I opened up DragonDraft3D, I ended up looking at my Condor prototype. I pored over it, looking for flaws other than the ones I'd put in. There were none. The dragon was perfect, and if I wowed them as much as I expected, it would win an exception from the stupidly arbitrary points system. More importantly, it should give me what I needed to prove that Connor's mutation was pathogenic. The physical manifestation wouldn't appear for some time, but under a microscope, the muscle fibers would look abnormal. As for what would happen if and when we sold fliers that slowly degenerated, well . . . that was a problem for future Noah.

On the day of the demonstration, we met in the coliseum-style outdoor gallery. Evelyn had sent a company-wide invite and wanted to this to be a flagship event for her department. No pressure. Most designers were present, of course, but a lot of the executives showed up, too. Sales and Customer Service sent a few people. We even had a couple of dragon-tamers from Herpetology on hand. They stood over to the side, away from everyone else. Their appearance set them apart, too: dungarees and wide-brimmed hats didn't mix with the tailored suits in the stands.

All of those were welcome surprises. The armed guards were another matter entirely. They cradled automatic rifles and stood off to one side, speaking quietly with Ben Fulton. I tried not to think too much about their purpose here.

It might seem insane to go outside in Arizona in the middle of the afternoon, at least to outsiders. But the heat was good for the hatchlings. Besides, if you lived in the Southwest, you developed a certain tolerance to it. At least, that's what Arizonians told ourselves.

The hatchery staffers wheeled the eggs out on sturdy carts. They seemed larger than I remembered. God, I hoped none of the bigwigs would notice. If they knew how far I'd pushed past the restrictions, they might scrap this demonstration before it even got started. The hatchers team-lifted their eggs into a massive stick-and-straw nest. The materials were hardly necessary, but the people at Build-A-Dragon liked a good show.

Even as I watched them, one of the eggs quivered. The dragon inside was wakening, growing restless. I felt the surge of nervous anticipation I always got before a prototype hatching. "I hope this goes well," I whispered.

"Don't worry, Noah," Korrapati said.

"Yes, you design good dragons," Wong added.

"Thanks, guys," I said. It was good of them to come out and support me. O'Connell and the Frogman hadn't bothered. Then again, if things went well, my prototype would be replacing their Pterodactyl, so maybe it was for the best. I had a lot riding on this demonstration, though. If it went well, I'd probably get free rein with design resources, and undoubtedly the invitation to develop another prototype. The promise of freedom beckoned.

Evelyn sat with the execs, looking so like them in her tailored suit that I almost didn't notice her. She straightened the hemline of her skirt every few seconds. My eyes slid past her to the man in the middle, the only one not in a suit. Robert Greaves lounged in the direct sun, totally at ease. Dressed all in black, too. Making an open statement that the heat didn't bother him.

Everyone in the gallery was watching him, though they tried not to show it. I did, too, out of a sort of morbid fascination. Evelyn acted as the go-between for between him and the designers. Not that we couldn't approach him on our own, but I still hadn't worked up the nerve. Today might be the first time we interacted directly. I hoped it would go well. There was, unfortunately, no sign of Simon Redwood. I felt a twinge of disappointment at that, even though it wasn't surprising. Rumor around the coffee machine was that no one had seen the guy in over a year.

The first egg rocked back and forth, tearing my thoughts away from Redwood. A hairline split cracked it almost from top to bottom. Smaller fractures spiderwebbed across. Then the egg shattered into a hundred sky-blue fragments, and I laid eyes on my newest creation.

It extended dark-green wings, first. Then its whole body uncoiled. The head came up, and the dragon met my gaze with narrowed eyes. Of everyone there, it looked at *me*. Two more of the eggs began trembling.

Two hatchery staffers approached with the meat tray. I'd wanted to do this part myself—to make sure that everyone knew whose dragon design it was—but Evelyn overruled me. She said that any deviation from hatching protocol carried a risk. We wanted everything to be optimized for success.

The dragon watched the meat-bringers with an unreadable expression. It waited until they'd retreated before standing up. No shakiness to the legs. There shouldn't have been, with the muscle tone I'd given it, but I was relieved just the same.

The dragon folded its wings along its body and climbed out of the nest. It moved with effortless grace, like a snake weaving through the grass. I drew in a sharp breath and hazarded a glance at Greaves. He'd put his phone away. He was watching. Meanwhile, the dragon tore through two pounds of raw meat like a starved hyena. Ten, maybe twelve seconds until the tray was empty.

Now all the executives were riveted. A couple of them even cast a nervous look towards the security guards. These were all ex-military types, and they held their M-16s with the practiced air of readiness.

We shouldn't need them with a flying model, but the company took no chances.

A dragon won't fly unless it wants to. Build-A-Dragon had learned that the hard way. The old adage about kicking a bird out of the nest just didn't apply. To get a dragon off the ground, you had to put something that it wanted up in the air. Mourning doves usually did the trick. Their pear-shaped bodies and explosive, panicked flights were like a siren's call to apex predators.

Normally, the hatchery staff handled this part, but Evelyn had gotten permission for me to do it instead. I stood at the edge of the field holding her tablet and trying to look confident. This was my chance to prove myself, not just to the rest of the team but to the company leadership.

The other dragons were starting to crack out of their eggs, but the first one had dried its wings and eaten. He was ready. I sent a release signal to one of the cages. A red strobe light flashed atop one of the steel boxes at the edge of the field. The dragon's head swiveled toward it. Then two doves shot up and out, shedding white feathers.

"Go get 'em," I whispered.

But the dragon just watched the doves fly past.

Oh, God. I'd been so focused on designing a dragon that *could* fly, I hadn't considered whether or not it would even want to. I thought I could leave that to instinct, but biology was never certain. If they didn't fly, this whole demo would crash and burn. And here I was, standing in front of everyone like a dumbass. I cursed my own stupidity.

Then the dragon's scaled legs bent and it leaped into the sky.

Its gossamer wings flapped faster than I'd have thought possible. Faster than even the simulator had predicted. It was twenty feet off the ground and still climbing. Forty feet. Far higher than the doves, which had leveled off and made a beeline for the desert horizon. The dragon glided over them, folded its wings, and dove like a falcon. He snapped his jaws around the first bird and grabbed the second with a clawed foot.

"Sweet," I breathed. The crowd in the stands murmured approval.

Three or four dragons had broken out of the shell. Hatchery staffers moved around to feed them. But I had the executives' attention, so I sent another release signal.

Two more doves made a mad dash for the sky. The dragon banked smoothly and went for them, caught them lower this time. Didn't bother eating them, either, but dropped them down for his siblings in the nest.

I'd set up something special for the third cage. A real challenge. One of the most despised birds known to woodlands, a bundle of noise and distraction that irritated hunters and outdoorsmen to no end. A bird with which I still had some unfinished business.

The red-headed woodpecker.

I hit the release. The woodpecker yelped as it flew out; the raucous cry echoed across the yard like a challenge. The dragon reacted instantly, twisting over and back like a swimmer at the wall.

The woodpecker flew better than the doves, though. More cleverly, too. It flitted to the edge of its cage. Then to the side of a stone column. Rather than making a blind break for freedom, it zigzagged across the yard, making that call again. The sound set my teeth on edge.

The dragon twisted and turned in pursuit, not quite able to catch up without crashing into the columns.

Come on, catch him! I'd given the dragon every advantage, but the woodpecker continued to elude it. Continued making its cry, too, which rapidly began to feel like the taunts of a bully.

At last, the dragon gave up and broke off its pursuit. Worse, it shot over the edge of the coliseum roof and out of view.

"Son of a bitch!" I said under my breath. Well, *mostly* under my breath.

"Where did it go?" Korrapati asked.

"Over the rim," Wong told her.

The woodpecker had been a huge gamble, and I'd blown it. We'd not only lost the dragon but managed to make the entire design team look like morons.

The woodpecker poked its head out from behind a stone, then took off in the opposite direction. It landed on the edge of the coliseum roof. Paused there, just to cackle at us. The urge to kill that thing burned inside of me. If I'd had so much as a slingshot, I'd have used it. The armed guards fingered the handles of their automatic rifles. Part of me wished they'd open fire.

The woodpecker cackled again, basking on the cusp of freedom. It spread its wings, turned away.

And flew right into the dragon's jaws.

Crunch.

I stood in shocked silence. Then I pumped my fist in the air. "Oh *yeah!*"

The executives cheered. So did the guards and the dragon handlers.

I still couldn't believe my flier had pulled it off. He must have swooped around the wall. Probably flew thirty, forty miles an hour to reach the other side so quickly.

Now, seeing no more airborne targets, it banked its dark wings and glided back to the nest. Settled in among its siblings and preened, knowing we were all watching. The stands thundered with applause. Evelyn and the other executives all wore smiles and shook hands in decorous celebration.

I kept my eyes on Greaves. Only his opinion truly mattered here. He was quiet and unreadable behind his sunglasses. He leaned over to say something to Evelyn. She beckoned to me.

"Oh boy," I whispered.

"Be confident," Korrapati said. "That dragon speaks for itself."

Wong nudged me and grinned. "Remember us when you are *lao-bahn.*"

I tried to swallow, but my mouth was dry as a desert. "Yeah."

I hurried over, conscious of everyone's eyes on me. The sudden attention made me nervous as a kindergartener.

"Quite a dragon," Greaves said.

"Thank you." I felt out of breath, though I wasn't winded. I guess it was the thrill of talking to him. "Worked out even better than the simulator predicted."

"How much will it grow?" he asked.

"About forty percent larger."

He nodded. I still couldn't read his face. I waited him out and tried to remember to keep breathing.

"Did you see the agility?" Evelyn asked. "And the speed? I think it could be our best model yet."

Greaves nodded again, as if half-listening to her. "It ambushed the woodpecker. Did you plan that?"

"Wish I had, but no," I said. "That was pure instinct."

"More like *strategy*. And that means intelligence." He took off his sunglasses; his eyes were bright amber, like a wolf's. "You went outside the guidelines."

A twinge of cold hit my stomach. "Just a little," I admitted.

"How far?"

"Twenty points. It was the only way to meet the specs," I said.

He looked at Evelyn. "You signed off?"

"Yes," she said, with a touch of hesitation.

He nodded again and put the sunglasses back on. Then he stood. I still couldn't read his reaction, until he turned to his security chief and spoke two words.

"Quarantine them."

I didn't understand what he meant. I mean, I got the words right, but couldn't wrap my head fully around their meaning. Fulton signaled two of the dragon wranglers.

"Robert—" Evelyn began.

"You know the policy," Greaves said.

The wranglers marched toward the nest. The red-haired woman unpacked something from her burlap duffle bag. A weighted cast net. The first Condor, the one that had flown, watched them approach. Sensed their intent, maybe, because it hissed and took off.

Greaves looked at the guys with the M-15s. "Shoot it down."

"Wait. What?" I couldn't believe it.

They raised their guns.

"Is this a goddamn *joke*?" That was my dragon up there. It was pretty amazing. Everyone in the coliseum had to admit as much. I took two steps toward the security dudes. Surely they'd listen to reason.

Fulton materialized in front of me. I tried to squirm past him, but he laid a tree-trunk arm on my shoulder and held me fast. "Don't get in the way, son."

"Come on, man!" I struggled with no result. Then I looked him right in the eyes, desperate. "You *know* it's wrong."

"Look around, Parker," he said quietly. "Neither of us can stop this."

I craned my neck to look past him, to where the guards were stalking steadily.

"No." Fulton put both hands on my shoulders. "Eyes on me."

The *crack-crack* of gunfire echoed in the silent coliseum.

The dragon groaned. A long, low sound. It tore at something inside of me. I had to look. The Condor's perfect glide faltered. I watched as it tumbled downward out of view beyond the roof of the coliseum. Darkness pressed in around my vision. My greatest creation, gunned down like it was nothing. I just couldn't believe it. Couldn't *fathom* it. My legs gave out on me, but Fulton held me up. I hated him for it.

Meanwhile, the wranglers had the five still-wet hatchlings crammed together in their net. The bearded wrangler cinched it tight, and then the two of them dragged it away.

CHAPTER THIRTY-SIX
Corporate Retaliation

I had to go home after that. I didn't even go up to get my stuff. My feet carried me to the parking garage on their own. I let the Tesla take me home and just sat there, in a daze. Didn't even turn on the radio. Too much sound would hurt me. I needed the soft hum of the Tesla and nothing else.

Those dragons had been special. Not just because I'd made them, or because of what they meant for Connor. Everyone on the demonstration field had seen the promise of what these creatures could be without point restrictions. Strong, graceful, and clever all at once. An image, even, of the mythical dragons that Connor was always geeking out over. Greaves had seen all of that and ordered it locked away. The worst part was, my fliers were intelligent enough to understand what quarantine meant. That they would never have the freedom of the skies they'd been made for.

All of it was my fault, too. I should have seen Greaves' reaction coming. All the evidence was there. Now those fliers would spend their lives in purgatory.

I should have known better.

When I got back to my condo, I found Octavius watching the television.

"What the hell?"

He gave me an honest-to-God guilty look, like a kid caught sneaking a cookie.

"Is this what you do every day when I go to work?"

He shrugged his scaly little shoulders and turned back to the screen. They were running a puff piece about hypo-allergenic cats, and the joy they brought to the feline-loving-but-deathly-allergic segment of the population.

No wonder my channels were never the same when I turned on my TV after work. "You little rascal," I said, but my heart wasn't in it. His cleverness knew no bounds.

My flier had been clever, too. So clever that Greaves gave an order to shoot it down, as easily as some people order lunch. I didn't want to care about dragons, but those were mine.

Those dragons felt different.

I took my sweet-ass time getting in to work the next day. Part of that was my reluctance to face the other designers after the disastrous demonstration. Beyond that, I was hardly eager to start churning out one custom dragon after the other. When I got off the elevator, I even imagined that my badge might not work at the security doors. I pictured the red-light-and-buzzer combination, and then the awkward conversation with the security guard. Greaves had fired people for lesser offenses than going outside of the points system.

Termination might even be a relief. Better a quick death for my scientific career than a slow, agonizing spiral. I approached the door to the hatchery. *Moment of truth*. I held my breath and waved my badge in front of the scanner.

Nothing happened.

My heart sank, but there was a chance I wasn't close enough. I tried it again. The light blinked green, and the door hissed open. Thank God. I tried not to let my relief show as I hustled through the hatchery, dodging the occasional egg cart. The design lab lay in cool, productive silence. No one noticed my arrival, or if they did, they were nice enough to pretend otherwise. I was actually starting to cool off a bit when I got to my pod.

I reached in to flip on the lights, which is how I noticed a red LED on the back wall. "That's new."

I leaned closer to inspect it and saw the unmistakable round glass lens of a security camera. "What the hell?" I leaned my head over the divider. "Wong?"

He rolled out in his chair and raised his eyebrows.

I pointed a thumb back at my camera. "Do you believe this?"

"We all have them." *Because of you*, he didn't have to add.

Build-A-Dragon had hundreds of security cameras—in the hallways, in the elevators, watching all the main entry and exit points. I passed at least a dozen just going from my car to my chair. I'd stopped noticing them a long time ago. But this one was pointed at me. Well, technically it was pointed at the God Machine, but I'd be in the frame. It didn't have the angle to read my screens, or I'd have refused to work outright. I could just picture Fulton down in his security office, watching us with unblinking eyes.

"Unbelievable," I muttered.

"Not good for us," Wong said. "But still better than Shenzhen." He rolled back into his station.

"Noah?" asked a soft voice. Korrapati had tiptoed over. "I'm sorry about the Condor."

"Oh. Thanks."

"It flew wonderfully."

"Yeah, it did."

She glanced surreptitiously at the camera. "Well, see you."

She scurried away. Not that I blamed her. No one in their right mind wanted to be associated with me at the moment. I was toxic.

I sighed and logged in at my workstation. There were already two messages from Evelyn telling me to come to her office as soon as I got in. That rankled me a little bit, too. Yet another little corporate power-move she had picked up from the execs: summon someone to your office first thing, like they have no higher priority in the world.

Her door was open, but she had her back turned. I knocked on the glass. "You wanted to see me?"

She smiled, but it wasn't convincing. "Come in, Noah."

I sat down, and she activated her doorseal. Technically, the engineers put that in as a safety measure, but all of us quickly discovered that the hermetic seal provided wonderful soundproofing, too. The perfect thing for awkward conversations.

I almost blurted out a question about the camera, but I held my tongue. *Let's see if she brings it up voluntarily.* Something told me she wouldn't. She knew me enough to guess how I'd feel about up-close surveillance.

"I was just talking to Robert about the flier demonstration," she said. "He is not very happy with us."

I barked a laugh. It sounded as spiteful as I felt. "Yeah. Well, the feeling's mutual." I still couldn't believe he'd sent my fliers to quarantine.

"This is his company."

"I thought it was Simon Redwood's company."

She bit her lip, as if nervous. "Robert oversees the day-to-day operations."

"I'm aware." A spark of anger flared up in me. "You know, you could have backed me up out there."

"What do you mean?"

"With the point limitations. You didn't even make our case for an exception."

"You went so far outside the limits. I couldn't deny it," she said.

You were meek, I wanted to tell her. *You let them slaughter him.*

"That dragon was perfect," I said. "There's no way to design one without bending the rules. Not with the specs that you want."

"I think we should let one of the other designers have a crack at it."

"What for?"

"We need to keep you out of the spotlight for a while."

"So what am I supposed to do?" I demanded.

"Work on the customs. Keep your head down," she said.

"This feels like a punishment."

"It's not. It's . . . a strategy for us."

A part of me knew she was doing the right thing, that she was protecting me and my not-so-secret temper from doing something brash. But it *was* a setback. Instead of winning freedom with Build-A-Dragon's resources, I'd managed to win a double-secret probation and additional scrutiny.

"I'm thinking about your career," she said.

"Mine, or yours?"

"Noah . . ." She sounded hurt.

I waved my hand in something that might have been an apology. "It's fine. I can stay busy." I turned to the door and stood there, waiting for her to release the seals.

"The dragon wranglers couldn't find body of the flier," she said.

I turned back. "What?"

"The one that flew the demo." She shrugged. "They never found the body. It may have gotten away."

"It doesn't stand a chance alone in the desert." I forced myself to keep the anger on my face. To give nothing away. Because the tiny, fleeting hope that my prototype might have escaped into the desert was something I could cling to. I cleared my throat. "I should get to it."

She sighed quietly. Something had changed between us, and she knew it. Still, I refused to look at her. Then the seal hissed open, and I stalked out.

CHAPTER THIRTY-SEVEN
FREQUENTLY ASKED QUESTIONS

To better serve our customers, Build-A-Dragon's support team has compiled answers to some of our most commonly asked questions here. Even though we know you won't bother, we still encourage to read this guide in its entirety before contacting us with a question.

Which dragon should I choose?

That depends on what you want. If you're looking for a family pet or in-home companion, you probably want our bestselling model, the Rover. This model grows up to four feet long, weighs less than eighty pounds, and will be a loyal friend to your family. If you live in a small space and the idea of an 80-pound pet scares you, take a look at our Laptop model, which is designed for urban living. It can even fly short distances and has minimal cleanup. Plus, a customized Build-A-Dragon dragon tote comes with every purchase.

If your heart is set on a flying dragon, we offer two fantastic options with more endurance than the Laptop. The first is the Pterodactyl, our long-range flier. Don't believe everything you've read about it online. This dragon can soar. Does it crash into the occasional stationary object? Sure. But no more often than the average delivery drone. For a nimbler flying dragon, consider our Harrier model, which balances endurance and airborne agility.

Still here? You must be a discerning customer, indeed. May we recommend our premium dragon customization program? You give us the specs, and we design a dragon to the best of our ability that will meet them. Every customized dragon is unique and one-of-a-kind. Pricing available upon request.

When will my dragon arrive?

Once you've placed your order, it will enter Build-A-Dragon's product fulfillment queue, for completion as soon as a dragon becomes available. Build-A-Dragon's products are generally first come, first served. It may take 4-6 weeks until we're able to fulfill your order. You'll receive an e-mail notification when this happens. Add another 5-7 business days for delivery.

I placed a custom dragon order. How does that affect things?

Custom dragon design is a premium service provided by our Dragon Design department, the same team that brought you the bestselling Rover dragon. It may take 1-2 months before they can get to your design. Once you receive notification that your egg has been printed, it will arrive in about a week. We understand that this is a long time to wait and appreciate your patience. That's also why it's important that you be the first one in your family and/or group of friends to place a custom dragon order. Then you can lord it over your peers as they settle in for the long haul until delivery day.

How do I get my dragon egg to hatch?

You follow the detailed instructions we provide to you, that's how. Dragon eggs must be warmed to and maintained at a consistent temperature in order to hatch on time. We recommend a Build-A-Dragon HatchRite heating lamp (sold separately) for this purpose.

We cannot stress enough the importance of having fresh (raw) meat on hand to feed your dragon upon hatching. Newly born dragons are ravenous, and they need to eat right away to replenish energy stores after the strain of hatching. Furthermore, this simple act—providing your dragon with food—establishes the link between a dragon and its human master. It's critical to ensuring that your dragon accepts you as its owner. We ask that you kindly not screw it up.

If desired, Build-A-Dragon offers assisted hatching and imprinting with support from our highly trained personnel. This premium service is currently only available at our headquarters in Phoenix, Arizona. Pricing is available upon request.

I don't want my dragon anymore. Can I return it?

Build-A-Dragon's standard models are eligible for return for the first 30 days following delivery. Please call our customer service line for instructions on how to complete the return. Fair warning: it will involve giving your dragon a powerful sedative in the form of a suppository. This is the only condition under which we could persuade shipping providers to transport them. Returned dragons are housed at The Farm—our desert facility with specially designed enclosures and full-time care—until we can find a new home for them.

Unfortunately, due to the unique nature of custom dragons, most are not eligible for return or exchange. That's why we encourage you to specify your custom design with the utmost care.

What can I feed my dragon?

The best way to make sure your dragon gets what he needs is to only feed him with RepChow, our specially designed dragon food. If you prefer to provide your own food, you should administer a RepVite tablet or the RepViteWater beverage to your dragon at least once a month.

With the exception of the Guardian models, our dragons should not be taught to hunt food on their own. That might enable them to escape captivity and live in the wild where they have no natural predators. Reptiles ruled this planet once. It is in everyone's best interests to make sure that doesn't come to pass once again.

CHAPTER THIRTY-EIGHT
Strategy

To get anything done, I needed my printing rights back. And that meant acting like a happy cog in the corporate machine, doing exactly what they wanted. It's one of the hardest pills I've ever had to swallow, walking into the design lab every day to put in the work with the failure of the flier demo hanging over me. My reputation had taken a serious hit, and everyone knew it. Invitations to lunch from Wong and Korrapati ceased. O'Connell and the Frogman acted like I was no longer even worthy of their attention.

Build-A-Dragon cut back my clearance levels, too. The parking garage helped me figure that one out. For as long as I'd worked there, the gate had opened the second it detected my Tesla's RFID tag. Now it held fast across the entryway and acted like I wasn't there. I guess that in all the quiet curtailing of my security privileges, some numbnuts in IT didn't realize that I still had to park my car somewhere.

Well, I sure as hell wouldn't park my baby outside. Most security measures had weaknesses, and I was good at finding them.

I backed up and over until another car pulled in. The driver must not have been on Greaves' shit list, because the gate lifted just fine when he pulled up. I hit the gas and followed him in, bumper to bumper. The gate started to close, but it ground to a halt to let me slip through. Easy as pie.

It still ticked me off. I paid an exorbitant monthly fee for garage parking. I ground my teeth while the Tesla circled up to my spot. I stomped right up to my office and filed a support issue with the facilities group first thing. Subject line: PARKING ACCESS ISSUE.

No doubt they'd get in there, figure out what had happened with my clearance adjustments, and play it off as some sort of mechanical failure. Fine. But I wasn't going to play cat-and-mouse with the gate every day just to get to work.

I desperately wanted to open up the design for my flier model and run it through my simulator. It had flown better than I dreamed it would. But I didn't dare bring any more attention to what Robert Greaves considered a design failure. If someone scrutinized the model, they might see the extra genetic variant I'd introduced deep within its design, in the reptilian version of Connor's gene. It would be hard to explain. So would the tweaks I'd made to my simulator code to conceal the variant's long-term effects from its modeling. It wasn't easy, but I resisted the urge to even touch my flier design.

A few orders had come in overnight, so I got to work on those. The first was another birthday dragon. Powder blue this time, so obviously not the same customer who'd ordered the pink-and-white job.

I cranked out the design. It wasn't my best, because my heart just wasn't in it. But it was good enough, so I sent it to Evelyn for approval. The next one was more entertaining: someone wanted a watch dragon for yard security. We didn't have a regular product line for these, so they were among our most popular custom jobs. Junkyards, storage facilities, and other places with high fences around raw materials had embraced dragons as the new Rottweiler. A mean dog is intimidating, sure, but nothing discouraged trespassers like the glowing eyes of a hungry reptile.

DragonDraft3D wanted to automate the process—we'd done plenty of these dragons before—but I went the manual route because I wanted the distraction. This time I started with a more aggressive base model, but traded some of its speed for stamina, and a lower metabolism. A watch dragon's job was like a security guard's—occasional bursts of excitement buffered by long periods of boredom. I upped the starch tolerance, too, since a junkyard wasn't likely to have a supply of raw meat lying around. I sent that design off to Evelyn, too.

It drained me so much—physically and emotionally—to keep my head down and act like everything was fine. The work became almost mind-numbing in its boredom, its simplicity. Losing the flier was a setback on my secret plan, too. Then again, based on my argument with Connor, maybe it didn't matter. Thinking like that made me wonder what the hell I was still doing at Build-A-Dragon. I liked the work, sure, but I'd liked it much more when I had a purpose.

Summer was the only thing that helped me get through it. Whenever I had a dark moment, I'd let my thoughts drift back to her. How she looked, how she sounded. Whether or not we might beat Big Mesa the next time we tried. Our alliance to beat that cache had also meant a ceasefire on the constant sniping-back-and-forth. With that out of the way, I'd kind of enjoyed spending a few hours with her.

That shitty week seemed to last forever, but the weekend came at last. Friday night, as Octavius and I were making our battle plans out on the balcony, it occurred to me that I'd spent all week obsessing about something that was loosely planned at best. It's not like Summer and I had set a time, or even officially agreed on the meeting place. For all I knew, she was only being polite after Octavius saved her pig. Finally, I couldn't stand the angst and made myself to go to bed. Whatever was going to happen, I'd find out soon enough.

Saturday morning, I got to the rock-strewn parking lot a good fifteen minutes early, so I laced up my boots and played hide-and-seek with Octavius. His favorite game, and he kept getting better at it. Half the time, I couldn't even find him. There were just too many places for a little dragon to hide. The Arizona desert, inhospitable as it might seem for humans, was well-suited to dragons.

A deep rumble announced the arrival of Summer's Jeep. The parking lot had a long, looping driveway entrance, but Summer ignored it. She drove off the shoulder, across the drainage ditch, and over the median like it wasn't even there.

"Oh yeah." I gave her a thumbs up.

Riker jumped out to greet us before the Jeep stopped moving. There were no doors to keep him in, I guess. He grunted once, but in a friendly way, and ran up to nudge my foot with his snout, like he wanted to be petted.

"Hey, Riker." I'd never petted a pig before, but I couldn't turn him down. The portly little guy was starting to grow on me. I reached down and gave him a timid pat on the head. His coat was like chinchilla fur. "Whoa, you're soft!"

"I know, right?" Summer said. Her voice sent an inexplicable thrill into my chest. She wore khaki cutoffs and a white top. Desert colors.

"Hey there," I said.

I couldn't come up with any more words, but Octavius saved me by gliding down to greet Riker. The pig made a soft whine and licked him on the snout. I think it caught Octavius by surprise; he reared back and shook his head, sputtering. Riker hopped forward and licked him again. Summer and I laughed.

"I guess they're friends now," Summer said.

"A last alliance of pigs and dragons," I said.

"Nerd."

"Whatever, Number One."

There was no denying that we made a strong team, though. We found the last waypoint—Riker dug it out from under a cactus. With all five in hand, we could calculate the coordinates of the final cache. Summer and I crouched in the shade of a big saguaro while I crunched the numbers on my phone. She was right next to me, close enough that I could smell her perfume. Vanilla and roses. I inhaled it softly, losing track of the numbers for a second. I shook my head a little and buckled down. Took me a few minutes, working the numbers, to resolve the final coordinates. I read off the solution.

Summer punched it into her watch. "There it is. Half a mile south of us." She flashed me a wicked grin then. "Race you!" She bounded off.

"Hey, wait!" I scrambled after her, but my feet caught on something and I fell on my face. *What the hell*? She'd tied my shoelaces together. She was going to beat me to the cache and log it before I got there.

"Son of a bitch!" I shouted.

She and Riker disappeared around a rock formation. I heard her laughing.

I fumbled my laces apart, tied them, and tore off in pursuit. "Come on, Octavius!"

We chased them the whole half-mile, while my legs turned to lead and my lungs burned like fire. Couldn't catch up, though. Both she and Riker were apparently in better shape. I jogged through a switchback (rattlesnake-free, thankfully) and my watch beeped the arrival. Summer stood twenty yards to the right, with Riker at her feet. She had the clear plastic case in her hand, the final cache.

"Finally," she said.

"What the—" I managed, and then had to cough up half a lung. "Hell?" I finished. We had an alliance, dammit!

"Oh, settle down. I didn't log it yet."

Relief flooded over me. I had to laugh at her sheer audacity. I stumbled over to her while she pried the case open. She held the microdrive out to me. I reached for it, half-convinced she'd yank it away. But she didn't, and we both held it for a moment.

I let go of it. "Ladies first," I said.

She smiled and plugged it into her phone to record the find. I did the same right after her. We were inside the two-minute window, so this counted as a team find.

There were other files on the microdrive, too. Image files from cachers who'd taken selfies. Summer and I flipped through them.

"Should we take one?" she asked.

"Absolutely," I said. I set the ten-second timer. "Octavius, sky shot!" He plucked the phone from my hand and circled up, flapping his wings like crazy. We grinned up at it, the shutter clicked, and Octavius brought it back down. He circled down and dropped my phone into my hand.

"That's a nice trick," Summer said.

"Thanks." *We only broke two phones mastering it.*

The photo was perfect, and the way it was taken from above would add some mystery for future geocachers. And it had me in the company of a pretty girl, which wouldn't hurt the old reputation. I gave it a caption: *Tied for first.*

"Let me see it," Summer said.

"Got your phone?" I asked.

She did indeed, in a hot-pink case tucked into some kind of athletic armband. I beamed her the pic.

"Aw, Riker looks cute," she said.

I hadn't even noticed the pig. I was looking at her in the picture, the way she'd kind of leaned in against me and smiled. I liked the way we looked. It hit me, then, that we'd only agreed to work together until we found the cache. Technically speaking, the alliance was officially over.

But I wasn't sure I wanted it to be.

CHAPTER THIRTY-NINE
The Squeaky Wheel

Our victory out in the desert gave me a new burst of productive energy when I went back into work. I needed that, even if I was kind of obsessing over Summer. *Stay focused*, I kept telling myself. Difficult as it was, I had to put the flier behind me and concentrate on getting my printing rights back for the God Machine. One way to do that would be as Evelyn said: keep my head down, work efficiently, color within the lines and never step outside them. That would probably do the trick, but it could also take six months or a year before someone paused and said hey, Noah's not so bad after all.

Connor didn't have that kind of time, so neither did I. Instead, I went with plan B. I started cranking through custom orders as quickly as I could. The queue was deep enough to keep me busy, and I also took some orders off Wong's and Korrapati's plates, since they'd done the same for me. One good thing about designing the flier was that it upped my game in DragonDraft3D. I had the menus memorized, and my fingers knew the shortcuts on their own.

Every time I finished a design, I fired it off to Evelyn for approval. At first, she'd take ten or twenty minutes for each one, which told me she was checking over the designs and running them through my simulator. But as I kept blasting them into her inbox, the time to approval shortened to five minutes. Now she was probably just glancing at the design, making sure I stayed within the guidelines.

Within a couple of days, she was approving them almost as soon as I hit "Send." The God Machine whirred constantly.

I waited until Friday to approach Evelyn. I wanted to march right into her office and *demand* my egg-printing privileges back, but that's what the old Noah would have done. The old, rebellious, rule-breaking Noah. The new, obedient, cog-in-the-machine Noah knocked meekly on her office door. "Hey, Evelyn."

She turned and peered around her projection monitors. "Noah." She smiled. "You have been busy."

"Just doing my part," I said. "Did you get my last two customs?" I knew she'd probably seen them but hadn't had time to grant the approvals.

"Sorry, not yet." She shook her head and sighed. "I feel like I spend my entire day in meetings."

I held up my hands. "It's all right, I can come back."

"No, stay." She brought up yet another projection monitor and pulled up my designs. "Very nice. Oh, look at that one!"

"The silver one? Yeah, I had fun with that." The customer was a stage magician in Vegas and had wanted a custom dragon that would really dazzle the crowd.

"These are good, Noah." She put in a key sequence to approve them. I heard the distant hum of the God Machine swinging into motion back in the design lab. *Perfect.*

"Sorry to add to your plate," I said. "I know you are busy."

Her eyes went back to screen number four. Then five. Then three. "It's good. You are being productive."

"Thanks," I said.

I went back to my desk and tackled the incoming request. It was a complaint disguised as a support ticket; I'm surprised the customer service people didn't catch it. I read the summary:

We've only had our new dragon a couple of days. My daughter just loves it! But the first time we left it alone, the thing attacked my tabby cat! If I hadn't heard her hissing and crying, I'm sure he would have eaten her. Please make sure your pet dragons won't try to eat the other pets in the household.

"Yeah, right, lady," I muttered. Dragons were apex predators. There was no taking that away; it was coded into their DNA far deeper than the little tweaks that I could make. If you leave an apex predator alone with a not-so-apex predator, the order of things will be asserted no matter what I did.

I wrote up a brief memo to customer service, telling them that we understood the complaint and suggesting they send her a copy of the Rover manual with the "Dragon Safety" section highlighted. That would remind her to read the damn thing, which most of our customers didn't bother doing.

Wiping that one out of my queue felt good. I took a little break and texted Connor, to see how he was doing. We'd sort of made our peace by pretending our fight never happened, though I hadn't been over since. He was busy studying for finals anyway. Rumor had it, even the video game console had fallen silent at the Parker residence. I was glad to hear about him going after something for once. Planning for the future and all that.

In the meantime, I had to keep up my ruse as a happy cog. So I dove into the next custom design. A rancher out in Montana wanted a dragon that would keep the wolves away from his livestock.

Behavioral traits easily ranked among the most difficult things to adjust in a custom dragon. Take this rancher's request, for example. He needed a dragon dangerous enough to threaten a pack of wolves, but that also won't eat the livestock it's supposed to be protecting. Dragons come with all sorts of animal instincts; some we gave them intentionally, and some just manifested on their own.

I fully admit that there were some forces at play that we didn't entirely understand. But I used whatever tools and knowledge I could to dance among the DNA patterns, finding one that would make everyone happy.

And keep our customers satisfied, of course. Because that was Build-A-Dragon's top priority.

I knew what I had to do for this rancher's dragon, but I didn't like it. My fingers seemed to fight me the whole way. It was wrong. It was downright unnatural. But it was the only way.

I had to turn a dragon into a vegetarian.

This wasn't as hard as it sounds, because we knew which enzymes broke down animal fats and proteins in the dragon's digestive system, just as we knew the ones that handled starches. If you knocked out the former, the dragon wouldn't be able to digest meat. I did permit an active copy of the gene that conferred lactose tolerance. If the dragon had to, it could digest milk.

That handled the problem of a dragon eating its flock, though it might still kill them for sport. To counter that I relied on a different sort of biological property: maternal instinct. With the right balance of hormones and a carefully timed imprinting exercise, this dragon would think of the rancher's livestock as his own children. Montana wolves knew better than to come between a mother and her children when it came to rival predators; the grizzlies of Yellowstone had taught them well.

If they thought mother bear was fierce, just wait until they met papa dragon. I smiled just thinking about it as I walked to Evelyn's office. She perched on the edge of her chair. At least two more holoscreens hovered in front of her.

"Hey, boss," I said. "I know you are busy."

"Twice in one day, Noah?" She smiled at me between two screens. "It must be a special occasion."

"I sent you another design. The one for that Montana rancher," I said.

She opened a seventh screen and pulled it up. "Looks pretty good. Wait, a vegetarian diet?"

"Otherwise it might eat the livestock."

"Ha! A clever solution."

"Just thinking ahead."

"I'm surprised you were willing to make an herbivore."

"It rocked my very core, but it was the only way." I paused and tried to make my tone casual. "You know, I could probably be even faster if I could print directly."

She looked away from her screens long enough to give me a puzzled expression. "What?"

I sat down on one of the backless leather stools in front of her glass desk. "If I could print eggs without your approval, like before, we would go faster."

"I don't know..."

"Look, you've got enough to do without me adding to the workload. I can tell you're stressed."

She pursed her lips. She was tempted. "You may have a point. I will see what I can do."

"I want another shot at the flying model, too."

She winced.

"Come on," I said. "We both know I'm the only one who's gotten close to specs." This was an educated guess based on the amount of cursing O'Connell had been doing over the last week. It sounded he was right on track to create another Terrible-dactyl.

"I don't think Robert will approve," Evelyn said.

"It doesn't hurt to ask, does it?" I asked.

She sighed. "I suppose not."

Undoubtedly my constant requests were interfering with her grand ambitions with the company's top brass, but at this point I didn't care. She'd capitalized plenty on my design achievements. This was the least she could do.

I expected an answer from Evelyn pretty soon. Maybe even that afternoon. She had a regular Friday meeting with Build-A-Dragon's executives over lunch. Most of them had offices on the other side of the building, where they could look out at the more scenic Scottsdale vista. This suited everyone on the lab side just fine. Designers like myself usually kept to our semi-private workstations by the God Machine, and the hatchery staffers pretty much only cared about eggs.

I could count on one hand the number of times a higher-up had set foot in our design lab. So when I looked up and saw Robert Greaves standing outside my cubicle, I didn't really know what to say.

"Afternoon, Noah." He wore the characteristic outfit, loose-fitting pants and a long-sleeve shirt, all black.

"Mr. Greaves!" After a second's hesitation, I stood up. Sitting while Build-A-Dragon's CEO stood seemed like a faux pas.

He flashed the same smile that graced most of our company's literature. "Please, call me Robert."

"All right." I hadn't seen him face-to-face since the failed demonstration of my Condor model. *Best not to think about that.*

"Evelyn tells me that your last several designs have been spot-on," he said.

"Oh." It rattled me a little to learn that Evelyn was reporting on me. Did she know he was here now? Probably not. If she had, she'd have been hovering. "I'm doing my best."

"Good, good. We're reinstating your print privileges."

"Thanks." So far, this was good news. However, I sincerely doubted the head of the company had come to tell me everything was hunky-dory.

"A talented designer like you shouldn't be punished for a mistake," Greaves said.

"That's . . . nice of you to say." It took a major effort not to bristle at my Condor being written off as a mistake.

"Still not happy about that, I'm guessing," he said.

I opened my mouth and shut it again. There was no point in denying what he could clearly see on my face.

"Look, man, I get it." He wandered back and stood facing me, with my chair positioned between us like a buffer. "Anyone who loves dragons wants to see the fairy tales brought to life. But it's dangerous to create something you can't control."

Control. That's what mattered to someone like Robert Greaves. As Simon Redwood had undoubtedly learned after inviting him in to run the company.

"I put a lot into that design." I looked away from him and shook my head. "It seemed like a terrible waste for such elegant creatures."

He waved an arm dismissively. "It's not as bad as you think. They'll get to live out their lives at the Farm, and you got to learn the importance of coloring inside the lines."

The dragons went to the Farm. I'd been trying so hard to forget what happened on demonstration day, I didn't think through what he'd meant by ordering the dragons to quarantine. "Does that mean I'll get another shot at the flying model?"

"We want you to focus on the custom orders, at least for the time being."

That meant no. It didn't hurt as bad as it could have, because I'd expected as much. There was a sliver of hope and I clung to it. "I can do that. I like them."

He gripped my shoulder. "And you're good at them. Keep at it, all right?"

"I will," I said dully. He was looking at me, and I could feel the weight of his gaze. I summoned a bit more enthusiasm. "Thanks. And sorry about . . . well, you know."

"It's water under the bridge." He gave me a nod and strode briskly out of the lab. I took what felt like my first full breath since he'd arrived.

A shadow detached itself from the wall beside the door. Ben Fulton gave me a little nod before following Greaves. *What was he doing here, anyway?* Maybe they thought I was unstable. Which wasn't the worst possible guess. Or maybe he'd come to support me. Either way, it didn't matter. I'd passed the test.

And more importantly, my flying dragons were still alive.

CHAPTER FORTY
Denials

The Farm was Build-A-Dragon's desert facility. I'd never been there before, nor had any of the designers. Hell, I didn't even know where it was. It couldn't be far, because that's where they sent all the problematic dragons—the returns, the failed prototypes, the custom jobs that didn't turn out. Or in one case, dragons that turned out a little too well.

I sincerely doubted I'd be granted permission to visit if I asked. Evelyn wanted me to keep my head down, and Greaves clearly felt we should put the whole matter behind us. That being said, if some of my Condor models were still alive, I had a good chance of obtaining the samples I needed to finalize my experiment. If I could get close to one of them, it just might work.

The problem was that I had no idea where to go. I wasn't about to ask someone down in Herpetology where it was. Or Evelyn, for that matter. She'd have too many questions, and she'd pull up the dragon design to figure out what I was looking for. No, if I wanted to see my Condor models, I'd have to do it on my own. Without anyone even realizing I'd done it. Then all I had to do was take a tiny sample for a biopsy. I could almost certainly get one of my former labmates at ASU to do the biopsy and tell me whether or not the muscle fibers showed any sign of dystrophy. But first things first: I had to find The Farm.

Wong was out, so I wandered over to Korrapati's workstation on the other side of the God Machine. She sat delicately in front of her screen, working a custom job through DragonDraft3D. As I watched, she ran her current design through my simulator. The dragon looked like a Rover model, but shorter and more rotund, with stocky legs. "What is that, a corgi?"

"Hey, Noah!" She looked past my shoulder and lowered her voice. "What did Greaves want?"

"To give me my printing privileges back."

"Really?"

"I guess I'm off double-secret probation."

"Well, good. That whole thing was *ridiculous*."

"Yeah, it was." Funny how she never thought to say so when I was going through it, though. "Hey, you know one of the dragon wranglers, don't you?"

"Yes." Her cheeks colored. "Peter."

I hadn't been terribly plugged into the company rumor mill, but it was fairly common knowledge that Korrapati was dating one of the wranglers. Now I had a name to go with the dungarees. "Does he ever go out to the Farm?"

"Sometimes. He doesn't talk about it much."

In fairness, neither did we. No one liked the idea of dragon designs going awry. "I imagine it's far away."

Her brow furrowed. "It can't be too far. He's gone there and been back before the end of the day."

"He has?"

"At least a few times."

"Gotta be out in the desert somewhere, I suppose," I said, while the wheels turned in my head. "Well, anyway. You should introduce me to him the next time he stops by." I smiled and winked at her, which only made her blush even more.

"Okay, um . . . sure."

"See you." I went back to my workstation, thanking my lucky stars that Korrapati had caught a dragon wrangler's interest. He made it to the Farm and back within a day. That meant it had to be a four-hour drive, tops. But four hours covered a lot of desert territory. I'd never find it without help from a wrangler. But I could hardly follow one of them without being noticed. The Tesla drew too much attention. Which is part of why I loved it, but that's beside the point.

But I didn't have to follow the handlers, if I knew where they went.

The first step was to identify the vehicles of the Herpetology staff. This was the easiest part, because the dragon wranglers' vehicles stood out just as much as the wranglers themselves did: sturdy old pickup trucks with mud on the rims and desert dust everywhere else. I tagged each of them with a stamp-sized magnetic GPS tracker. Fourteen trucks overall.

Then I had to do something I'm not terribly proud of. I had to make a defective dragon.

The order, ironically, was for another child's pet, a vanilla-type Labrador retriever dragon. Docile, loyal, protective—I mean, clearly the parents wanted a dog but couldn't talk their little boy out of a dragon.

I started with the Rover model but curtailed the development time for teeth and claws. After putting in the necessary pigmentation changes, I tackled the delicate stuff: balancing endorphins and neural feedback. That's where I effected some sabotage, an edge case that even my simulator code wouldn't necessarily catch. I modified the dopamine transporter, which normally helped modulate the neurotransmitters for pleasure and excitement, so that it would react not just to dopamine, but to other biological amines.

Now the chemical signals underlying emotion—joy, pain, fear, hunger, guilt, or anything—would act like a hit of dopamine to the brain. The result, by my guess, would be a dragon that was overstimulated almost all the time. I didn't dare try to model this in the simulator, but I could guess that its defect would be pretty obvious.

I hit the Print button and put in my transfer ticket. The egg was charcoal gray, with little flecks of scarlet throughout. I'd never seen a design like it before. I felt a little stab of guilt, knowing that the creature within was doomed to a life in quarantine, but I reminded myself that this was just a means to an end. This was about something more important than dragons.

At least, that's what I told myself as the staffers wheeled it away.

I set my watch so that I wouldn't miss the hatching. *That'll be one hell of a show.*

CHAPTER FORTY-ONE
Triangulation

On hatching day for the sabotaged dragon, I took my lunch to the glass-paneled observatory room. I figured I had half an hour to eat before the egg cracked. But I hadn't accounted for the gung-ho attitude of a perpetually eager dragon.

I was halfway through my peanut butter and jelly when the purple snout broke through the egg's surface. Most of our custom jobs take two or three minutes to fully escape the eggshell. This one squirmed free in less than thirty seconds. It scampered over to lick the gloved hands of the hatchery staff.

They nudged it toward the bowl of raw meat. Newborn dragons usually needed a quick infusion of protein; the instinct to eat meat was so powerful that we relied on it for the imprinting process. This one couldn't settle down long enough to eat, though. It kept leaving the bowl to wander about the room. Jim and Allie were in there trying to clean up, and the thing just wouldn't leave them alone. At one point, Allie tried pushing the dragon's head away.

Big mistake. In my mind's eye, I could see the neurotransmitters flooding synapses, and the neurons firing in a self-multiplying fireworks finale. Every emotion amplified a hundredfold.

The dragon reared back, put its two front paws on her shoulders and licked her full-on in the face. Big, wet, *slimy* licks. This wasn't normal behavior; anyone could see that. Jim came up behind the dragon and gently slipped a catchpole over its neck. He eased it over to the food bowl and held it there to eat. Meanwhile, Allie went to the phone and made the call to Herpetology.

I went back to my desk as if things were normal. Half an hour later, I got the summons to Evelyn's office. I'd kind of developed a reputation for not being the most prompt communicator, mostly because I lost track of time when I got deep into DragonDraft3D. So I gave it ten more minutes before I moseyed over.

"You needed me?" I asked.

Evelyn glanced up. "Yes, come in."

I stepped inside, and she sealed the door. So that's how it was going to be.

"There's a problem with one of your custom dragons," she said.

I feigned surprise. "Which one?"

"The purple birthday job."

I knew I didn't have much of a poker face, so I thought it best to fall back on a role I knew well: touchy, defensive artist. "What kind of problem?" I demanded.

"Behavioral. It wouldn't leave the hatchery staff alone."

"It's supposed to be a child's pet. You don't want it friendly?"

She pursed her lips and hit a few keys on her keyboard. "Here's the vidfeed."

A new opaque rectangle appeared in the air, showing security footage from the hatching I'd just witnessed. I winced at the close-up view of the purple dragon's wet tongue sliding up Allie's face. *Yech.*

"I guess I see what you mean," I said.

"Did you use a stock design for this one?"

"No. The simulator said it would be fine, but I didn't run a comprehensive battery." Because I'd known it might show up.

"Will you check the design again?" she asked.

"Sure. I'll do it right now." I made to leave, then turned back. "What's going to happen to that one?"

"Probably just a quarantine. It's not that the dragon is dangerous. But something didn't quite work," she said.

I sighed, maybe a touch too theatrically. "Yet another dragon wasted. I'll take a look at the design." Then I left, not trusting myself to keep a straight face. I went back into my design and readjusted the transporter gene so that it would function normally. We still had to fill the order, after all.

Sure enough, the simulator code predicted the desired result: a dragon that was friendly but not over-the-top. Then again, that's what it had said about the first one. This time, however, the guy who wrote the simulator wasn't trying to fool it. I sent the new design to Evelyn with a note:

Think I found the problem. One of the serotonin transporters. I fixed it and put this one through the works. Sorry about that.

It took twenty minutes for the egg printer to turn on, which told me she'd probably run my new design through the simulator herself. I wasn't worried, though. It would be exactly what the customer wanted.

With luck, the defective one was already headed for The Farm.

I stayed at work bit later than usual, not because I was busy but because I didn't like driving the Tesla in heavy traffic. It had collision-avoidance systems and real-time maps and such, but that didn't stop some moron on a cell phone from sideswiping me on the freeway. My baby was pristine, and I wanted her to stay that way. Only Wong was still there by the time I left,

"*Tai t'yen, Wong Xiansheng*," I told him.

"Yes, see you later," he said.

"Don't work too late." Sometimes I wondered if he ever stopped working at all.

Traffic had relented a little by the time I got onto the freeway. I got home just before dusk and found the condo dark. Usually, that meant Octavius had settled somewhere for a nap.

"Octavius?"

A soft noise came from the kitchen, the unmistakable sound of dragon claws on stone tile. I walked in, thinking I'd find him on the floor amid a destroyed box of cereal. But the floor was clean and empty. Octavius dropped down from the ceiling like a ninja assassin. He put his wings over my face, too, effectively blinding me. I cursed and swatted at him until he flew off to perch on top of the micro-refrigerator.

"Missed you, too, buddy." I rubbed the dry patch of scales on the back of your head. "You're going to help me clean this up. Then we've got work to do."

I wolfed down some Asian-Mexican fusion leftovers—that food truck had really gotten a hold on me—and then parked myself in front of the computer to get started. The GPS tags were linked to a tracking app that Octavius and I used to log our geocaches. My watch synchronized with it, as did the tracking tags I'd placed on the handlers' trucks. I pulled up the paths and overlaid them with a map of Phoenix, centered on the company headquarters.

Over the last several hours, the tags had rolled out of the parking garage and headed in a dozen directions. I traced most of them to residential complexes on the outskirts of Phoenix. Interesting that none of the handlers lived downtown, even though it was closer to work. They seemed to prefer the fringe of the desert.

Tag number six was the only one that went far beyond the city limits. In the early afternoon, that vehicle had made a straight shot northeast of Phoenix into the desert wilderness near Gila National Forest. I tried to zoom in on the satellite imagery, but it became blurry when I did so. I zoomed out and moved around to be sure. Sometimes that happened in areas with poor satellite coverage, but I doubted that was the case here. Not this close to a major city, and neatly ensconced between national forests that the federal government liked to keep eyes on. No, this had the stink of paid exclusion to it.

For an exorbitant fee, imaging and mapping companies removed the high-quality satellite coverage of certain sensitive areas. Corporations and wealthy individuals who valued their privacy were all too happy to pay.

Say what you want about the Freedom of Information stuff, but it came in handy from time to time. Especially to those of us who were computer-savvy enough to pay attention. First, I went to the property maps website for Phoenix County. Working back-and-forth between that and my mapping program, I found the property record for the parcel of land where the truck had gone. A few more clicks and I was looking at the details on the property's registered owner.

Hello, Reptilian Corporation.

That sealed it, for me. Build-A-Dragon had no reason to own a second swath of land out in the desert. Certainly not one that the dragon handlers would visit.

The location was going to be a problem, though. There was a

single two-lane road going in and out. No real reason to be on that road unless you were headed to the facility. I couldn't be sure that I'd tagged all the handlers' vehicles, either. They were all dusty old trucks and jeeps. My red Tesla would stick out like a sore hallux. That's a big toe, by the way.

I didn't love the idea of taking my baby on an unfinished road, either. If only I still had the jalopy. That thing would have blended in just fine. The thought gave me an idea. Two ideas, really. An excuse to call Summer, and a halfway-decent cover story for if we got caught.

CHAPTER FORTY-TWO
TECH SUPPORT

Build-A-Dragon Support Chat Transcript
Operator: Li-Huei Chang
Date: May 17th

System: We appreciate your patience. A support operator will be with you in one minute.

Charles Smith (trainee): Hello and thank you for contacting Reptilian Corporation. May I have your name, please?

Guest 1: Bill Middleton. I'm at the Mala Mala Game Reserve in South Africa.

Charles Smith (trainee): Good afternoon, Mr. Middleton. How can I help you today?

Guest 1: We're having some trouble with the three dragons we bought for the park.

Charles Smith (trainee): What seems to be the problem?

Guest 1: We've advertised them as a sort of main attraction.

Charles Smith (trainee): Excellent choice, sir.

Guest 1: We thought so at first but turns out they're extremely hard to find during daylight hours.

Charles Smith (trainee): That's true of most predators, sir.

Guest 1: Well, the tours aren't seeing them. We've fielded numerous complaints.

Charles Smith (trainee): If I understand your problem, sir, you'd like your dragons to be seen more by the park visitors?

Guest 1: Ideally, yeah.

Charles Smith (trainee): You must have other apex predators in the reserve as well, do you not?

Guest 1: Before the dragons arrived, most of our visitors came to see the lions.

Charles Smith (trainee): And how do you lure them out to be seen?

Guest 1: We used to tie a carcass on the back of a jeep and drive it past them. But that never works on the dragons.

Charles Smith (trainee): I'm afraid they do prefer live prey, generally speaking. But perhaps the lions could serve as your main attraction until you're better able to study the dragons' habits.

Guest 1: We don't have any lions left. The dragons got 'em.

Charles Smith (trainee): I'm sorry, sir, do you mean to say that the dragons killed your resident lions?

Guest 1: That's correct.

Charles Smith (trainee): Surely your lions were aged. And sickly, perhaps?

Guest 1: No, these were prime males and females. Four to seven years old.

Charles Smith (trainee): How many lions did you have in the pride, if I may ask?

Guest 1: Twelve.

Charles Smith (trainee): I'm finding it difficult to believe that three juvenile dragons took on a pack of mature lions.

Guest 1: Oh, they didn't challenge the pack. That'd be suicide. They picked 'em off one at a time.

Charles Smith (trainee): I see.

Guest 1: The lions weren't used to being hunted. They didn't stand a chance.

Charles Smith (trainee): So sorry for the inconvenience, sir. And you're sure it was the dragons behind these killings?

Guest 1: We never found the bodies, but Dr. Kandoth sure seemed to think so.

Charles Smith (trainee): I presume you're referring to Dr. Gaurav Kandoth? Our records show he's your chief zoologist.

Guest 1: Right. He was.

Charles Smith (trainee): Is he no longer with you?

Guest 1: He thought if he caught one of the dragons, it might draw the others out into the open. We never found his body, either.

Charles Smith (trainee): I'm sorry to hear that, sir.

Guest 1: Dr. Davis moved up to replace him. She was the assistant zoologist.

Charles Smith (trainee): Perhaps I could speak to her?

Guest 1: Well, one of the tours radioed that they saw a dragon and it looked injured, so she took a jeep out to investigate. The dragon must not have been hurt, because it mauled her pretty good.

Charles Smith (trainee): Oh, no!

Guest 1: Yep. Happened right in front of the tour group.

Charles Smith (trainee): Well, at least they got their money's worth. So, who's heading up the zoology team now?

Guest 1: I guess I am.

Charles Smith (trainee): Ah. So you're a zoologist as well?

Guest 1: Eh, I'm kind of in a different branch.

Charles Smith (trainee): Wildlife biology?

Guest 1: Park security.

Charles Smith (trainee): You're a *security* guard?

Guest 1: Not such a redundant job now, am I right?

Charles Smith (trainee): Bravo on the career choice, sir. So, there's no one else with you?

Guest 1: The guides ran off. Everyone else is missing.

Charles Smith (trainee): Oh, my goodness. How did this happen?

Guest 1: One at a time, just like the lions. Those are some clever dragons you sold us.

Charles Smith (trainee): Very kind of you to say, Mr. Middleton. Would you mind staying put while I contact the South African authorities?

Guest 1: I'm not going anywhere!

Charles Smith (trainee): Sir, I'm pleased to report that four game wardens are en route to your location.

Guest 1: I hope that's enough.

Charles Smith (trainee): To summarize, you had a problem getting your dragons to come out into the open, and it seems like we've solved that now. Thank you for choosing Reptilian Corporation.

CHAPTER FORTY-THREE
Trespassing

I met Summer in the parking lot for Big Mesa in early afternoon. I'd tucked my Tesla in the corner and activated the super-alarm. There were three parts to that: a verbal warning in a voice that sounded like Mr. T, followed by an ear-piercing alarm siren, and lastly an alert that went to my phone by satellite.

I could pull up a live feed from the six cameras positioned around the car. None of this would stop a determined car thief from taking my Tesla, but I hoped it wouldn't come to that. Deterrence was the name of the game. With luck, we wouldn't be gone more than a few hours.

Summer rolled in at a good clip, and parked haphazardly—front wheels in the lot, back wheels on the median—even though there was plenty of room. The Jeep was badass. *She* was badass, and I found that very distracting.

"You ready?" she asked.

"Yeah." I climbed into the passenger seat and beckoned to Octavius. "Come on, buddy!"

He trilled at me with uncertain tones.

"It's all right," I said.

Come to think of it, he'd never ridden in a car other than mine before. No wonder he was nervous.

"I'll be right here the whole time."

Nothing.

"We can stop for food," I said, hoping that was all right with Summer. She'd probably insist on some Vegan artisanal crap that he wouldn't touch, but I left that part unsaid.

The promise of food enticed him enough to glide onto my lap. It took another minute and talk of dessert to coax him into the back seat. He folded his wings, all prim-and-proper, and edged as far from Riker as possible.

He was probably afraid of getting licked again. Knowing Riker, that was a distinct possibility.

"Thanks for doing this," I told Summer.

"Where are we headed?"

"East on 60," I told her.

The Jeep rumbled to life. She didn't back up but made a U-turn and drove right back over the median.

Like I said, *badass*.

While she drove, I synced my GPS watch with her dash computer. It pulled up the route, about an hour and fifteen minutes.

"That's the middle of nowhere," Summer said. "Are you taking me out there to kill me?"

"You know, I was going to, but I could never drive this Jeep to get back."

"Seriously, there's not a cache within fifty miles."

"There's going to be." I dug the plastic container out of my pocket and held it up so she could see. It was transparent and watertight, about the size of a PB&J sandwich. I'd already loaded it with paper, pencils, a G.I. Joe, an arrowhead, and the all-important microdrive.

"Ooh, I've always wanted to make one," she said.

"Me, too. I thought we should do it before I pass you up and take first place."

She scoffed. "Never gonna happen."

"I should disclose that we have a second mission, too."

She gave me a side-eye. "Oh yeah? What's that?"

"Build-A-Dragon has a facility out there. I want to pay it an unofficial visit."

"Oh my God, you want to do *work* stuff? It's fricking Saturday!"

"It's not work, not really at least. There's just a dragon that I need to see. It'll only take a second."

She sighed. "What kind of facility is this?"

"We call it the Farm. It's where they send the failed prototypes, the returns, all of that."

"Um, I don't want to go anywhere near a place that's crawling with defective dragons."

"They'll be in fenced enclosures. Totally safe." I'd dug up an old set of blueprints for The Farm on Build-A-Dragons intranet server. It looked like a high-end kennel, complete with roomy pens for each dragon and an exercise yard. Describing it that way made it sound vaguely like a prison. *Best not to think about that.* But I figured they wouldn't have anyone working on the weekend, so I might be able to sneak close.

"I don't know." Summer's face had that scrunched-up look that she'd had when the rattlesnake was about to bite Riker.

I had to give her something, and I really didn't want to lie to her. I took a breath. "There's this one dragon I need to see. A flying model that I designed."

"What, one flying dragon's not enough?"

"This was a prototype to replace the Pterodactyl."

"The terrible-dactyl?"

I scowled. "I hate you."

"No, you don't."

"*Anyway*, my prototype flies better than all of our mainline models. It's awesome."

"Then why is it out in the desert?"

"We're not supposed to give any one dragon too many advantages."

"Of course not. Why would you want to give dragons *advantages*?" she asked dryly.

"I know, right? But those are the rules, and I broke them. So Greaves canceled the design before I could get a sample." *A sample that I've invested years into.*

"What do you think a sample of a dragon is going to tell you?" she asked.

"You can tell a lot from looking at the muscle fibers under a microscope." I knew, because I'd seen Connor's biopsy results several times. Muscle fibers were similar across the animal kingdom, so it should be easy to tell if the dragon's looked like his.

"So you just want to stop by and perform a brief surgery on a wild reptile."

"They're not wild, they're domesticated." *Thanks to me.* "And it won't be surgery." I dug the slim metal case from my pocket and flipped it open. Inside lay a steel-and-glass cylinder about the size of a cigar. "This is a robotic biopsy arm. Quick, painless, and automatically seals the sample in an airtight container."

"Will it hurt the dragon?"

"There's a local anesthetic included." Which did not quite answer her question, but I hoped would be good enough.

"You have this all planned out, don't you?"

"Just the black-market equipment part of it. I'm a sucker for high-tech gear."

My obsession failed to impress her. She just shook her head. "Why did you even call me for this?"

My first thought was that I didn't want to go in my own car, but if I said that, I was pretty sure I'd be walking home. I was too chicken to tell her that I'd wanted to an excuse to see her. So I settled for a middle road. "I don't know what the terrain is going to be like, and . . ."

"And what?"

For a second, I almost glimpsed the old Summer coming back. Yikes. I spread out my arms in desperation. "And you're the best hiker I know."

She bit back what was probably a cuss word followed by *you.* "I don't want to get arrested again."

"*Again?*"

"Don't ask."

Oh, I was going to *have to* ask. But that could wait. I shrugged and looked out my window. "It *is* a fair hike into the desert. I'll understand if you're, you know, not up for it."

She snorted. "Anything you can do, I can do."

"Oh, really?"

"Probably faster, too."

"Ha! Well, now you can prove it."

She didn't protest, so we got to talking about other things. She caught me up on the last year or so of her life which was far more interesting than mine. After moving out from Jane's place, she'd gone to Costa Rica for a few months. Supposedly the mission trip was to teach kids English, but it sounded like there was a lot of beach time involved.

I figured Octavius had fallen asleep, but every time I looked back,

I found him staring at up at the open sky as if hypnotized. I'd never taken him in a car with an open top before. His bright eyes never wavered. He wanted to be up there, flying free.

And I probably couldn't blame him.

"So. What does one do for a living, after a long Costa Rican vacation?" I asked.

"As I keep telling you, it was a mission trip!"

"Right, mission trip," I said, in the most dubious tone I could muster.

"I work for an architecture firm in Paradise Valley."

"Oh, bullshit."

"I'm serious."

"Wow." I tried not to show how much that impressed me. Architecture had a lot in common with engineering. I'd considered going into that myself, except Connor didn't have a broken house.

"What did you think I did for a living?" she asked.

"Hemp fashion design."

"Oh!" She glared at me. "Only *you* would say that."

I held up my hands in mock surrender. "All right, fine. You're an architect. What do you design?"

"Mostly green projects, like energy-efficient condos. Things you'd hate, in other words."

"*Actually*, I live in one of those."

"Which one?"

"Scottsdale," I said.

She looked at me sidelong for a second, then shook her head. "And here I thought you didn't care about the planet."

"Hey, I drive an electric car!"

"A Tesla." She made it sound like an accusation.

"Well, they make the best ones. Better than this gas-guzzler."

"It's biodiesel, thank you very much."

My mouth fell open. "Are you serious?"

"I converted it myself. Well, my dad and I did."

I shook my head. The more I learned about her, the more she impressed me. But there was still tension between us, from way back, and I wanted it gone.

"You know, I . . . I'm not sure why we didn't get along, before," I said.

"When you were with Jane?"

"Right. I wasn't very nice to you."

"No, you weren't." She said it so fast, so readily, that I felt like the biggest jackass ever.

"Well, for what it's worth, I'm really sorry about that," I said. And I meant it.

She nodded, and we rode in silence for a second. I knew that one apology might not be enough. *Why did I have to be such a jerk?*

"I had my own issues, back then," she said. "Jane and I used to feed off each other, you know?"

Toxicity by association. I knew it too well. "We did that, too. It wasn't healthy."

Summer cleared her throat. "I don't know if you're aware, but she was, um, *not well.*"

I laughed. It felt good. "You're kidding!"

"Crazy as a loon."

"I had *no* idea."

"You don't know the half of it."

"I know enough," I said. "But I'm still sorry."

She smiled at me, took her hand from the stick-shift and put it on top of mine. "It's in the past."

She moved her hand away, but the feel and the warmth of it lingered. I looked out the window so she wouldn't see my face—I'm sure it had turned bright red—and I just held on to the memory of what it felt like.

CHAPTER FORTY-FOUR
Shadows

We got to the turnoff at nine thirty, about fifteen minutes faster than my GPS watch had predicted. Summer had a bit of a lead foot. Or maybe she was anxious to get this over with and be rid of me for good. I couldn't be sure. She pulled over to the shoulder at the head of the unmarked road leading north.

It was hot by then, Arizona hot, but I really felt it when the Jeep stopped. The desert heat hit like a wall. Riker started bouncing around the back seat as if he could sense the excitement. Octavius chirped in annoyance—in danger of being squashed, too—and flew up to the Jeep's rail.

Summer and I both peered down at the single-lane unpaved road that led down off the highways and into the saguaros. The satellite map coverage for this part of the desert was suspiciously over ten years old, but based on the terrain, it couldn't be far.

I looked back at her. "What do you think?"

"Are you sure there's something here? Looks pretty abandoned."

"No. Look at the tire tracks." A set of them led unerringly down the road, and they were fresh enough that the wind hadn't blown the sand flat.

She looked doubtful. "Anything could have made those."

I knew what had made them—a stout pickup with an aluminum cage in the back, hauling a defective dragon. "That's it."

"All right, so we're here. What now?"

"Well . . . this thing has four-wheel drive, doesn't it?"

She snorted, spun the wheel, and floored it. We bounced off the shoulder and plunged downhill.

"Whoa!" My stomach dropped. I grabbed the *oh shit* handle.

She kept the jeep in first gear so we wouldn't skid down the slope. Smart. We leveled off and followed the winding track through a maze of cacti and craggy boulders. Maybe half a mile from the road, after it doubled back on itself, a jagged ridge rose up to one side. Up ahead, the track appeared to make a hard turn, leading through a gap in the ridge. And something lay beyond that. I couldn't see what, but once we reached that turn, we'd be exposed.

"Hey, why don't you stop here?" I asked. "I don't want to surprise anyone." *And I don't exactly have permission to be here.*

We both had our hiking boots on—it was kind of our thing, to wear our gear when we went somewhere—so we set out at an easy pace down the road. Riker kept pace with us, snuffling the rocks and debris along the edge of the road. Octavius wanted to fly overhead, but I made him land and ride on my shoulder. If there were other dragons here, live ones, they might attack without warning.

We approached the turn, where it looked like the land opened into a small canyon, with cliffs rising up on either side. The terrain lent the area some natural privacy.

"How big is this place?" Summer asked.

"Maybe a few hundred square feet. We don't have that many failed designs." Again, I felt a stab of guilt that I'd created a defective dragon just to find this place.

"Let's find it, then. I don't want my baby out in the sun all day."

I grinned at her. "I'm fine, actually."

She elbowed me in the side. "I was talking about Riker."

"Oh, right."

We reached the turn and looked right. I was expecting a small structure, maybe a dozen fenced enclosures. Instead, a massive complex sprawled from rim to rim across the floor of the vale. Solar panels glittered on the roof over what had to be *hundreds* of enclosures, all of them occupied with dragons. A boxy metallic robot—almost like a warehouse bot—moved on a track that encircled the building, dispensing something into the cages in systematic fashion. Food and water, probably. The whole place must be automated. There was no sign of any human workers, other than the ruts of Jeep tracks from where the wranglers turned around after making deliveries. Which they obviously did far more often than I realized. It would take forever to find my fliers in that maze.

Summer shaded her eyes. "It's . . . a little bigger than you said."

"Yeah." I was too shocked to even make the obvious joke. Then Octavius dug his claws into my shoulder. "Ow! Knock it off!"

The moment I loosened my grip, he launched into the air. *Shit.* "Don't go too close!" I called after him.

"He's acting weird," Summer said.

She wasn't wrong. Octavius paid almost no attention to the huge desert vivarium but glided off to the right, toward a jumbled mound of wood almost two stories tall. It was strange to see that much timber in the desert. We had rocks and saguaros, but not a lot of real trees. Octavius circled it twice and then returned rather abruptly. He folded his wings and practically crashed into my shoulder. If I hadn't caught him, he'd have plummeted right to the ground. He made a sound I'd never heard before, a low-pitched moan.

"What's wrong?" Summer sounded apprehensive.

"I don't know." I cradled Octavius against me and stalked over to the stack of discarded trees. But they weren't trees. They were bones. The closest one to me, about ten yards away, was a Laptop model. I could tell from the size and the teeth. Farther off I saw the lean, lithe skeleton of an attack dragon. The sun had bleached the bones to pure white. They looked so tiny, so *delicate*. Yet there was a wrongness to them as well. The Laptop model was larger on one side than the other, a genetic condition called hemisomia. The attack dragon was missing a rib, even though the rest of the skeleton looked undamaged.

How can this be?

I'm not sure how long I stood there staring. I just couldn't fathom it. My mind knew what I was seeing, but I didn't understand how it could be real.

Faint footsteps approached from behind me. "Oh my God," Summer whispered.

Octavius sighed against my chest. I held him close to me and stroked his back. I felt like I should say something to comfort him, but words failed me.

Summer slipped her hand around my elbow. "Come on, let's go."

I let her pull me away, then. I felt like I was walking through gel. Everything moved in slow, terrible motion. Riker took the lead without being asked, picking a way for us among the jeep track. Summer pulled me along. Thank God for them. I don't know that I would have made it out before nightfall. We climbed into the Jeep without a word. She cranked it up and flicked on the headlights, because the sun was rapidly dipping beneath the horizon. How did it get to be dusk already? A little part of my brain pondered that, but the rest of it was numb.

So much of what I thought I knew about Build-A-Dragon was a lie.

CHAPTER FORTY-FIVE
Ghosts

I tried to keep my mind on the little things while Summer drove. The sound of Riker's heavy breathing from the backseat. The feel of the sun-warmed seat at my back. The blur of yellows and greens out the window as the desert landscape rolled by, painted in twilight. Then something black and gray flashed past my window. It jarred me back to active consciousness. "Stop!"

Summer let off the gas and glanced at me. "What?"

"Stop for a second, will you?"

She gave me a weird look but jammed the brakes. The Jeep ground to a halt on the rough dirt road.

I stuck my head out to look back the way we'd come, and there it was. A gray metal post mounted in the ditch beside the road, topped with a dull steel lockbox. A black wire ran out of this down to the ground, toward the road. It looked a lot like the sensors that parks use to measure visitors, but this box had a stubby transmission antenna on top. "Shit."

"What's wrong?" Summer asked.

"It's a road alarm. I didn't see it on the way in." That explained why there wasn't a locked gate sealing off this road from the public. Locked gates drew attention. Rough jeep-tracks into the desert did not.

"Maybe no one's—" Summer cut off as headlights splashed against the ridge ahead of us where the road turned. A car was coming.

I thought about telling her to gun it, but the road was probably too narrow. "Pull over!"

She wrenched the Jeep over onto the rocky shoulder. The other vehicle came into view; it was a dark SUV with tinted windows. If they hadn't spotted us already, they would in a minute. *They can't catch me out here.* If they did, I'd have a lot to explain. Greaves might guess my real reason for coming out here. If he didn't, Evelyn certainly would. I needed a plan. I needed time! But my brain wouldn't work. Not after the shock it had just received.

Summer threw on her parking brake and turned up the music.

"What are you doing?" I shouted.

She grabbed me by the front of my shirt and pulled me to her. Then she was kissing me. It caught me by surprise. Total surprise. My brain still wasn't operating, but my survival instinct died. A new one kicked in. I slid my hands around her waist, wrapped my fingers in the belt loops of her jeans, and pulled her in tight. She was warm and so *soft*. The road and the ghost-images of dragon bones faded into the background of my mind. Summer became my entire world.

A horn blared from very close by, and a man's voice intruded. "Hey!"

Summer and I broke apart, doing our best to seem flustered. Which didn't take a lot of acting on my part. The dark SUV had pulled alongside us. A man in security fatigues and aviator sunglasses stared at us through his open driver's side window. The others were too tinted for me to see anything.

"Oh my God." Summer sounded breathless, and I decided to believe it was because of how I'd kissed her. She turned the radio down. "Uh, hi."

"This is private property," the man said. There was a second guy in the passenger seat, but the interior of the SUV too dark to see their faces. I kept my own in the shadows, on the off chance that they might recognize me. I didn't dare glance back at Octavius, but I prayed he'd stay asleep. If they spotted him, this would go south in a hurry.

Summer twirled a strand of her hair between two fingers. "Oh, sorry. We were just, um, talking." Her cheeks flushed. "I swear."

Damn, she was good.

"Yeah, sure." The man glanced at his companion, who spoke into a phone. "False alarm. Just a couple of kids."

I might have bristled at that a little bit, but I damn well kept quiet.

The guy with the phone hung up, and the driver made a shooing gesture. "Move it along."

Summer made a big show of flipping her hair and thanking the "gentlemen." I wanted her to floor it, but she drove off slowly. The SUV just sat there. I watched them in the rearview, waiting for them to whip it around and come after us. I didn't breathe again until the Jeep's tires crunched across the shoulder gravel and rolled onto the quieter highway.

We didn't say a word until we'd put some distance between us and the SUV. At last, I couldn't hold out anymore, and turned around to look behind us. The desert was all inky darkness. I let out a heavy breath. "I think we're clear."

"God. That was close," she said.

"Yeah." Some of the tension drained from my shoulders. "You're a hell of an actress."

"Oh, do you like that?" She did the hair-twirl again.

"Heh. I kind of did," I admitted.

She gave me a side-look, and I could have sworn *she* was blushing.

Then I remembered what we'd found in the desert valley, and the little bit of happiness faded.

Summer must have seen it on my face. God love her, she kept the music off and just drove.

I stared out the window and tried to make sense of the screwed-up world.

We rode in silence back to the parking lot for Big Mesa. My Tesla was there, apparently undisturbed. The usual thrill of seeing it was muted, now. Summer shut the engine off and helped me disentangle Octavius from Riker.

I put my thumb on the Tesla's biometric scanner to disarm the security system. It beeped in soft recognition.

"What are you going to do?" Summer asked.

"I don't know."

"I'm sorry. This really sucks."

"Yeah." I wasn't ready to talk about it yet. I tucked Octavius into the passenger seat. He was so small and pitiful then, still fast asleep, as if trying to dream the visions away. Then I felt her hand on my shoulder and turned. She surprised me with a hug. A real hug.

I hugged her back. "Thanks for coming. Sorry it was, well, you know."

She sighed. "Yeah."

I didn't want to let her go, but I'd already exceeded the proper hug duration. I let my arms fall against her sides. Maybe a little slowly. She eased back. Our faces brushed against one another. I held my breath.

Then her lips found mine and for three heartbeats, I forgot everything.

She pulled away, looking about as surprised as I felt. She was smiling, though. "Call me, okay?" She hopped into her Jeep. The engine roared to life, and she drove off with a wave.

I stood there like an idiot for a couple minutes, watching the Jeep disappear in a cloud of sand-dust. Then I saw Octavius, still asleep. He'd have ended up in the valley facility too, if I hadn't smuggled him home with me. I brushed his rough back with my fingertips, lightly enough that I wouldn't wake him. So little, so defenseless.

Dragons had never had a champion of their own, someone to look after them. Maybe they should. But it wouldn't be easy to advocate for them without catching all the wrong kind of attention at the company. I could defend dragons, or I could work quietly on Connor's problem. I probably couldn't do both.

CHAPTER FORTY-SIX
Crises

Mondays are never great, but the next one sucked. I dragged myself into work at the usual time. The other designers were busy and hard at work. The God Machine hummed with activity. Orders were piling up in my queue, too, but I couldn't bring myself to create another dragon when it might end up imprisoned out at the Farm. Or worse, a pile of bones bleached white by the sun. The images kept playing through my mind. Dragons packed like sardines in tiny cages. Misshapen skeletons.

So I sat and tinkered with designs without ever finishing anything.

My phone rang right as I was packing up to go home. Mom again. I'd ducked her last two calls and felt bad about it, so I hit the green button.

"Hi, Mom," I answered.

"Connor is in the hospital."

"What?" A heavy foreboding settled in my gut and leeched all the warmth from my body. "Why?"

"He collapsed. I had to call an ambulance."

I scrambled to find my keys, pressing the phone against my ear so I wouldn't drop it. "What hospital?"

I let the Tesla drive me there, because I didn't trust my hands to drive. Or my foot, to keep it below a hundred miles per hour. I parked in the visitor garage and hustled inside.

249

The harsh utilitarian style of the university hospital makes me long for the children's hospital in Tempe where we spent so many days when Connor was younger. Pediatric hospitals are warm, friendly places with all kinds of kid-friendly nooks and crannies throughout. Visiting Connor there was almost an adventure to discover new things—animal statues in the halls, or the soft tweets of electronic birds beneath the artificial trees.

The university hospital is a colder and less welcoming place from the entrance, with its massive and permanent sign about washing hands because *It's Flu Season.*

I've always hated the way the hospital smells. From the moment you walk in the door, you're assaulted with countless harsh odors. The antiseptic cleaners, and the hand-soap in the scrub-in room. The dusty-dry smell of the sterile cotton gowns. There's a sound in the hospital, too, a muted white noise from the machines. The air feels thicker somehow, as if gathering in the wide overhead spaces to press down on those who wait uncomfortably for any sort of news.

Normally, Connor's hospital room bustled with activity. He reigned from the hospital bed like a prince, always jovial, laughing and joking with the staff. The nurses and medical techs all loved him. Even when they had to put in an I.V., you'd have to watch closely to see the discomfort flicker across his face before the smile returned. He took it a hell of a lot better than I would, I'll say that much.

This time, an uncommon quiet reigned. My eyes drifted past my mom, who was half-asleep in her usual seat by his bed, to where my brother lay with his eyes half-closed. His chest rose and fell in slow breaths. The only sound came from the soft, persistent beep of his monitors.

"What's wrong with him?" I demanded.

My mom sprang to her feet. "Noah."

She tried to hug me, but I fended her off. "Why isn't he talking?"

"He's resting, but the doctors think he'll be fine. They were worried he had a myocardial infarction. That's a—"

"Heart attack, I know," I said irritably. It had been a long drive, and I felt like she weren't giving me information fast enough. "Did he?"

"The troponin test came back normal."

That was something. "Where's the doctor?"

"He went home for the night."

"He went *home?*"

"Shush. You're going to wake Connor."

But he was already awake. His eyes were moving. They flitted from us to his bed to the vital monitors on the walls. Confusion wrinkled his brow.

Mom made her voice calm, but it sounded forced. "It's all right, honey. You're in the hospital."

He leaned back a little and groaned. I knew that groan. It twisted my heart a little more than usual. Maybe because we'd argued the last time I saw him. Maybe because while I was chasing that dream of getting him a diagnosis, I really hadn't been around. Now all I wanted was to distract him. To take his mind off it for a moment.

I put an overconcerned look on my face. "Hey, buddy. Listen, if anything happens . . . do you mind if I take your gaming system?"

"Noah!" Mom smacked my arm.

A little smile played at the corner of Connor's lips. "You couldn't handle it."

"I mean, clearly I'd have to upgrade some of the janky equipment. But I think I could make it work."

He coughed. "Janky? You have no idea what you're talking about."

"Listen." I put a hand on his arm, still mock-serious. "I'm going to play under your username, in your honor. People will be astonished at the skills."

"You wouldn't last thirty seconds."

Mom sighed. "You boys. I'm going to see if I can find the doctor on duty."

She walked out slowly, sort of hunched over. She seemed so old all of a sudden, so frail. Connor's never-ending medical crises must be taking more of a toll on her than I realized. He caught me looking at her and must have seen the look on my face. He could always read it like a book.

I couldn't quite meet his eyes, but I said, "Hey, man. Sorry about last time I came over."

He waved me off. "It's cool."

"I'm just not ready to give up on what I set out to do." I bit my lip. "No matter what I have to stomach."

"Did something happen?"

I laughed, but without humor. "You don't want to know."

"Come on. I'm going to be stuck here for hours. It's basically your job to entertain me."

"Well, I designed this prototype that Greaves hated, so he sent it to the farm. That's what we call the desert facility, where they send the returns and failed prototypes."

"Okay, I'm with you."

"Where is it?"

"Out near Gila."

"Whoa, that's remote."

"Not by accident," I said. "So Summer and I get out there, and suddenly—"

"Summer?" he interrupted.

"Oh, yeah. She's new. I met her while out geocaching."

"That's the nerdy thing you do with compasses and stuff."

I blinked. "It's not *nerdy*. It's like desert survival with GPS."

"My mistake," he said, with a hint of sarcasm.

"*Anyway*, so we get out there, and—" I paused and looked around, to make sure no one else was within earshot. Mom could be sneaky when she wanted to, but she hadn't come back yet. She'd probably found a private place to drink one of those bottles in her purse.

"And what?" Connor demanded, impatient as ever.

"The place was massive. They must have hundreds of dragons living in captivity out there. It was . . . a lot bigger than I thought."

"That's what she said."

I laughed. "Yeah. But it gets worse."

He shook his head. "I mean, I knew you probably sucked at designing dragons, but—"

"Whatever, dude. But it gets worse. There were piles of bones out there, too. Dragon bones."

The smile fell from his face. "*Shit.*"

"I know. It's bad news."

"What are you going to do?"

I shrugged. "Not sure I can do anything. I wasn't even supposed to be there."

"So they're just leaving the dragons out there to die?" He shook his head. "That's messed up."

I had a dark suspicion they were putting the dragons down, not simply leaving them in the desert, but I didn't say as much. "It is, but I can't really afford to rock the boat. If I come under more scrutiny, they might figure out my secondary agenda."

He sighed. "Still with that?"

"Yeah, still with that. I'm making progress, too." I clenched my fist. "I was so close."

"Dude, you've got bigger problems now. What that company is doing to dragons . . ." He trailed off and shook his head. "Somebody's got to stop them."

I wanted to tell him that I didn't give a shit about dragons. The words were on the tip of my tongue. But I saw the color coming back to his cheeks and didn't have the heart to do it to him. I mean, Connor *loved* dragons. "But I have no power there."

"That doesn't surprise me," he said.

"Hey!"

"Seriously, man. All you gotta do is find someone who does. Someone who cares more about dragons than profits."

Something about the way he phrased it made a name pop into my head. A crazy-ass idea of a name, of a crazy-ass inventor.

Simon Redwood.

CHAPTER FORTY-SEVEN
TECH SUPPORT

Build-A-Dragon Support Chat Transcript
Operator: Li-Huei Chang
Date: March 28th

System: We appreciate your patience. A support operator will be with you in five minutes.

System: We appreciate your patience. A support operator will be with you in three minutes.

System: We appreciate your patience. A support operator will be with you in one minute.

System: We appreciate your patience. A support operator will be with you in five minutes.

Guest 14: You gotta be kidding me.

System: We appreciate your patience. A support operator will be with you in two minutes.

System: We appreciate your patience. A support operator will be with you in one minute.

Charles Smith (trainee): Hello and thank you for contacting the Build-A-Dragon company. May I have your name, please?

Guest 14: It's Johnny.

Charles Smith (trainee): Johnny . . .

Guest 14: McMann.

Charles Smith (trainee): Good afternoon, Mr. McMann. How can I help you today?

Guest 14: Got a problem with my dragon. It's defective.

Charles Smith (trainee): I would be happy to help you with that. Do you have your order number?

Guest 14: Yeah. 474638.

Charles Smith (trainee): Just a moment.

Charles Smith (trainee): I see that you ordered one of our attack dragons, with an intelligence upgrade. In, oh my, hot pink?

Guest 14: Right.

Guest 14: Bought it for my wife.

Charles Smith (trainee): I see.

Guest 14: She never wants nothing. I figured, how 'bout a pink dragon?

Charles Smith (trainee): Well done, sir. I'm sure your wife was pleased.

Guest 14: We just got separated.

Charles Smith (trainee): Ah.

Guest 14: Told me I was "selfish." Then she lit out while I was at work.

Charles Smith (trainee): I'm sorry to hear that, Mr. McMann.

Guest 14: Took the good TV, too. Who's selfish now?

Charles Smith (trainee): Did you say there was a problem with the dragon, sir?

Guest 14: Yeah. It ate the cat.

Charles Smith (trainee): What kind of cat?

Guest 14: I don't know. My wife's cat.

Charles Smith (trainee): How did it get into the dragon's cage?

Guest 14: Cage?

Charles Smith (trainee): All Build-A-Dragon orders for attack dragons ship with a reinforced metal cage.

Guest 14: Oh, that. We ain't using it.

Charles Smith (trainee): May I ask why, sir?

Guest 14: Had to keep letting the dragon out and putting it back. Lot of work.

Charles Smith (trainee): If you read the dragon ownership manual, you'll see that we recommend keeping the dragon in its cage. Particularly for this model.

Guest 14: Well, she's real pissed about the cat.

Charles Smith (trainee): Did you discipline the dragon, afterward?

Guest 14: Damn right I did. Haven't fed it since.

Charles Smith (trainee): That's not quite the guideline we've laid out in the manual. May I ask how long ago this occurred?

Guest 14: 'Bout three days.

Charles Smith (trainee): To clarify, sir. You haven't fed your dragon in three days?

Guest 14: Right.

Charles Smith (trainee): Sir, our dragons must be fed on a regular basis. It says so in the manual.

Guest 14: Never got around to reading that. It was, like, a lot of pages.

Charles Smith (trainee): Forty-two pages to be precise, sir. But that was important information.

Guest 14: Who cares? She don't want the dragon anyway. I'll send it back, and you guys can put it down or whatever.

Charles Smith (trainee): I understand, sir. Can I ask what the dragon is doing now?

Guest 14: He's sleeping on the ... oh. Guess he's right here. God, they're quiet when they want to be!

Charles Smith (trainee): I'm sure the cat would agree, sir.

Charles Smith (trainee): Did you say the dragon is right beside you?

Guest 14: Yeah.

Charles Smith (trainee): Mr. McMann, are we on a secure channel?

Guest 14: What do you mean?

Charles Smith (trainee): Can the dragon see your computer screen?

Guest 14: Guess it can. So what?

Charles Smith (trainee): It's just that you ordered one with the intelligence upgrade, sir.

Guest 14: Well, I still want to return it.

Charles Smith (trainee): That's not what I meant, sir. I'm concerned that the dragon might have followed our conversation.

Guest 14: What's your point?

Charles Smith (trainee): My point, Mr. McMann, is that you have a fully grown attack dragon beside you. And it may have learned that you're planning its demise.

Guest 14: Think I'm afraid of this little guy? Doubt he weighs a buck twenty-five.

Charles Smith (trainee): Our attack dragons are bred for killing. A single one can take down a mature lion.

Guest 14: Bull**** [off-color content suppressed]

Charles Smith (trainee): I'm quite serious, sir.

Guest 14: For real? Didn't know that.

Charles Smith (trainee): Do you have the Build-A-Dragon sedation kit with you?

Guest 14: Yep. Got it right here.

Charles Smith (trainee): Open it up, if you would.

Guest 14: Okay. What is this, a pill?

Charles Smith (trainee): It's a suppository.

Guest 14: What!?

Charles Smith (trainee): A suppository. You have to put it—

Guest 14: I know what a goddamn suppository is.

Charles Smith (trainee): Glad to hear it, sir.

Guest 14: But why would you do that?

Charles Smith (trainee): We've found it discourages returns.

Guest 14: No shit.

Charles Smith (trainee): Good one, sir.

Guest 14: That wasn't what . . . never mind. I'll give it a shot.

[Brief period of inactivity]

Guest 14: No dice.

Charles Smith (trainee): I'm sorry, sir?

Guest 14: Couldn't do it. All I did was piss him off.

Charles Smith (trainee): Try holding him by the safety harness.

Guest 14: Huh?

Charles Smith (trainee): The safety harness, sir. It should give you a better grip on the dragon.

Guest 14: You mean the leather and chain thing?

Charles Smith (trainee): Exactly, sir.

Guest 14: Yeah . . . I don't have that.

Charles Smith (trainee): I'm sorry?

Guest 14: My soon-to-be-ex-wife dropped off the dragon this morning. She didn't give me the harness.

Charles Smith (trainee): Sir, are you saying that you have no way to restrain your dragon?

Guest 14: Nope.

Charles Smith (trainee): Uh . . .

Guest 14: He's kinda staring at me.

Charles Smith (trainee): I must advise you to vacate the area as quickly as possible.

Guest 14: He's jlkkl,.,kllk/////////

Charles Smith (trainee): Mr. McMann?

Charles Smith (trainee): Sir?

[Brief period of inactivity]

Charles Smith (trainee): It sounds like we've resolved your issue. I'll be closing the chat window now, sir.

Charles Smith (trainee): I've put in a request to have another copy of the manual sent to you. Thank you for choosing The Build-A-Dragon Company.

CHAPTER FORTY-EIGHT
Celebrity Stalker

Back when the Dragon Genome Project wrapped up, a dozen startups were established, all of them vying to create a living creature from the recently assembled dragon genome. But Simon Redwood had a key advantage: access to a curated version of the dragon reference that was much higher quality than the public release. Yet even with that, the eggs he created from it were sterile. It seemed like no one would be able to bring the creature of myth to life.

Right up until Redwood built his Codex. That wire-and-plastic fire hazard ensconced at the heart of the God Machine made dragon eggs *viable*. I still hadn't figured out how. Evelyn was fuzzy about the details.

My guess is that it had something to do with the epigenetic code—various chemical modifications of DNA that didn't change its sequence, but controlled which genes were activated, and when. The epigenetic code was like Mother Nature's special sauce: a series of subtle changes required for life. It would take a half-crazy genius to figure out how to replicate it.

After Robert Greaves had ousted him from the management team, Redwood basically took a leave of absence and retreated to his home out in the desert. That's where I'd have to find him.

The problem, of course, was that no one seemed to know where he lived, and asking too many questions about him might draw attention.

Luckily, Simon Redwood's status as a kind of celebrity meant I didn't have to do all the legwork myself. I disabled the "safe search" options on my phone and plunged into the dark, obsessive corners of the internet.

Deep in a forum on celebrity stalking, I found my first clue: some nut calling herself "FutureMrsRedwood" had tracked down the man's residence in Arrowhead Ranch. The post was a couple of years old, but that was about as warm a lead as I could get. A late-night, caffeine-fueled data-mining operation followed. To his credit, Redwood surfaced from the waters of insanity long enough to guard his privacy rather well. I couldn't find a single property registered in his name in Arrowhead Ranch, nor anything with obvious ties to Reptilian Corporation.

I dug deeper.

Arrowhead Ranch's elite, gated neighborhoods had evolved and expanded into a few distinct communities over the past two decades. The most desirable and exclusive of these was the Enclave. Roughly speaking, the cheapest house there cost about ten times what I'd paid for my condo. *Yowza*. Now, to the satellite imagery. God bless all those spy satellites with their high-resolution cameras. Twenty or thirty houses sprawled inside the Enclave's luxurious borders. I pored over them, looking for something that fit my mental image of the old kook.

Most of them had the immaculately trimmed hedges and perfect landscaping that spoke to hired gardeners. Redwood wouldn't have manicured lawns or sculpted stone lions. All of these did. Then I spotted a stone mansion set apart from the others, surrounded by rugged terrain in the southernmost edge of the Enclave. I'd almost missed it because there wasn't even a driveway leading up to the house, just an old gravel road hardly wide enough for my Tesla. Between that, the haphazard landscaping, and the general feel of abandonment to the place, I figured I'd found the home of our company's founder.

Who probably didn't want to be found.

Next up, infiltration. Gated communities were fine and good until you had to reach someone on the other side. Quietly. The ironic thing, though, was that the gates only restricted vehicle access on the main road. They counted on the rugged desert terrain to deter anyone from trying to enter on foot. Fortunately, negotiating such terrain had recently become part of my skill set.

I parked the Tesla in a bank parking lot between a Mercedes and another Model S. I figured it'd be as safe there as anywhere else. *Luxury car camouflage.*

The Tesla wasn't the only thing I wanted to keep out of sight. The courier's jumpsuit I'd ordered from the internet was olive green—a recognizable corporate color that just happened to blend in with the desert landscape across the road. I tucked a narrow rectangular package—completely empty—under my arm and plunged down a narrow trail into the scrub-brush. My GPS watch started beeping, a soft, persistent tone. I had it on passive tracking mode, with Redwood's house already plugged in. I wouldn't even have to look at it—the beeps increased in frequency while I stayed on track.

On a difficulty scale, the buffer land around the Enclave scored closer to "picturesque" than "challenging." Compared to some of the terrain I'd crossed for my geocaches, it was a walk in the park. *Hell, I didn't even need my hiking boots.* What a relief that I'd not brought Octavius. He'd never let me live it down.

Stucco walls loomed ahead, and the beeping of my watch reached a fever pitch. I'd come within a hundred yards. I hit the reset button on my watch and skirted southeast. Where was the door? I was focused so much on it that I didn't see the dragon until the last second. Its brown-and-green scales made it hard to see against the landscape.

"Whoa!" I froze. "Uh, hey there."

The dragon made no reply but crouched with a jaguar's readiness. Its dark eyes narrowed. That, and half a dozen other telltale signs told me this wasn't one of our domesticated models.

It's a prototype. Like one of the dragons Evelyn had shown me when I first interviewed at Reptilian Corporation. I forced myself to meet its gaze, then I backed off. Nice and slow. Hoping, praying that it wouldn't follow. Its tongue flicked out once, twice. Then it rolled into a slow, steady step toward me.

I kept backing up and reached behind me to flail around for the boulder I'd just passed. If I slipped around it and out of view, I'd have a few seconds out of the dragon's view to make a break for it. The only good thing about the wild prototypes is that they had short legs. They could run fast in one direction but weren't good at turns. I might be able to zigzag away fast enough to reach the road.

My hand found the edge of the boulder. I edged around it, on the cusp of my break for safety. A flicker of movement from behind made me stop short. A second dragon crept into view, cutting off my escape and boxing me in with the first one. Almost like they planned it. *Son of a bitch.* I scooped up a fist-sized rock from the ground and tried to look threatening. They stared at me, tongues flicking in and out.

A whistle shattered the quiet of our little standoff. A *human* whistle. The dragons both cocked their heads at it, then bounded off in unison. Startled me doing it, too. I turned back toward the house, where a man in an honest-to-god brown bathrobe stumbled toward me on shaky feet. I watched in paralyzed fascination as he shuffled closer to me.

"The hell are you doing here?" he demanded. The bathrobe was stained and torn; it couldn't be less than a decade old. But the grizzled white face rang familiar to me, as if seeing someone I'd known in elementary school.

Oh my God. It's him.

CHAPTER FORTY-NINE
The Founder

For a minute, I didn't know what to say. This was a moment I'd been waiting for most of my adult life. I'd daydreamed about how it would go, and what I might say. How I'd impress him.

Somehow I forgot all that and blurted out an obvious question. "Are you Simon Redwood?"

He gave me a guarded look. "Who's asking?"

"I'm Noah Parker."

"Never heard of you."

"I work at your company. In Evelyn Chang's group?"

"It's not my company anymore."

It'll always be your company, I didn't say. "I have some bad news, actually. Turns out that Build-A-Dragon is doing some horrible things."

He snorted. "What else is new? That's what happens when the money-grubbers get involved, son. People sell out."

"But they're killing dragons."

"What?"

"They're—"

He held up a hand to stop me. "Not here."

"It's all right. I came alone."

He scanned the sky, a nervous rabbit wary of hawks. "They have eyes and ears everywhere. Satellites, you know?"

"Okay." I didn't think satellites could eavesdrop on conversations, but I figured this was his show. I bit my tongue.

He spun and marched back the way he'd come. "Safer to talk in the house."

I glanced back the way the dragons had gone but didn't see them. Their natural coloring matched the Arizona landscape surprisingly well. Idly, I wondered how many of our native reptiles had gone into the DGP. Evelyn would know that by rote; she was good with numbers.

I stumbled on a rock and nearly fell into the waiting spines of a cactus. *Focus on the here and now.* Redwood lurched over rocks and around bushes, his bathrobe flapping behind him like he was an escaping mental patient. Which he might very well be, for all I knew. His great stone house loomed overhead. The south wall bore no windows or markings of any sort, but Redwood marched right at it like we were going in. And then he walked right through the wall and disappeared like a goddamn ghost.

I skidded to a halt. "What the—"

I'm hallucinating. Maybe because of the heat. That seemed like the only rational explanation until Redwood's head appeared out of the stone. "You coming?"

The stone around his head shimmered. I reached out and my hand went right *through* the wall. Like it wasn't even there. *Holy crap, a holographic door.* It matched the house's exterior color and texture perfectly. I put a foot through and forced my body to follow. Darkness enveloped me on the other side of the threshold. I took off my sunglasses and paused to let my eyes adjust.

Redwood grimaced. "Whoops, I should have warned you about the hologram."

I couldn't resist sticking my hand through the opaque screen. It disappeared up to the wrist, and the bright sun on the other side warmed my fingers. "That is so cool."

Metal screeched as Redwood yanked open a battered white screen door that clashed rather nauseatingly with the house's aesthetic. He held it open. I followed him in and let it creak shut behind me.

"You might need some WD-40 on that," I said.

"Ha! You know what the WD stands for?"

I grinned. "Water displacement."

"I'll be damned, you *are* an engineer."

So much preparation, all for this moment. Part of me still couldn't believe I was in Simon Redwood's house. The storm door led to a long hallway lined with doors, all of them closed. Not just closed but bolted shut with biometric locks. Who knew what treasures lay on the other side? The hallway opened into an alcove with stairs leading up. I had to step around a leather-and-metal contraption that looked like a backpack with a pair of charred mufflers at the bottom. A pair of antique pilot's glasses dangled tantalizingly over the corner of it, their lenses coated with desert dust.

Oh my God. "Is that—is that a *jetpack*?"

Redwood marched up the stairs without answering. I fought the urge to snap a photo with my phone and ascended behind him. The staircase opened into a huge, bright atrium. Sunlight streamed in through the far wall, which was entirely made of glass. Cactus-topped dunes rolled away at a slight incline—we must be facing away from the highway—and I wagered the sunsets must have been pretty spectacular. I could see the route I'd hiked in from the highway, and the boulder where I'd encountered the dragons. *No wonder he saw me coming.*

But the real question was whether he'd simply witnessed what happened, or somehow ordered those dragons to intercept me. Wild dragons didn't take anyone's orders, or so I thought. Granted, something had seemed different about those prototypes. In the early days we'd always kept dragons isolated because of their innate aggression. This was the first time I'd seen a pair together. Not just in proximity but working as a coordinated team. Like pack hunters.

"What exactly do you do for the company?" Redwood settled into a sandalwood chair that faced the window-wall and gestured vaguely toward the matched one beside it.

I honestly didn't think the thing would hold my weight, but it didn't even creak as I settled into it. There were no joints or seams or visible bits of hardware.

"I'm a genetic engineer. I design the customs and the new prototypes."

He grunted. "Hack jobs."

"I'm sorry?"

"You're just a code-tweaker." He stared off at the dunes, as if I wasn't even there. "Developing the first prototype, now that was a challenge."

I bristled at his casual dismissal of what Evelyn and her entire group did. "Well, we did crack domestication."

"That was you, huh? Never saw the point of it myself."

"Not everyone wants a pet that'll kill them as soon as look at them," I said.

"Dragons aren't meant to be pets."

"That's funny, coming from a guy who owns a couple."

His brow furrowed, as if my jab confused him. "Oh, the ones outside. I don't own them. They just showed up here, one day."

"They're *ferals*? That's impossible."

"Why, because they're man-made?" He snorted. "Thought you knew genetics."

I bristled even more at that, because I *did* know genetics. I knew it well enough to carry out my own little experiments in the dragons I designed. My few little acts of rebellion were nothing compared to Build-A-Dragon's overall production. If enough dragons were left to die, some might manage to survive. "Unless there were compensating mutations. Or some rare, hidden resiliency."

"Given how many species went into the Dragon Reference, it's inevitable," Redwood said. "Nature likes to find a way."

"How many are there? Just those two?"

"No, I've seen others. They're drawn to the desert. And to me." He said this as a simple fact, not trying to brag or anything.

The meaning behind it struck me like a sock full of pennies. Either some fey biological undercurrent drew wild dragons to their inventor, or the dragons somehow *knew*. Somehow were aware of Redwood, and where to find him, and felt that they should go there. The two that had ambushed me weren't screwing around, either. They sensed a threat and had just about eliminated it. *Damn.*

It was a vote of confidence, the dragons protecting him. It meant they trusted Redwood, and that made me realize that I should, too.

"Mr. Redwood, I came because I need your help. The company's got this desert facility."

"The Farm."

"You know about it?"

"It was my idea."

It took me aback to think that Redwood himself would have conceived the place. "It was?"

"Of course. Made sense to have few state-of-the-art pens to observe our creations away from prying eyes."

Well, he's got the state-of-the-art part right. "Well, the company's grown a lot since you were running things. And so has their dumping ground for problematic dragons."

His face darkened, but his eyes narrowed as if I'd confirmed something rather than broken the news. "How certain are you?"

I told him everything: my Condor design, the field trial. The huge scale of Build-A-Dragon's desert facility, and the pile of bones nearby. He let me talk for the most part, interrupting only now and then with a gruff question. Nothing I said shocked him, but by the end of it he'd fallen silent.

"So Connor wants me to tell someone else what's going on. Someone with actual clout," I finished.

He barked a laugh. "And you think that's me?"

"You started the company, didn't you?"

"I did," Redwood agreed, but he sighed. "It wasn't supposed to become a corporate monstrosity."

"What did you want it to be?" I asked.

"A workshop of sorts," Redwood said. "A place where we could dream up more solutions to the world's problems."

God, I would kill to work with him at a place like that. "So what happened?"

"Same thing that usually does. People figured money was more important than anything else. And based on what you're telling me, it's only getting worse."

"I'd try to stop it myself, but I've got zero power in that place."

"That's no accident. Greaves designs companies to keep down the little people. Reinforces the chain of command, with him at the top."

I ran my hand through my hair, because he was right. "I didn't know who else to tell. I figured, it's your company."

"Used to be my company."

"Still, you've got to have some sway there."

Redwood harrumphed. "Not as much as you think."

"People will listen to you."

"Why?"

"Because you're *Simon Redwood*. You probably have a lot more fans than you realize. Greaves can't ignore you."

"Maybe you're right." He gave me a crooked grin. "Besides, I owe him a lump or two."

CHAPTER FIFTY
Moves

I left Redwood's compound feeling better than I had in a while. It was like a huge weight had been lifted from my shoulders. You couldn't ask for a better ally than Simon Redwood. He knew this company and Robert Greaves better than anyone. And he could go right to the board. And if not, he could call a press conference. Reporters would fall all over themselves in the rush to get a moment with Simon Redwood.

My own glow after basking in the crazy old coot's presence finally gave me the confidence to ask Summer out. She and I had done the geocaching thing a few times, but most of those outings ended up with some kind of natural disaster. So I went out on a limb, and asked her to come over for dinner. Granted, it took me half an hour of writing and rewriting the text until I was happy with it. I held my breath and hit Send.

Waiting for your phone to ring is like self-inflicted torture. You want to go on with your day and forget about it, but you can't. Then you have that odd moment of panic: maybe your message didn't go through. Maybe your phone switched off or the volume was down, and you're missing that all-important return call *right now*.

I wanted to call Connor and tell him about meeting Simon Redwood. He'd gotten out of the hospital, but the doctors warned that the sort of medical collapse he'd experienced might rear its ugly head again. He was still convalescing at home under Mom's somewhat-too-attentive care. She wouldn't want me to get him all riled up about anything, so that would have to wait.

Waiting. It was the absolute worst. I tried reminding myself that Summer had a regular job and probably wouldn't answer me before she clocked out. That didn't help, especially when that little voice kept telling me she might not write back at all.

I was on my way home, driving with the windows down and Steve Perry playing on the radio, when Summer texted back. The Tesla's computer took the liberty of reading it off to me.

Sounds like fun! Can I bring Riker?

I told her fine—Octavius would be disappointed, otherwise—and gave her directions to my condo. Which I nearly killed myself preparing for her arrival. The whole time, I kept sweating with nervous anticipation. But when I opened the door for Summer, it was totally worth it.

"Hey guys," I said.

"Hi." She wore a little summer dress in peach and white. Desert colors, but softer somehow. A waft of vanilla and roses swept across my face. She looked even better than I remembered. It was funny how everything between us had changed. This was a *date*, and we both knew it.

Riker was there too, on a leash, already snuffling the threshold of the door as if he smelled truffles.

I grinned, and hoped it looked welcoming rather than awestruck. "Come on in."

She stepped across the threshold so I could close the door and crouched beside Riker to unclip his leash. "Is it all right if I . . . ?"

"Go for it," I said. "He probably wants to find Octavius anyway."

"Where is he?"

"Hiding."

"Aww, he's shy all of a sudden?"

"Oh, not at all. This is his favorite game."

"All right." She took the pig's snout in her hands. "Riker, find the dragon!"

Riker yipped and ran into the kitchen, his nose already working the floor. My eyes met Summer's. They were this perfect shade of green, and she'd put on some dark eyeliner that really brought them out.

Oh, the date was *so* on.

"Hi," I said.

"Hi," she said. She hugged me, and excitement warred with the disappointment that she hadn't kissed me instead. Or that I hadn't been brave enough to kiss her. Maybe that kiss hadn't meant anything. Maybe it was just her way of being nice, to someone who just found out his employer had been lying to him about almost everything.

I wasn't giving up yet, though. "Want something to drink?"

"What do you have?"

"Everything," I said, because it was true. I had at least one of every juice, soda, beer, and wine that she could possibly want. The mini fridge was full to bursting. "But I was thinking margaritas."

She drew in a sharp breath. "Oooh..." she said, in the way that meant *I shouldn't, but I'm going to.*

"Heh. That's a yes." I headed back to the kitchen, where Riker snuffled around the pantry door. "Not there," I told him.

He moved over to the base of the refrigerator.

"Now you're getting warm," I said.

He reared up on his hind legs but couldn't see over the top of it. He even tried to hop up higher, which for a pig was pretty funny. I busted out laughing, and Summer did, too.

"I think he's got you, Octavius," I said.

Octavius uncoiled from the little fruit basket on top of the fridge. He stretched languidly, as if just waking up. His eyes flicked open, and he acted all surprised to see us. He even gave me his good-morning chirp, like he was up and ready for breakfast.

"You little ham," I said.

"So, what are we eating?" Summer asked.

"Tacos. Is that okay?"

She gave me a dubious look. "You can cook?"

"Uh, I'm a scientist."

"I never saw you cook anything," she said.

"We were in college. I lived on pizza and cheap beer."

She laughed softly. "Didn't we all?"

Talking about the old days still had the edge of discomfort to it. Even if we didn't say her name, Jane was our common denominator. I didn't want to relive the bad moments, which seemed to drown out the good as time went on. So I steered clear and changed the subject.

"Do you want fish, or chicken?" I asked. "I have both."

"What, no tofu?"

Oh, God, was she a vegetarian? I'd never considered that. "Seriously?"

She was biting her lip not to laugh. Her eyes sparkled.

"You're screwing with me," I said.

"Totally. I wouldn't last a day without meat."

I shook my head and turned on the stove. "You were almost dead to me."

"What kind of fish do you have?"

"Mahi-mahi," I said. Wild-caught, too, not the crap that they farm-raised in China. I'd spared no expense on this dinner. There was too much at stake. The deep thrill of just having her here started to well up in my stomach. I forced it back down.

"I love mahi," she said. "How about fish *and* chicken?"

"Attagirl."

"Need any help?"

It was tempting, but my kitchen barely had enough room for me. And I was a little worried I'd screw something up. "Actually, would you mind letting Octavius out onto the balcony? He likes to watch the sunset."

"I suppose I owe him one." She took her margarita to the balcony. Riker and Octavius wandered out after her.

I hardly touched my own drink. Tacos were my favorite thing to make, and I didn't half-ass it. Ten minutes later, she came in for a refill. That gave me another butterflies-in-the-stomach feeling, because I knew she meant to stick around a while. I took the meat off the stove, just as Riker trotted in to do his begging routine. Perfect timing. Summer just laughed and shooed him away. Octavius winged in to the top of the mini-fridge and trilled at me. He wanted in on it, too.

"All right, it's coming." I flipped him a few pieces of meat I'd set aside.

"Can't he go out and . . . hunt birds or something?" Summer asked.

My mind went to the Condor, and the way it had handled itself so beautifully during the field trial. The memory sobered me. "He's got limited range."

She raised an eyebrow. "Mm. Sounds like his genetic engineer screwed up."

I snorted. "I did it on purpose."

"You love to play God, don't you?"

"Maybe just a little."

We ate out on the balcony while the sun painted the desert in crimson hues. Riker and Octavius tore into their little bowls of cubed meat and were done in about thirty seconds. They settled down on the stone while Summer and I ate. I suppose I could have gone with the tablecloth-and-candles type of meal, but it just didn't feel right. Come on—this was tacos, and we were sharing the meal with a pig and a dragon.

Summer sat perfectly straight in her chair, with her plate balanced on her lap, and took these adorable teeny-tiny bites.

"You're so proper," I said.

"My parents were pretty strict about table manners."

"Oh yeah?"

"In case we had dinner with the Queen someday."

I nodded, as if that made perfect sense. "How's that coming along?"

"No invitations yet, but I'm hopeful."

"You know, the royals came and toured Build-A-Dragon last year."

Her eyes went wide. "Shut up!"

"They brought in their daughter to see her dragon hatch."

"Did you get to meet them?"

"Me? Oh, hell no. Greaves wanted all of us automatons in the background. Want to hear something cool, though?" I leaned closer to her and lowered my voice. "I designed her dragon. The daughter's, I mean."

Summer put her plate aside, turned to face me, and said, "Tell me *everything.*"

We talked for hours, while the sky grew dark and the margaritas melted. The desert air brought its usual nighttime chill, but the balcony's heat-retaining concrete kept us comfortable. Riker and Octavius had curled up in the two outer corners where it was warmest. Their bodies rose and fell in the slow rhythm of sleep.

I got up, quietly as I could, to clear away the dishes. Summer brought the margarita glasses. I started loading the compact autoclave. All my dishes were high-heat stoneware; with all the water shortages, autoclaves had replaced dishwashers almost entirely. The Pyrex margarita glasses went in, too.

It only took about ten minutes, everything being small and close-together as it was in my kitchen. We tiptoed back to the balcony door to check on Riker and Octavius. They were still out. Summer slipped her arm in mine and pulled me back. I turned and she was there, I mean *right there,* kind of giving me a little smile.

Instinct took over. The next thing I knew we were kissing.

We moved to the couch, fumbling for it because we wouldn't separate. I thought that if we did, it might stop. So I ended up crammed against the back of the cushion, with her soft slender body right up against me. My neck was at an almost painful angle, but I powered through.

We kept at it, until I let my hand stray down to her waist.

She pulled away just a little. "I should get home," she said.

"You can stay," I whispered. I tried pulling her back to me, but she put a hand on my chest, and kept a little distance between us.

"It's really late."

I may have pouted a little, but I let her go. She stood up and sort of straightened her clothes. Riker poked his head in and gave a little high-pitched whine.

"Ready to go home?" she asked him.

I walked them to the door. "I'm glad you came," I said.

"Me too. Thanks for dinner."

I kissed her again on the threshold. And I loved the fact that I could do that. It wasn't a peck, either. It was a warm, lingering kind of kiss that had me hoping she might come right back in. Which I wanted so, so bad right then. After a minute, she eased back, out of reach.

"See you," she whispered.

It physically hurt to watch her leave, but after I closed the door, I reminded myself that it had gone well. Really well. If I kept this up, Summer and I might even become a thing. A warm twinge of excitement washed over me at the thought of it. Between that, and the help from Simon Redwood, things were looking up. For the first time in I don't know how long, I could actually draw a full breath.

CHAPTER FIFTY-ONE
Extreme Measures

The events of the last couple of days put me into a dreamy, weightless haze. Food tasted better. The air seemed fresher. Hell, I didn't even mind the omnipresent heat of the Arizona sun as much. I got back into my work again and found that I rather enjoyed it. Even if there was a slight chance that any dragon I designed would end up in the killing heap at the "farm."

I wondered how Redwood would execute his plan. He had a lot of options—going to the press, or the in-house counsel, or even the board. The hour or so I'd spent with him still felt like a dream. I reported bits and pieces of it back to Summer, but kept remembering these little details—an offhand comment he'd made, or a funny little machine I'd spotted in the corner of his greatroom—and they never seemed to end.

To her credit, Summer put up with my incessant fangirling. Only once or twice did I catch her in a half eye-roll when I'd say, "Did I tell you what Simon Redwood said about this?"

Of course, I didn't dare tell anyone at work what I'd done. It wouldn't take an above-average IQ to connect the dots when he brought the hammer down. I didn't want to go down in Build-A-Dragon's history as the guy who tattled to Simon Redwood. So when Wong popped his head over the wall between their offices, I tried to play it cool.

"Noah Parker," he said, with that infectious grin. "Did you hear the news?"

"What?" I gave him a fleeting glance from the custom I had up on my simulator.

"Simon Redwood is coming to the board meeting."

"Get out! Seriously?"

"Yes."

"When?"

"Thursday."

Redwood wasn't wasting any time. "Where did you hear this from?"

"Friends."

Friends meant Wong's network of Chinese connections in the company. I liked to give him trouble that he seemed to know every Asian person in Phoenix, but sometimes I wondered if that really might be the case.

"Wonder what he wants," I breathed. *And how Greaves will take the news.*

Thursday morning, I left my condo earlier than usual to head to work, figuring that the press would make everything chaotic. Redwood's presence brought them like flies to a picnic. He'd warned me not to contact him before he made his move, or to show any undue interest. *Build-A-Dragon monitors everything*, he'd said.

Traffic was heavy, but I managed to beat all the news vans downtown. In fact, I didn't see a single one parked out in front of the building. That seemed a little off. I cracked open the door to the main floor lobby, figuring the crowds must be inside. Cool, dim emptiness awaited me instead. Where was everyone? Surely, I wasn't the only Redwood fanatic working at the company he'd founded.

I spotted Virginia at the information desk and strolled over to her. "Did they move the press conference, or—" I trailed off when she looked up at me. Her eyes were moist and red-rimmed. A single tear traced a translucent streak in her normally perfect makeup. "Oh, what's wrong?"

"I was supposed to meet him today," she whispered.

"Meet who?"

She dropped her eyes to a wooden cube on top of her desk. It was about four inches to a side. Inside its thick wooden frame, a ball bearing danced in perpetual circles between two conical magnets.

Balanced Infinity. That was the name of the child's puzzle, and I recognized it because I'd memorized every one of Simon Redwood's inventions.

A chill of uncertain dread crept down my spine as it all came together: the lack of media, the empty vans, the somber pretty redhead. *Oh, no.*

"What happened?" I croaked.

"There was a fire at his house."

I wondered if she was having a stroke, or maybe I was having a stroke, because her words made no sense. "When?"

"Last night." She sniffed and dabbed at her cheeks with a tissue. "They said it was the wiring or something."

Bullshit. I'd been to Redwood's house. That guy could have done the wiring on an F-15 if he wanted to. And if he did, it would fly better than the current F-15 did. "It doesn't make sense."

"I know."

"Well . . . is he all right?"

She let out a little sob and shook her head. "They're still searching, but the place burned to the ground."

Oh my God, the house. There went the jetpack, and who knows how many other Simon Redwood inventions? Damn it all. What a waste.

This wasn't a freak house fire. I knew damn well that someone got word of his plans and took action before he could make the fight public. The grim realization knocked the wind out of me. I leaned against the information desk, too shaken to move.

"It's not fair." I whispered.

Virginia said nothing, but sobbed softly, her slender little frame trembling. I sagged against the cold steel of her reception desk. My legs didn't have the strength to find the elevator, even if I wanted to. Which I absolutely did not.

When Virginia's phone rang, I sucked in a breath and turned tail for the parking garage. *They can charge me a personal day. I don't give a shit.*

My childhood hero was gone, taking so many of his wonderful creations with him. Even worse, the best chance of righting all the wrongs at Build-A-Dragon had been cut away.

And I couldn't help but think that it might be my fault.

✢ ✢ ✢

I don't remember giving my Tesla the destination, but it took me to my mom's house anyway. She was at work, of course, it being mid-morning on a Thursday. But Connor was home. The door buzzed open even before I could ring the doorbell. He must have been watching the cameras, must have known I was coming. I'd have known it, too, in his shoes. Call it some kind of brotherly intuition.

I found him in the living room, sprawled out on a chair, still in his pajamas. The wheelchair sat beside him. A set of medical monitors glowed on a portable nearby. That was new. His face looked like I felt. Bewildered, exhausted, and angry at the world.

He already knows. "Hey," I said.

He gestured at the projection screen, which had four news channels running at once. Three of them were on mute. The one with volume showed Casey Quinn, the beauty-queen anchorwoman for channel five, her face schooled to somberness. "On a sadder note, Phoenix lost a visionary inventor today. Simon Redwood is believed to have passed away tragically in a fire at his home."

"Oh, damn." I wasn't sure I could stomach hearing about this again.

"You believe this shit?"

"I know, man. It's messed up."

Casey continued, "We're being told from a source close to Redwood that old wiring sparked the three-alarm blaze, which left his mansion in absolute rubble."

Connor muted her and shook his head. "That's crap. Redwood never does anything less than perfect."

"He could have run the NSA from that house." I sensed the hand of Build-A-Dragon's powerful PR department once again. Spinning the story. Turning the unpalatable tragedy into an understandable accident. The type of thing that could happen to anybody. But this wasn't just anybody. This was the white knight who was going to turn it all around. More legend than man. Untouchable, or so I'd thought.

"So what happened?" Connor asked. "I thought you were going to try to talk to him."

"Oh, I talked to him. Right after some of his dragons nearly ripped my face off."

He sat up straighter. "You *met* Simon Redwood?"

I pointed at the screen, which showed news-drone footage of Redwood's mansion before it had burned. "In that house."

"Bullshit."

"I'm serious. That's where we hatched the plan."

"What was he going to do?"

"He called a meeting with the board." I shrugged. "I guess he was going to confront Greaves about the desert facility."

"Christ. No wonder they had him killed," Connor said.

Hearing that brought a chill to my guts. I'd dismissed the fire as a likely cover story without really thinking it through. Someone *had* killed him and set the blaze to cover their tracks. Someone with a lot to lose. Someone like Robert Greaves. Well, no, the rich and powerful didn't get their own hands dirty. They had people for that. People like Ben Fulton's faceless security goons.

"Of course, there is an alternative explanation," Connor said.

I'd have given anything for a new narrative about what happened to my hero. "What would that be?"

"You went to his house, didn't you?"

"Yeah. So?"

The corner of his lips twitched, as if he were fighting a smile. "Well, you're a little clumsy sometimes, so it's possible that . . ." he gestured as if for me to fill in the blanks. "You know."

I gave him a flat look. "I did not start the fire that killed Simon Redwood."

"Can we know that for absolute certainty, though?"

"Oh my God." I laughed, because the sheer ridiculousness of it all was just too much.

"Seriously, man, what's going to happen now?"

I shrugged. "I guess they'll get away with it."

He pointed at me. "You could say something."

"Oh, because that went so well for Redwood."

"Redwood called a public meeting. They saw him coming."

He had a point. Redwood had a brilliant mind for invention, but human interaction wasn't his strongest suit. Still, the guy had serious clout. "I'm just a cog in the machine." An idea struck then. A crazy, foolish idea. "You may have stumbled on a good point, though."

"Which is what?"

"Well, accidents *do* tend to happen around me."

He pursed his lips, as if giving the idea serious consideration. "An accident at the right place and time could be most inconvenient for some people."

"And the best part is, I can probably play dumb," I said.

"Definitely." Connor kept his voice casual. "I mean, for you, it's not really an act."

CHAPTER FIFTY-TWO
Spirals

That night, I pored over the satellite footage of the area surrounding the killing fields. Even with a paid upgrade from GeoEye, the area that might otherwise show a massive animal care facility just *happened* to remain blurry. It had to be some kind of paid exclusion. Greaves was no fool. He didn't want high-res satellite imaging of Build-A-Dragon's dirty laundry out there for the world to see. I stayed up too late, obsessing over the desert facility and what secret might be there that was worth killing over.

Though the next morning came painfully early, I had to return to work like everything was normal. That was the shittiest part of all. Lots of people missed work the day Redwood died—he had plenty of acolytes at Build-A-Dragon—but *life must go on*, as Greaves put in his company-wide e-mail lamenting Redwood's death.

"*Nihao*, Wong," I called over the wall as I got into my workstation.

Wong rolled out in his chair. "Noah Parker. *Ni zěnmeyàng*?" How are you?

"*Mama huhu*," I answered. Just so-so.

"Yes," Wong said. "Very sad day yesterday."

"Did you come in?"

"Of course."

I shrugged. "I just couldn't."

"It was hard. But I take no chance with visa."

"How was it around here?"

283

"Quiet. Like a ghost town."

I sighed. "Guess I should get to work."

"Same." Wong gave me a crooked smile and rolled back into his workstation.

I plugged away at design work. It was slow going. I tried to do right by the designs that came in, and I delayed as long as I could before printing new eggs. The week seemed to pass in slow motion. I trudged through it like a ghost. Finally, around lunchtime, my phone buzzed with an incoming phone call. It brought an instinctive feeling of dread. Few people called. Lately it seemed to be all bad news.

Then I looked at the display, and saw it was Summer. That perked me up a bit. I hustled out to the stairway, because we weren't supposed to use phones near the God Machine. "Hello?"

"It's Summer," she said.

Her voice made me smile. "Hi, how are you?"

"I'm fine."

The feeling of dread returned. "What's the matter?"

"Nothing. I just wanted to make sure you're still alive or whatever."

"That's nice of you," I said, though her tone absolutely had a chill to it. "I'm okay."

"All right. Well, I gotta go."

Damn, she's pissed. I couldn't imagine what for. "Summer, wait!"

"What?"

"What's going on?"

Silence.

"Did I say something to upset you?"

She sighed. "I admired him too, you know."

"Who?"

"Simon Redwood."

"Oh." A slow breath escaped me. "I didn't know."

"You're not the only one having a shitty week, is all I'm saying."

Oh, hell. "I'm sorry. I just got caught up at work."

"So you're still working there."

"It's a long story."

"Is it? You work for a company that kills dragons. Whose founder just died in a mysterious fire."

I wanted to tell her what I was really doing here. What I could do for my brother, if I could only get my hands on the right dragon. But the steady LED of the staircase surveillance cam stared at me like a baleful eye. Maybe I was being paranoid, but I could practically feel Fulton watching me on his monitors. "I can't talk about it."

"I guess we don't have anything to talk about, then."

"Summer—" I started.

The line went dead.

I tried to get back to work, but the Summer thing gnawed at me. I tried calling her a few times that afternoon but got no answer. She was pissed, and it was my fault. I hadn't realized that she might be upset about Redwood, or about my coming back to work. I'd only been thinking about myself. From her point of view, we'd been getting close and then I suddenly ghosted her. The realization brought a tightness to my chest. I suppose I could have given her time to cool off and then try again, but every minute I spent knowing that she was pissed at me made my stomach hurt more. I could practically sense the gulf forming between us.

That was the emotional straw that broke the camel's back. Everything started to spiral. I'd failed my Condor, failed my brother, and now I'd failed Summer. The one bright spot in my recent existence—Simon Redwood—had been ripped away from me, too. No, not just me. From the world.

All those failures had one thing in common: Build-A-Dragon's desert facility. If Greaves had secrets, that's where they were. The more I thought about it, the more I *obsessed* over it, the more I convinced myself that I had to go back there.

But the place was huge. I'd never be able to cover it by myself, at least within a short enough time period to avoid any security patrols. Octavius would help, of course. It still might not be enough. I needed four or five of him.

Four or five of him.

That gave me a crazy idea. A small act of rebellion that would lay the groundwork for a much larger one. It was time for me to start printing dragons.

CHAPTER FIFTY-THREE
Shell Game

My plan for building a small army required going to work every day like everything was normal. It was harder than I imagined. At the best of times—in the middle of the domestication challenge, or just before my Condor's field trials—I looked forward to work. Some days I even jogged from my car to Build-A-Dragon's shining front door. Now, a heavy non-specific dread replaced the excitement when I passed through the lobby on my way to the elevators. Virginia took a leave of absence, and they replaced her with a matronly woman who glared at me like I was a trespasser every time I walked by. She glared at everyone that way but losing Virginia's warm smile rubbed salt in my emotional wounds.

Build-A-Dragon's design floor got busier than ever. We had some new ad campaign running, and the orders were rolling in. Hatchery staff bopped in and out constantly, moving eggs from the printer to the hatchery. Evelyn scurried across the design floor no less than a dozen times a day. There was an uptick in tours as well, and the tour guides *loved* our floor. Every time I turned around, there were twenty faces pressed to the glass, staring at me. Pint-sized kindergarteners, gangly high school students, even stooped elderly folks from the nearby senior centers. I felt like a museum exhibit. So did my fellow designers. We hid behind our workstations as much as we could.

The good news was that I had my printing privileges back. Evelyn was probably monitoring my activities, but she was far too swamped to pay close attention. The bad news was that we'd gotten a new accounting system to manage the workload. Every egg that came off the printer had to be linked to an order. One dragon requested, one delivered. I could have gotten into the systems code and spoofed some false orders, but that was risky. The company had various auditing systems and double-checks in place to prevent fraud. I couldn't circumvent all of them, and any changes would leave an electronic trail pointing right back to me.

The Design group did have a company account that we used to print new prototypes. I could create an order with that, no problem. But the moment an egg rolled out and hit the scale, its weight would be compared to the expected value from DragonDraft3D. If they matched, the account would be charged, and Evelyn would get an invoice. That would raise a red flag no matter how busy she was. Everything in that system was pretty much locked down to me, except for one part: the scale that verified eggs as they came out of the God Machine. It had failed before—that's how I ended up with Octavius.

Whenever no one was around, I started tampering with it.

O'Connell still had the new flying model assignment—which sounded to be shaping up like a Terribledactyl 2.0—so custom orders and support requests dominated my daily work. It amazed me how many customers wanted dragons that resembled very specific dog breeds. If I had to guess, they were filling a void that their departed dogs had left behind. In the space of three hours, I designed somewhat obvious reptilian versions of a golden retriever, a dachshund, and a labradoodle. All of those were too big for my needs. Even so, by the time I'd printed the eggs, my scale was off by half a kilogram. Then I came across a custom order for a light green Laptop model that was "extra clever." *Couldn't have asked for a better subterfuge.* Rather than starting with a Rover model, I imported the specs of the design used for Octavius. I balanced the traits a little more—moving some intelligence points to claws, teeth and agility— but kept the diminutive size. DragonDraft3D estimated the egg would weigh 0.48 kilograms. *Bingo.*

I checked over the design one last time, and then ran it through the simulator. The predicted dragon could have been Octavius's older brother. Slightly stockier, perhaps, and a shade less clever. Probably how Connor considered me. I chuckled, though it sounded nervous to my ears. Now came the riskiest part: a shell game with my now-inaccurate egg scale. I went back to DragonDraft3D and hit the print button.

The God Machine's hydraulics kicked in. The metallic printer-arm danced around for a couple of minutes, and then the thing beeped. I rolled my desk chair to put myself right between the output tray and the surveillance camera. I couldn't keep it from hitting the scale entirely—that's why I'd been tampering with it—and I had to make sure the egg didn't show up on camera, either.

The God Machine fell silent. The egg rolled out. I didn't make a grabbing motion or anything, just sort of let it tumble up into my palm. It was only a shade bigger than Octavius's egg had been. I leaned forward to cover the motion of slipping it into the pocket I'd sewn into the inside of my lab coat. If anyone was watching the feed, I wanted to look confused. I peered up into the God Machine, like I was still waiting for the egg to come out.

Then I shrugged and went back to my workstation. I even glanced back over my shoulder a couple of times, like I couldn't figure out what had gone wrong. DragonDraft3D had gotten the error message from the printer by that time and prompted me on whether I wanted to try re-printing the egg. I looked pointedly up at the clock and chose "No." Then I started typing up a support ticket to the robotics group, the geeks that kept all our machinery running. I didn't send the ticket but kept it up on my screen in case I had to explain it later.

I stood, stretched, and walked to the break room. Build-A-Dragon stocked a full refrigerator with drinks and had plenty of snacks. Another little perk of working here. I'd stashed my insulated lunch box behind the refrigerator, right where the hot air coming off the coils would hit it. I tested the temperature with my palm. Still toasty warm. Perfect.

I slipped the egg inside it, carried it back to my desk, and set it down by my backpack. My workstation beeped with a message: a new order had come in.

I decided to roll with it, and act like the new order suddenly became my top priority. I minimized the window with the robotics ticket, switched to DragonDraft3D, and got to work. The customer wanted a courier dragon, a fleet little flying model that could see in the dark. Oh, and it had to spout flame, too. Most customers could never resist checking that little box on the form. I worked on the design for a couple of hours, while the design floor cleared out and Build-A-Dragon's windows darkened. I'd print the egg first thing Monday morning. I loaded my lunch bag into my backpack as if everything was normal.

Out of sheer paranoia, I took the stairs instead of the elevator. You never knew who might pop on, and I couldn't count on a good poker face when I was smuggling a dragon egg out of the building. When I entered the stairwell, the odor of fresh paint hit me like a wall. Uh-oh.

I only got two floors down before I ran into the paint crew. They had a scaffold up so they could paint the ceiling. Seriously, who paints the ceiling? I couldn't get around it without squishing my bag, so I had to cut over through the main part of the second floor.

This took me through the customer service department, a sea of grey-walled cubicles that buzzed with the sound of a dozen telephone conversations. It was after seven, Arizona time, but a lot of our customers in East Asia were just waking up. And they demanded perfection from their dragons. It must have been a cultural thing. I caught snippets of conversation as I passed.

"I'm sorry to hear about your trouble."

"And how many hamsters do you think he ate?"

" . . . made it clear that custom-made dragons can't be modified once they've hatched."

Yet another unwanted dragon in the world. Perfect.

Octavius knew I was up to something the moment I walked into the condo. He'd been waiting for me just inside the door, which he did sometimes when he didn't feel like playing hide-and-seek. Maybe he noticed the unusual weight of my lunch bag, or just read the expression on my face. He hopped over and started nuzzling around my legs. His version of a body search.

"What's got you so excited?" I asked.

He took to the air and began zooming around me, bumping my backpack with his nose.

"Hey, stop that!" I swatted at him but missed. *Damn, he's getting quick.* "All right, settle down and I'll show it to you."

I drew the curtains first and made sure the door was locked. Put my phone and laptop in another room, just in case. I sat down at the table and eased the egg out of my lunch bag. It was the color of limestone and dappled with gray and ochre.

I eased it to the center of the table and held it there so that Octavius could have a look. His claws clicked on the wood as he approached it, hunched low, pink tongue flicking out every few seconds. He circled it a few times, then settled down on his belly. He looped his tail almost all the way around it and made a new sound: a soft, undulating buzz from deep in his throat.

"Are you purring?" I didn't know dragons could even do that. Yet another quirk of biology that our simulations didn't predict.

I carried over the old-school desk lamp and set it up. Octavius slapped it almost lazily with the end of his tail to turn it on. He stretched out then, enjoying the heat. You couldn't ask for a better egg-sitter.

Just like that, I had the first of my little dragon army. Over the next four days, I smuggled out four more the exact same way. They incubated in the warmth of my old lamp while I tried not to think about my next utility bill. In the meantime, I surveyed the target using every terrain and satellite map I could find. The current satellite images might be restricted, but I was able to pull up older imagery from the archive. Taking the direct road into the facility wouldn't work. I'd gotten away with it once, thanks to Summer's quick thinking—just remembering it brought tandem flashes of excitement and dismay—but now Greaves would probably have his security people on high alert. The archived maps revealed an old highway that wandered in from the northwest, maybe a mile and a half from the field itself. It might be close enough. Of course, a mile and a half of raw desert country might take hours to cross. I didn't like the idea of trying it alone. I had a couple of weeks before my reptilian strike team would be ready. That might be enough time for me to win back the best geocacher in Phoenix.

CHAPTER FIFTY-FOUR
Reparations

Summer had effectively ignored my efforts to reach her so far. Ghosting me was only fair, I suppose, but each passing day made it more likely that she wouldn't stop. I needed to do something bigger. A grand gesture.

I considered going to her house, but that seemed overly aggressive and creepy. Especially since I didn't know where she lived. Yes, in the modern information age, I probably could have figured it out. Few things remained hidden anymore. But I hadn't looked. I wanted to come by it honest. All that being said, her work was fair game. She'd told me about it already. Her architectural firm had a small but elegant building on the edge of Scottsdale. Summer wasn't a send-me-flowers-at-work kind of girl. I might not know her through and through, but I knew that much. Instead, I resolved the send her the most persuasive messenger I knew.

The Courier, Build-A-Dragon's smallest mainline prototype, offered a reasonable cover story. It was a cute thing—a Wong design, as a matter of fact—but sales had been slow for the first few months. Then some talk show host had sent one to her friend on national television or something, and suddenly orders blew up. Now it wasn't unusual to encounter little Couriers with their recognizable message tubes flapping overhead on city streets, or even swooping down an office hallway.

I put in a request with Sales, under the guise that I was doing product support and needed an example message tube. Then I went down to Chinatown, to find one of those little hand-carved puzzle boxes that would fit inside the tube. Cost me a small fortune, because the damn things were apparently harder to make small. But I figured out how to open it and put a little handwritten message inside. Mostly numbers: time, date, GPS coordinates.

She worked at the main branch, on the third floor. I saddled up Octavius with his courier tube, explained what he had to do, and smuggled him into the building in a backpack. I let him out on the third floor and hustled out of there; it would blow all the drama and mystery if she spotted me.

I told myself that Octavius should be fine in there. Most people gave Courier dragons a lot of leeway. The little reptiles were easy to recognize with their trademark message tubes.

I kept running this through my mind while I waited for Octavius. In truth, I was worried he might be found out. He was an unlicensed, unregistered dragon. I'd already learned what Greaves did to those.

I loitered outside the building. Getting more nervous by the second. Wondering if maybe I'd made a big mistake. Grand gestures were fine and good, but my little dragon meant the world to me.

What was I thinking? I shouldn't have risked him on this. What if he got hurt, or someone reported him? I'd be up to my eyeballs in crap at Build-A-Dragon. Even worse than that, they'd take him away. And probably send him to the desert facility, to die out in the unforgiving desert sun.

Damn it!

A shadow crossed the sidewalk. There he was, gliding languidly down from the building's upper level.

"Octavius!" I snapped.

He saw me and banked over, taking his time about it, before landing on my shoulder.

"Took your time, didn't you?" I couldn't keep all of the hurt out of my voice.

He crooned noncommittally, as if he'd done his job and didn't want to hear any complaints.

"At least tell me that you got the message to her."

He trilled an affirmative.

My stomach did a backflip—one half excited, and the other half sick with nerves. Either I'd just earned a shot at winning Summer back, or I'd screwed things up for good.

Saturday morning, I waited in the Tesla at the coordinates I'd sent to Summer and hoped to God she would show. Things weren't looking good, though. I'd said nine o'clock, and it was already ten after.

Not once in our time together had she arrived late.

By 9:15, I had to accept the inevitable. *She's not coming.*

My heart sank. I don't know why it surprised me. I'd been a total ass to her. Again. Girls like Summer didn't stick around when you were an ass. They didn't have to. There were ten guys like me who hadn't screwed up yet and would be happy to swoop in. Just the thought of it twisted my stomach in knots. *Stupid.* I pounded my steering wheel in frustration.

Thunder rumbled in the distance and grew steadily louder. No, not thunder. A car engine.

I didn't dare to hope until Summer's recognizable Jeep rolled into view. *Yes!*

She had the top down, which explained her wind-tossed hair. She was no less gorgeous for it, though. We met in the empty space between our cars. Octavius took off to do a little circuit of the area but chirped a greeting at her as he passed.

Summer wore a pair of white strappy sandals, the first non-hiking-boot footwear I'd seen her in. How did she manage to get her feet perfectly tan? No sign of Riker, which made our greeting slightly more awkward. *Never underestimate an overzealous pig's ability to break the ice.*

"Hey." I wanted to hug her, but I could tell from her body language it wasn't going to happen.

"Hey."

"I'm glad you got my message. Was Octavius a convincing courier?"

"He missed my desk and landed in the trashcan."

"Oh jeez. Sorry about that." *But not really, because it worked.*

"So, I'm here," she said. "What do you want?"

I did my best not to wince at her tone. "Well, I invited you for three reasons. First, I wanted to apologize for not calling you sooner.

The Redwood thing...it just totally crushed me." My voice shook a little. It wasn't acting. "I didn't know it did the same to you, and I'm really sorry."

She looked away. "It's fine."

When a girl said something was *fine*, was not fine. I knew that much. I sighed to myself, because I didn't want to burden her with this, but she clearly wasn't going to be impressed with remorse. "I don't think he died in an accidental fire. I think the CEO of my company had him killed, so he wouldn't intervene."

"Shit. Really?"

I shrugged. "It adds up. Redwood had called a meeting with the board. It was supposed to happen on Thursday. The day *after* the fire."

"Damn."

"The worst part is, I think it's kind of my fault."

She shook her head. "It's not. Even if that's why he died."

It meant so much to me that she said that. It made me brave enough to confess reason number two. "Second, I wanted to say that I missed you. A lot."

She looked away from me, out toward the desert. "It didn't seem that way."

"I know. But I really did."

She pressed her lips together but said nothing.

"I even missed Riker a little."

"Oh, now I *know* you're lying," she said. But a hint of a smile betrayed her lips.

"I'm serious. Pigs aren't as bad as I thought."

"All right, what's the third reason?"

"This." I held up the little watertight tube that we'd meant to set as our geocache, on the day we found the desert facility. *The day we first kissed.*

She brightened. "Our geocache. I almost forgot."

"I didn't. Do you know where we are?"

"On the southeast edge of Tonto."

She meant Tonto National Forest. Which was technically correct, but not what I was going for.

"We are at the exact midpoint between the Tortilla Flat cache by the Salt River, and Red Rock Run in Sedona."

She gave me a look that I can only describe as guarded. "Tortilla Flat was my first geocache in the league."

"I know. Red Rock Run was mine."

"How did you find that out?"

"Because I studied you, SumNumberOne. I know everything about your storied geocaching exploits."

"So basically, you're a stalker."

That caught me off guard. I started stammering a protest. Then I noticed she was biting her lip. "You're messing with me, aren't you?"

She giggled. "Little bit, yeah."

"You are *mean*." The time felt right, so I hugged her. She hugged me back, and it was the most wonderful feeling in the world. I moved back, aware of the big dopey smile on my face but powerless to fight it. "Well, crap. The only problem is, I forgot to tell you to bring boots."

"They're in my Jeep."

Relief flooded through me. "You brought them."

"I never go anywhere without them."

What a girl. "I like the way you look in those sandals, though."

"Oh, shush."

We hiked about a quarter mile from the road, cresting two shallow ridges that ran parallel to one another. After the second rise lay an almost-impenetrable wall of saguaros. Right in the middle was an ancient one absolutely riddled with woodpecker holes. Summer and I grinned at one another, because it was somehow fitting to put our cache in there. We climbed over to it, and both took a pinpoint reading on our watches. I took her hand and compared the numbers to make sure we got it right. Nothing was more frustrating than reaching someone's cache but not being able to complete the end-goal.

"Looks good," Summer said. She laced her fingers into mine and smiled at me.

Yes it does. "I'll upload everything to the database tonight," I said. "It should go live in a couple of days."

"Aw, I feel bad making you do all of the work."

"There's a way you can make it up to me."

"Well, that didn't take long. What do you need?"

"You," I answered quickly. "And Riker, if you want to bring him. To help me get back to the desert facility."

She gave me a side-eye, but it was a playful one. "You need us to find a place you've already been?"

"So much." I squeezed her hand.

She laughed. "All right. Count us in."

CHAPTER FIFTY-FIVE
Desertscape

The following Saturday, I sat in my car on the shoulder of the old highway, watching the sun rise over the desert. I'd managed to arrive first but only by asking Summer to meet me half an hour later. I told myself it was so I could scope the place out first. In truth, part of that was simply an eagerness to get Octavius and his new siblings out of my condo before they destroyed it. Hadrian was emerald green. Titus, a fiery orange. Nero was amber and Otho a darker brown. Marcus Aurelius was supposed to be yellow but looked more gold in the light of the early morning sun. Despite their young age, they nearly matched Octavius in size and could fly pretty well. Watching them bond had been fascinating. The hatchlings not only accepted Octavius as a littermate, but also seemed to confer him the eldest-sibling authority. He helped keep them in line, admittedly with mixed results.

A familiar and distant rumbling grew louder behind me. Summer coasted past and parked on the shoulder in front of me. There were no doors on the Jeep. Only a seatbelt and her hand on the wheel kept her from falling right out of the vehicle. She was *hardcore*.

"Hey!" she called.

"Hi there." I grinned. Her casual confidence gave me a boost. I climbed out of my car and jogged over. "I don't know if you realize this, but your doors are missing."

"Doors are for amateurs." She killed the ignition and reached back to unbuckle Riker, who bounced with excitement.

I patted his head. "Hey, buddy."

Octavius flew over, landed on the edge of the Jeep, and flicked his tongue out at the pig. All his siblings followed, swooping down on the Jeep's rail with the eager clumsiness of toddlers. Riker snorted in alarm.

"Are all these yours?" Summer asked.

"Octavius wanted some siblings," I said. "Meet Nero, Otho, Hadrian, Titus, and..." I looked around in a moment of panic. "Marcus Aurelius, get back here!"

The little golden dragon was gliding out toward the saguaros with an air of casual innocence. He dropped his head guiltily when he heard me and turned around. He zoomed down to join his fellows, knocking Nero from his perch and onto Riker's head. The pig snuffled him, to the amber dragon's obvious alarm. He scrabbled back to find refuge on the spare tire.

"Wow," Summer said.

"It's been a long week."

She laughed. "I'll bet. So, are you ready?"

"One hundred percent," I lied.

"Do you think this is a bad idea, going back there?"

"Probably. But I've got to do *something*." I saw the uncertainty on her face and added, "You don't have to go, though. This is my fight."

She snickered. "You wouldn't last five minutes in the desert without me."

"Oh, really?"

"Really. Where are we headed?"

I beamed the coordinates to her watch. She oriented herself, and then pointed. "That way. About a mile and a half."

Riker jumped to the ground and trotted off in the direction she'd pointed. The dragons all took wing and followed, chattering excitedly.

"We'd better take it slow." I waved to Octavius. "Keep everyone close, buddy." *You might not be the only dragons around.*

Summer and I hiked mostly in silence, checking our watches every few minutes to stay on track. The terrain forced us to make occasional sidetracks—around a pile of boulders, or a thick clump of cacti—but I fought to keep heading southeast. There was a constant breeze out of the north, dry and warm and smelling faintly of creosote.

I kept looking ahead, trying to catch a glimpse of the facility. The satellite imagery for this part of the desert was sparse, even in the archives. The scrub-brush obscured our view. Half a mile out, we still couldn't see much of anything. I was about to step around a tangle of scrub-bushes when Riker gave two sharp grunts.

"Stop!" Summer said.

I froze mid-step. "What?"

"That's his warning grunt." She bent to put a reassuring hand on the pig's back. "What is it, boy?"

Riker gave a little whine and rolled his eyes at the bushes.

I shaded my eyes and peered into them. When I saw the round shadow that hung there, I went cold inside. "It's a beehive!"

Summer's face paled. "Shit." She grabbed Riker's collar and pulled him back.

I crept after them, all too aware of the humming undercurrent from hundreds of insects. Africanized hybrid bees had colonized the entire southwest, despite numerous government-led campaigns to eradicate them. They were more aggressive and more likely to swarm than regular honeybees. Most people knew them by another name.

Killer bees.

I'd never been this close to a nest before. If they thought we were a threat, hundreds of bees would swarm us in seconds. Blood pounded in my ears. My whole body tensed. The raw, animal survival part of my brain screamed at me to break and run for it. But that might draw them out. We had no viable shelter, no nearby water. We'd be completely exposed.

That dark thought reminded me. *Where the hell are the dragons?*

I'd lost track of them when Riker grunted. Now I scanned the sky, growing more frantic each second. At last, I spotted them gliding lazily around a boulder.

"Octavius, get over here!" I beckoned him with short, frantic gestures.

He ignored me, or maybe didn't hear me. His siblings followed him in a lazy circle right toward the hive. Totally unaware.

"Octavius! *Scorpio!*" That was our code word for emergencies, one of the first things I taught him. And thank God, it worked. He banked over and swooped back toward me. The other dragons chased him, thinking it was a game. That was fine. Octavius landed on my shoulder, and I took Summer's hand. We backed away one step at a time. It seemed to take forever. Finally, we got far enough that we couldn't hear the buzzing.

"We'll, uh, give that area a wide berth," I said.

Summer hugged Riker tight against her. "Damn right we will."

I tapped Octavius. "Keep everyone high up, okay? Warn us if you see anything."

He launched himself from my shoulder and chirped orders to the other dragons. They followed him up higher, maybe thirty or forty yards, and fanned out ahead. It unnerved me a little to have them so visible, but I never wanted to come that close to killer bees again.

The terrain grew rougher, jumped with rocks and razor-sharp cacti. Summer and I had to keep our eyes on the ground. We covered maybe a quarter mile and then I heard a sharp hiss from above. Hadrian, the emerald dragon, hovered in place and ducked his head toward the ground.

"Shit," I said. "Looks like another beehive."

We backtracked again. Ten minutes of hiking, and then got another warning from above. Octavius made the spot this time.

"This can't be a coincidence," Summer said.

"No." They were spaced too evenly, and in a straight line. *Almost like fence posts.* Whether they were placed to keep trespassers out, or the dragons in, I couldn't be sure.

It was midmorning by then, and the desert was really heating up. We called the dragons in and took a water break. Summer didn't say it, but I could tell what she was thinking. If things kept going this way, we'd have to quit. Nothing at the desert facility was worth trying to sneak past killer bees.

We moved east again, and the landscape changed. A wide, angular rock formation rose up out of the desert scrub. Two stories tall, but not terribly steep and free of scrub. Most importantly, no apparent beehives. I even sent Octavius up and over, to check it out. He came back humming to himself, undisturbed, which I took for a good sign.

I looked over at Summer. "You ever do any rock climbing?"

CHAPTER FIFTY-SIX
Jailbreak

It was almost ten by the time we set foot on level ground on the far side of the rock formation. It was strenuous, if not technically challenging. The hardest part was watching Riker negotiate the rocks with apparent ease. I told myself that his lower center of gravity gave him an unfair advantage. We rested in the shade beneath an overhang and drank more water. The heat had grown from mildly unpleasant to stifling. Though Summer and I carried two water bottles each, it was going fast. We hiked over the top of the next ridge, which turned out to border the vale of the desert facility. It looked much the same as I remembered it, a broad steel structure of holding pens beneath a sea of solar panels. Our elevated viewpoint revealed what I'd suspected the last time: there were holding pens on every side. That made for hundreds of them. The massive track-robot that tended them was on the left side, moving steadily clockwise.

"Let's wait until it turns the corner," I said. It looked automated, but it probably had at least one video feed.

Summer nodded and bent down to hold Riker in place. She'd sweated through her tank top and was covered in dust from our climb. And just as attractive.

Focus, man. I forced my eyes away, back to the facility. The robot turned the left-side corner and started moving out of view. "Let's go."

The terrain offered few challenges here—it was uneven but less rocky and had little slope to it. I told Octavius to keep his siblings close by. It was hard to predict how they'd react to seeing other dragons, especially ones in cages. But as we got nearer, I began to appreciate the scale of the massive complex. I didn't like it, but I was going to need all of them.

I called Octavius closer. "Okay, buddy. Are you ready?"

He trilled an affirmative.

"Find the Condor!"

He winged off, chirping at the other dragons. They spread out into a loose formation, gliding low across the tops of the shallow ridges. I'd used my simulator to give them an idea of what the Condor models looked like. They were larger than most other prototypes, which would help. Summer and I picked up our pace as we neared the cages. The nearest one held a purple-and-green Rover model. It was eating noisily out of a stainless-steel bowl but looked up in interest as we approached. It seemed more curious than wary.

"That's a Rover," I told Summer.

"Those colors are a crime against nature."

"I know, right?"

"It's not your Condor, though."

"No." Not one of my designs at all; of that I was certain.

"You want to split up?"

I opened my mouth to protest, but she was right. This place was massive, and my Condors could be anywhere. "All right. Just for this row, though."

She turned right and moved at a fast walk past the row of cages. I went the other way. The next cage held one of the stout police dragons, the K-10. After that was a steel-gray Laptop model with stunted wings. I wondered if that was an intentional choice from the designer, or yet another biological accident.

"Is this it?" Summer called.

I spun and jogged down the row of cages. She pointed at a large flying dragon. I had a brief surge of excitement and then a blanket of disappointment. "No, that's a Pterodactyl. See the small head? A Condor is a bit smaller and leaner, too."

I turned back around. Summer walked to the next cage. "All right, what about this one?"

It took a minor effort not to roll my eyes. *She doesn't have to be here helping me,* I told myself. But I turned around anyway and checked the cage. There, right on the other side of the bars, was one of my Condors. It lay in the middle of its holding pen, ignoring its bowl of food, its large wings wrapped neatly around it. The wings were probably what had caught Summer's attention, but for me it was the eyes. They'd haunted me since the day of the field demonstration. "You found it," I breathed.

The Condor watched us but didn't move. I couldn't believe that we'd come this far and found it. Octavius returned and circled overhead, trilling happily down at us. They'd found another one.

Meanwhile, Summer had moved closer to inspect the door of the holding pen. "These are hydraulic. There should be a control panel somewhere that opens them."

I looked left and right but saw no control tower or any structure. Just a long line of holding pens. "All right, but where?"

"It'll be flush with the wall. Probably on one of the corners."

"Stay here." I jogged past her, counting cells as I went. After I hit fifteen, the cells ended, and I came to a large metallic plate set in the wall. Maybe two yards wide and one tall, covered in a grid of heavy-duty buttons with green LEDs above them. And here I'd been concerned the controls might be too complicated to figure out. I started at the rightmost switch and counted back fifteen, then found the next one over. I waved at Summer and shouted, "You ready?"

She pulled Riker back away from the cages and waved back.

I jabbed the button. A deep motor thrummed behind the wall. Octavius and his mates had located another one down the right-hand side. With luck, the control panel would be right around the corner rather than the far end of the other side. My first Condor was emerging timidly from its cell as Summer and Riker watched in fascination. *Yeah, it does have that effect.* I jogged around the corner and the panel was right there. But fifty yards down the line, so was Ben Fulton.

"Parker!" he shouted.

Shit. What the hell was he doing here? I had no time to carefully count the switches. I made a guess and jabbed the button. Then, on impulse, I pushed several more.

Fulton cursed. "What are you doing, kid?" He broke into a run.

I ducked around the corner, preparing to shout to Summer that we had to go, we had to run. But I looked up and saw she was already up. Pulling Riker toward us, and in the custody of two men. They wore desert-style fatigues and heavy combat boots, the kind you could walk right over a cactus wearing and not feel a thing. Sunlight glared from the assault rifles in their hands.

CHAPTER FIFTY-SEVEN
Dark Wings

I refused to acknowledge the men with rifles who stood over me and Summer. We'd been ordered to sit on the ground. Fulton stood off to the side, talking on his phone. To Greaves, almost certainly. It was midday and blisteringly hot. I could feel the heat of the sand through my clothes. Summer clutched Riker against her chest. Octavius and his mates wheeled overhead, chasing one another, completely oblivious. They still thought this a game. There was no sign of the Condor I'd set loose. A few Rovers were milling around the metal tracks, probably waiting for the big food-delivering robot to return.

Fulton hung up his phone and marched over. "It's not looking good for you, Parker."

Of course, it wasn't. If that was Greaves on the other end, my plans were well and truly borked. "How did you find us?"

"I saw you tagging the dragon wranglers' vehicles in the parking garage," Fulton said. "Thought I might find out why."

Well, shit. I'd forgotten his surveillance obsession. "It's Saturday. Do you work seven days a week or something?"

"When someone trips an alarm on a secure facility, yeah." Fulton frowned at me. "This is private property, son."

"We didn't know," I said flatly.

Fulton gestured up at the small cloud of dragons circling overhead. "You want to tell me where you got those?"

"Right after you tell me where you got yours," I answered.

"I don't know what you're talking about. If I had an unlicensed dragon, I sure wouldn't be stupid enough to bring it onto someone's private property in front of witnesses."

I shook my head wordlessly. There was nothing for me to say.

"Call them down to you," Fulton said.

"What are you going to do to them?"

"Well, it just so happens we have some vacancies at this desert facility."

No. He didn't just mean the dragonets, either. He meant Octavius. Keeping my smart little dragon in a steel-barred prison cell would be worse than torture.

"Don't make me ask again," Fulton said.

I met his eyes, pleading. "Come on, man."

"It's better than the alternative, Parker. Trust me."

Behind him, and out of his view, the two gun-toting psychos both made a strange gesture, putting two fingers to their right ear. *Who's talking to them?* I didn't know what that was about, but a heavy sense of dread pooled in my gut.

"I understand." I climbed to my feet. "Octavius! *Gemini!*"

Octavius wheeled and chirped at his fellows. I closed my eyes and prayed he'd remember what to do. I felt Summer's hand slip into mine. I squeezed it and closed my eyes.

It took Fulton a second to realize what I'd done. "Oh, hell."

Octavius and the other dragons had scattered, bolting for cover. *Gemini* meant *go to ground.* I only prayed they'd reach shelter and stay hidden.

His men cocked their rifles. The harsh, metallic sound echoed among the boulders.

Fulton waved at them. "Stand down. Those little dragons won't get far."

The guard on the left, the one with the square jaw who'd shot my Condor at the field trials, shook his head. "Orders, sir."

Fulton rounded on him. "You get your orders from me, and I said *stand down.*"

"Sorry, sir. This comes from the top."

They lifted their rifles and began firing. The noise was *deafening.* Summer screamed. I did, too. My mind started to go. Apparitions swept across the pale desert sand behind Fulton and his men. Sleek reptiles crested the ridge on clawed feet, their tongues flicking in and out. Dark shapes rose into the sky behind them, gliding over the ridge and down on silent wings.

I'm hallucinating. I knew it when I saw my own Condor with them. Not the one I'd freed, but the one from the field trials. Twice as large, twice as majestic as I remembered. If only that were possible. *Visions, then.* These were the dragons of my past. All my failures had come back to haunt me. They were beautiful, though. I didn't regret having made them. The ground trembled as they charged at us. My Condor passed in front of the sun, casting us in shadow.

Fulton glanced back over his shoulder. His eyebrows shot up. He opened his mouth, closed it, and took two slow steps away from the ridge. Was he hallucinating, too? I still doubted what I saw, until the wind from the Condor's wings rose to a tempest and on my face. *Oh, shit!* I dove on Summer and Riker, carrying them to the ground.

Fulton's men spun around. The sun went dark. Then light bloomed again, and a man screamed.

The square-jawed mercenary squirmed on the ground, clutching his face with bloody hands. The Condor swept around to make another pass. But the element of surprise was gone, and the remaining mercenary trained his rifle on it. The *crack-crack-crack* of the rifle made the Condor fold its wings and drop behind rocks for cover. More dragons were pouring over the ridge, but they scattered when they heard the gunfire. The Condor swept back into view, flying almost straight up into the sky. My heart sank. The mercenary spun and tracked it with his rifle.

He did not see the shadow ghosting toward him on the ground. It had a lean, muscular body and flowed over the rocks with a serpent's grace. An attack dragon. The gunman got off two shots at the Condor. Then he must have sensed the danger. He tried to bring the gun down. The dragon slid in like an assassin's knife. Its jaws closed on the man's thigh. Then it wrenched its whole body in a violent gesture. Blood fountained across the sand. The man bellowed and went down beneath a blur of teeth and claws. His bellow became a scream. A high, terrible scream. I had to look away. A wave of nausea swept over me and made my knees week.

I felt Summer's arm around my chest. She pulled me back and away. Something *snapped* with a wet crunch. The man no longer moved. The attack dragon coiled itself over him and looked around. Its catlike eyes fixed on us. All of us froze.

Fulton looked down at the ground beside him. One of the rifles had fallen there, almost at his feet. Fulton flexed his hands.

"Don't!" I whispered.

"Stay where you are," Fulton said. Whether he meant me or the dragon, I couldn't be sure.

"That's an attack dragon. If it sees you as a threat..."

He glanced at the gun again but straightened and backed toward us.

The dragon looked from Fulton to me. I met its gaze. Not challenging but acknowledging.

It flicked its tongue in and out, smelling me. Smelling us.

"We're friends," I whispered.

The dragon cocked its head, as if it heard my fervent prayer. Then it hissed and advanced on us.

Small energetic wings flapped in my ear. A familiar weight settled on my shoulder. Octavius curled his tail around Summer's neck and crooned two short, high notes.

The attack dragon halted in its tracks. Then, almost in slow motion, it turned its eyes to Fulton, who stood apart. Who didn't have his little dragon friend to vouch for him. I knew what would happen next, but there was nothing I could do to stop it.

Fulton dove for the gun. The attack dragon reached him before he could fire. It pivoted and lashed out with its back leg. A three-inch killing claw slashed Ben Fulton's throat. He groaned and sagged to the ground.

The attack dragon gave Summer and me one last look, then bounded off.

I ran forward and crouched by Fulton. Blood stained the front of his shirt. I ripped off the bottom half of mine to try to staunch it, but there was just *so much*. He was still alive. He looked at me and tried to say something, but only a gurgle came out.

"Hold on, man. Just hold on."

He gurgled again. Two syllables. *My house.*

"Your house?" What did he want? My brain wasn't working. Neither were my efforts to stop him from bleeding. It was pointless.

Fulton looked at Octavius, who still clung to my shoulder. Then I understood.

"He's at your house?" I asked.

Fulton gave a nod, and then coughed blood.

"I'll look after him."

He stiffened, then went completely still.

I don't know how long I stayed there, kneeling in the sand beside Fulton. Summer had come up and put her arm around me. A shadow fell across us both, and we looked up. An old man with a shock of white hair and a beard to match stood before us.

It can't be. Maybe I was having heatstroke. Or the psychotic break had finally come.

"Looks like you were right about this place," he said.

I stared up at him. "Thought you were dead."

"Son of a bitch," Summer blurted out. "Are you Simon Redwood?"

"Who's asking?"

I scrambled to my feet. "This is Summer Bryn. She's a friend."

Redwood looked from me to her. "Yeah, I'm him. Or I was, at least."

"Your house burned to ashes," Summer said.

It was a nonsensical thing to say, because obviously the man knew it. Then again, I'd been just as eloquent the first time I met him.

"Yeah, how in the hell are you still alive?" I asked.

"I was warned a minute before the arsonists set fire to my place." He raised an eyebrow at me. *By the dragons*, he seemed to be saying.

"That was lucky," I said.

"Got out just in time."

I had the sudden and completely irrational urge to ask him if he'd escaped with the jetpack. Because it would be such a Simon Redwood thing to do. Before I could, he looked down at Fulton.

"What happened?"

"It was an attack dragon."

"A custom?"

"Yeah." *One of mine.*

"I'm sorry. We didn't always see eye to eye, but I liked him."

"Me, too," I said.

A pack of small flying dragons—Laptop models and Couriers, as best I could tell—arrived and began circling overhead, chattering excitedly. Octavius and his mates had flown up to perch on the roof of the facility in a row. They watched the new arrivals with rapt admiration.

Redwood cocked his head. "My friends tell me that there's something inside the facility that we need to see."

CHAPTER FIFTY-EIGHT
Ghosts

We made an odd procession as we hiked around the perimeter of the desert facility. Redwood led the way, accompanied by a motley assortment of dragons. Some were recognizable Build-A-Dragon production models—most commonly Rovers and K-10s—but others had a wilder look to them, like the ferals I'd encountered at his house. The facility's layout reminded me of a medieval fortress, with the long lines of holding pens as the outer walls. Redwood's dragons led us to the middle of the southern edge where there was a gap.

Summer hesitated on the threshold and glanced behind us.

"What's wrong?" I asked.

"The tracks don't come in here."

"Maybe they don't keep dragons on the inside."

She furrowed her brow but said nothing. We passed into the inner ring. There were no enclosures on the inside of the walls. Only the tall, unmarked steel inner walls. There was another building within, a dark hexagonal building whose glass-and-steel walls reminded me, strangely, of Build-A-Dragon's office downtown. It had an oddly corporate feel that contrasted sharply with the rugged vivarium. The air around was hot and still, but the building itself hummed.

"What's in there?" I asked.

"No idea," Redwood said. "It wasn't part of the specs for this place."

The dragons were acting strangely. They perched on the vivarium's inner rooftop, or sat on their haunches below, keeping some distance between themselves and the black building. There was a single door on the front with a metal frame and tinted glass panels. I saw the access panel beside it and felt a wave of disappointment. *A biometric lock.* All this time, all this way, and now we'd never know what lay at the center of this odd place. Time was running short, too. I could sense it. Whoever Fulton had spoken to on the phone would be trying to reach him, demanding an update. When he didn't respond, they'd send another team.

I approached the panel and touched it with a knuckle. The screen flickered to life and confirmed my fear. "It's a biometric lock. I'm sure I don't have access." There was someone who probably did. Ben Fulton. But I knew what that would probably take, and I didn't have it in me. "Damn."

Redwood stumped up next to me. "Here's a crazy idea." He put his hand on the scanner. The light scanned it, and two wonderful words flashed in bright green letters. *Access Granted.*

I stared in disbelief. "How?"

"Funny thing about being dead. No one thinks to remove your profiles from the biometric locks."

A buzzer sounded, and I yanked the door open before the system could change its mind. A roaring cacophony sounded from the opening, a noise so loud and unexpected that I nearly let go of the door.

"Is that—" Summer started to say.

"Dogs barking," I said.

The dragons around us shrank back even more, hissing and unfurling their wings. And no wonder. It was a daunting, staccato sound that no dragon had ever heard. I pulled the door open and walked in. Motion-activated lights illuminated the entryway as Summer and Redwood followed me in. The light quieted the barking some and made its source clear. Holding pens lined both sides of the central corridor, and each one of them held a dog. A *living* dog. The first one was a black lab. Beyond that was a small terrier, then a yellow lab, and then . . .

"Ooh," Summer breathed. "A golden." She reached through the bars and scratched him behind the ears.

"I'm not sure we should—" I started, but there was no point in protesting. Summer laughed as the retriever panted and basked in her attentions. God, I'd forgotten the warm fuzzy feeling that a joyful dog brought, even to the darkest of times.

"It's probably all right," Redwood said quietly at my shoulder.

"What about the disease?"

"See the scars on his muzzle?"

I saw them just as he said it, the hairless furrows along the bottom jaw. "He's already got it." I felt a pang of sadness, remembering when the unmistakable signs of fate had marked my own dog.

"*Had* it," Redwood said. "Those scars are old."

"So he got better?" That didn't sound right. Dogs didn't survive the epidemic.

Summer glanced back at us. "How is that possible?"

Redwood scratched his head. "If I had to guess, this dog was successfully treated." He marched forward, checking the other enclosures. Each one held a dog of a different breed. I couldn't pick out the scar on the bulldog, but they were plain on the snouts of the German shepherd and the beagle.

"I feel like I'm watching the AKC dog show," Summer said.

She was right. I shook my head, still amazed. "It's like, one of every major breed." I turned to Redwood, who'd pursed his lips in thoughtfulness. *So why isn't he surprised?* "What is this place?"

"A ghost of Robert's past."

"What?"

Redwood turned to face me. "You seem to know your recent history, so let me ask you this. Do you know what Robert Greaves did before he came to Reptilian?"

"Biotech," I answered. "One of the big pharmas. I can't remember which."

"Bingham Pharmaceuticals. He ran the Canizumab trial."

Which failed right after he left. I still remembered the news cycle from that week. We'd been waiting for them to announce the trial's success, which would mean that every dog still alive had a shot at effective treatment. Instead, Canizumab totally failed, and the collective dismay robbed the world of any meaningful enthusiasm for finding a cure. That was the week we knew dogs were doomed. "These are the test cases. The ones that got the medicine."

"Why would he intentionally sink his own trial?" Summer asked.

"Because if dogs come back, we'll sell a lot fewer dragons," I said. Redwood pointed at me and touched a finger to his nose.

"What an *asshole*," Summer said.

"Seriously." I turned to Redwood. "So, what are we going to do?"

"Don't ask me." He grinned. "I'm dead, remember?"

"You're kidding."

"I assure you, I'm not. Death suits me for the time being."

I chewed my lip, thinking. *Well, we need a record of this at the very least.* I took out my phone and took a video of the healthy, boisterous dogs as we walked back to the door. They must have sensed that we were leaving, because their barks grew to a near-deafening level. I was forced to stop my video to cover my ears.

We stepped back out into the Arizona sunlight. A welcome respite, or at least it would have been, were it not for the full-on animal brawl happening outside the door. I'd totally forgotten: we'd left Riker alone with all the dragons.

Two of Redwood's dragons had pinned Riker up against the wall of the inner building. They were lean, muscular things. Big, too. *Guardians*. The original hog-hunting dragons. Of course, they'd go after him. They were bred to hunt wild hogs. They'd have killed him already, except for the handful of little dragons barring their way. Octavius and his five littermates formed a protective half-ring around the pig, wings spread and fangs bared. The Guardians circled and snapped at them but couldn't get through. I would have intervened, but Summer took two steps and kicked the nearest Guardian right in the chops. It grunted in surprise and hissed at her. Summer wound up *again*. The dragon thought better of it and ran off. So did its fellow. Summer glared after them.

"Where did you find her?" Redwood asked me quietly.

"Out in the desert."

"Don't let her go."

I laughed softly. "Not planning on it."

"Something tells me I should take my dragons out of here before any of them are injured."

"Probably a wise idea." I turned at him and shook his hand. "Thanks for . . . everything."

Summer hugged him goodbye, and I tried to suppress the natural flare of jealousy. Then he put two fingers in his mouth and whistled. He walked back up the ridge where he'd first appeared. Most of the dragons followed. It was like watching the end of the strangest parade ever.

"We should get moving," I said.

"Yeah. Wait, did you get what you needed from the Condor?"

The biopsy. I shook my head. "They're long gone."

"Let's find the others."

"We don't have time. If Greaves sent another team, they'll get here any minute."

Summer eyed the route back to the rock formation and our cars. "They might see us if we're on the rocks."

She was right, and if they did, they could drive around to intercept us before we reached the highway. Granted, we could hide at the base of the rock formation and wait them out, but that would put us in the direct sun for hours. With virtually no water. I jogged over to the control panel where the lights still shone steadily green over most of the switches. I picked twenty or so buttons at random and pushed them in. *You know what? Screw it.* I pushed the rest of them. The hydraulics whirred into motion.

I jogged back to Summer. "That ought to keep them busy for a while."

An hour later, Summer and I crested the final ridge and saw our cars waiting for us. Talk about pure euphoria. It was like hatching-my-first-dragon euphoria. Or first-kiss-with-Summer euphoria. We grinned at one another, both of us nearly dancing with relief.

"Uh, I hate to ask you this," I said.

"You can come over to my place."

"How'd you know?"

"Your company knows where you live, don't they?"

"Absolutely," I said.

"Do they know about me?"

"I don't think so."

"You didn't go bragging about me to your coworkers?"

I felt my cheeks turning red. If I'd thought I was allowed to brag, or had someone to brag to, I would have. Because Summer was totally bragworthy. "I don't really talk about personal stuff at work."

"That's good," she said, but she didn't sound like she meant it. She muttered something about how I "could have bragged a *little*." Then she beamed her address to my watch. I disabled the Tesla's alarm, opened the door and dug my flashlight out of the console. Then I knelt on the ground and used it to look up under the car.

"Son of a bitch." There it was. A black rectangular shape with a rubber antenna, and a blinking green LED. I squeezed my shoulder under the car, grabbed it, and tore it loose. They'd had to use an adhesive, because the Tesla's frame was a non-magnetic alloy.

"They tagged your Tesla," Summer said.

"Taste of my own medicine, I guess."

Later, halfway to Summer's place, I pulled into a gas station to get rid of the tag. The first lane offered an appealing option: a mud-spattered 4x4 plastered with bumper stickers for energy drinks. The owner was probably inside stocking up on some of those. Or a six-pack. It looked like the start of a promising off-roading expedition out in the desert.

I tossed the tracker into the back and zipped away. Greaves would need a Jeep to track that one down. Or a helicopter.

My last task made me a little sad. The Tesla's GPS and computer were on the same circuit. I wouldn't put it past Greaves to have someone hack the system as a backup. I pried off the lid of the fuse panel.

"Just what do you think you are doing, Noah?" asked the car.

I laughed. God love the engineers at Tesla for that little Easter egg. "Sorry about this, beautiful," I said. "I have to pull your fuse for a while."

"Tampering with the fuse panel will void your warranty."

"I know." I half-expected her to keep up the classic dialogue. *I'm sorry, Noah, I can't let you do that.*

But she made no further protests. I pulled the chip and the screen went dark. Everything was manual now: no autopilot, no navigation, no traffic avoidance. Back to the basics.

Summer had a condo in a green development in Scottsdale. She swiped me in to the underground parking complex so I could stash my car. We rode the elevator up to her floor, with our animals in tow. We didn't talk. She probably sensed that I needed quiet to figure out what to do next.

Summer's condo was roomy compared to mine. But with water

prices being what they were, the real perk was the eco-shower. It was a deluxe model, with no less than six cycles: spray, foam, mist, lather, rinse, turbine dry. I fed Riker and the dragons while she used it, and then I had a go myself. It was absolute bliss. No wonder she smelled so good.

By the time I dried off, Riker had fallen asleep in his crate. The dragons were all piled in a heap around it. Summer, meanwhile, had dressed in a pair of shorts and a skimpy tank top. Her damp hair was the color of shadowed honey.

"You forgot to close Riker's crate," I whispered.

"I never do. It's his little fortress of solitude."

"Even while you're at work?"

"Of course," she said. "He behaves himself."

"How do you know?"

"Piggy cam."

I started to ask where the camera was, but she twined my fingers with her and pulled me down the hallway. It seemed like a good time to avoid idle conversation. I followed her on cat feet, praying I wouldn't trip and wake the pets. She pulled me into the dimness of her bedroom and eased the door into the doorframe. *Snick.*

I slid my arms around her waist and pulled her up against me. She let out a soft little breath and leaned back so I could kiss her. She started to turn around, but I held her there, kissed her again. Slid my hands up under her shirt. She wasn't wearing anything under it. Her breath was hot against my cheek. She turned around then, and her hungry lips found mine.

My phone rang. I fumbled with one hand to try to turn it off, but Summer heard the incessant buzzing and pulled back. "Is that your phone?"

"It's not important." I tried to kiss her again.

She dodged me giggling. "You'd better check it."

I sighed dramatically and dug it out of my pocket. *Connor.* He and I rarely had phone conversations that lasted more than two minutes, so I hit the button to answer. "Hey, C-biscuit."

Summer tried to slip away but I held her around her waist. She protested silently. I struggled not to laugh.

"N-terminal. Need you here, pronto." His voice had a strange sense of urgency to it. Excitement, maybe.

God, what now? "What for? Is something wrong with Mom?"

"Mom's on wine tour, dummy. I just need you here, *Aquarius*."

Connor and I had code words, too. It had been years since we talked about them, but I still remembered. Aquarius meant *no more questions*.

I put the phone to my chest and whispered to Summer. "Connor needs me."

"Go," she said.

"Be there in twenty," I told Connor, and then hung up. *And this had better be important.*

CHAPTER FIFTY-NINE
Latent Abilities

I parked out front and jogged up to the door to Mom's house. It buzzed open. I entered, inhaling the familiar smell of the place where I'd grown up. It calmed my nerves a little. "Connor?"

"Out back!" he called.

We had a decent-sized yard that, like virtually every other yard in the area, couldn't keep grass alive. Connor was out on the wide deck that Mom had had built as a consolation prize. I slid open the door and stepped out. "So, what the hell is *so* imp—"

The rest of that sentence died in my throat, because Connor was sitting in the ancient tri-fold lounge chair between two coiled-up dragons. Not just any dragons, either. *My Condors.*

"Hey man, glad you could stop by," Connor said, with a casual air.

My mouth worked, but I couldn't seem to formulate a proper sentence.

Connor grinned. He was clearly enjoying this. "So, what's new?"

"Where did they come from?"

"You tell me, bro. They just showed up."

"What?"

"Dropped into the yard like a couple of dive-bombers. Nearly wet myself, if I'm being honest."

"When?"

"I don't know. Maybe an hour back," he said.

"You only called me twenty minutes ago!"

He shrugged. "They seem like they know what they're doing. I assumed you were going to show up after. When you didn't, I thought I'd give you the heads-up."

There were so many questions. How had they found him? Why had they come? I shook my head before I went down the rabbit-hole searching for answers. *First things first.* "I need something from my car. Nobody fricking move!" I said, addressing Connor and the dragons both. They blinked at me and didn't seem to be in a hurry to leave, but I ran anyway. Some jack-wang had double-parked by my car, so I threw open the passenger side door, grabbed the biopsy tube, and hustled back inside.

Connor feigned surprise. "Oh, you're back? I was just chilling here with these dragons."

"Yes, yes, you're super cool." I held up the tube. "Know what this is?"

He squinted. "Isn't that your Swedish-made p—"

"Shut up. It's your future. A biopsy pen."

"I've had enough biopsies for two lifetimes, thanks," Connor said flatly.

"It's not for you. It's for them." I pointed. "These are the flying dragons I designed, you dummy! With your mutation in them."

Connor's mouth fell open, and for the first time in recorded history, he had nothing to say.

"I have no idea how they found you, but I doubt it was an accident." I watched the dragons as I said this. They stared back with those too-knowing eyes.

"Did Redwood send you?"

The dragons snorted and shook their heads.

"Redwood?" Connor grabbed my arm. "Wait, Simon Redwood? Is he—"

"Alive, yes. He saved my ass today."

"I knew it!" He pumped a fist.

"Keep it to yourself." I looked at the dragons. "You came on your own."

They did not disagree.

I exhaled slowly. "Oh my God."

"This is unreal," Connor said.

"And it's your lucky day. Because we're going to prove once and for all that your mutation is pathogenic."

Connor laughed. "You think you're going to give one of them a biopsy? Dream on."

The dragon on the right uncoiled itself and approached me. I'm not sure what I expected to happen. But it knelt in front of me in open invitation.

I looked at Connor. "You were saying?" I crouched down and ran my fingers along the dragon's thigh. The thicker the muscle, the easier this would go.

"What do you call this model, anyway?" Connor asked.

"The Condor."

"Aw, you named it after me?"

"I named it after the bird."

"Sure, sure."

I rolled my eyes. Then I met the dragon's. "Are you ready?"

It gave me the unblinking stare that seemed to mean *yes*, so I jabbed down on the plunger. The Condor stiffened momentarily. Then the tube sealed itself, the sample tucked neatly inside.

"All done." I inspected the leg. There was a tiny red pinprick of blood where the needle had gone in, but that was all. I rested my hand on the dragon's leg. "Thank you."

Meanwhile, Connor had moved over and managed to take a selfie with the other Condor.

"Dude!" I said.

"Mom's always saying she wants more pictures of us."

"Don't post that anywhere."

"Don't worry."

I stood up and examined the biopsy tube. "I have to get this into a freezer." I looked at the dragons. "You two should get back to the desert."

The nearest dragon crooned at me with unmistakable attitude.

Connor laughed. "I think he just called you a dummy."

Both dragons stood and unfurled their wings. They leaped off the deck and flew across the yard, gaining speed, before gliding up into the sky between the next row of houses.

Connor stared off at the direction they'd gone. "I'm going to remember this day. This was the best possible day."

I clutched the tube against my chest. "Can't argue with that. Keep your phone on."

I left him on the deck and left by the front. On the way to my car, I shot Summer a quick text that things were fine and I was on my way back. When I went to get into my Tesla, the double-parker was still blocking me in. It was a black SUV, and the engine was running. Probably some moron on his phone. I moved to the passenger window so I could politely tell whoever it was to get out of my goddamn way. The window was already open and staring at me through it was Robert Greaves.

Some primal instinct made me freeze, as if Greaves were a T-rex that could only spot movement.

"Get in," Greaves said.

I looked around. The street was deserted, other than us. I could run, of course, but he already knew where my car and my mom's house was.

"No need to panic, Mr. Parker. I just want to talk."

Dr. Parker, I thought, but managed not to say. I lifted the handle and climbed in. The tinted windows cloaked the interior in dimness, but not so much that I couldn't pick out the wood paneling and fine leather. It smelled brand new. I pulled the door nearly shut behind me but kept it from latching.

Greaves looked mildly amused. "You're a cautious one, aren't you?"

"I try to be."

He peered past me at the house. "That's your parents' place, huh?"

"My mom's." I cleared my throat, aware of how nervous it sounded. "She's due back any minute now."

"Do wine tours offer door-to-door service now? That's news to me."

I clamped my mouth shut before another obvious lie snuck out. Greaves was too smart to be so easily fooled.

"How's your brother doing?"

"Great," I said, because in one sense it was true.

"I had a younger brother, too. Did you know that?"

I looked at him to try to get a read on his face, but it might as well have been invisible. "I did not."

"Michael. Two years younger. He died when I was eight."

I'm sorry to hear that would be the polite and expected thing to say, but I refused to give it to him.

"We lived in a house a lot like yours. Had an elderly neighbor, Mrs. Benkert. She never said no to an animal in need, so the shelter persuaded her to foster a couple of terriers."

I wondered where this was going but didn't ask. The longer he babbled on, the more likely people were to notice us here, and the safer I'd be.

"You probably don't know this, but *terrier* was a loaded word in the animal rescue business. They'd call a dog a terrier mix when trying to find it a home. Ninety percent of the time, that meant something else."

"Pit bull," I said.

He raised his eyebrows. "That's right. I forgot I was talking to the guy who cracked domestication. Well, the dogs they pushed on Mrs. Benkert were obviously pit bulls. My brother and I didn't know. One day we wandered into her yard, and they came out of nowhere." He pushed up the sleeves of the black shirt he always wore. Scars from animal bites decorated them like tattoos. "A hundred and eight stitches. And I was the lucky one. My brother didn't make it." He tugged his sleeves back down.

"That . . . really sucks," I said, fighting the sense of empathy before it became any stronger.

"Yes, it does. And I think it might help you understand why I have no interest in allowing dogs to return to this world."

"That's not your decision to make, though, is it?"

"You're absolutely right. At the moment, it's yours." He picked up a sheet of paper from the dashboard in front of him. It had the Build-A-Dragon letterhead. "I've got two letters here. This one is the notice of your termination and forfeiture of your stock options. There's also an affidavit on trespassing and destruction of property that will be forwarded to the local police."

Yikes.

"I think you might prefer this letter," Greaves said, lifting the second sheet from the dash. "This is your promotion to senior designer, with authorization to develop several new prototypes. There's also a considerable budget to support your independent research projects." He paused and looked at me. "Up to and including human therapeutics."

Human therapeutics. That meant gene therapy, or customized

small molecules. Maybe even a trial, and I could pick the patients. Connor would be at the top of that list.

"There's also a memorandum in which I recommend you for a seat on the company's board of directors, in the newly created position of employee advocate."

"Is that a voting membership?" I asked.

He chuckled. "It wasn't, but it can be."

I nodded but didn't say more. My head was spinning.

Greaves stacked the two papers on top of one another and handed them both to me. "I want you to come in Monday morning, and bring whichever of these letters you want me to sign."

I got out of the car, clutching both letters in my hand, and watched the dark SUV drive away.

CHAPTER SIXTY
WHO LET THE DOGS OUT?

PHILADELPHIA, PA—The American Kennel Club announced today that its annual dog show will resume next year on Thanksgiving Day. The beloved event, which had been on hiatus since the onset of the canine epidemic, will include sixteen of the world's most popular breeds and feature entries from around the world. Dog lovers everywhere celebrated the news.

"This is a dream come true. It really is," said Katherine Oliver, a two-time category winner who specializes in German shepherds. "I'd just about given up hope."

The event will be sponsored by Bingham Pharmaceuticals, whose biologic drug Canizumab received approval last month to treat the devastating canine facial tumor disease (CFTD). Hundreds of breeders have already received the drug and permission to administer it under compassionate-use exemptions. The reports thus far have supported an almost complete protective effect when delivered in the first sixty days of a dog's life. With these encouraging results, breeders have taken their mating pairs out of expensive "clean facility" vivariums and brought them home to encourage, well, *rapid production*.

"We have a waiting list a mile long," said one breeder, who declined to give his name.

Meanwhile, conservation agencies have begun delivering Canizumab to the few remaining gray wolf populations that have survived in the wild using specially baited "traps." Experts caution, however, that the recovery of wild animal populations affected by CFTD will be measured in years, not days.

Recoveries in financial markets, however, have been rapid. Animal supply companies reported their best quarter in three years as investors jumped to capitalize on what is certain to be a booming market. On the other end of the pendulum, stocks of companies in the so-called dog replacement sector continue their sharp decline. Leading them is the Build-A-Dragon Company, a legacy of the late inventor Simon Redwood, whose board voted last week to remove Robert Greaves as CEO. He was replaced by Evelyn Chang, who headed the company's genetic engineering team.

Dr. Chang admits that demand for some of their production models had diminished. "Even so, there are a number of niche markets where a dragon still holds tremendous appeal," she said.

The bevy of good news has largely overshadowed a still-unresolved mystery. How did a "record-keeping error" cause one of the country's leading pharmaceutical companies to misplace critical subjects from their efficacy trial? Where were they kept, and how did this serious mistake come to light? There is much to celebrate, but this reporter would still very much like to know.

Who let the dogs out?

CHAPTER SIXTY-ONE
New Directions

The call came on Saturday morning, when Summer and I were on a special geocache at the Apache Wash trailhead. An unusual cold front had kept the temperatures down, but we still started early in the morning. I wasn't sure how long this would take, and I wanted to make the most of Summer's off-hours—being at home while she was working had started to drive me a little crazy. That was one reason for starting early. The other was the fact that we were trying something new this time, and I really wanted it to work.

I pulled up behind Summer's Jeep and put it in park. The dragons shot out of my car the second I opened my door, Octavius in the lead, and Benjy at his shoulder. I never got his name from Fulton, so I'd named him in the man's memory. He and Octavius were born troublemakers and had grown especially close. Perhaps not as much as Nero and Otho, who could communicate almost silently. Hadrian and Titus, the green and orange dragons, acted more like rivals than bosom buddies. And last of all there was Marcus Aurelius, who had to be cajoled out of his doze in the backseat. It astonished me that genetically similar dragons could have such diverse personalities.

But they were a herd, all of them, and they'd even adopted an extra member outside the species. Riker lumbered out of Summer's Jeep and was swarmed instantly in a hail of flapping wings. I skirted around the tangle of pig and dragons to hug Summer. "Hey you."

"Hey." She smiled that dazzling smile and hugged me back. "Did you bring it?"

"Yep."

"Is this going to work?"

"One way to find out." I jogged back to my Tesla, activating my bluetooth headset. "Call Connor." The phone connected and barely rang once.

"N-terminus," he answered.

"C-string."

"Are we go for launch?"

"Give me a second." I threw open the trunk and lifted out a quad-copter drone, careful to keep the rotors away from my car's frame. Supposedly, this was one of the more durable camera drones available to civilians, but given how much Connor and I had spent, there was no need to test that claim at the moment. I set it on the ground two yards from my Tesla. Then I thought better of it and moved it another three yards. I pressed the power button, and green LEDs flashed in response. "All right, the drone is live."

"Stand clear, please," Connor said.

I called Octavius to my shoulder, which usually helped to keep his mates close. Summer clipped Riker onto his leash. Then the drone's rotors spun and it ascended ten, twenty feet into the air. It held that altitude and rotated as Connor tested the controls. Octavius flicked his tongue in and out, watching it.

"Looking good," I said. "How are the controls?"

"Smooth as silk," he answered in my ear.

"Try the video."

"Already running. Nice hat."

Well, the video was working. "Thanks."

"The first waypoint is about point-six miles down the trail. You ready?"

"Just about."

The drone banked and zoomed off. Octavius clawed my shoulder.

"Ow! Fine, you can go. But don't get too close to that thing," I said.

He launched himself and winged off after the drone. The other dragons chirped excitedly and took off after him. Even Riker hurried forward, practically dragging Summer across the gentle dunes.

I couldn't believe I didn't think to try this before. Connor could use his ridiculous computing setup to be part of this from home, at least until he could get out here in person. The muscle biopsy that the

Condors had allowed me to take showed classic signs of muscular atrophy, and genetic sequencing confirmed that Connor's mutation was the only possible explanation. Dr. Sato helped me write up the research report and get us on fast-track for publication. A week later, Mom got a call from Connor's doctor. They'd changed his variant's classification to likely pathogenic. The irony continued to amaze me: it had been classified as uncertain because it was never seen before, and only changed classes when we told people that we'd seen it.

But the lab did us a solid—they connected Connor with a doctor in Ohio who was running a gene therapy trial for his form of SMA. Connor got in, and he was showing some improvement. All that because of two Condors who presented themselves to him like a gift from the sky. I hadn't seen them since, but sometimes I had the eerie sense that they were near. Watching over us.

Connor's voice came in my ear, bringing me back to the task at hand. "Could you move any slower? I'd like to get there before nightfall."

"Don't make me kill the drone's power," I replied. We set out into the desert, six dragons, two geocachers, one pig, and one camera drone. This geocache didn't stand a chance.

We'd just gotten back to the parking lot, still flush with victory, when my phone buzzed with an incoming call. Scottsdale area code, and the prefix looked familiar. "Connor, I'm getting another call. Hold on."

"Make sure you put my drone back in its case. And a seatbelt."

I rolled my eyes and switched over to the incoming call. "Hello?"

"Noah Parker," a woman said.

I knew that voice. Funny how much I missed hearing her say my name that way. "Evelyn Chang." I looked at Summer, whose eyebrows shot up. "How are you?"

"Well, thank you."

"I should hope so. Allow me to express my congratulations to the new CEO." *And to the board of directors, God help you.*

She laughed. "Oh, please don't."

"Fine. But I'm glad for you."

"Thank you. Hey, are you free for lunch?"

"How soon?" I asked, mostly to cover my surprise.

"*Mah shang,*" she said. Right away, or literally *on the horse.*

I put the phone to my chest and whispered to Summer. "She wants to meet for lunch."

"So meet her," Summer said.

"I already promised you peanut butter and jelly."

"We can do that tomorrow."

"Are you sure?"

"Yes."

I got back on the phone. "Lunch sounds good. Do you mind if my girlfriend tags along?"

"Of course not." Somehow, I knew she was smiling.

"How about Phan Boi Chau's?" I asked. That was a Vietnamese place in Scottsdale near the HQ. Good food, private booths, and always quiet.

"Perfect. See you at noon."

Summer and I got there early, so we waited out front. A luxury sedan with dark windows pulled up to the curb. A driver hopped out to open the back door for his passenger.

When I saw it was Evelyn, I just had to smile. "*Nihao.*"

"*Nihao,*" she said.

Introductions have all kinds of rituals in Chinese culture. For whatever reason, that part of the audiobooks stuck with me. *Always say the name of the more important person first.* Luckily, Evelyn and I no longer worked together, so it was no contest.

"Summer, I'd like you to meet Evelyn," I said.

They shook hands and said, "Nice to meet you."

Evelyn smiled at me, her eyes twinkling with either pride or amusement. "Noah Parker."

I shrugged and felt my cheeks heating. *I know. Totally out of my league.*

We settled into a quiet booth near the back. Summer and I had the booth side. Evelyn took the chair.

"It's good to see you again," she said.

"You, too," I said. "How does it feel to have the reins?"

She shook her head. "I'm just helping the board figure things out."

"Sure you are." I winked at her.

"You know me too well."

"How's Wong?"

"The same."

"That's good." At least he hadn't been sent back to China. I missed the guy and his crooked grin.

Evelyn and I both ordered our favorites: a curry dish for her, green beans and garlic for me. Summer ordered the soup like an absolute *pro*. Yet another hidden talent of hers; I'd been to Phan Boi Chau's a dozen times and still hadn't worked up the courage.

"So, Summer, what kind of work do you do?" Evelyn asked.

"I'm an architect at Evans and Meyer."

"Ooh, that's a good firm. They built our headquarters."

"Yes, we did."

I half-choked on a crispy spring roll. She'd never told me that. Summer slapped my back a couple of times.

Evelyn leaned back, watching us. "You two are a good match."

"Thanks." Summer had kept her hand on my back and rubbed it softly. "I think so, too."

I kept my mouth shut, and just enjoyed the moment.

We were halfway through the pot stickers by the time Evelyn finally got down to business.

"Listen, Noah. Build-A-Dragon is struggling," she said.

I fought a smile but failed. "So I hear." *Sorry, not sorry.* Greaves had given me what I thought was a hard choice. Summer and Connor were quick to point out that it really wasn't. Bringing dogs back impacted the entire world. It was unfortunate that Build-A-Dragon had to pay the price for that. I knew things were tight, but the company really did have a fighting chance. There were still plenty of dragon lovers out there.

"With Robert gone, we have been discussing removing the points system to allow for bigger, better dragons."

No points system. What a novel idea. I bit back a snarky comment. "You could really try some new things. Aerial guard dragons, maybe even seeing-eye dragons." I had to stop myself from mentally designing the prototypes. *Old habits die hard.*

"We have a lot of work to do." Evelyn agreed.

"Good for you."

Evelyn smiled. "We are going to need our best designer."

Oh, that's clever. It was so perfectly subtle, so wonderfully

Chinese, that I nearly laughed. But that wasn't the way this game was played. "Did Korrapati leave?"

"You are very polite, Noah Parker."

"When he wants to be," Summer said. She winked at me, which took the sting out of it.

I looked at Evelyn. "I do miss it."

"And we miss you."

I smiled sadly. "The manner of my leaving was..." I trailed off, because so many words could have ended that sentence. Sudden. Awkward. Embarrassing. But perhaps even righteous.

"Unfortunate?" Evelyn offered.

We shared a laugh.

"That's a great way to put it." I felt the smile leave my face. "Still, I don't know how to come back after that. Or why they'd let me."

"They?"

"The board of directors." *Where I could have had a seat.*

"They brought me in because they want results," Evelyn said. "And I made it clear that my acceptance came with some conditions. One of them was you."

A wonderful sense of elation bubbled up inside of me. I hadn't known how much I wanted it. "So...I can have my old job back?"

"Not exactly," Evelyn said.

"Oh." Those two words crushed me. The elation fizzled as quickly as it had come. It crushed me a little, but I understood. It's not like I could waltz back in and rejoin the ranks of the design team. "What, then?" I suppose I could come back and do something else, but design was all I knew. All I wanted to do.

"I was thinking *my* old job," Evelyn said.

Oh my God. I inhaled slowly. Director of Dragon Design. It had a certain ring to it.

Evelyn smiled. She probably thought she had me. Before Summer, I'd have jumped at the opportunity. But that was part of why I brought my new conscience along.

I looked at Summer. "What do you think?"

Summer frowned. "I didn't like the idea of engineered dragons in the first place."

"I know." Truth be told, I hadn't imagined getting to go back to Build-A-Dragon after everything that had happened. But the real surprise was how much I wanted it. *Maybe I care about dragons after all.* It's hard to let go of your dreams, especially when they're staring you right in the face. Beckoning to you. But Summer mattered more. I tried to hide my disappointment. "I get it."

"You know what, though?" She squeezed my hand. "I'm starting to come around."

Author's Note

Dear Reader,

Thank you for reading my book! *Domesticating Dragons* combines two of my favorite things: genetics research, which has been my avocation for nearly two decades, and dragons, which I've loved for as long as I can remember. I had a hell of a time writing this and hope you enjoyed the ride. If you liked it, please consider leaving a review at your favorite online retailer. If you *really* liked it, tell your family, friends, coworkers, and followers. Reviews and word of mouth are vital to newer authors like me, but they're very hard to get.

If you're a fan of realistic sci-fi, you might enjoy the Science in Sci-fi blog series (http://dankoboldt.com/science-in-scifi). Each week, I invite scientists, engineers, doctors, and other real-world experts to discuss their area of expertise as it applies to science fiction. To receive updates about new blog posts and my future books, please join my mailing list at http://dankoboldt.com/subscribe.

It means so much to me that you took a chance on my book. Thank you!

Sincerely,
Dan Koboldt
August 2020

Acknowledgments

When I first started writing this story in 2014, I had no idea how many people would help shape it into the novel it became. Insightful critiques from Dannie Morin, Sonia Hartl, Rachel Done, Michael Mammay, Ryan McLeod, and Chris Kerns improved it at every turn. My agent, Paul Stevens, applied his sharp editorial skills to several iterations, and also helped land this book at the right publisher.

I'm deeply grateful to the team at Baen Books. Tony Daniel and Toni Weisskopf acquired the manuscript and offered thoughtful edits; Christopher Ruocchio, Libby O'Brien, and David Afsharirad helped transform it into a marketable book. Thanks also to Dave Seeley, the artist responsible for the absolutely splendid cover.

The writing community has inspired and supported me from the beginning. I would not have come this far without my friends in the Clubhouse, Codex, SFWA, Impulse Authors Unite, and the Pitch Wars community. Last but not least, I would like to thank my family for their unwavering tolerance of my writing adventures.